HAVENWOOD FALLS
VOLUME NINE

A HAVENWOOD FALLS COLLECTION

EMILY CYR   T.V. HAHN   JD NELSON

ABOUT THIS BOOK

Three paranormal fantasy novellas (books 28-30) in this multi-author shared world of Havenwood Falls, home to sexy men, strong women, and neighbors who bite.

Fate's Demand by Emily Cyr

Lana Velis always knew she might one day inherit the powers and duties of the Oracle of Delphi, but the inheritance arriving in the middle of her last-ever college final wasn't something even she could predict. With a power she never wanted and her testy cat, Lana must leave her best friend behind and make her way to Havenwood Falls to take over the never-ending petitioner list her ya-ya left behind. If only it were that easy. The gods are angry, and the Fates demand a soul in place of the one Lana accidentally stole —or all of Havenwood Falls will suffer the consequences.

The Wu & the Wand by T.V. Hahn

Sequel to *The Ward & the Wanderers*—Trying to get back to her simple Havenwood Falls life, Teeny Weeny Tahini enjoys nothing more than her morning teas at the Broastful Brew, but that seems to be where trouble always finds her. This time it's a tantalizing Asian gentleman who has all of Teeny's senses on full alert. When her friend Nina suddenly disappears, Teeny is certain Mr. Wu has the answers. She never expects what she learns, though, and now it's up to her to not only save Havenwood Falls, but an entire dynasty of another place and another time.

A Demon's Redemption by JD Nelson

For six hundred years, demon Rayonus Rixa has used his destructive power to fund his nomadic, mercenary lifestyle and hasn't had the time or inclination to care about someone other than himself. When the demon hierarchy tasked him with a job unlike any other, that all changed, and the moment he met Penelope Osbourne, he changed. She's sassy, beautiful, and a little crazy for her favorite TV angel. In her, Rayonus has finally found a future that doesn't include death or general mayhem. And then, in typical demon fashion, he promptly screws it up ten ways to Sunday.

HAVENWOOD FALLS BOOKS

Forget You Not by Kristie Cook

Old Wounds by Susan Burdorf

Fate, Love & Loyalty by E.J. Fechenda

The Winged & the Wicked by T.V. Hahn & Kristie Cook

Alpha's Queen by Lila Felix

Ink & Fire by R.K. Ryals

Lose You Not by Kristie Cook

Tragic Ink by Heather Hildenbrand

Nowhere to Hide by Belinda Boring

Flames Among the Frost by Amy Hale

Rock Me Gently by Susan Burdorf

From the Embers by Amy Miles

Defying Gravity by Kallie Ross

Break Me Not by Kristie Cook

How the Dead Lie by Stacey Rourke

The Lurkers Within by Danielle Bannister

The Collector: Awakening by Kristie Cook, R.K. Ryals, Belinda Boring & Nadirah Foxx

Addicted to You by Belinda Boring

Affliction Mine by C.J. Pinard

The Ward & the Wanderers by T.V. Hahn

Toil & Trouble by Melissa Wright

Of Salt and Stars by Seven Jane

Redefined by Morgan Wylie

Betrayal Among the Frost by Amy Hale

Forever Loyal by E.J. Fechenda

Fate's Demand by Emily Cyr

The Wu & the Wand by T.V. Hahn

A Demon's Redemption by JD Nelson

Also try the YA line, Havenwood Falls High; the historical paranormal line, Legends of Havenwood Falls; the darker, sexier side of town, Havenwood Falls Sin & Silk; and the local supernatural college, Sun & Moon Academy.

Stay up to date at www.HavenwoodFalls.com

FATE'S DEMAND

EMILY CYR

~ A Havenwood Falls New Adult Novella ~

HAVENWOOD FALLS

FATE'S DEMAND

EMILY CYR

BOOKS BY EMILY CYR

The Lightning Witch Trilogy:

The Lightning Prophecy

The Lightning Legacy

The Lightning Progeny

The Vampire Favors Series:

Push and Pull

Give and Take

Fight or Flight

Sink or Swim

Stand-alone books:

Hotline to Hell

Mended

Blackened Magic

Coming soon:

The Lone Wolf

Back and Forth

For Jess. Everyone needs a Jess in their life.
I'm glad I have mine.

CHAPTER 1

*T*he way her short silver hair kissed that slim neck of hers sent chills throughout my whole body. That neck I'd spent two years loving, spent two years brushing my lips against. Now? Just what was I supposed to do? I was expected to just pick up the remnants of my shattered heart and move the hell on. How could anyone be expected to do that?

She knew I was there. I could tell by the way she hung all over the other woman. The one I'd caught her with. I was so stupid for still loving her, but apparently, she'd moved on long ago.

"Lana. You can't keep doing this to yourself." It was Jensen chiding me. It was always Jensen. Her kind voice had always been a balm to my soul, ever since we were kids. Now, here we were only a few finals until we graduated from college. She with a degree in education and I in graphic design. But as it was, none of that mattered, not when my heart had been so viciously ripped out.

"Earth to Lana," she prodded again. This time I glanced at her. She looked so much like the child she used to be, I couldn't help but smile at her. Her light brown skin was such a contrast to her vivid green eyes. Her spiraled ringlet curls hung around her face, making her rounded features stand out even more. She was beautiful. I was always so jealous of her. She stood at a whopping five foot seven, whereas I was five foot two on a good day. My skin seemed so pale in comparison to her richly tanned color, even though my Greek heritage gave me an olive complexion. However, she always said I never appreciated my pin-straight dark brown hair. She was right, as usual. My eyes were always my favorite feature. They were a bright blue and against my dark hair they stood out even more.

I sighed. "I know, it's just, I—" I choked on the words.

Jensen held up a slender hand in a stopping gesture. Her brow and lips tilted up slightly, causing her features to soften slightly. "I know you do. But you deserve better, girl."

Of course, she was right. "I know." There wasn't a whole lot more I could say.

"Come on, we have a final to get to. Did you even study? Greek history—shouldn't you be an expert? You being Greek and all?"

Glancing down at my phone, I realized she was correct. It was the only class the three of us shared, so it wasn't like it would be awkward or anything.

"Fuck no!" I exclaimed. I tried like hell to recall the last semester's worth of Greek history. "What were the three Fates' names again?" I blurted.

"Girl, if I have to tell you that, you're totally screwed." She laughed, shaking her head.

We walked to class as we always did, her trying to make me laugh, me brooding while trying like hell to remember the Fates' names and everything else I needed for that damn exam.

"So, what? Are you going to go back to dudes now?"

Her question caused me to choke on my own saliva.

Half coughing and half laughing, I looked at her and explained, "That's not really how it works. I'm bi. I kinda just love who I love."

"I know it's not, but I heard a laugh or two around that cock you were choking on just now, so hashtag worth it." Her crazy ass seemed to preen as her face lit up.

"You're the most inappropriate person I know." I laughed, rolling my eyes at her.

"Oh, that's so not true. You've met my mother."

"You win!" I cackled as we rounded the corner and walked into class.

This was it. My last final I'd have to take before real life would come crashing down on me.

We made our way to our seats and got settled in. My phone buzzed, and I looked down to see the text.

It was from my dad. Like I'd done for the last five years, I hit ignore. The absolute last thing I needed right then was my alcoholic father hitting me up for yet more money.

"Let me guess, your dad or ya-ya? Still letting them walk all over you?" It was her. My whole body froze at her words, not because of what she said but because of who had said it.

"Don't you have a rock to find, Cassidy?" Jensen taunted in a venom-laced tone.

Cassie looked at her in confusion.

"What?" Cassie spat. Her eyes were laser focused on Jensen.

"Oh, you know, the rock you crawled out from under and need to return to?" I heard several shocked inhalations of breath from around me at Jensen's dig.

I swear to Hades's bouncing balls my jaw hit the fucking tile floor with an audible clack.

The look of shock and hurt flashed so fast across Cassie's face, I questioned if I'd seen anything at all.

"See, this is why I found something better. You're no better than the company you keep. Remember that, Lana." She was so condescending. Come to think of it, she'd always been like that, not just to Jensen but to me as well. And her words were nothing more than a slap in the face meant to hurt me and Jensen. Then, under her breath, she said the words I thought I would never hear from someone I'd once loved: "No wonder your dad's an alcoholic."

I was so shocked I just sat there for a heartbeat. Then rage took over, and I stood to face her eye to eye. I'd had enough. Not because I actually cared about my father, but for the sheer fact that she had the gall to blame me for something I'd always blamed myself for—something she'd known. She had the audacity to use my own insecurities against me? Yeah, fuck that.

"You know, Cassie, as I recall, I broke up with you. And, as I recall, you were trying to sext me, what, just last night? So really, who's the lucky one?"

She opened her mouth to speak, but fuck that. I wasn't having it.

"So, you want to give me advice?" I continued. "How about I give you some? You are what you eat."

The whole class was listening, including the TA and professor. I should have cared about the audience. But for once, I didn't care whom I offended or who heard my dirty laundry.

"What?" she said dumbly. Looking around for a split second, I saw the same look on nearly everyone's face.

Smiling my very best *eat shit and die* expression, I intoned, "You are what you eat. Me? I last ate a bagel. What did you eat? A rotting, stinking pus—" The world tilted and went black. But not before I saw Cassie's horrified expression. I couldn't help but laugh. Well, at least I thought I did.

CHAPTER 2

"*There must always be an oracle.*" The words swirled around me like a physical haze, something that could be heard but never touched.

Voices broke through the darkness like the lapping waves of a lazy ocean. My body felt fuzzy, as if my whole nervous system were replaced with a live wire. I felt like electricity was being pumped through my veins.

"What—" I tried to speak, but only a garbled sound came out.

"You fucking sack of dog shit!" Jensen screeched so loud, I honestly thought she was a pissed off parrot rather than her joyful self. *Is she yelling? Of course she is.*

"Hi." This time, while it felt and sounded garbled, the word was at least clear. Well, clearer.

Raising my hand to my throbbing head, I felt my forearm catch on something. Glancing down, I saw just what kept my hand from reaching my face—an IV. *What the hell?* It was only then that I took stock of where I was, in a hospital if the beeping monitors and machine-operated bed had anything to say about it.

"What the hell happened?" I croaked. I was so confused.

"How much do you remember?" Jensen inquired as she

nibbled her bottom lip. Her obvious nervousness caused me to worry.

I tried to think back to the last thing I could remember, but every time I did, a massive headache would slam into me with the force of a damn Mack truck.

"Um, I remember going in for our final, then Cassie being a dick. Then—" I groaned as pain spiked in my head. "Nothing," I rasped.

Jensen shook her head, walked over to the bed, and sat down on the not-so-comfortable mattress. Her green eyes searched my face as her lips went from a soft smile to a worried line. Whatever it was, it was bad.

She took in a deep breath and explained. "You told Cassie off, which by the way, was epic. You should have seen her face when you said she was what she ate. Priceless." Her mouth turned into a slight smile, but then she looked at me fully and her smile dropped.

"Then you just dropped to the ground and started having a seizure. Do you have epilepsy? I didn't think you did, but I mean I—"

My eyes went wide as I blurted, "Wait, what? I had a what?"

There was no good goddamn way I'd heard her correctly.

"Uh, um, maybe the doctor should come and talk to you?" she suggested, looking from me to the door and back again.

"Also, um, your dad has been calling you, like, a lot," she added as she walked to the head of my bed.

"Wonderful. Sounds like a cherry on the shit sundae." I groaned.

She reached out to cup my face, a thing she'd done only four million times in our lives. But this time, as soon as her skin touched mine, white-hot pain shot through me like I'd been struck by lightning, or what I thought equated to such a thing. My whole body glowed with a bright white light, though that didn't scare me. It wasn't until I saw Jensen that I realized just what had happened.

I saw Jensen, but it wasn't her. I mean, it was, but it wasn't. I could see Jensen, the one I knew and loved, but there was another version of her. Time—well, the time I knew—seemed to slow to a near stop as the scene played out in front of me. It was like there was a hologram of her in the background of what I knew was real.

She is in a stunning white dress that hugs her slim body, then flares out at the bottom. Her image in the mirror and the smile on her face are so real I can feel them in my heart. I can feel her feelings and hear her thoughts.

"Jensen!" her mother called, causing her to turn from the mirror.

"I know. It's time. Just give me a second!" she calls back, returning her attention to her reflection. "Please don't be a mistake," she whispers to no one, though deep down in her soul she knows it is.

The present slammed into me, knocking the breath out of me. My chest burned as I tried and failed to suck in much-needed gulps of air.

"Lana! Are you okay? You just glowed! Like, your skin!" Jensen screamed as she went to grab me.

"NO!" I blurted. I couldn't take another vison, not right then.

She froze without touching me. We both just looked at one another.

"Jensen, I have a lot to explain, but I can't right now. I swear I will, but for now I have to call my dad." I was out of breath, and every part of me felt raw and exposed.

Her face twisted up in disgust. "Lana," she intoned in that chiding way of hers.

"I know, but I can't explain until I talk to him."

She looked at me for another long moment before making her way to the door. I knew she was feeling dejected, but I had to talk to my dad. As soon as the door clicked shut behind her, I reached over to the floating table and fumbled for my phone.

I clicked it on and saw forty-six missed calls. All from my dad.

Without checking for any messages, I called him.

"Lana? Oh, thank the gods." I hadn't spoken to my father in five years; even still, his voice took me back to all the times he'd yelled at me for dropping a fork or one of the number of other things a child does. Or the times he'd come home drunk and angry. From the way he slurred his words, he was likely currently inebriated.

"Dad?" It was an all-encompassing question.

"She's dead. Your grandmother is dead."

Not that I needed him to tell me. I knew by the power I felt running through me that felt like pins and needles, as if my skin had fallen asleep and was waking up.

"I know. How?" I rasped.

My grandmother wasn't my direct grandmother. She was my great-great-great-great-grandmother. While normal women of her age would be long since gone, mine was the sacred oracle. I'd always known this was a possibility, as the power traveled down the matriarchal line, but I honestly never thought it would happen. From the time I was little before my mom died, she'd told me about my grandmother and how she'd been blessed with a gift from the gods, as she'd put it. We could trace our bloodline back to that of the Oracle of Delphi. Our bloodline was created long ago by the gods themselves, to offer a link between the people and the gods. This was a secret story in our family; one I knew but never fully believed. Well, by Hades's bouncing balls, I believed now, that's for damn sure.

"I, uh, don't know. I tried calling you. Where are you?" His third-degree line of questions rankled slightly.

"The hospital. I had a seizure in class." I sighed nonchalantly.

"You need to get out of there and get to, uh, where was that town she lived in?" He rambled, not caring one bit about the fact that I was in the damn hospital. I had to grit my teeth at him telling me fuck all. To say that we had a rocky relationship would be putting it lightly. The man had no idea about Havenwood Falls or on most days his own damn name.

My grandmother lived in a small town in Colorado. This was a special town, as it were, a place where supernaturals ran rampant and outsiders were discouraged. The whole town even had wards so no one could wander in without someone knowing about it or leave without forgetting it. I was sent there when I was seven to visit with my ya-ya and came home with a small tattoo so that I'd have the memory of how to get back if I needed to, though I would only regain those memories should my ya-ya ever die. Under normal circumstances, if someone in the town left, the tattoo would disappear along with their memories, but my grandmother petitioned the Court of the Sun and the Moon to have the Luna Coven weave a more permanent magic into my tattoo, one that would activate when she died. The Court rejected the petition at first, but she offered them something in return that seemed to change their minds, though I never knew what. Clearly my ya-ya's insistence that my mother force me to go made sense, despite how pissed my mom was when she found out her ulterior motive. The knowledge and memories of that time with my ya-ya were so clear now, I felt a little dizzy.

"Yeah, I know." I didn't know what else to say. My whole life was over. I'd always known it was possible the power might shift to me, but given my ya-ya had been the oracle for so long, I thought it wasn't likely. I thought I'd get to live a life that was all mine, one I picked. Glancing down at my tape-coated hand and legs covered by a scratchy thin sheet, I realized just how over my life really and truly was.

Then there was Jensen. I'd have to leave her behind. That thought alone caused my eyes to burn with hot tears. She'd been my oldest and best friend. I couldn't just leave her. But really, what choice did I have? It wasn't like I could bring her. She had a future, a life to live. My mind flashed the vision of her in that white dress. She had a wedding. Maybe once I settled down, I'd try to convince her to come up there.

"Lana, you there?" my dad wondered.

"Not really." It was the truth. I was somewhere, but my head was swimming and I couldn't cope.

"I want to see you." They were only five words, five words that snapped me back to reality.

"I haven't spoken to you in what? Five years? You know what you said to me?" It was a rhetorical question, one I didn't even give him a breath to think about. "You said, and I quote, 'Hey Lana, you owe me for those years I spent taking care of you.' You mean raising me? Or better yet, me raising myself. Remember that, Dad?"

"Lana—"

"No. You call me for money to spend on booze. Dad, I've been just fine without you, without mom, without anyone."

"I've changed—"

I hung up the phone and did the one thing I should have done nearly five years ago—I blocked him. I had no idea why it took so long to cut off such a toxic person, but it felt like a weight had been lifted off my chest.

I let my head fall back against the pillow, praying like hell I'd sink into sleep.

"Ms. Velis?" a male voice asked from what I assumed was the doorway.

"Unfortunately, yes," I muttered in a melancholy tone. *Just when I was trying to sleep or die, one of the two, ugh.*

The middle-aged man with thinning hair walked in to the room without meeting my eyes and started speaking. "Ms. Velis, we've done some tests, and everything we saw was normal."

He was glancing and flipping through some papers, still not meeting my eyes. I was a patient right in front of him, but he was treating me like a subject.

"Really? Normal? How odd, considering I'm half goblin and survive on nothing but Jell-O." He didn't even look up at me. I rolled my eyes so hard I thought I might actually need medical attention.

"I'd like to run a few more—"

"I'm going to stop you right there, Dr. Hubert." I had no idea what the hell his name was, but it didn't matter, as I was feeling slightly stabby. The use of his clearly incorrect name finally caused him to look at me for the first time.

"That's not my name," he interrupted, like a petulant child.

I held up a hand and shook my head.

"Well, it's not like you took the time to introduce yourself, did you? But that doesn't matter, because I'm out of here," I said coolly, as I glanced down at the IV on the side of my wrist. Pulling it free, I explained further, "There's nothing wrong with me. And yes, I know what AMA is and will sign whatever paperwork you'd like stating as much."

As I pulled the IV free, there was a small pinch and a tiny welling of blood. Pressing my thumb to the tiny hole in my skin, I looked at the wide-eyed doctor.

"Ma'am, I'm sorry, but I think you fail to grasp—"

"Oh, I grasp," I cut him off as I swung my legs over the side of the bed. It was then I realized I had no pants on. Glancing from my bare legs back to him, I decided I had zero fucks to give and, well, yolo.

Getting up, it wasn't until I bent over that I realized I hadn't been wearing panties that day. Well, either that or someone set the air conditioner to turbo. I whirled around to find the man looking at the spot my ass used to occupy. Wonderful. This day just kept getting better and better.

Gathering all my shit that had been stuffed into a too-small bag in my arms, I turned to face him.

"Trust me when I tell you, my health is the absolute least of your worries." *My sanity, though, is suspect,* I didn't add.

Brushing past him, I slipped on my flip-flops and cracked the door but paused at his frantic rambling.

"Ma'am, I, um could you please um, put pants on."

"I don't have time for your—" I paused when I realized that in that short span of time, I'd forgotten I didn't have pants on, again.

After pants and paperwork, I broke free from the hospital. I made Jensen leave earlier for her last final, so I had to figure my own way out. My exit was complicated by brushing past a homeless woman and seeing her future. I concealed my silvery white glowing self with my large book bag and ran out to my Uber as if my ass were on fire.

On the way back to the apartment I shared with Jensen, I called her to be sure she was at home. She was, and boy was she pissed I'd checked myself out of the hospital.

After I hung up with Jensen, I spent the rest of the drive trying to come up with a million and one explanations. But as I sat down right in front of her, none of them seemed to make sense or be good enough for my friend. They just seemed like a pack of lies she didn't deserve.

So there we sat in our living room that was filled with furniture we'd gotten from many weekends of thrift store shopping for a home we'd built together. I began feeling sick. This wasn't supposed to happen. This was supposed to be just like my mom: I'd get to live my own life. Even if she did die long before she should have, she at least had a life that was her own.

"You just going to sit there and ignore the white zebra in the room?" she puzzled as she glared at me.

"I think you mean white elephant. And isn't that a Christmas thing?" I quipped, hoping to prolong the inevitable.

Rolling her eyes, she huffed, "You know what I mean, so stop stalling."

"I'm not stalling." I was absolutely stalling. We both knew it.

"Listen here, you turd muffin, I don't know what's going on or why you checked yourself out of the hospital—"

I opened my mouth to tell her I hadn't, a lie. But she held up a hand, staving me off.

"Don't even try to tell me you didn't. Don't lie to me." She was beyond annoyed. She carried that tone she always had when she knew I was lying.

"Jensen, I—" The words caught in my throat. I didn't need to possess the power of the sacred oracle to see what was going to happen. I could see it play out in front of me.

Then something my ya-ya told me the only time I met her washed over me with the force of a rogue wave.

"You can't keep her forever, Lana." She sighed as she touched my hand. *My ya-ya should have been old and covered with wrinkles that told the tale of a well-lived life, but the power of the oracle kept her young and ageless.*

"Huh?" I questioned, looking back up at her. *Her blue eyes that matched my own showed her many many years of life, yet there was a spark of knowing.*

Cupping my face in her hands, she smiled down at me before she placed a soft kiss on my cheek. Her deep chocolate hair tickled my ear as she leaned in to whisper.

"You'll know what I mean when you're grown."

Over the years, I thought about that moment often. I even thought it might have been Cassie. But looking at this moment with Jensen, I knew it was now. I knew it was her.

She sat there and studied my face for a long moment. I wanted to tell her that I had to leave everything and everyone behind to become an oracle. Not that that would sound crazy or anything. Damn, how I wanted to tell her the truth. I almost did at least a hundred different times. I knew I couldn't. This wasn't the life I wanted.

"I don't want this." The words left my lips before I could stop them.

"Don't want what? Lana, you're scaring me." Her voice was shaking. I was scaring myself, if I was honest.

"To leave you." The words came out garbled and on a half sob. By the look on her face and the tears rolling down her cheeks, she understood everything.

"I—" she started, but her voice cut off in a squeak. "I don't understand."

"My ya-ya, she died. I have to—"

"Oh, that's all?" She looked relieved, then seemed to realize her words. "No, I mean I'm sorry she passed, but you look like you're leaving forever."

I just looked at her for a long moment.

Her eyes went wide, and she stood up abruptly, causing her cell phone to clatter to the wood floor.

"You are coming back, right?" I could nearly feel her accelerated heartbeat in her voice.

"No," I whispered. The word hung in the air between us like a crowbar prying us apart.

Turning her back to me, she walked to the front door and reached for the knob.

"Wait!" I nearly yelped.

She did.

"Please let me explain?" I begged to her back. She didn't turn to face me but didn't move either.

"My ya-ya has a home and family business that I have to go look after. It's not really what I wanted either. But I have to go."

Turning, she crossed her arms over her chest.

"Fine," she snapped. "I'll just come with you."

Smiling and cocking a hip out, I reminded her, "You have to graduate, and you already got a job at that uptight private school, where you'll teach the rich and obnoxious, remember?"

"Nope. I'm good. I'll quit," she snipped back.

"You can't! But how about you give me a year? Just one. That way it won't look bad on your résumé. Then if you still want to come, we'll figure it out."

Strained silence fell over us again, but this time there was a feeling to it that was warm and tender.

"Deal. But will you come and visit?" she asked, dropping her arms and opening them to me.

Walking into her embrace, I held her tight. While I hugged her, I was careful not to touch her skin. I couldn't really control, nor did I understand exactly, what was happening to me.

"I will if I can. But we'll figure something out. I promise," I assured her, even though I knew how unlikely that really was.

We both just stood there and held on to the last thread of our friendship as though it were a lifeline, and in many ways it was.

There was a loud hiss and meowing that rang out, followed by a bright streak of white fur.

"What are we going to do with Hades?" she wondered as we both looked at my insane cat.

Hades had been my oh-my-god-my-biological-clock-is-going-wacky-despite-being-in-my-early-twenties adoption. The stark white cat flopped on his back and started kicking his back legs against the lace bra—

"Hey! Asshole, that's my bra!" I hissed. He just looked at me, glared his *eat shit and die* look, and kept up the lacy assault.

"Yeah, you're so taking him with you." She laughed. "I'm not going to miss having to buy new bras every week," she added as she pulled away.

"Yeah, I guess Hades is coming with me." The thought of shoving his big-balled butt into a carrier had me mentally looking for the Band-Aids and ointment.

"I love you. That won't change. And I promise as soon as things calm down, I'll be sure I get your ass up for a visit," I assured her. It was then I realized I'd likely never see Cassie again. That thought normally would have devastated me, but now I really wasn't bothered by it. Leaving Jensen, though—that would be a hell of a lot harder. She was my everything for so long, but I had to let her live her own life.

"I know. I love you, too."

Hades meowed so loud the downstairs neighbors banged on the floor.

"I won't miss that, though," she added. We both laughed like wild hyenas, and that caused the neighbors to pound again.

Then we both broke out into our best Michael Flatley imitations with shitty Irish dancing. Ah, got to love being petty.

CHAPTER 3

"*H*oly shit." My jaw dropped to the floor. I'd been to Havenwood Falls one time for all of a single day. So my memories of the small Colorado town were fuzzy to say the least. I certainly didn't remember my grandmother's house being this uh, well, clearly she was a hoarder. Either that or she sold all kinds of wooden, porcelain, glass, or you-name-it dolls. Creepy dolls, the stuff nightmares are made of.

Huffing, I set Hades's carrier on the floor and went to flip another light on. Pausing, I thought better of it. There was no way on earth I really wanted to see the billion and two eyes of the scary-ass doll things looking at me.

"Okay, Hades. We're home, er, home-ish."

He hissed. *Yeah, we're both just pleased as punch to be here.*

Opening his small cage, I prepared for his release, but he didn't budge. I peeked in to find him eyeing the small dolls that seemed to line every single space of the house.

"Same, buddy. Same." I sighed as I stood up. There was a stack of mail on the side table that caught my attention.

Flipping through the envelopes, I realized they were all addressed to me. *Just how long had the crazy lady known she was going to die?* Then I realized there was a small journal with a post-it note stuck to the front that read, "Step one, read me."

Picking it up, I laughed. "I thought step one was to cut a hole in the box."

Well, according to Justin Timberlake anyway. *Guess it's not that kind of party. Pity.*

Hades growled in response.

"Man, I hate it when no one is around to hear my jokes. It's just a shame, honestly." I sighed again.

I grabbed the book, decided all the shit in my car could wait, and walked over to the flower-covered couch.

"Oh man, there's going to need to be a serious purge in our future, Hades," I commented as I sat down. Hades finally decided to leave his cage and jump up on my lap.

Stroking his short silky fur with one hand, I opened the book with the other. Ya-ya's handwriting wasn't familiar to me, but by the time I finished this instruction manual, I would never be able to forget it.

Lana,

I've known this day was coming since the moment you were born.

"Of course she did," I murmured as my eyes rolled.

Don't be snotty. It's not nice.

My eyes squinted at the paper. Had she just? Hades picked that moment to protest loudly about the fact that I'd stopped petting him.

I read on while stroking the testy cat.

I know you had plans—big ones. You planned to get your degree in graphic design and land a job at that advertising firm, the one that tends to hire only women. I'm sorry things didn't work out the way you'd hoped.

"Understatement of the century, Ya-ya."

But the one thing I'm truly sorry for is Jensen. I know she's been your rock for many years, especially after your mother died. So for that I truly am sorry. But I have a feeling that loss will only be temporary.

I had to bite my lip to keep from sobbing.

Lana, I know you might have a few questions, so I will do my best to answer them. First, as to how I died. After I'd been the oracle for so long, the gods saw fit to give me a choice for all my years of service. I could relinquish my duty so that a new one might arise. In doing so I would be granted an afterlife with the gods, to wander the afterlife and be reborn at a time of my choosing. Or I could remain the oracle, denying you your future.

"Denying me a future? Just what does that mean?"

I know you don't understand, but you will. Okay, moving on. Your power could manifest in a number of ways. Knowing you, my guess is you're a touch oracle. You can prophesy by touching someone. This is both good and bad. You won't be able to control the power. However, you don't have to touch people, so that's something, right?

Narrowing my eyes at the tightly packed cursive, I pursed my lips. Not touching people—great, there goes my nonexistent sex life.

There are some rules. First, if you see a future you may not do anything to affect that outcome. You must let the Fates cut their threads no matter what. This is the most important of our laws. You may not expound a vision unless that person, or persons, has been printed on the waitlist. Lana, understand the gods are great, but you are their link to the world. You are their gift to the humans. They will not hesitate to rain hell on earth should you break a sacred law.

Well, that sounded ominous.

You will find the list of petitioners in a spreadsheet on the computer in your room. I know, fancy, right?

I giggled in response. I wished suddenly I'd gotten to know my ya-ya more.

Okay, law two: you must be honest with each and every petitioner who comes to you. What they do with the information is up to them. Also, it's your duty to keep everything you see in utter confidence.

This was all a little too much information all at once. It was getting late, and I was beyond exhausted, but I read on. My grandmother went on to explain about the town and the deal she'd struck with the Court, which held dominion over the town.

Basically, if they allowed her to live in the town and live within the protection offered, and also allow her petitioner a day pass with memories intact of the oracle's reading, there would be a permanent place for the Court on the list, should they ever need it.

I know all of this is new and even a little scary, but you won't be in this alone. When there is a new oracle, she is granted a protector, a guard—"

There was a pounding at the door that sent my heart to my throat and Hades's claws into my thighs.

"Ouch!" I hissed, hopping to my feet. The cat tumbled to the floor, hissed at me, and sauntered off to wherever the hell cats go.

The next knock nearly caused me to pee my damn pants. I didn't know anyone out here so it wasn't like I could have pissed anyone off. *Oh, dear gods, what if it's a serial killer? I've never seen one before but based on every documentary ever it could be. Oh, I guess he wouldn't knock before serial killing. Wait, do they knock at all?* For fuck's sake, my thoughts were rambling.

Creeping over to the door, I crouched low, then realized what a freaking moron I was being and stood up. Reaching for the doorknob, I thought better of it and grabbed a particularly heinous looking brass doll that was sitting on a small bookshelf. If nothing else, I'd scare whoever it was away with bad taste.

"Who's there?" I coaxed, realizing the damn door didn't have a peephole.

"Pizza man," a deep, rolling voice crooned.

Pizza? I didn't order a pizza. I mean, if it's a mistake, I could just take the pizza. I do love pizza. Wait, no, that's dumb. By Hades's bouncing balls, I was being ridiculous.

"I didn't order a pizza," I called back.

Then the damn guy laughed. He fucking laughed at me! He had some nerve.

Tossing the door open, I shoved the creepy doll in his face and waggled it menacingly. Well, as menacingly as one could look whilst waving a bronze doll.

"Hey! I don't appreciate being made fun of. It's been a long day and—" My words were cut off when I finally got a look at the man behind the deep voice. He had long—by what I'd call guy standards—brown hair that hung in his eyes. From what I could see, he had light brown eyes that were a shade lighter than his hair. But it wasn't his eyes that caused me to pause. It was his smile. He had this wide grin that was a mix of sex and the Cheshire cat. He stood a full foot—if not more—taller than me, so I had to adjust my weapon's aim, not that'd I'd really call it a weapon.

My frantic waggling seemed to only amuse him. Dropping the horrific doll to my side, I cocked out my foot and put my other hand on my hip.

"You know, I spent a whole summer at karate camp when I was ten. And I'll have you know, I could kick your"—I let my eyes roam over him to gauge his size. While he was lean to the eye, he held himself like a man who knew how to use his body in all kinds of ways—"your tall ass from here to Sunday. So, unless you have a really, and I do mean *really* good reason for being here, I suggest you mosey on back to the underside of the bridge you call home."

Other than his eyebrows twitching up about a half a millimeter and his lips tilting up slightly, he looked utterly unfazed.

"I think I have a pretty good reason. I'll let you be the judge, though." His voice oozed cockiness. *Oh, this is why I never dated men. Well, never say never, but that's certainly why I didn't date men like this douche goblin.*

Reaching a hand out to me, he gave me a wide smile before adding, "Hi, I'm Damen Costos, the new guardian to the sacred oracle."

We both just stood there for a moment too long, him with his hand out and me like a moron, just looking at it. *There's no way I can shake his hand. He's going to think I'm a douche. Oh well.*

Lifting his hand, he ran the large fingers through his long dark locks instead.

"Well, you are the new oracle, aren't you?" he queried, now

looking a little confused. He did, however, take a very long look at me.

"Yeah, I am. Sorry, come in. It's just been a long day, and I'm a little frazzled." Understatement of the century. There had been a lot of those lately. I pivoted so that he could enter. His eyes went from me to the area behind me, then back to me.

"Not really a decorating choice I'd make, but to each their own. How about you show me to my room?" he mumbled, just before walking in.

There are these moments in life when everything slows down, and you're met with perfect clarity. This wasn't that moment; in fact, this was just the opposite. Everything hit me all at once and spiraled out of control. The reality was I'd erected an emotional dam, and all the shit had piled up.

"Are you fucking kidding me?" Dam broken.

I held up a hand, stopping him from speaking.

"You know what? I don't even care if you're kidding me or not. But I'm done. I'm so freaking done. I don't want to be here. I had everything ripped from me. I was moments away from graduating. I had to leave my best friend behind. And I caught my girlfriend cheating on me about a week ago. You just walk into my house, informed me you're my new roommate, and you're worried about whether or not I fluffed your pillows? Do you even know my name? You know what, go take a flying fuck!" I was heaving and huffing, I was so pissed.

"Wait," he called as I turned my back on him. Damn him if he thought I'd give up one single tear on his account. I did stop, though.

"You're a lesbian?"

I threw my hands in the air, hoping the gods would just go on and strike me down to put me out of my misery.

Facing him, I nearly exploded, "Really? Out of everything I just said, the fact that I was in a relationship with a girl is what you latched on to? The fact I date who I like—that's what you have an issue with? How about, 'Hi, my name is douche canoe,'" I mimicked in a mock male tone.

His eyes went wide for a split second before they returned to the indifferent expression he'd been sporting moments before. I, however, surely looked like the wild and crazy oracle I was. I was breathing hard, seriously pissed off.

Shaking his head, he replied, "No, it's not that. I'm from a small town, and no one is ever open like that. I guess it caught me off guard."

A thick silence fell over the small space, making it feel yet smaller. My anger began to ebb, and I realized just how out of line my outburst had been. This really wasn't the introduction I wanted.

"Listen, how about we sit down and start over? I'm coming across like a total asshole," he finally said, breaking the silence.

"Yeah, you are, but I'm not much better, so I agree. Let's start over."

An expression flashed across his face, but it happened so fast, I wasn't sure I saw anything at all.

"Hi, I'm Damen. And if it makes you feel better, I too had to leave a life behind," he greeted once more.

We sat down on the plastic-covered couch. Before I had time to reply, Hades rounded the corner and hopped up on the coffee table, likely to inspect the newcomer. The cat leaned forward to sniff the air near Damen. The tall man reached out to allow Hades to smell him. Hades, being the turd he was, drew in a little air, then hissed.

Yanking his hand back, Damen growled, "What's wrong with your cat?"

"Everything. Who knows, really? Hades isn't really a fan of people . . ." My words trailed off as the damn cat hopped off the table and onto Damen's lap, then curled up into a ball and proceeded to purr. The devil of a cat actually, honest to god, purred.

My mouth gaped open in both shock and betrayal. *Et tu, Hades?*

"Guess your pussy likes me after all."

I groaned at his play on words. This was going to be a really long night, er, eternity.

"Lana," I blurted out like a total moron.

"The cat's name?" he asked, as one eyebrow bolted upward and his brow furrowed in confusion.

"No, mine. I realized I never told you. He's Hades."

"Well, nice to meet you both," he stated, holding out a hand for me to shake. I just stared at it.

"Sorry, not to be rude, but I can't touch you. Apparently, that's how this lovely gift of mine has manifested." The girl who can't be touched. Sounds like an Amish romance title—groan.

Smiling, he assured me, "You can't see my future. So don't worry about that."

"Oh" was all I could say.

"Let me explain. I've been training for my role as guardian my whole life. Just as your power goes down the line of females in your family, the role of the protector of the oracle travels down the line of males in mine. We are granted the strength of Hercules. While we stop aging, like you, we aren't immortal. I was created to protect you—protect the gift the gods have given to the mortals. My life is now tied to yours."

He knew so much more about this life than I did. How was this possible? Well, if I was being honest, the answer was my mother. After the one visit I had, coming back with a tattoo, my mother wanted nothing to do with what she'd called the tall tale of our family, though I'd always known it was true. It wasn't like I had much time with her. Shortly after that, she left me with my drunk dad, then died a few years after that.

"You didn't know any of this, did you?" Concern was threaded in his question.

"Not really. I came up here one summer for one visit. My ya-ya told me about the power she had. She said someday I might get it. Then she petitioned the Court to give me a tattoo. They put it here." I lifted my hair up, exposing the back of my neck. "Once my mom found out about my new ink, that was it. My mom refused to hear anything about Havenwood Falls, our family power, or anything. I never heard anything more from my grandmother until recently, but I guess I thought it was disrespectful to my mom's memory, so I ignored her." I rubbed the bridge of my nose, hoping that the headache forming would ebb. Looking back on my actions, I realized how utterly stupid and childish I'd been. Hindsight really was twenty-twenty.

"So what do you know?" He lazily stroked Hades's velveteen ears.

"Honestly, I knew I could possibly get the power. And I knew of Havenwood Falls; well, I did after I received my power anyway. Oh and it wasn't like, boom here's your power and cookie, nope, not for me. I had a full-on seizure in class, then I saw the future of my best friend when I touched her. Other than that, I have no idea what I'm doing."

Running a big hand through his long hair, he sighed.

"You might have wanted this. But I didn't."

His brown eyes went wide, then narrowed slightly at my words. "I never said I wanted this. I wanted to make music. I wanted to perform. But I have a responsibility to my family, to the gods, to humans, and to you. Hell, you at least had a tattoo, making it somewhat easy to get here. I had a hand-drawn map my grandfather left me. I'd never even met the man before. Despite all of that, I very much take all of this seriously."

"And I don't?" I snapped. It came out way harsher than I'd meant, but damn, was he saying I didn't care? I was here, wasn't I?

"That's not what I'm saying," he hurried, his expression hardening.

"Listen I don't think anything you or I say at this point is going to help. How about we just go get some sleep? I think there's an inn somewhere in town." I let the statement fall off at his raised eyebrow.

"The guardian lives with the oracle. I have to be near you always," he explained, raising an eyebrow.

"You are *not* sleeping with me!" I very nearly screamed. My tone must have been surprising, as Hades jolted off of his lap, but by how Damen's face was contorted, he'd left him a parting gift with all of his claws before vacating.

"You say that now, princess." He winked as he stood up and brushed the fur off his lap. His eyes tracked over to the cat, who sauntered off.

"Holy big balls, Batman!" he exclaimed.

"Yeah, it's a whole thing. They're fake. It's a really long story." I groaned.

I had a new weird power with all kinds of rules. I had to leave everything I knew behind. I lived in a town where I knew absolutely no one. I had a new house and a massive list of people to see. And to top that shit-coated cone? I had a new roommate.

I glanced at his ass as he walked through the room to explore what I guessed was his new home. With a behind like that, it couldn't all be bad, could it?

"Take a picture. It will last longer," he hollered.

Yeah, I guess it could be that bad. Ugh.

CHAPTER 4

"Oh, for the gods' damn sake, would you hurry the hell up?" I screamed at the closed door. Not that I was really angry at the door itself, rather the man behind it. He'd been in there since the beginning of time, so needless to say, I was over it.

"What kind of house only has one bathroom?" he grumbled in an almost inaudible tone.

"I didn't exactly pick the layout, if you must know. However, I'm about to pee myself so—" My words trailed off as the oak door swung open. In a plume of steam stood Damen with only a towel that hung low on his hips. I couldn't have stopped my eyes from trailing down his well-defined chest to his oh by Hades's bouncing balls—

"Sorry. As I'm sure you can see, perfection takes time." His voice dripped cockiness. It would have been seriously impressive had it not been so infuriating.

I groaned so hard I might have actually seen stars from the lack of oxygen.

"Yeah, well, in that case you might want to hop your happy ass right back in there." With each word I spoke, his smile grew. Clearly my joking amused him.

"I like you." He chuckled before walking away.

Men are so confusing; I might have to stick to women.

A shower never felt so damn good. The heated water almost made me forget that I had an unwanted roommate, an unwanted power, and an unwanted life.

"Ugh, now I'm just being whiny," I said to absolutely no one, but nevertheless it was true.

Hades meowed a long drawn-out howl as if in reply. Clearly, he agreed even though he wasn't asked. But he was kinda right.

Sticking my head out of the shower, I spotted the white cat splayed out in, of all places, the sink. Lucky for him, the water wasn't on.

"Okay, Hades, I swear, from here on out I won't do the woe is me. And I'll try to have a more positive outlook on this whole situation. And I need to apologize to Damen. He hasn't deserved my hostility one damn bit. Happy now?" I assured the cat while blinking the water from my vision.

He picked that moment to tuck his head down and hike his back leg up as he proceeded to lick his massive manhood, er, cathood. I took that as a yes and finished my shower.

When I came out of my room, I saw Damen sitting on the couch, strumming an acoustic guitar.

I couldn't quite tell what he was playing, so I sat down and listened to him.

The melody was haunting and had such an old-world feel that it caused my whole body to break out into goose bumps. As the speed of his fingers picked up, the intensity of the song built to a fever pitch. My heart mimicked the frantic beat. I could feel myself leaning toward him for something more, anything more. Fuck, just more.

Then everything just stopped. His fingers froze, hovering just above the cords. The only thing I could hear in the small space was my own heartbeat. His gaze was locked on mine, and for a moment, I felt solid and grounded. I didn't feel like I'd just float away, for once.

Hades came skittering into the room. He paused, looking at the two of us, hissed, and ran back out.

"That cat has some serious issues."

"Are you a bard?" The question just kind of fell out. I thought it was possible, considering how enraptured he had me.

"No, but I'm glad you liked it, because I wrote it."

Silence fell over the small space, making it seem even smaller.

"Listen, I'm sorry for my attitude. I won't try to justify it. I'm dealing with things the best way I know how and took it out on you. Just give me a little time to adjust. Everything has happened so fast." He deserved an apology. He didn't deserve the crap I'd given him over the past day.

Laying down his guitar, he moved so that he was crouched in front of me. I had no idea why, but butterflies erupted in my stomach. *Stupid insects.*

He offered his hand to me, but I didn't move. I couldn't. I knew he'd told me that I couldn't see his future because it was tied to mine, but I wasn't sure. There were so many rules that I still knew nothing about.

"Trust me. You don't have to, but I want you to. Our lives are intertwined, but you still have a choice. And I want your choice to be to trust me." I knew he hadn't meant to, but his words gutted me. They were nearly the same words that Cassie had fed me so long ago. I couldn't help my body's reaction—I flinched.

His hand and head dropped at nearly the same time.

"Someone said those same words to you, didn't they?" He didn't meet my eyes.

"How?" was all I could croak out.

"I don't have to be an oracle to see pain." Then his eyes met mine. Offering me his hand again, he added, "Just give me a chance to earn your trust."

I couldn't allow the sins of another to cloud how I saw him, and that's what I was doing.

Taking his hand, I nodded. It was only when I felt his warm skin against mine that I realized that this had been the first person, since Jensen, I'd touched. It made me sad to think how careful I'd have to be. Would I be able to touch anyone again?

He didn't pull his hand from mine. He only squeezed it reassuringly.

While I couldn't see his future directly, icy fear washed over me, causing me to pull my hand from his.

"We need to get going." I half coughed.

"Where to?" he asked, standing up.

"We have a meeting with the Court of the Sun and the Moon. We have to go over the compact we have with them. Just to be sure we're allowed to operate the same way my ya-ya did." Hell, for once, I sounded like I knew what the crap I was talking about. Hey, fake it till you make it, right?

The town really was adorable, from what little I was able to see of it. It'd been so long since I'd been here, and I mostly remembered my mom and Ya-ya fighting, so I never really took note of the town. The place had a quaintness about it, though my skin pricked with the amount of supernatural energy pulsing through it.

I moved around a lot as a kid, never really staying in one place for too long, so I knew when a town had a heartbeat. This one did. The people seemed to move around as if they were blood flowing in veins, giving the place life. I couldn't help but smile. *No, it hadn't really been in my plan to give up my hard-fought college degree at the very last second, abandon my best and only friend, and—* Nope, I wasn't going down this trail of thought. I was going to make the best of this and make the active choice to be happy.

"Earth to Lana." Damen's voice cut through my thoughts like the annoying squeal of a cat in heat.

"Sorry, what?" I was perplexed, looking from his eyes to the object he held out to me.

"Here, before we do a whole lot, I want you to put these on," he instructed me, sternly waggling the gloves at me.

Raising an eyebrow, I puzzled, "Uh, why? It isn't even that cold out. It's August, for crap's sake." If I put those babies on, I'd end up with major clam hands.

"Because when we meet with the Court, I'd like you to not be rude and be able to shake their hands. Plus, we don't know the extent of your abilities. What if you touch a door handle after someone else. Could you get a reading that way? Do you know?"

I paused at his words. The truth was, I had no idea. This was all so new to me. I had my ya-ya's journal, but when the power moves from one oracle to the next, it becomes unique to her. I looked at him. I half expected him to have a smug, knowing smile ready to gloat that he was right, but what I saw in him caused me to stop. It was genuine caring I saw staring back at me. His job was to protect me. He was under no obligation to like or even care about me, but he did.

"You're right." I sighed.

I grabbed the slender leather gloves and slipped them on.

"Come on, short stuff, I saw a bakery not far from here. We'll get some food and OJ." Grabbing my hand, he pulled me along. Under normal circumstances, I would have objected, but I found my fingers curling around his without much thought. *How peculiar.*

"Daily Knead. That's such a cute name."

"Let's hope they have something to feed the bear, because I'm hungry!" Damen half laughed as he pushed the door open.

A delightful tinkling sounded as the door swung open. The bright white of the tile made the small space seem bigger than I knew it was.

"Welcome to the Knead!" a cheerful voice called out. As much as I wanted to return the gesture of greeting, the pictures that lined the walls caught my eye. There were several black-and-white images of the town that seemed to span who knew how many years. Finally, after what was far too long, I glanced to the left side of the shop. There behind the counter stood a dark-haired girl who couldn't have been more than about eighteen, whose name tag read *Meghan*.

"Hi! Thank you. Sorry, I got so distracted by the pictures. They're beautiful," I explained, looking over to the opposing wall. There, where I'd just come from, stood Damen, who also seemed captivated by the photos.

"Aren't they? I swear every time I come in here, I see something I haven't seen before." She giggled with a wide smile.

We both grinned. She had a kind of sweet innocence about her that led me to believe she had to be fully human. Not that that was a bad thing.

"What would you like today?" she asked, looking up at the menu posted behind her.

My eyes went wide at all the options.

"Oh my gosh. Wow, you guys have a ton!"

"Yeah, Michelle is practically a witch in the kitchen." She laughed at her own joke. There was just something so endearing about her.

"How about a cinnamon roll? And—"

"Make that two, and two cups of orange juice. Please and thank you!" Damen chimed in.

"Got it," she replied brightly.

Taking the cash Damen handed her, she popped the register open, then turned to walk to the back of the store.

"Shall we sit?" I asked, walking over to a small round table.

A few moments later, Meghan walked over and set down our food and drinks. "I hope you enjoy it!"

"Thank you," Damen replied.

Without another word, we both dove in. It was the perfect mix of sweet meets cream meets spice. It was far and away the best cinnamon roll I'd ever had.

A soft chuckling pulled me out of my cinnamon-induced stupor. Opening my eyes, that at some point I'd shut, I saw Damen's grin.

"What?" I questioned, frowning.

"Oh, nothing. Just figured out the way to your heart is cinnamon rolls."

Scoffing, I replied indignantly, "Nuh-uh." I know—not my wittiest reply, but hey, I was mad he was right. But what he didn't know was any sweet would do.

Then, out of nowhere, he reached out and swept a thumb across my bottom lip. My heart sped up for some crazy reason.

Raising his finger up, he smirked. "Icing." He then dipped his digit in his mouth to clean it off. A fucking meteor could have hit the whole damn town and yet my attention would still have been glued to him.

"I hope you guys are enjoying your food." The woman's voice was like a bucket of ice water, one I clearly needed.

Sucking in a gulp of air, I looked over at the new woman. She had long wavy dark hair and kind brown eyes. If I had to say, I would have pegged her for somewhere north of thirty-seven or so.

"Oh my gosh, I think these are the best cinnamon rolls I've ever had. I don't know who made them, but they need a raise." My mouth watered at the idea of ordering seconds.

The woman let out a loud bark of laughter. After a moment, she said, "Well, I'll be sure to take that under advisement, considering it was me."

"Oh!" It was then I realized her name tag read *Michelle*. The either literal or metaphorical witch in the kitchen.

"Are you guys new to town?" She smoothed down a flour-coated apron.

"Yes, ma'am. Just got here yesterday," Damen mumbled around a gooey bite of sugary confection.

Shaking my head, I said, "Please excuse his manners. He was raised in a barn by wild hogs."

"True story!" he hollered, while raising a hand with a clenched fist. The action sent something flying from his lips to the table. By Hades's bouncing balls, he was an absolute mess.

Michelle, however, just giggled.

"Well, welcome. I'm Michelle Price, and you already met Meghan." She smiled, sticking out a hand in greeting.

I returned the gesture. "It's nice to meet you. I'm Lana, and this reprobate is Damen. Like he said, we just got here last night. We live in a cabin on the outskirts of town. My ya-ya died, and we came to uh, take over her business," I tried to explain, but my words came out in a jumbled mess. It was hard to tell if she was human or something else. While I might have been human, I was god-touched. I was a gift, as were my abilities.

She gave me a knowing smile, and I swear I saw her wink.

"Well, let me know if you need anything. Oh, I almost forgot. I think there will be a ghost tour tonight. It might be a great way to learn more about our lovely town."

"Oh, that would be fun!" I sang in a bright voice. I knew in that moment this might be a place I could fall in love with.

"Thanks!" Damen garbled, sending a half-chewed chunk of cinnamon roll flying across the table to land smack dab on Michelle's apron. Oh, good gods, please no.

Nearly choking, Damen coughed, cleared the possible obstruction, and rasped, "Sorry, it's just so good."

She smiled at him, then me as I mouthed, "I'm sorry." She just chuckled as she walked away.

"Damen, if first impressions were left up to you, I think we'd be sincerely screwed."

"Who's to say we aren't?" he moaned suggestively, while waggling his eyebrows. The poor tufts of hair looked like scared caterpillars quivering on his forehead. I groaned as if in pain. And this was what I had to look forward to for eternity. Fucking lovely.

CHAPTER 5

"*D*ude, relax, would you? You're making me nervous," Damen whispered, so close to my ear I felt the warm puffs of air from his words against my skin, sending a shiver up my spine.

"You're not helping!" I snapped. I couldn't help it. I was so stressed about this damn meeting. If they didn't agree to the compact, we'd have to move. I mean, what if I screwed the whole thing up? Where would we go? I had a job to do and a billion-year-long, ever-growing petitioner list.

"I can practically hear your thoughts," he added annoyingly.

Glaring at him, I opened my mouth to reply, but the double doors swung open. I swallowed hard, hoping that would ease the lump that had formed in my throat. No such luck.

Damen grabbed my arm as we were getting up and pulled me to him.

"I feel what you feel. That's our connection as oracle and guardian. I'm here to protect you. I won't let them, or anyone, hurt you. Trust me." His words acted like a balm to my overreacting anxiety. His eyes studied me, and in that moment, his words hit me full force. He was so many things, but he'd always be here to protect me.

I nodded and relaxed slightly.

"There's my girl." He sighed with a smirk, which didn't cause a bazillion and six butterflies to erupt in my stomach or anything.

"Ms. Valis?" a small feminine voice rang out.

"That's me!" I exclaimed, like a total moron.

"This way, but your, uh, friend will have to stay."

I felt Damen stiffen at her statement.

"I'm sorry. I'm afraid that's simply not possible. This is Damen. He's my guardian. If I go, he goes. If he stays, I stay," I stated with absolute authority. Even my own tone shocked me, but this was my place in life now. I had to abide by the rules set on the oracle.

"Fine," the woman sneered, before moving out of the way and gesturing toward the open room.

This was it, now or never. Damen placed his hand at the small of my back and lightly pushed me. We both walked in.

Eleven members of the court sat down behind a long table. Eleven separate pairs of eyes sat staring back at me disapprovingly. Well, maybe not all of them, but some of them did for sure.

"Uh, hi?" It came out a question. Fuck, I was such an idiot. *Uh, hi? Ugh.*

A woman who looked to be my age with dark brown hair and an odd gray-green stare smiled softly at my words. My grandmother had listed the names of the Court members, but there weren't any descriptions, so I really had no idea who anyone was.

"You're the new Oracle of Delphi?" a dark-haired man scoffed. This time I was pretty sure there was disapproval in his tone. There was something in his blue eyes. Maybe it was the way he looked at me or maybe it was my own insecurities, but I suddenly felt like an ant under a magnifying glass, and this prick was the kid holding it.

"Uh, either that or I need to be heavily medicated." *Ugh!* My hand flew to cover my mouth. Shit was just coming out without my permission.

"Oh, for crap's sake, Roman! Could we just not scare her?" the smiling woman from before snapped.

"How about we just introduce ourselves and you can do the same. Let's start there," a slender woman sporting some seriously big hair groaned. In turn, they all gave their names. The smiling girl was Michaela Petran. She looked to be my same age. I couldn't help but smile at her when it was her turn to talk. She was engaging and had a strong air about her, someone I wanted to get to know.

Not everyone on the Court exuded her gripping personality. The gruff man was Roman Bishop. Frankly, he scared the shit out of me. However, I thought that's just who he was, very intense. Damen didn't seem to have a reaction at all, except to one man.

When Lawrence Mills addressed me, I could feel aggression and disgust waving off of the man. Damen's hand gripped mine tightly, and he even shifted slightly as if to ready himself. It was an action I was sure wasn't missed by the rest of the Court.

After the Court finished the introductions, it was my turn.

"I'm Lana Velis. I am the oracle, gift of the gods to the mortals. I'm new to all of this, as my mother made the choice to keep me away for so long. My ya-ya and her guardian passed away recently, and the power of the oracle has passed to me. While I'm long-lived, I am granted a new guardian. This is Damen Costas. We're here to renegotiate the terms of the compact that was signed by my grandmother and this Court many years ago." My voice may have been steady and confident, but my heart was beating like the hooves of a wild horse.

There was an uncomfortable pause before Roman spoke up.

"So just because your grandmother had a contract with us, we're supposed to grant you one?" While he came off kinda like an asshole, I thought his question had merit.

"In the end, that's up to you. What I'm asking for is a place to live. My grandmother left me her home, on the outskirts of town. I would like to reside there, honor the petitioners who are on my official list, and do my job," I explained, though I knew there was more to it.

"And what exactly would our town get from allowing something like this? Letting outsiders flood our borders with their memories intact sounds like it would be a crack in the foundation our town is built on," Ric Kasun asked. While his words were stern, his eyes glittered with kindness.

"The Court will have me. As with my grandmother, the Court will have a permanent place on my petitioner list, and should the need arise, I will be at your disposal. The way it works is I have a list. This list is incredibly, exceedingly, annoyingly, and infuriatingly long. The petitioners come in, I will do my thing, they will be able to stay in the town, bringing in money and such, then when they leave, they will lose their memory of the town, but not the reading they were given. I have laws I am bound to, so if someone isn't on my list and I see a future, I can't help them. If I see something damning, such as a threat to the town, my hands are bound. If the Court does not agree to these terms, there will be little I can do." Silence fell again as each member thought about my words. I could tell it wasn't so much that they didn't want me here, but that they had a big responsibility of protecting this place, the way of life, and the people in it. In an odd way, that thought alone helped me both relax and gave me the urge to be part of such a thing, such a community.

"Was that a threat?" Roman intoned calmly. Though his words were even, his glare was pointed, and his lips were pursed into a flat white line.

"Not at all. It was an explanation of power," I clarified.

Damen shifted to my right slightly, the same direction Roman sat. Roman's eyes, ever watchful, tracked the slight change, and he smirked.

"How do we even know she's got any kind of ability at all?" Roman added the question in a bored tone.

"He makes a good point. She was a human until days ago? What's to say anything has changed?" Lilith Blackstone added.

"Why not let her show you?" Damen snapped. I whipped my

head to meet his gaze. I gave him a look that conveyed, *What the fuck are you thinking?* But he clearly didn't get it. He had no idea I'd only ever done this twice, and both were totally an accident.

"Oh! Yes!" Madame Tahini clapped her hands excitedly. Her motions sent her long, nearly black hair sliding in front of her face. She blew out a long breath, causing the strands to fly outward. "How about Mr. Loud Mouth? Mr. Roman could use an omen!" She was clearly pleased with herself.

"Well, I can't very well read anyone unless they agree, and . . ."

My words fell away as I saw Roman tent his fingers under his chin and a wicked smirk slowly spread on his face.

"I'm not a coward. Come, Lana, read me. Let's see if you can tell me something no one else knows." His words dripped with challenge.

Fuck my life. I stood there for a solid thirty seconds, unable to move. What if all I saw was that he was going to have a peanut butter and jelly sandwich for dinner? Or that he was going to break my face? Oh, by Hades's bouncing balls, I had to find a damn backbone and get the hell over this.

Finding that backbone I'd been missing, I walked over and removed my glove.

"I just need your hand," I informed him, unable to hide the shaking in my voice.

With utterly no emotion, he stuck his hand out for me.

Taking in a deep breath, I reached out and laid my hand on top of his.

A crash of crystal and china rang out as they fell to the floor, flooding the expensive-looking Persian rug with wine. He didn't seem to even notice the mess he'd made. His vibrant blue eyes were focused in such a way that went beyond obsession; he was like a shark stalking his prey. The woman sat on the edge of the table, her breathing shallow. There wasn't fear in her eyes, not the way they fell into a golden color then back again.

"Lie back," he ordered, his tone rough.

She paused at his words, and her breathing hitched.

Reaching back, he grabbed a fistful of her hair, angled her face to his, and snarled, "Lie. Back."

She allowed him to guide her back until she was splayed out for him like a goddamn meal. Releasing his grip on her hair, he took a slight step back to observe his prey. To feast with his eyes the meal he would devour. He could feel his need for her, and it only seemed to anger him.

"Part your legs." This time she didn't hesitate. She knew that tone. She knew that intent. Slowly she spread her thighs until her lace-clad sex was bare to him. She had to stop her shiver. He'd only see that as weakness, and fuck if she'd ever show him anything other than strength.

He slid fingers up her silken thighs and she had to stifle a moan. He let his too-warm fingers dip down past the hem of her panties and yet lower. A moment later he pulled the lace down and stuffed his prize into his pocket. He could wait no longer. He needed to taste her. Without breaking away from her eyes, he slid his finger into his mouth.

He needed more. He'd have everything, all of her. He slid his hand back to her core. Parting her slightly, he found her clit and rubbed slow circles. Her eyes rolled back and her head fell lightly back to the hard wood table. It was then she felt his warm breath on her core. His mouth covered her as he began a slow feast of her. She didn't stifle her moan. There was no fucking way she could have.

I sucked in a deep breath of air as the erotic scene ended abruptly. I yanked my hand from his without much thought, just praying I wouldn't be pulled back in. I had to blink rapidly to coax my vision back. I could feel more than see everyone's gaze on me. I glanced down at my exposed hand to see its bright white glow begin to fade back to my normal tanned color. As the white glow receded, my face flooded with heat from such an erotic scene. I could feel everything he felt, everything she felt. It left me panting and embarrassed to have seen such a thing in front of so many people.

"Well," Roman's lips twitched. "Other than lighting up like a light bulb, what did the great Oracle of Delphi see?" His question was laced with a mix of amusement and disbelief.

"Uh . . ." I started, but stopped myself. Was this information something he really wanted spread far and wide? I could feel heat rush to my face. I had no freaking idea what to do. I glanced to Damen, who just stared at me. He was no help.

Taking a deep breath, I mumbled sheepishly, "Uh um, I think I'd like to tell you in private? This particular vision was, um, rather personal." I stammered around the words.

His eyes raised ever so slightly, something I would read as shock for this hard man. However, in others possibly, I would have questioned that I'd seen anything at all.

Roman nodded and motioned for me to walk over to him.

"Did Roman's omen turn him shy? Oh my!" Tahini giggled.

Roman shot her a death stare that it seemed she couldn't care less about.

Leaning down, I retold him everything I saw. While he didn't seem to have any reaction verbally, his hands tightened into fists.

Once I was done, I began my retreat, but Roman's hand flew out like lightning to snake around my wrist. Thankfully, he took care to keep his hand on the edge of my lightweight sweater. My heart rate went sky high as I heard Damen shuffle up. I reached out a hand to stop him. Looking over my shoulder, I caught his rage-filled gaze.

"I'm fine," I mouthed. While I knew it likely wouldn't matter, he did pause. Was his body getting bigger? I blinked, but returned my attention to Roman.

"Tell no one," he hissed, so low I thought it doubtful anyone else heard.

"It's my duty as sacred Oracle. All things are held in confidence," I assured him in a smooth confident tone that told nothing about the quivering mass of Jell-O I was feeling inside.

Clearly satisfied, he let me go, but not before glancing—and smirking—at Damen. It was the kind of expression that was meant to taunt him.

"Stop antagonizing him," I snapped at Roman. The words flew out of my mouth before I had a moment to stop them.

Michaela erupted in laughter. "Oh man, I like her. She's totally got my vote!"

"Please step out and allow us to debate and then we'll call you back in," Mathilde Augustine instructed politely.

As soon as the door closed, Damen snatched my hand and inspected it.

"I swear to the gods, if he hurt you . . ." he mumbled.

"I'm fine," I assured him. My words, however, didn't seem to stop him from fussing over me like a mother hen. It was both odd and a little exhilarating to have someone fuss over me. I was sure I'd never had anyone do that. Well, other than Jensen. My mother had left so early on, and my dad was always useless.

"Well, you look fine. But I'm here to tell you if he lays another hand on you . . ." He let the threat hang thick in the air.

"Did you, uh, get bigger back there?" I pulled my hand from his.

Running a hand through his hair, he nodded.

"Yeah, that happens when I see something as a threat to you. Well, I mean I knew it would, but that's the first time." It was then I realized this was all new to him, too. Just as unsure as I was, he was likely the same.

Cupping his face, I pulled his gaze to mine.

"You don't have to be okay with this. There isn't a rule or law that says you have to be. You know that, don't you?"

I couldn't explain it, but I could feel an overwhelming sense of peace fill me even at my own words. We always hear people ask are you okay; I'd always felt like I had to say yes and believe it.

His brown eyes searched mine for a long moment. For the first time, I saw the same fears and uncertainty in my own gaze reflected back at me.

"You can come back in." A voice wove its way into the spell that I'd unknowingly created. Neither of us moved right away.

After a long moment, I dropped my hands and backed away.

47

Just as soon as I let go, I felt his hand tug on mine as he laced our fingers together.

"Come on, oracle."

Where he led, I found myself following, and oddly I was okay with it.

CHAPTER 6

The Court voted ten to one in my favor, though I didn't think Roman Bishop had been the one against.

With that meeting behind me, I was able to relax slightly. I had a place to live and a job to do, but for now I could just have a little fun and go on a ghost tour. Well, after a certain Damen got his fancy new tattoo. I didn't need one, as I'd already had mine at such a young age.

"Do you have any tattoos?" I inquired of Damen as we neared the exit of the Court chamber, stopping at the back of the room.

"No, you? I mean other than the one." His voice had this deep tone that reminded me of the distant rumbling of thunder rolling as a storm grew closer.

"Yeah, I have one other," I replied absentmindedly.

Reaching for the doorknob, he paused and quirked up an eyebrow in question.

Smiling, I reached for the door and opened it myself. Just before walking through I added in a flirty tone, "I guess you'll just have to find out what and where it is."

I had no idea what had possessed me. I couldn't help it.

He smirked and quipped, "Game on then, oracle."

Walking through the doorway, I saw a girl sitting at a small desk. As soon as we walked in, she smiled at us brightly. She had the kind of smile that made me want to smile back at her. Her light brown hair was in a mess of a bun atop her head, but there was a red bandana tied lovingly around her head in that way I'd seen a lot of pinup girls had done way back when. As if in direct contrast, her nose ring, black-rimmed glasses, and tattoo-covered arms seemed to stand out more.

"Hey there! You my first victim? Oh, I mean customer?" She laughed at her own joke, and I joined her.

Running his big hand through his shaggy hair, Damen coughed nervously. I narrowed my eyes at him. Was he afraid? Maybe he didn't like needles? I opened my mouth to jab at him, but then thought better of it. This man wanted to always put out a strong front.

"Yeah, I guess that'd be me." He half coughed.

"Well, I'm Addie, and I was the one over in the corner scribbling notes earlier. It's nice to meet you two, you know, not in a meeting." She smiled at Damen.

"Well, not in a formal setting, I'm Lana. And this is Damen," I introduced brightly as I stuck out a hand in greeting.

"You're making a statement with those gloves. I can dig it." Before I could say anything else, she turned to Damen and asked, "Well big guy, what do you want? I can do pretty much anything. Just leave the magic part up to me." She winked at him to add emphasis.

She went on to explain that he could have whatever, and wherever he wanted, even if he wanted it to be invisible. He showed her an image on his phone, and she just smiled.

"Fuck yeah. Step into my office," she agreed, as she escorted us around to a large chair and her official tattooing station.

Addie took some time to set up everything. She made a stencil, placed it on Damen's forearm, and seemed to weave her own brand of magic as she pulled out her inks and got everything ready.

"Do I get to know what you're getting?" I asked Damen.

"No, you can wait," he cooed, pretty much dismissing me.

Groaning, I turned away, respecting his wishes even if it was just to annoy me.

"So Lana, Damen, tell me about yourselves," Addie instructed as she began her assault into Damen's arm. I could hear the telltale buzzing of the tattoo machine.

"Well, I'm basically a what-you-see-is-what-you-get kinda guy. I was gigging and writing music before I was called up to be this one's guardian," he explained. I couldn't see anything but could hear a little pain in his voice. While he'd trained for his position, he too had to leave a life behind.

"What about you, Lana?" Addie asked as the buzzing continued.

"Well, I was almost done with college. I only had one final left. Then I'd have my degree in graphic design. I love to draw and create logos and all kinds of things."

"Hey, that would be useful around here. There are a surprising number of businesses around here. Maybe I can give a nudge in the right direction, I mean if you're up for that kind of thing."

"That would be great!" I nearly cried with excitement.

"And Damen, you should ask Willow at Coffee Haven or Michelle over at Daily Knead, about doing some music days. I can ask around about open mic nights too. Oh snap! There's also Music in the Square on the third Thursdays of the month in the summer. I can send you the details."

"I'd appreciate that."

I thought back to Damen on his guitar and the spell he'd seemed to weave. It would be a shame for the world to be deprived of his talent.

"How are you guys liking our town?" she asked.

"Everyone has been amazingly nice and welcoming. Well, aside from that meeting. It was kind of intense," I admitted, looking at a few photos on the wall.

"Yeah, the Court can be like that at times. But in the end,

think of us as a family. A fucking dysfunctional family." She chuckled.

"I believe it," Damen muttered.

"So, Lana, talk to me. You're the new oracle? What's that like?" she asked.

"Well, I can see anyone's future if I touch them. Hence the style choice." I wiggled my fingers.

"Ah."

"But honestly, I don't know what I'm doing. I feel like I've been thrust into this whole thing and I'm just going on fumes." My voice cracked but I refuse to let it take me over.

"Yeah, we've all been there. Even though we might have grown up knowing what we were, we all have times where we are trying to find out what's unique about ourselves and how to be us. Life isn't a straight line. We all have to find our own path."

I hadn't expected such insight from someone my age, but her words caused me to pause for a long moment.

"Well, I'm done here. And if I do say so myself, it's pretty fucking awesome," she announced confidently.

"Can I see?" I chirped, bouncing on my toes.

"It looks good. Fine, oracle, come and see." He sighed as if I'd asked him a million times.

Turning, I saw Addie with her arms crossed, beaming with pride. Damen held his arm out, and I was able to see the image. I froze, unable to formulate a response.

"Do you not like it?" Addie asked in a worried tone.

"Lana?" Damen hedged. After a long moment, I met his gaze.

"You wouldn't believe me unless I showed you," I intoned.

I slid my hands down to my jeans and unbuttoned them. Pulling down the waistline, I exposed the only other tattoo on my body. Silence fell in the small room as we all just looked.

When I turned eighteen, I got a small tattoo on my left hip. It was a Delphian epsilon sitting on the sun. It looked like two curved "E's" that were a mirror image and a line separating them.

It was the symbol of Apollo, the god of music and poetry, from whom it was thought that my new power came.

Sitting freshly inked on Damen's arm was the same symbol. While the art differed, as they were done by two different artists, the symbol was just the same.

"Well, that isn't the weirdest shit I've ever seen, but it's pretty far up there," Addie said.

"I guess I don't have to hunt for that tattoo now. But yeah, that's weird as hell," Damen joked.

"Well, if there's nothing else, I have some things to do. And I hear you have a ghost tour to get to," Addie added.

"I hear that as well. Thanks a ton for everything, and I hope we get to hear from you soon about some open mic nights," Damen reminded her as he shook her hand.

"I'm on it! Oh, Lana, I almost forgot. Here's my number." She handed me a card. "Call me for lunch or something. I might have some personal work we could collaborate on."

"I'd love that!" I was excited by the prospect of a friend. I had the feeling Addie would be a good one to hang out with. Hey, I was always down for a friend; I could use all the help I could get at this point.

"So, you're really set to go on this tour, aren't you?" Damen grumbled as we walked down the sidewalk.

"Yes. Come on, you'll have fun!" I gushed brightly, practically dragging him along.

"It's just so touristy," he groaned, as if in pain. I rolled my eyes. I mean, I really couldn't help it. He was being an infant.

"Well, sorry, big guy. We're going! Maybe there will be a stop at a bar, and you can get a beer. Will that make you happy?" I snickered in a tone I'd use with children.

Narrowing his eyes at me, he poked me in the ribs. I yelped and slapped at his hand.

"Hey! That tickled!"

"That's the point, oracle."

We walked along the center square until we came upon a small white trolley. On the side were the words *Moon Light Ghost Tours*. From what I could see, there were only about ten people on the bus, which made me feel better. Less chance of accidently bumping into someone.

We walked up to the bus where a tall dark-haired man, dressed head to toe in black, stood leaning against the white metal.

His gaze shifted to mine, and I had to stifle a gasp. His eyes were like nothing I'd ever seen before. The whole of his right eye was black. It looked as though it had been dipped in black ink. His left eye was a rich sapphire blue.

His grin was the kind of smile that under most circumstances would have had me dropping trow. Now, however, cock-blocking Damen was still complaining behind me.

"Why, hello there." The too-hot-for-his-own-good man seemed to roll the words more than speak them.

"Hi!" I replied, sticking out my glove-clad hand.

Glancing down at it, he smirked.

"Fashion statement?" He took my hand in his.

"Something like that," I joked.

He raised the back of my hand to his lips and placed a soft kiss on it. I felt blood rush to my face and knew I was blushing.

"And what's your name, beautiful girl?" His mouth was still so close to my hand, I could feel his words through the thin leather of the glove.

"Lana," Damen spat from behind us. Somehow the damn brute managed to make my name sound like a curse word. I had no idea what had gotten into him.

Still holding my hand in his, the man flicked his eyes behind me. Whatever he saw caused him to smile in what I would call a challenge.

"Lana, beautiful name. I'm Rayonus. Please call me Ray. I will be your tour guide. Do you happen to have your ticket? Or will you be paying me directly?" He released my hand. The way he said the word *directly* made it sound like a naughty proposition. His little wink didn't help his case in the slightest. Or did it?

Nodding and absolutely not blushing, I handed him our two tickets.

Pushing his way past me, Damen shoved me over and took my place. I let out a little huff and glared at him.

"I'm Damen. And, personally, I think it's far prettier a name." He spat the words as he stuck his hand out.

Ray took the hand and shook it. They both stood there just shaking hands. Something, I wasn't sure what, passed between the two, but the macho-ness of it went way above my pay grade.

"Okay, not that this is awkward or anything, but I'm getting on the bus." I rolled my eyes at their shenanigans as I went up the stairs.

I found a seat up front, next to the window, and sat down. A moment later Damen walked in and sat next to me, of course.

"What the hell was that about?" I hissed in a low tone.

"Nothing. Just didn't like how he looked at you," he grumbled.

Turning in my seat slightly, I crossed my arms over my chest and looked at his sandy brown eyes.

"Damen, we're stuck together for like ever. We have to find some common ground here. I will get hit on. I'll even date. You cannot scare away anyone who wants to come into the same zip code as me."

"It's my job to protect you." He crossed his arms, looking bored.

"I know, but don't protect me into submission. I'm a big girl. Let me live a little, okay, grandpa?"

That caused him to erupt into barks of laughter.

Soon, Ray got on to the bus and the tour started.

The trolley stopped and started a number of times in a number of places within the town. If I had thought the place had magic during the day, at night the place seemed to be reborn into something entirely different. Gone was the innocence of the sun. It was replaced by the taunting moon and the trickster stars.

Ray was absolutely mesmerizing as he told the stories about each of the historical sites of the town. He seemed to know all of the juicy bits of every story. It made me wonder just how old he was. I knew people in this town weren't always what they seemed. While he looked to be in his late twenties, possibly early thirties, I knew there was a good chance he was far older.

He used voices, cracked jokes, and was an absolute shameless flirt. I instantly liked him. In the game of fuck, marry, or kill, he'd firmly be in the fuck category. That line of thought had my eyes shifting to Damen. *What category would he be in?* I'd seen him in nothing but a towel and he had a great body, so the fuck section was possible, but he was also tender and wasn't afraid to show his emotions.

"What?" he blurted.

I just blinked at him, wondering if I'd spoken aloud.

"You're staring at me."

Damn it!

"Oh, sorry," I mumbled.

The trolley slowed to a stop, just as it had done a number of times. This time, however, it wasn't at a store, old home, or even abandoned building, but rather we stopped at a line of dense trees that ran across the southernmost edge of the town. I looked at Ray, who sported a devilish grin. His pink tongue darted out and ran across his lower lip. He was the definition of trouble.

"I know some of you might be confused as to why we stopped here. There are no sordid stories, no murders, and no hauntings to tell you of." He paused for what could only be assumed to be dramatic effect. "However, there is a myth. Now, whether or not you believe it is up to you."

Motioning to the tree line, he began weaving his tale.

"Just beyond these trees, you will find a dirt path. Along this path it's said you'll see the trials of your own life in some fashion. It has been reported that people walking down it have heard the tinkling bells of children's laughter, though no one quite knows why. At the end of the path, you will come upon a small pond." Ray's one black eye seemed to glint in the light of the moon, making it seem as if it too were a star.

"I heard from a man who went on this journey that if you gaze upon yourself in the waters of the still surface of the pond, you can stare directly into the blind eyes of the Fates themselves and see the moment of your death. Now, I don't know how credible this man was, but he said that if you can find the Fates, they will offer you a boon in return. The last I heard of him, he was still in search of the three hags."

The night around us seemed to grow so still that had a single cricket chirped, it could have been heard for a hundred miles. I had no idea how long we all sat there in silence, letting Ray's words echo into the inky darkness. I didn't realize we were moving until we were nearly back to the center of town.

"Well, gentlemen and"—Ray paused, looked at me, and winked—"ladies, that's the end of our tour. I hope you've enjoyed the very real haunts, stories, and ghosts of our fair town. But be careful—you never know what things might be hunting you in the night."

We all started clapping; even Damen joined in. Everyone filed off the trolley, talking about the tales they'd heard and whether or not they should go hunting them.

Passing Ray, I waved a goodbye and turned to go. I felt a hand grab mine. Forgetting about my gloves, I went to yank my hand back but thought better of it. I turned to see Ray on the other end.

"Hey there, Ms. Lana. I hope you enjoyed the tour."

I opened my mouth to assure him I had, but I didn't get the chance, as Damen shoved his way between us.

"Hands off," Damen snarled.

Letting go of my hand, Ray peered around Damen to meet my eyes.

"I don't think your lapdog likes me very much."

"I don't think I like him very much either," I agreed in an annoyed tone.

Damen whirled to face me. His gaze was fixed, and his lips were peeled back slightly.

"I'm here to protect you," he growled between clenched teeth. "What don't you get about that?"

Putting one hand on my hip and the other one gesturing to Ray, I hissed, "Does it look like I need protecting?"

His jaw turned into a white line of strain.

"Yeah, boss, trust me. My intentions are purely"—he paused and licked his lips—"honorable." How he made that word sound utterly sexual was beyond me. That's when I understood. Ray was baiting Damen. And Damen was falling for it. His arms and chest were growing in size. I had to figure out a way to defuse the situation before it became a thing.

I was going to hate myself for how much of an absolute dumb girl I was about to be, but it was all I could think of.

Internally I rolled my eyes, then I stepped off the curb and mock twisted my ankle.

"Oh, ouch!" I complained loudly.

Damen sucked in a breath, fell to his knees, and put his hands on my foot.

"Lana! Are you okay?" he fretted in a worried tone.

Sliding his hands from my foot to my ankle, he inspected the supposed wound.

Ray gave me a knowing smile, winked, and walked away. He was absolutely fuckable, but not a bit marriage material.

Damen slipped his arms under me and lifted me up, cradling me. I was one hundred percent capable of walking, but I let myself sink a little deeper into his hold. Besides, it wasn't like he'd ever know I wasn't really hurt.

CHAPTER 7

I had thought my biggest hurdle to overcome would be getting the Court's approval to renew the compact. Whoo boy, was I wrong!

"Have you even made a dent in it?" Damen wondered, looking over my shoulder at the illuminated screen.

I let out a huge breath and pinched my brow in frustration. He was referring to my petitioner list. I'd been in Havenwood Falls five days before I started seeing people, and that had been two weeks ago. I wasn't even close to catching up to the forever long list.

"No." I breathed the word. Staring back at me was the list. The long as hell, hundred-years-long freaking list.

I let my head slump slowly down until I felt it hit the keyboard.

"Could you see more people?" Damen suggested, knowing full well the answer.

"No," I groaned. "I'm pretty wiped out if I see more than five a day. Remember the day we thought we could bump it up to ten?"

As if in answer, I felt his hands touch my shoulders. He brushed his fingers so lightly against my bare shoulders, it was as if his touch was a question. I froze, wondering where he was going.

His grip tightened and then loosened. He was massaging my overtired and overworked muscles.

I couldn't help but melt into his hands. I swear someone even started moaning. Oh wait, yeah, that was totally me. I should have stopped him, told him I was fine, told him I could take care of myself. But that would have been a lie. I shouldn't have taken comfort in him, or at least I held some convoluted idea I shouldn't take comfort in a guy I hardly knew.

"You think too much," he whispered. Sometimes I wondered if he shared a little of my powers.

I knew he was right. So in that moment, I just shut my brain off and enjoyed someone else taking care of me. I found myself drifting in and out of consciousness. It felt as if I was falling in a slow cradle-like descent to the ground. But for whatever reason, I wasn't afraid of falling. I fell for what seemed like hours, until I felt something hit me. I opened my eyes and didn't understand what I was seeing. I was standing smack dab in the middle of the Havenwood Falls downtown square, except it was fully night and I couldn't recall how I'd gotten here.

Something zipped past my ear, making a whistling noise as it fell to the ground. I glanced down and saw a glowing red ember. What the—

I had a sinking feeling. Turning around, I sank to my knees and my hand flew to my mouth in horror. Fire was raining down on the town, people were running, and buildings were burning. I tried to scream, but the heat from the building blaze stole my voice away. I couldn't move. I couldn't help as the people tried to drop and roll to put out the fire on their bodies. They were burning. Everything was burning.

This time I was able to scream. This time my voice rang out, shattering everything.

"Lana! Lana!" a voice echoed. I felt myself shaking and sobbing. I was out of control. I thrashed against my restraints, but nothing changed. I was trapped by iron.

"Lana." This time the voice was soft, feather light. It was a pause button to my wild emotions and caused me to still.

Finally, after a long moment, I opened my eyes. Looking back at me was Damen. He suddenly felt like an anchor, something tethering me to the earth, keeping me from flying away.

"You okay?" I rasped. His features were pulled tight and his skin slightly pale.

"Me? You're the one asking if I'm okay? You're a trip," he scoffed, as he ran a hand over my sweat-soaked forehead.

"What happened?" I hesitated. I was a bit confused. I'd had visions, but this was unlike anything I'd ever seen before.

"I was rubbing your shoulders and you fell asleep. I carried you to bed then went to bed myself. I heard you screaming—" His voice cracked slightly, but he coughed as if to hide something. "I tried to wake you up but couldn't. Then you just stopped once I started whispering to you."

I couldn't look at him. I couldn't tell him what I'd seen. Hell, I didn't really even know what I saw.

We both sat there on my bed, him holding me and me letting him. After a while he moved to get up.

"Wait!" I panicked. He froze at my words. He looked down at me, and there was something in his expression that I couldn't name. He seemed to be holding his breath.

I had no idea what possessed me, but I reached up to his face and pulled him down to me. Brushing my lips against his, I felt him tense under my fingertips. What in the gods' names was I thinking? I pulled away. *I'm so dumb!*

Suddenly, he crushed his lips to mine. Gripping his hand in my hair, he tilted my face up to his as if to give himself better access to me. My heart felt as if it would jump out of my chest, it was beating so quickly.

I parted my lips and let him explore me. When I'd kissed Cassie, she'd always been quick to retreat, never taking the time to let us explore one another. But this was so different. It was as if with each lick and each nip he was trying to learn what I liked and what would steal my breath away. I leaned up to him, pushing my chest against his. I couldn't get close enough to him. I wanted to rip our clothes off just so I could feel his skin next to mine. His hand snaked up to my breast, and he found my nipple in short order. I would have sucked in a breath of surprise or even moan in pleasure, but he just swallowed every emotion I had.

Knock knock. We both froze. After ten or so seconds the knocking returned, and with it my brain reengaged.

"You have a night petitioner, don't you?" he huffed, breathlessly.

I nodded as he dropped his hands from me. They fell onto his lap with a disappointing slap.

"I forgot." I panted.

Getting up, Damen walked to the door. I couldn't help but notice his slight shift in the groin area. Nor could I help the smirk plastered on my face.

Just before he walked out of the room, he intoned, "Don't think this is over, oracle."

My smile faltered, and heat flooded my whole body. Now it was him not trying to hide his smirk.

"Come on, you have a petitioner." He laughed half-heartedly as he offered his hand to me.

Getting off the bed, I took the hand he'd stuck out.

I paused, causing him to look back at me.

"Is that a promise?" I flirted huskily.

In answer, he just squeezed my hand and pulled me to the door. I had no damn idea how I was going to get through this without him distracting me, but I had to. Then there was that dream. I'd never seen anything like it before, but I had a bad gut feeling that it meant something. Trouble was, I didn't know what.

I walked into the front room and sat down. I gave Damen a nod, and he opened the door.

"Hello and welcome to the home of the sacred oracle. While I understand you might have your own rules, I will have to ask a few things. First, all weapons must be left outside. This is a home of neutral territory. Any acts of violence toward the oracle will be dealt with swiftly. Second, no shifting, use of magic, or biting of any kind. Leave your bad attitudes at the door. And last, while the oracle is a gift to all beings from the gods of old, she will never ask for payment. I, however, as her guardian, ask that you make an offering. Just remember, we have to eat," Damen explained to my last visitor of the day. I'd heard this same spiel a number of times. While it varied here and there, the intent was nearly always the same.

"I understand and accept your terms," a rumbling male voice sounded.

Metal clanged against concrete, leading me to believe that some kind of weapon had been dropped on the floor.

A tall thin man with salt-and-pepper hair rounded the corner. He had sharp features that looked as though he'd been carved by someone who shouldn't have given up their day job.

Standing up, I stuck out my newly gloved hand in greeting. "Hello, Mr. Roth. I'm Lana."

He scowled at me for a moment but took my hand. He grimaced as if I'd been covered in garbage. *Well, this is going to go swimmingly, I can just tell. Ugh.*

"Thank you for seeing me. I only had to wait seventy-three years, three weeks, and five days. The last two weeks and five days being past my scheduled time." If a voice could sound both oily and pissed the fuck off, his did.

Damen stepped a little closer to me as if he was warning the man.

"I am sorry for that. But as I explained on the phone, the last oracle died, and I had just come into the power. I needed the time to get my life situated so I could see petitioners as soon as possible," I added, my own irritation showing, and I didn't feel a bit bad about it.

"Excuses aren't very becoming for a new oracle," Roth snapped.

"Sir, the oracle has been very patient with you, but I won't be.

If you continue to be rude, you'll be asked to leave without what you came here for," Damen said in a cool and dispassionate tone.

The man's deep black eyes flashed a red color, but nothing else gave away a single emotion.

"I'm sorry," the man finally groused, though his words were empty. The man blinked as he looked around the room. I could nearly hear his judgment through his disgusted look. *Yeah, well, you and me both, buddy*, I didn't say in reference to the creepy-as-fuck dolls. I should probably do something with them, but I never seemed to have my motivation and time line up.

I slid my glove off and looked at him fully. I knew nothing about the man other than his name. I didn't know what race, breed, or creed he was; I liked it that way.

"I have no control over what I see. Anything I tell you is the truth. Anything I see will not be disclosed to anyone other than you. These are my vows, and I take them seriously." He nodded at my words. "Please feel free to visit the town of Havenwood Falls. But please follow the rules that have been emailed to you prior," I added.

He again nodded.

I removed my glove, reached out, and requested, "May I have your hand, Mr. Roth?"

He placed his cold hand within mine.

Warmth spread throughout my body, and I sank into my vision.

Roth sat in a large red velvet chair. Crackling and snapping of burning logs came from somewhere behind him. The glow of the fire cast everything in a flickering amber hue.

At his feet lay a crumpled mess of cloth and pale skin. Roth sipped at his drink for a moment before setting it aside. His attention never left the bloody body at his feet, despite his best efforts.

Taking in a deep breath, he kneeled by the corpse, grabbed a handful of hair, and angled her face up to his. He lovingly brushed the woman's dark hair from her face, leaving smears of blood streaking across her pale skin.

"Oh, daughter mine. You'll forgive me for this one day. On the day when I meet you at the gates of hell." His voice was soft and echoed a deep-set pain.

I gasped for air and blinked rapidly, hoping for my vision to return. After a few hard blinks, everything came into focus.

"Well? What did you see?" Roth demanded impatiently.

I'd only been seeing petitioners for a short time, but this one had shaken me to my core. I glanced over to Damen, who studied me. I tried to convey my worry to him, but wasn't sure he picked up on it.

Taking a deep breath, I explained everything in great detail. Roth bombarded me with three hundred questions. I did my best to answer him, but with each one, he seemed to get more and more irate.

"Who killed her?" he huffed for the third time.

"Mr. Roth, I don't know. I saw no one else in the vision but you and her."

"Are you saying I killed her?" His fists slammed down on the table.

Damen stepped forward and grabbed the man by the wrist.

Yanking Roth off his seat and to his feet, Damen explained in a cool tone, "And your time is up. If you have an offering, leave it on the doorstep." From the way Damen's outline swelled and how tight his clothes grew, I knew he took this threat deadly seriously.

"Let. Go. Of. Me," the man huffed, doing some yanking of his own. Damen didn't let the man go until he'd made it perfectly clear that he—and he alone—controlled the situation. Once free of Damen's grip and outside the door, he turned to face the small home and brushed his clothes off.

I walked over to the door and stood just behind Damen. The tall man met my eyes for a long moment before turning and walking away. I could feel Damen's rage coming off him in waves.

Shutting the door and turning around, Damen mumbled, "Asshole."

Maybe it had been the dream I'd had, the vision, the rude guy, or even the kiss, but the enormity of everything began to hit me all at once.

I gave up everything to do a job I knew nothing about. I read journal after journal explaining the laws as set forth by my gods, and now I was faced with people constantly using me. I was nothing more than a tool. For what exactly? For people to treat me like I owed them something?

"Why do people feel like they can use me and then toss me out like garbage? Like I'm not even a person." I realized only after I'd spoken that the words had come out loud. I could feel myself slipping down a rabbit hole of loss. I was losing myself and letting the oracle take over. Maybe this was how it was supposed to be? I was granted this power to be of use, nothing more?

"Lana—" Damen started. But my hand flew up, stopping him.

"Damen, I don't want your pity," I snapped, and immediately regretted it. "I'm sorry."

"No, I get it. That guy was an ass and you feel used."

I wished that was all. I wished I could be more like him. He'd been preparing for this role his whole life. All the while I'd been running from it.

"I just want to go to sleep." It was late, and I just wanted to forget that guy. I just wanted to forget everything. I just hoped I could find my place, find my reason and stop feeling like something to be used.

"Okay, well I'll see you in—"

"Wait! I want you to sleep with me," I blurted out. As if it could have somehow shoved the words back in, my hand flew up to my mouth.

He cocked an eyebrow at me, and his expression of worry was replaced by one of intrigue.

"Well, I thought you'd never ask," he crooned as he waggled his eyebrows. Those poor caterpillars were getting the workout of their lives.

"No, I mean, uh, I want you to just be there. Not like

anything, uh, um." I stammered. I couldn't seem to get the words out.

Chuckling lightly, he softly grabbed my hand and led me to my room.

"Come on, oracle. Let me protect you while you sleep."

And as though his words had a direct line to my stomach, butterflies once again erupted in a panic.

After slipping into my grungy shorts and my three-sizes-too-big top, I crawled into bed. I was drained and after that last guy, I just wanted to close my eyes and sink into sleep.

"What's your favorite food?" Damen puzzled as he sank into the spot next to me. This should have been awkward or at least felt somewhat wrong, but it didn't, and that fact alone should have scared the shit out of me.

"Coffee." I yawned.

"I know you want to work hard to get caught up, but how about we go get some tomorrow? We have an hour break. It would be nice to do something different."

I opened my mouth to reply, but Hades let out a loud meow and hopped onto the bed. The white cat circled a few times, trying to find a spot. Once he realized his normal place was taken, he looked at Damen and hissed.

"There's something wrong with that damn cat." Damen sighed.

"You're not wrong," I agreed, as Hades curled up in the small space above my head.

"Let's worry about tomorrow, tomorrow," I yawned sleepily. As much as I wanted to be positive and embrace all of these changes, I didn't know how much more I could take.

Slowly, I let my mind clear and sank into a dream-filled sleep.

CHAPTER 8

Coffee Haven was located on the south side of the town square and, in my opinion, was one of the most unique spots in the whole town.

"Wow," I breathed, looking up at the menu. They had everything from herbal teas to specialty lattes and every snack in between.

"I still think we need to go back home. I can't believe you forgot your gloves." Damen sounded like a disapproving brother—well, what I assumed one would have sounded like.

"I'll be careful. Plus, I need coffee," I whined as I stuck out my bottom lip.

"It's noon, Lana," he moaned as he playfully tugged on my pouted lip.

"And I need coffee. I fail to see how the time affects whether I should have coffee. What's the saying? It's five o'clock somewhere?" I explained indignantly.

"I'm not too sure that's how it works."

Was I in a cinnamon mood or caramel? Hmmm.

A little voice screamed, causing me to turn around. It happened so fast, I didn't even have time to think about my reactions. A little boy no more than five came directly at me, his soft red hair floating in a crown of flames as he flew toward me. He was looking back at his mother, or the woman I assumed to be his mother, who was chasing after him. However, he was paying far more attention to the little girl with silver white hair who was toddling after him. The little girl let out a joyful shriek of excitement.

"Jacob, Arabella, look out!" the woman with bright red hair called. The little boy ran smack into me and bounced against my leg to the floor with an audible thud. And in short order the little girl followed, tripping over the pile of little boy.

I couldn't hide the grimace on my face as the little one looked up at me. Like flipping a switch, he started crying, alligator tears and all. Arabella looked from me to him and back again, then she too broke out into tears.

"Aw, babies, it's okay." I bent down and tried to reassure them. Without warning, Jacob launched himself at me, wrapping his arms around my neck. Arabella just sat on the floor, still crying. A thin woman with the same light blond hair as the little girl, who'd been standing with the other woman, walked over to the crying girl.

"Arabella, it's okay, love. You should know better than to play tag with Jacob inside the shop." Meeting my gaze, she smiled a shy smile and added, "Sorry, they don't get a lot of time together. I'm Willow Fairchild. This little one is Arabella. You've already met Jacob, and his aunt Aster McCabe is just over there." She pointed to a red-haired woman who was walking over.

"It's totally fine! I just hope they're okay," I said as the little boy still hugged me.

"Jacob, you're fine, buddy! Let go of the poor woman." Aster chuckled as her green eyes squinted in a half smile.

Jacob relaxed slightly, allowing me to release him. He gave me a crooked smile framed by a dusting of adorable freckles. The little boy slid his small warm hand into mine, and that's when I realized my mistake. Images of the little boy's future took me over.

Wild and floating fire red hair sprung to life as the little boy jumped from one foot to the other as he munched on a sugar cookie in the shape of a purple flower. In his other hand, the boy gripped a napkin tightly.

"Jacob, come on, come get my hand," his aunt called after him. Her bright green eyes peered at her nephew, so full of love and a fierce protectiveness.

However, a strong gust of wind snatched the napkin from Jacob's hand and sent it flying into the busy street. Without thinking, the boy went running after it. Neither he nor his aunt saw the blue SUV coming.

He lay on the ground bleeding, his once lively fiery hair lifeless and his expression no longer full of joy and energy. His aunt let out a scream so loud that if emotion alone could have kept that little boy tied to this earth, hers would have.

Time was irrelevant; a surge of people ran to help as the little boy lay still on the pavement. His cookie was still clutched in his tiny lifeless hand.

I gasped for air, clutching the small child's hand in mine. I could feel the heated streaks of tears that were streaming down my face.

"You okay, Jacob?" his aunt said cautiously. It was then I realized how strange the scene must have looked. I was grasping her nephew's hand tightly and glowing. Thank god it was daytime and my glow was harder to see.

I let the boy go, and he went running to his aunt. Wiping his face clean of tears, Aster placed a small kiss on the tip of his nose.

"Come on, let's get you a cookie. We have purple flowers today. I bet if you're really good, we can talk Willow into giving you one while we visit!"

My heart sank at her words. I hadn't seen too far into the future because he had none.

"Willow! Don't you know a day off means a day off? As in, you don't need to come in?" the shaggy-haired man behind the counter joked, sporting a crooked grin and fixing his thick black rimmed glasses. Looking to Aster, he added, "Always good to see you, Aster. You're missed around here and left some big shoes for me to fill."

"Lana," Damen whispered in my ear, "you saw something, didn't you?"

I could only nod as I watched the two women with the children approach the marble countertop and talk with the man behind the counter.

"He's about to die." I nearly choked on the whispered words.

"Fuck. Lana, don't do something stupid," he spat.

I knew what he meant. I couldn't actually say anything. I was bound by the laws of the gods. If he wasn't on my list, I could not affect his future. But how could I possibly sit back and do nothing? How could I watch him die twice?

The words my ya-ya had written flashed in my mind. *They will not hesitate to rain hell on earth should you break a sacred law.* Had that been what that weird dream was about? But why was it a law? Who made these laws? Well, other than the gods themselves.

The little boy's clothes were the same, the cookie was the same, and his aunt handed him a small white napkin. How? How could I be asked to do nothing? How could I be expected to sit back and watch a child die?

"Damen . . ." I intoned.

"Lana, don't do this." There was resignation in his tone. I think, in some way, he knew I didn't have a choice.

"Damen, what choice do I have? I can't let him die," I whispered.

I met Willow's aqua-colored eyes for a moment. Her brow was pinched, her expression drawn. I didn't know her, but for whatever reason, she seemed to react to my fears and worry. However, just when I thought she'd say something, she turned and gave Aster a hug and cupped Jacob's freckle-filled cheek.

Jacob and Aster were leaving the store. I didn't have much time to make this choice. This was a sacred law; this was one they would punish the hell out of me for. I glanced at the little boy's bright copper hair and how it seemed to be full of just as much life as he was. I could never forget his small hand gripping that cookie.

The door shut as the pair walked out of the coffee shop. I was officially out of time.

Without further thought, I raced after them. Swinging the door open, I looked to the right, but saw nothing. Then I looked to the left and spotted the little boy balancing on a curb. I froze, giving what I was doing a second thought. The napkin flew out of his hand and into the street.

I went as fast as my feet could carry me. I glanced at the oncoming car. I'd waited too long. I wouldn't get there in time. A strong gust of wind blew by me, causing my hair to fall over my face. Clearing it, my eyes went wild looking for the boy who I just knew would be— The sound of screeching tires caused my heart to skip a beat.

"No!" I screamed in horror. I rushed over to the small crowd of people who'd gathered to see—nothing but a crushed cookie on the ground. Just beyond the car knelt a panting Damen, who cradled a small figure with fluttering red hair.

"That man just came out of nowhere. If—if he hadn't been there, Jacob would have been hit!" Willow gasped right next to me.

Meeting my tear-filled gaze, she breathed, "You?"

I blinked, and a tear rolled down my cheek. I couldn't speak. I just couldn't formulate the words. She knew. I didn't know how, but she did. I ran over to the other side of the street, where Damen sat hushing the scared little boy. His aunt ran over only moments before I had. He'd done it even when he'd told me not to. He knew just as much as I did what this meant. But why?

"Jacob!" Aster screamed.

Letting the boy go, Damen made his way to his feet. I ran full force at him, and like I knew he would, he caught me just as I jumped at him. I didn't even try to hide the sob that escaped my lips.

"Shh," he crooned reassuringly, as he rubbed his big protective hand against my back.

"Why?" I croaked. I was not a pretty crier, so I was grateful my face was buried in his shoulder.

Running his hand through my hair, he whispered, "You were right. I couldn't stand back and do nothing. So whatever the punishment is, we're in it together."

And the snot-pouring, hiccup-producing, slobber-dripping sobs took me over.

"Wow, I can tell you're an ugly-ass crier," he joked.

I tried to laugh, but it only came out a gurgling mess of unintelligible sounds.

"Come on, oracle, let's go home and figure out how to hide from a bunch of old Greek gods."

He set me down, and I ran a sleeve over my runny nose. Looking over my shoulder, I saw Jacob and Aster walking toward us.

"I—" Aster started but was cut off by a small sob. Her delicate features were pulled taut with what I was sure was a mix of fear, relief, and everything in between. Her pale skin and green eyes seemed to stand out more with her extreme emotions. Getting herself under control, she tried again, "I cannot thank you enough; you . . . you saved Jacob." Glancing at me, she seemed to ask me if it was okay. I simply smiled in agreement. She threw her arms around Damen with Jacob still tightly clutched in her arms.

"Ma'am, no need to thank me. I was just in the right place at the right time."

My heart swelled at his words. I was so proud of him.

"I—I used to work here." She gestured toward the coffee shop before adding, "Please, if you ever need anything, anything at all, don't hesitate to ask for help. Gosh, I didn't even get your names. And I'm totally rambling."

"I'm Damen and this is Lana. We're new to town," he replied, his voice wavering slightly. His body shifted back and forth. I blinked as I realized he didn't like being the center of attention.

And in that moment, I decided he was firmly in the marry category. Okay, marry and fuck.

"Well, I'm glad you're here! I mean, not just because of this. Oh man, I just can't thank you enough. I don't know what I'd do without him! I, just, his dad, my brother—" Her words broke off as tears began streaming down her flushed cheeks. She hugged the little boy tightly to her chest.

"Aunt Aster. I can't. Breathe!" the little boy croaked.

Releasing her hold on him, she bent down so that she met the little boy's eyes on his level.

"Jacob, I love you. I wouldn't be able to live with myself if something happened to you." She pulled the boy to her and sobbed into his rust-colored hair. Willow ran over, her little girl in tow. She threw her arms around Aster and Jacob but met my eyes.

With tears in her own eyes, Willow mouthed, "Thank you," to me, not Damen. She knew. Whatever doubt I held, it was utterly quashed in that moment.

A bright flash of light was followed shortly by two immensely loud cracks that brought my hands up to cover my ears. The sound caused me to sink to my knees. I actually had to pull my hands from my ears to be sure I wasn't bleeding. Everyone who'd been gathered in the square scattered to avoid the sudden turn of the weather. I, however, knew better. That wasn't the lightning of an impending thunderstorm. Rather it was the warning of an angry god or gods. A flash of fire raining down covered my vision, but when I blinked, there was nothing but the street and square.

Damen and I locked eyes and blurted at the same time, "We need to go."

All I could think about on the way back to our little cabin was how I was going to talk my way out of this one. One thing I knew for sure was I would be taking the fall for this. No matter what it was, it wouldn't be Damen. It was my fault, not his. I forgot my gloves, I took the risk, and I failed.

"Damen," I sighed.

"Oh, no you don't. You aren't taking the blame for this. I'm a big boy. I can make my own mistakes. I can pull up my own big boy panties."

"How'd you know? Wait, panties?" I stammered as we walked into the house. Did he just say panties? Did he wear them? Oh, I hoped not.

"It's written all over your face. I could see you plotting in the car, and knowing you, you were devising some plan to take the fall. And more the metaphorical panties, not literal."

"Well, if I hadn't forgotten my gloves . . . had I just listened to you and gone back, we wouldn't be in this mess." I sighed.

Walking slowly over to me, he slid his hand behind my head and tilted my face to his.

"Yes, but then Jacob would be dead. And, oracle, I deem that as a worthy fuckup," he said, just before lowering his lips to mine.

What had started as a soft kiss quickly turned into something more frantic. He cupped my ass so firmly against him that I could feel the hard press of his erection against my belly.

As if I'd done it a million times before, I hopped up and wrapped my legs around him. I ground my hips against his in search of friction—fuck, anything more. He in turn grabbed my ass harder and held me as though I belonged there. We fit. It was actually a little scary with how well we fit together. He stumbled backward for a second, but then walked his way through the small home to my bedroom.

I couldn't seem to stop myself from kissing him. From nibbling his full bottom lip. From rubbing myself against him, praying for some feel of his skin, his cock, anything.

Breaking our kiss mid-nip, he groaned. "Fuck, girl, if you keep grinding on me like that, I'm going to have a mess to clean up before we really get this show on the road." *Now, there's a thought.*

My face must have shown how intriguing I thought that idea was because he dropped me on the bed so hard, I nearly bounced off the other side.

I let out a little huff as I landed. Suddenly, he grabbed either side of my favorite Cowboy Bebop shirt and ripped it down the center as if it'd been made of tissue paper.

Looking down at myself, then back up at him, I crooned, "Did you just . . . ?"

Giving me a wicked grin, he replied, "Yeah, I totally did." He then tossed off his shirt and threw it to the floor.

By Hades's bouncing balls, his body was the real gift from the gods. Every single move he made, whether it was twisting or simply breathing, seemed to cause every muscle to ripple. It was like a kaleidoscope of strength the way his body moved. After the last however many years that I'd been strictly dating women, looking at him made me remember how attractive the human form could be, male or female.

It was then I realized that he was looking at me with about as much awe as I was looking at him. I couldn't help but feel a little self-conscious. I went to cover up my exposed flesh.

"Don't you dare," he snarled in warning. "Just let me look at you." He licked his lips and kept on staring. I felt like his meal.

Feeling suddenly bold, I arched my back up and un-hooked my bra. I slid the lacy material off, leaving myself topless. He didn't move a muscle, only his eyes tracking me.

"Damn, woman," he hissed, as if in pain. However, I knew better.

Leaning down, he pressed his mouth to my collarbone and placed a small kiss on the skin, leaving gooseflesh in his wake. He trailed his soft kisses all along my chest before pausing just above my nipple. He didn't move, but he was so close, I could feel his warm breath teasing me. *Oh, fuck this.* I arched up at him, brushing the pebbled flesh against his lips.

Slipping a hand beneath my back, he pulled my nipple into his mouth. Heat exploded throughout my whole body, and a moan escaped my lips.

Without my permission, my hips bucked up, searching for some kind of friction.

"Need something?" he teased, before returning his mouth to my other nipple. He was playing with me, taunting me.

"Please." I wasn't above begging or guiding him to what I needed.

My nipple still in his mouth, he moved his hand from under me to the waistband of my pants and flicked the button open.

"Thanks for not ripping these. I really like them," I breathed.

He released the suction he had on me and raised an eyebrow.

"I could change that, ya know," he threatened in a deep rumbling tone.

However, he pulled my jeans off me and tossed them over his shoulder. All that lay between him and my complete nudity was a small scrap of black lace.

Sitting back on his heels, he looked down at me and sighed, "Fuck me."

Raising an eyebrow, I purred, "I plan on it."

I leaned up and ran my fingers along every bump and valley his gracious body was made of. Meeting his eyes, I flicked open the button on his jeans. That tiny movement caused such a big man to suck in a breath. *Is he trembling under my fingertips?*

I let a finger slide a little further south and— His hand grabbed mine as I felt the head of him press lightly against my finger. Holy gods, I hadn't expected that. He had to be big, really big.

"Oh god!" I whispered as my eyes went wide.

"I've been called a lot of things. God I'm okay with," he joked in a cocky tone.

"No, I just—I could get pregnant. Um, I mean do you have a —a condom?" I hadn't had to think about that kind of thing lately, as my last two relationships had been with women.

"Oh, uh yeah, I thought, never mind. Yeah, I got it covered." Something, I couldn't name what, flashed across his face, but just as I thought I'd seen it, he leaned in and kissed me full on the mouth. Sliding my hand down further, I unzipped him, and his pants fell to the floor.

My eyes went wide at the sight of him. Oh holy night, that thing was just—just too much. There was no possibility on the planet I could even contemplate doing anything with that weapon.

"You're staring at me," he pointed out nervously.

"Oh, sorry," I mumbled, pulling him on top of me.

The press of our naked bodies lit a fire deep within me, one that I'd never really experienced before. Every inch of my body needed him, the press of his heated skin, the lap of his wet tongue, even the bite of his teeth. Now it was I who was starving.

He kissed me, taking in my taste and learning how I liked to be touched. He took his time allowing me to become accustomed to both how I wanted him to touch me and how he wanted to touch.

With every stroke of his fingers and caress of his taut silken skin, he was stoking a fire deep inside me that only grew in intensity. I'd never been so wet in my life. He was driving me out of my mind with need.

"I can't take this anymore." I moaned as his fingers dipped low to cup my sex in his heated hand.

"Shh, I know. I'm going to give you the world." He kissed me lightly.

Suddenly, he got off the bed. It had been the first time ever in my life that someone's absence left me feeling hollow and unfulfilled. I knew in that second that whatever was blooming between us was unlike anything I'd ever experienced.

He appeared again at the foot of the bed and crawled his way up my body one painful inch at a time. He paused at my core. Spreading me open with one hand, he took one long lick of me. We both moaned in approval. He licked again, and again. And I was being pushed to my peak. I was being hurtled toward a precipice one lick at a time, and I wanted nothing more than to dive off headfirst.

Likely knowing I was close, he stopped. I moaned in protest, as I'd been so damn close. But he just kissed his way up my body until he came to my lips.

"Do you want me to wipe my—" I cut his words off, my lips devouring his mouth.

I let my tongue explore him. It darted in and out of his so much like the sex act that I had to let out a moan.

He broke the kiss and gazed down at me.

"I like the way you taste," he breathed.

"I like the way I taste on your lips," I added breathlessly.

"Fuck, that's sexy." He growled as he pressed himself against me.

I lay back and let my legs fall open around him in both supplication and invitation.

He leaned back, and I heard the rustling of a foil packet. A moment later he hovered over me.

I needed him. I needed him and everything that went along with being with him.

He rubbed himself along my folds, allowing himself to breach me for only a moment before retreating and starting over again. It was maddening, this rhythm he was building, then tearing down.

"Please," I pleaded.

He laughed a strained, almost pain-filled laugh. That's when I realized his need was just as strong as mine. It wasn't just in his laugh, but the pull of his lips and the focus of his light brown eyes.

This time when he breached me, he didn't move away. He slid in a little bit. My hands flew to his shoulders, and my eyes went wide.

"Did I hurt you?" he panted, his voice full of fear.

"No, just go slow. It's been a long time since I've been with a man." I couldn't help but be a little afraid.

Giving me a soft, knowing smile, he kissed the tip of my nose before rocking a little more inside of me. I gasped at the pain.

He reached down and found my clit in short order. He began rubbing the sensitive flesh with slow careful circles. A rush of heat and wetness surged through me. My body responded to his, welcoming him as he was able to slide further in. Any time I'd start to feel pain, he allowed my body to get something it needed to take in more. He played my body as if he'd known it for a hundred years, as if I was his instrument and he'd trained his whole life for this moment. After a few more strokes, he was buried deep in me.

Sweat began to bead up on his forehead, and his whole body trembled lightly. He wasn't moving; he was just there, looking down at me. I realized he was waiting on me to move.

Grabbing his hips, I began to move with him. He followed the pace I set. After a while, I was matching him stroke for stroke. I could feel my release building up to a fever pitch, waiting for that last spark before I flew apart into a million and one pieces of the old me I used to be.

"I . . ." I let the statement hang, unable to get the words out.

"I know." He seemed to understand that talking was an action I wasn't able to perform at the moment.

He plunged so deep within me that if I'd had a voice left, I would have screamed his name. I would have praised the gods for this moment. That was all it took to send me headlong into a soul-fracturing orgasm.

I could feel my pleasure pulsing, dragging him deeper into me. He shuddered against me as his orgasm overtook him. His rhythm became frantic, but his eyes never left mine. It was this connection that went further than sex, deeper than conversation. It was a feeling of a deep forever.

He collapsed on top of me, causing the little air I'd managed to suck in to whoosh right back out.

Hitting his shoulder, I croaked, "You're too big. I can't breathe!"

"That's what she said! OH AH!" He laughed before rolling over.

As much as I didn't want to laugh, I couldn't help it.

We both lay there for a long moment, basking in the afterglow of simply being with one another.

Finally, he got up, went to the bathroom and cleaned up. Once he returned, I did the same.

"I'm ready for bed. Thank the gods we don't have any more petitioners today." I yawned as I fell back into the soft mattress.

"Same. You wore me out today. Between saving kids, coffee, and other things." There was a smile of satisfaction plastered so big on his face, it could have been its own billboard.

"Oh, you loved it!" I huffed as I smacked his shoulder.

"Well, I know I enjoyed the show," a deep, rumbling male voice intoned. My heart nearly stopped at the sound of someone new in the room.

CHAPTER 9

*D*amen bolted to his feet, still on the bed, and still nude as the day he was born. While that thing could have been registered as a deadly weapon, I doubted it was going to be his best choice, in the moment. However, it did swing in the air like a pendulum.

"Stand down, guardian. I mean no harm to your oracle," ordered the man, whom I'd still not seen.

There was something in his voice. I knew I hadn't heard it before, but there was something deep within me that stirred at the sound of it.

"No" was all Damen warned.

A glowing blue light began to fill the room, like someone had put a light on a dimmer switch and began turning it. It was then I saw a man sitting in the black leather chair in the corner. He was a thin, lanky man with wild black hair and skin that looked somehow paler than milk. His eyes, though—they weren't an ice blue; oh no, nothing about this man, er, being was cold. His eyes were the same blue as the hottest part of a flame, and if I had to venture a guess, just as deadly. He was dressed in a tight-fitting suit, so tight in fact that I would be willing to bet that if he got a hard on, his pants would rip right in half.

At that moment, my damn cat jumped up on the strange man's suit-clad lap, turning around three times and settling down.

"Hades!" I hissed.

The cat looked at me with what could only be described as a *What?* expression.

At the same time, the man smiled a dangerous smile and also replied, "Yes?"

My eyes went wide, and not just at the sight of Damen's full moon.

"How about your guardian gets some clothes on and we all sit down for a little chat," the man I really hoped wasn't *the* Hades advised in an amused tone. And then he just disappeared. I don't mean that he ran so damn fast he looked like he'd just disappeared —no, he actually *poofed* gone. The cat looked just as stunned as I felt.

Damen just stood there while I still clutched the sheet to my chest. We both gawked at the space the stranger had just occupied a moment before.

"You don't think he's really . . ." I let the statement hang in the air as the whole disbelief of the situation dawned on me.

"Yeah, oracle, I really do." Damen sighed as he got off the bed and pulled his pants on.

As we walked into the living room, hand in hand, my heart felt like it was going to burst right through my chest and plummet to the floor. I had to stifle a gasp at the sight of the foreign man sitting on my sofa. *Was he reading my mail?*

"Hey!" I chided. I then thought better of it. Yeah, scolding a bazillion-year-old god, wonderful plan, said no one ever.

"Hello, oracle and her guardian," he replied, with absolutely no inflection in his tone at all. It was actually a little eerie.

"Uh, hi?" It came out more of a question rather than a statement.

"Come have a seat," he suggested, motioning to my couch. I had no idea why, but I was discomfited by the fact that he was inviting me to sit on my own damn furniture. However, I thought better of pushing my luck with the god of the underworld. For once I thought better of talking back. Yay, go me.

Damen and I did as instructed. The three of us sat in my living room just looking at one another, surrounded by creepy dolls. Well wasn't this exactly how every single horror movie ever started out? Ugh, I swore I wouldn't be the first one dead.

Hades opened his mouth to say something, but my cat took that as his cue to make his presence known yet again. Hades the cat jumped up on the coffee table and let out the absolute loudest meow I'd ever heard. He then walked over to Hades the god to inspect the newcomer.

The god of the underworld leaned in with his hand extended to let the feline take a sniff. My cat, the fickle being he was, hissed, did a slow turn around, waved his butt in the air, and jumped off the table.

"By Zeus's cock, that cat has the biggest balls I've ever seen!" The god eyed the cat as he sauntered off.

"Yeah, I got him fixed, but he was depressed afterward, so I had them put those fake ones in, you know, the neuticle things. Anyway, long story short, it was the wrong size, and he's now super confident. It was a whole thing." I was rambling; I did that when I was nervous. *Did I just tell a god about my cat's nuts? Oh, someone please save me from myself.*

The two men in the room just looked from me to the cat, who was sitting in the doorway, and back.

"I have no idea what that means, but all right," the real Hades admitted. He looked from Damen to me, then back at the space the cat occupied, scratching his head. Shrugging, he returned his attention to me. "Oracle, I have a little issue I need to discuss with you." His tone was deadly serious. My stomach dropped to my feet at his words, despite the fact that I knew this was coming.

"One Jacob McCabe." The way he spoke his full name sent a shiver down my spine.

I looked to Damen, whose attention was rapt on the god.

"Uh, yes. I know him." One thing my father taught me—well,

come to think of it, the *only* thing his drunk ass taught me—other than to never mix gin and vodka, oh and to clean up his messes—was to never admit to anything unless the accuser is direct.

The god narrowed his eyes at me, and I swore the temperature dropped about ten degrees in the room. I began hearing a rapid clicking sound, but after a moment, I realized it was the chattering of my own teeth.

"His soul was due in the River Styx today. Any idea why I'm a soul short?" He leaned forward, his arms resting on his knees.

"Miscounted?" I suggested in an innocent tone.

"Oracle, I have little patience for humans on a good day. Today isn't a good day." There was a clear warning, not only in his words and tone, but in the way his body conveyed the words.

I had to swallow to clear the lump that had formed in my throat.

"I touched him and saw he would die. I couldn't let a little kid die. It was my fault, and Damen had nothing to do with it. So if you have to kill me, then so be it." My eyes burned with unshed tears, and my chest grew tight with the frantic beating of my pounding heart.

"Hades, if I may—" Damen started, but was cut off by a flick of the god's fingers. Damen stood frozen, but still breathing. I just blinked at him. What had he done?

"I know neither he nor his family were on your list, so here is where the problem is." He leaned in, placing his palms flat on the coffee table. "You're new to this power, and new to being the intermediary between the gods and mortals. However, what you've done is broken the rules the gods set on the oracle and the laws of nature."

I knew this was serious. I knew this could be the thing that killed me. But all I kept seeing was Jacob's bouncing red curls lying lifeless on the ground. All I could see was a tragedy I could prevent.

"He was just a child. I saw something I knew was wrong, so I did something about it. How can you really believe his life isn't valuable?" I wasn't trying to anger the gods—well, anger them more than I already had. However, I wanted him to see my side of things.

"Oracle, that isn't something for you to decide. What if he grows up to be the very thing that ends all of mankind? When the downfall of mankind could have been avoided, how will you judge your actions?"

I hadn't thought of it that way. Holy shit! What if I'd doomed the world? I hadn't seen that far into the future. The truth was, I had reacted to what was in front of me, and that's it.

"I-I hadn't really thought of that." I was unable to meet his eyes.

"Oracle, I get a bad reputation for being an evil god. The truth is that death is just as important as creation. We can't have a beginning without something ending. There is a balance that is to be maintained." Everything he was saying made sense. But what I couldn't wrap my head around was why this had to happen to maintain that balance. Why children? Before I could ask, he went on.

"Some things live, and others die. There's no rhyme or reason. That's the job of the Fates. But we must maintain the balance."

"Why?" I asked.

"There's a trickle-down effect. If one life is allowed to be saved, then the balance is gone. If the balance is gone, that will throw the whole world off." It just kept sounding like he was saying the same thing over and over.

"I get it, balance, but what's going to happen?" I knew this was a stupid question, but I needed to know how bad things could get.

"Seventy-nine AD, 1346 to 1353, 1929—all years an oracle decided the laws we'd set upon them were flexible. Pompeii, the black death, the stock market crash on the modern world. The gods will punish the mortals; we will right the wrong you created." He stood up as if to leave.

"I wish I could tell you I was sorry. I wish I could tell you that given what I know now that I'd do something different, but in reality, I likely wouldn't," I admitted.

"I know, oracle. And because of that heart, I will give you two days. On the setting of the second day, if I don't have a soul to replace the one you stole, I will not stop the rest of the gods from raining down upon this land and killing everyone in it. I want a soul. One that's given freely. Or the soul of the child. Either will do."

"Take mine!" I blurted out with no thought as I stood to my feet. If I had to sacrifice myself for this town I now called home, I would.

The tall man turned, walked up to me, and cupped my face. His skin was warm, nearing hot. It was like he was running one hell of a fever.

"Oracle, it's not your time to die. Besides, I like you. I'm not ready to see your soul." He ran his thumb along my cheek, leaving overheated skin in his wake.

Glancing over to where the frozen Damen stood, he smiled menacingly.

"Too bad that brute got to you first. I tried to tell Zeus the line of Hercules would be too much, but hey, who listens to the master of Hell?" Did he just make a joke? He looked at me expectantly, like he was waiting on me to laugh.

Shrugging, he snapped his fingers.

"—interject for just a moment," Damen sputtered as he blinked, looking around. Frowning, he huffed, "Where'd he go?"

Then it was my turn to look around. He was gone.

"He left, I guess." I walked to the front door. I let my head fall lightly to the hard wood. Just what in hell was I going to do?

I could feel Damen's body against my back, his warmth easing the knot in my stomach slightly.

"What happened, Lana?" I didn't want to tell him, mostly because I didn't want him to do what I knew he would—offer up himself. However, keeping it from him felt dishonest, and I didn't want to start whatever was blooming between us on a lie.

Taking a deep breath, I turned around, and caged in his arms, I told him everything Hades had told me.

Neither of us spoke for a long moment. We just stood there, looking at one another. I studied every feature on his face. I let my eyes make memories of every freckle, the rich colors of his eyes, and the small scar that disrupted the dark brown of his left eyebrow. I had no idea why, but it seemed like this was the right choice in the moment, knowing him.

"Well, oracle, what do we do?" He rubbed his hands down my arms.

"I don't know."

It was the truth. It wasn't like I could go out and pick some poor shmuck up and kill them. This had to be someone who knew what would happen. It had to be someone who wanted to die.

"I could offer myself . . ." he offered, like I knew he would.

My chest hurt at the thought of losing him. I would never let that happen, but how could I stop it? How could I stop the wrath of the gods from raining down?

"We have two days to figure this out, right?"

I nodded as a yawn slipped out.

"Then let's go to bed and make a plan in the morning." He pulled me into his arms. I didn't want to take comfort in his embrace. I felt like I didn't deserve it. I'd gotten us in this mess, and I had to figure out a way to get us out of it.

Climbing into the bed, I let myself sink into his body. I wish I could say I fell into a contented dreamless sleep, but that wasn't at all what happened. Rather, I found sleeping to be a fruitless venture. I did, however, formulate a plan. Hades said they wouldn't take my soul, but what if they had to? There were no more females left in my family. The oracle would die with me. It was a shit plan, but I saw no other options.

CHAPTER 10

"Are you one hundred percent sure that murder is completely off the table?" Damen raised an eyebrow as he garbled the question around a massive bite of bagel.

Rubbing the bridge of my nose, I glared at him and sighed. "Yeah, pretty darn sure."

"Just checking," he replied defensively.

I knew he was trying to lighten the mood, but I was so stressed trying to figure out this whole mess, nothing really helped.

I searched the whole journal my ya-ya had left me, looking for anything she'd written that could help, but found nothing.

Letting my head fall forward, I lightly banged my forehead on the table. I let out a loud groan and flung my arms over my head.

"Lana," Damen called. I ignored him.

I felt his strong hand on the back of my neck rubbing circles. I wanted to just get my happy ass back into that room, strip the two of us down, and curl up and forget everything going on.

"We could leave." I breathed the thought, and somehow once the words had left my lips, I wished I could take them back.

"Lana, you know—"

"I know," I agreed, cutting him off. "We can't run from this, I know. I just have no idea what to do." Finally, I lifted my head up.

"I guess the Fates will always get their due." His words seemed to have a haunting tone to them. But there was something in them that caused my head to tilt to the side.

"Say that again?" The world stopped spinning for a single moment, and everything shrank to a single pin prick.

"The Fates, they always get their due?" He observed, though it came out more as a question this time, but then it hit me. The Fates. The three Fates.

"The Fates!" I screamed as I stood up. However, I must have moved too fast, as the momentum sent Damen flying back and then tumbling to the ground.

"Damn, sorry," I hurried, offering him a hand. While he took it, I knew he didn't need to.

"The Fates. You know the three Fates. What if we found them? What is the superstition? Find the Fates and they grant you a boon, right? That's what Ray said." My thoughts were scattered as the words fell rapid-fire from my lips.

"Uh, isn't that a genie and the lamp thing? Not sure how accurate that story is." He raised an eyebrow.

Shaking my head, I bolted up and out of the kitchen. I ran into the living room, past a confused-looking Hades, over to the bookshelf. I started rifling through the hundreds of books that lined the wall. If I glanced at a cover that wasn't what I was looking for, I tossed it over my shoulder and moved on. I knew I saw this damn book. Slipping out a red leather book, I glanced at the title, *Greek Architecture: The Base of Modern Plumbing*.

"Nope." I sighed and tossed it.

Hades hissed from somewhere behind me, but I kept on going. As I tossed book after book, I became more and more frantic. Why—

"Ouch!" Damen yelled as I heard a deep thud.

"Sorry, but I know it's here! I saw it!" I tossed three more in quick succession.

I grabbed a black leather-bound book that simply read, *The Fates*.

"I knew I'd seen it!" I nearly screamed, as I plopped to the floor and cracked the book open.

The tome started out with basic info.

"Three sisters, they are the Fates controlling the fates of mankind, they are hags, blah blah blah." This wasn't what I wanted. I was running out of time.

I flipped through the book, reading only about every fourth word, hoping like hell something would jump out at me.

My heart stopped when I saw the words.

"To find the Fates, one must but look to the north and call out their true names. If the speaker of words is deemed worthy, the Fates will reveal themselves posthaste. Though this might sound easy, it's anything but. The Fates are fickle and like to play games. What they say isn't always what will happen, as in the end, the Fates will always get their due," I read aloud.

"What the hell does that mean?" Damen blurted.

I wasn't honestly sure.

"I mean, I guess I just say their names? Then if they want to come, they poof?" It's not like there was an instruction manual for this kind of thing, beyond the book in my hands. The reality was that these books were written by humans who saw the living history of my people as nothing more than a myth. Within each of the pages of every book written, there were a million contradictions, doubts, and lies; then in the spaces between the words was the unknown. The truths that had been all but lost through time. Truths that became myths because we lost ourselves.

"Do you know their names?" he wondered, clearly thinking I didn't. *Oh ye of little faith.*

"I do, actually. But there's really no telling if it would actually work."

Hades strutted into the room tentatively. Likely to be sure he wouldn't be beaned with another book. He stepped onto my lap, turned around, and settled down. As crazy as my cat was, he seemed to know when I needed him.

"Well, what are you waiting for?"

"What if it doesn't work?" I whispered.

"Well, then go back to plan A," he remarked confidently.

"We cannot murder someone!" I sighed, rolling my eyes.

Taking a deep breath, I tried to clear my mind. This had to work because I wasn't sure what else to do. I didn't want to die, but I also didn't want anything to happen to this town.

"Clotho." She was the sister who dispensed the life threads of all mortals. "Lachesis." She was the weaver who was responsible for weaving the threads. "Lachesis." She was the sister who dispensed the threads. "Atropos." She was responsible for cutting the life threads. While together the sisters knew the lives of mortals, they couldn't see beyond their individual tasks.

After I spoke the last sister's name aloud, I wish I could say I felt the air around me change or that I reappeared somewhere else, but nothing. Hades let out a low warning growl, but that wasn't exactly new.

"Fuck!" I spat.

"Oh, she said a cuss word!" a small voice chuckled.

My eyes popped open in surprise. I flew to my feet, causing a seriously pissed off Hades to tumble to the floor.

"Aw, she's so mean to the kitty! Here, kitty kitty!" another voice called out.

Damen whirled around, and his eyes grew wide in alarm. Then I saw what he saw.

Three little girls all dressed alike, scattered throughout the small living space. They wore fluffy pink dresses with a kind of white lace trim. One darted after Hades. One sat on the floor cross-legged, rifling through the books, and the other was jumping on the couch as if it were her own personal trampoline.

"Holy shit, when did this turn into a daycare?" Damen shrieked, eyeing the jumping girl.

"I don't even know what's going on right now." I was completely dazed.

The little girl flipping through the books gazed up at me. She had a full face topped with wisps of featherlight white hair. But it wasn't her pale skin or white hair that caused my very soul to shake. It was her unfocused red eyes.

"Did you not call upon us, oracle?" She had a small angelic voice. Her words were so mature, yet her tone so young. It was so strange.

"Oh, uh, I mean, I called on the Fates?" It came out as a question mostly because this was not at all what I'd expected.

"That's us! We really liked your cat, so that's the reason we came." The one who'd been chasing Hades giggled. She walked into the room cradling the large white cat.

"Oh, be careful. Hades can be pretty temperamental," I warned. That's just what I needed, my damn cat scratching a Fate and then us all dying.

"Oh, kitty loves getting pets!" She laughed while stroking Hades's silky fur. And damn it if the flippin' cat didn't start purring so loudly I could hear it over the squeaks and groans of the poor couch.

"These are them? The three Fates? I thought they were old hags?" Damen wondered in a low tone.

The child on the couch stopped jumping for a moment to yell, "They are old hags! Just look at them!"

"Hey! That's not nice! I'm not a hag. You're a hag!" the one holding Hades spat.

After that, the three broke out into an argument over who was the biggest hag. My jaw pretty much dropped to the ground as my brain couldn't make sense of what my eyes were seeing. They were children, as in, they couldn't be more than a day over eight.

"I had no idea this would be a babysitting job," Damen whispered.

"Yeah, you and me both," I agreed, trying to keep count of just how many kids we had.

I thought this was my only chance to figure out how to get out of this mess, yet here I was with three bickering, er, scratch that, wrestling children. I had no idea what to do with this. I'd never really had any experience with kids, so I was kind of at a loss.

Clearing my throat, I screeched, "Excuse me!"

The three paused mid–arm bar and looked at me.

"I asked you here. Don't I get a wish or boon or something?"

"What do we look like, genies?" the three small voices cried at once.

"Ah, that's what I said!" Damen agreed. I cut him an angry glare, but he only shrugged.

"You're supposed to be on my side," I huffed indignantly. Taking in a deep breath and letting it out slowly, I said, "Listen, I just need your help."

The three untangled themselves, stood, smoothed out their frilly dresses, and looked expectantly at me.

The one on the left curtsied before saying, "Clotho."

Then the one in the middle did a little bow and chortled, "Lachesis."

The last triplet slowly walked around me, seeming to examine me. Once she stood back where she'd started, she added, "Atropos."

Of the three, Atropos was the one who gave me the willies. It was like she was looking for something only she could see, her eerie red eyes not really focusing on me, but somehow seeing through me.

"No one ever calls us to help them," Clatho whined.

"Yeah, they just call us to complain," Lachesis huffed as she crossed her tiny arms over her chest.

"Or to bring back the dead," Atropos added in a haunting tone. A shiver ran up my spine, causing me to shudder.

"Oh, I'm sorry. I guess I, um, messed up, kind of. Well, I mean, no, I totally messed up. I'm rambling. Let me start over." I couldn't seem to get my words to come out in any order that made any damn sense.

"Jacob. He's just a little thing. A baby really. It was my fault. I touched him and saw he was going to die. I saved him even though he wasn't on the petitioner list." My words were rushed and my throat tight with stifled emotion.

"Ah, yes. Hades was due a soul, yet when I tried to cut his life string, it would not cut. I thought it most odd." Atropos seemed to reminisce, her vacant red eyes staring at me all the while.

"Oh, I know he's mad!" Lachesis giggled.

"He said he either needs Jacob's soul or one given up freely. I want you to cut my thread," I instructed firmly.

"Uh, how about hell no!" Damen interrupted, like I knew he would.

"Shh," Lachesis snapped at him.

"Let her speak. I'm intrigued," Clotho ordered.

"I will allow you to cut my thread, leaving the human's will up to you, as I am the end of my line." I'd known from the moment I called upon the Fates that this would be my offer. The Fates had always hated the oracle. They saw the power of foresight to be in direct competition with their own divinity.

"Hmm, interesting indeed, sisters. We've never liked the powers the oracle was granted," Clotho said.

Damen grabbed my upper arm and pulled me to him.

"You can't do this. I won't let you. If you die, I die. Our fates are tied." I could hear the strain in his voice.

"But if you die, I don't." This time it was my voice that cracked.

"I have your thread, oracle. Would you like to see it? See your past?" The Fate's words caused me to whirl around.

"No," I whispered without thinking. I didn't need to see it. I'd lived it.

"What about Jensen's?" My heart nearly stopped at her words.

The Fate reached out in the air and seemed to pluck something. Drawing her pinched fingers back, she withdrew a long silver thread from nothing. The string seemed to glitter in the light as if made of liquid diamonds.

A twinkle of light caught my eye. It was Jensen's smiling face, and it caused my heart to hurt.

I felt a small hand cup my face as a heated tear tracked down my cheek.

"Oh, young one, you have so much living to do. As much as we would love to end the oracle, the gift no human should ever have, this isn't willing."

My heart sank at her words, mostly because she was right. I didn't want to die. But then we were back at square one.

"And guardian, don't think to volunteer. You have her to live for," Atropos added, a warning in her tone.

"I don't know what to do," I whispered, unable to trust my own emotions. My knees gave out, and I collapsed on my ass to the floor. "All of this because I forgot to put gloves on."

Clotho walked over and sat down next to me.

"Look, child, I want to show you something." I almost laughed at her calling me a child, but I went with it.

She pressed her forefinger and thumb together and then gently rubbed them back and forth. At first nothing happened, then a tiny light began to glow. It was faint at first, but soon it grew to nearly blinding. It was the most beautiful thing I'd ever seen. I could feel the life within it, feel the soul shining like a beacon. It seemed to cry out to my own soul. Suddenly, she stopped, but the light was still there. Now it glowed on its own.

She took her other hand and pinched the tiny spark and drew it out. There was a glittering thread, just like Jensen's had been.

"This is the birth of a soul," she marveled, her own voice filled with awe.

A moment later, her sister walked over and plucked it from her as if it were a ripe plum.

Lachesis ran her fingers along the thread of this new life while smiling and nodding. She then began making intricate knots along it.

"These are moments. Some may come to be; some may not. They may change; they may not, but this has potential." Her fingers flew along the string so fast I had trouble tracking them. Once she was done, she walked over to Atropos and handed her the new thread.

Atropos took the soul and inspected it thoughtfully. While her eyes didn't track along the thread in a way I could understand, I knew she could see the soul in her own way.

She took out a pair of what looked like well-worn shears.

While looking at me, she spoke, "Only I know the moment of death. This isn't out of hate, out of love, or out of predestination. It is because nothing in the mortal world is infinite. All things are born, and all things die." Then, near the top of the thread, she let the scissors hover.

"Wait! It's just a child, a baby!" I cried, lurching forward.

She cut the thread, leaving barely a half an inch between her fingers, and sending the rest to the floor. I fell to my knees, cradling the faded soul in my hands.

"Why?" I cried.

Atropos leaned down and cupped my face, and for once it seemed as if she really saw me.

"Child, weep not for the life that wasn't, but rather for the life that was lived and the love that was received." She offered me her hand. In it was the still glowing scrap of the soul that had just been woven.

"Send the soul to Hades, oracle. It's a privilege to do so," she instructed. I took the thread from her hand as if it were a precious and fragile doll. In a way, it was.

"What do I do now?" I whispered.

"Don't you know, child? Let your power guide you."

Taking a deep breath, I closed my eyes and focused on the feel of the barely there thread. I felt so stupid. I had no idea what I was doing, but then again, that had always been the case. I'd never known what I was doing, my whole life.

My mother had left when I was a kid, leaving me with my alcoholic father. When she died, I felt the same as I'd always felt—confused and lost. Even with dating and school, I'd never known what I was doing.

Opening my eyes, I sighed. "I don't know what I'm doing. I've never known what I was doing."

"You've lost trust in yourself. Trust your power and you'll see a clear path." Her voice was soft and soothing.

She was right. I closed my eyes and let go. Instead of looking for the answer, I let go of everything. Then the path was clear.

I raised my open palm to my lips and let out a long breath, blowing the tiny soul into the air. It fluttered for a few moments before floating off and disappearing. I knew it was on its way to where it was supposed to go. I knew this deep within my own soul.

"But why children?" My question was nothing more than a breath, but I knew they'd heard it.

"Because all things end. No matter the age or time, they all must end," Lachesis answered.

"So what do I do now? Hades needs a soul. One that must be freely given, or the child's soul. I can't just go out and ask someone for their soul."

"You can, though." The male voice came from behind me. I whirled around to face my father, who stood in the doorway.

Damen walked over to him, blocking his view of me.

"I have no idea how you got in here, or why. But I really don't care. My whole purpose is to protect the oracle. I'm going to need you to go before —"

He paused as I walked up and placed a calming hand on his shoulder.

"Damen, it's okay. That's my dad." Damen's back stiffened at my words. I'd told him about my past, but only barely. After a long drawn-out moment, Damen moved to the side.

There stood the man I'd not seen in close to five years. He looked so much older than I remembered. His whole body looked sickly, yellow even. It was likely all the years of drinking he'd done.

"Why are you here, Dad?" I narrowed my eyes, not inviting him in. How in the hell he'd even found this place with the wards up was beyond me.

"Your grandmother wrote me a letter and told me to come here at this time today. She said you needed me. She also included this pendant." He pointed to his chest. My guess was that was how he actually found the place.

"Okay, why now? What did her letter say?" Part of me felt so betrayed that my ya-ya had known this would happen, yet didn't warn me.

"Could I come in?" He was looking past me to Damen. For once he didn't seem drunk. He didn't seem angry. He just looked like a normal guy, which in itself was abnormal.

I nodded and moved aside.

The three Fates eyed my father with great interest.

There we all sat in my tiny living room. The sacred oracle, my guardian, the three Fates, and my dad, all surrounded by creepy-ass dolls. If this day got any stranger, I might actually combust. Oh, and the cat, the crazy-ass feline who kept darting in and out, his bouncing balls a testament to his greatness.

"Would anyone like any tea?" one of the Fates bubbled. I had no idea who was who anymore.

"Tea? You can make tea?" Damen asked in a confused tone.

"Yes, boy. I'm a Fate, not an imbecile." She huffed as the three walked into the kitchen.

"Dad, why are you here?" I asked again, just trying to make sense of it all.

He fidgeted for a moment, looking uncomfortable. A strained silence fell over us as we waited for him to say whatever it was he was going to say.

"I stopped drinking about a year ago, after I found out I was going into liver failure. I've been on the transplant list, but the reality is, because of my past, I'll likely never get one."

I shouldn't care. I shouldn't give a single damn about the man who'd put me through hell, but I couldn't seem to make myself not care. I said nothing as I felt Damen's hand slip into mine.

"When I got your grandmother's letter, I knew I had to come. She said you'd have need of me. And after hearing what I just heard, I'm here to help you. I want to give up my soul for the little boy's." The world stopped turning, and everything but him and me seemed to fall away.

My whole world shrank to this moment, to those words. All I could hear after this was the beating of my own heart in my ears.

"Why?" was the only word I could manage to get out.

"I've done nothing my whole life. Wasted every chance I've ever been given. You were the only good thing ever did, and even that I found a way to mess up. When your mom left, I was given a chance to be the dad you needed, and I failed. When she died, I was once again given a chance, and yet again I failed. Here I am, but this time—" He paused and looked at me fully. Our matching eyes met and locked. "This time I won't give up my chance to do the only good thing I've ever done."

He was serious.

"No." I couldn't even believe the word came out so firmly. I guess there was still a large part of me that wanted to believe in her daddy, that wanted to be loved by him. If he did this, I'd never get that chance.

"Tea?" one of the Fates called from the doorway.

My dad stood up nervously.

"I'm willing to give my soul in place of the little boy's. Freely given." His voice didn't even tremble.

"No." It was weak, but I spoke anyway.

"How very interesting," one of the fates mused. I thought this one was Clotho.

"Indeed, Clotho. Thoughts on him, Atropos? In the end, it's your choice if it will suffice," Lachesis said.

Atropos scooped up a still-purring Hades and walked up to my dad. She pursed her lips and began to walk a tight circle around him. She then handed Hades to my father, picked up the thread, and ran her small fingers along it. Her brow pinched and furrowed, and her bowed lips pulled taut as she inspected the thread.

"You can't be serious!" I tried to cross the small space to stop her, but felt two strong arms cage around me.

"Damen, let me go!" I ordered as I thrashed against him. He only squeezed me tighter.

"I'm so sorry." His whispered words did nothing to ease my concern.

"Don't. Do. This. Damen. Please!" I begged as my vision blurred with tears.

"I'm so, so sorry," he chanted over and over.

"This is my only chance at a dad, a real dad!" I screamed. That caused the Fate to look from me to my dad and back again.

Grabbing the cat from my father, she set Hades on the floor and patted him on his rump as if to say, "Move along." She then plucked out my father's thread fully for everyone to see. It didn't shine at all. In the middle it was worn, dark, and tattered, except for the barest bit at the end.

"His soul will do," she determined.

"Wait! Just wait!" This couldn't be happening! This was my mistake. One thing I'd done caused all of this. I should be the one to pay, no one else.

My father walked over to me, but looked at Damen, whom I was still fighting to escape.

"You take care of her. You hear me? You take care of her like I should have." His voice was raw, filled with pain. It was such an emotion-filled plea, I couldn't help but sob at it.

"Why wait until now? *Why?*" I screamed. My throat burned, but nothing mattered.

"Better late than never?" he joked half-heartedly. That only caused me to sob harder.

Cupping my cheek, he smiled softly. That smile I recalled seeing only a few times in my childhood, that smile I used to dream of getting to see again.

"Oh, peanut. I've done nothing in my life I could be proud of, aside from you. If this is the last and only thing I can do for you to be a good father, then please let me do it." With that, he turned his back on me and walked toward the Fate.

"I won't ask if you're ready for death, for no one should be," Atropos said.

He nodded and looked over to me.

She took out her shears once more and lifted them over the thread.

"Love you, peanut. Wish I could have been better." He choked as tears rolled down his cheek.

"DAD!" I was sobbing and thrashing. I tried like hell to stop this, but Damen wouldn't let me go.

"I love y—" He dropped to the floor in a heap.

My eyes flew to the fate who still held his life thread, except the glowing end had been cut and laid on the ground, fading.

I let out a scream that I'd only ever heard once, once in a vision of loss. Aster's scream of loss, the one that surely could have been heard by the gods, was really my own.

Finally, after I had no more voice, Damen let me go. I fell to the floor and scrambled over to the lifeless body that once housed the soul of my father.

They all just stood around me as I sobbed. I cried for a man I wished I could have known in the end, but mostly I cried for the little girl who still wanted her daddy, who wished he could have been the man he should have always been.

"Come, oracle, send him on his way home," Atropos whispered softly.

How could I be expected to do this? I didn't move at first. I sat there staring at the tattered thread.

Despite my tears and pain, I held out my hand as she dropped his thread into it. It felt heavy and warm. Unlike the last one, I could feel how worn the soul had been.

I took in a deep breath, but didn't let it out. If I let it out, I knew it would be like saying goodbye, something I wasn't sure I was ready for.

"Go on. Goodbye doesn't always mean the end." It was Damen's words that allowed me to exhale my father's soul to the underworld.

Suddenly, I felt hollow and raw. I just sat there and cried. I cried for the mistake I'd made and the sacrifice that was given. I cried and cried. I cried until I ran out of tears.

Between sobs I remembered the Fates telling Damen they would take care of everything in the house, but then they would have to leave.

Setting me in the bed, Damen kissed my head.

"I'm so sorry. I know you'll hate me. I hope someday you'll forgive me." His words were so full of heartache, it caused a tightening in my chest.

I wanted to hate him. It would be easier to blame him, hell, blame someone. But the truth was I could only blame myself.

"We have a lot of years for you to forgive me. I don't mind waiting. You're worth it," he added as he got off the bed.

"Damen!" I hurried. "Please don't go."

He stopped, his hand on the doorknob. He didn't turn, though.

"Damen, I don't blame you, and I don't hate you. Please don't let me sleep alone." The words burned my raw throat.

He opened the door and walked out. I'd never felt so alone in my life as I did in that moment. I had nothing, I had—

The door swung open, and Damen stood there in his silk boxer shorts that sported tiny flamingos.

"Just had to go get pretty for you," he joked as he heaved his big body over the small space and jumped on the bed.

"That wasn't nice," I chided, but my heart wasn't in it.

He only smiled and pulled me into his arms. Though my wounds were still fresh and raw, for once, I allowed myself to take comfort in him. In his arms, I felt safe and protected. I was finally able to release the breath it felt like I'd been holding for years. And just like that, I slid into a deep sleep.

CHAPTER 11

FOUR MONTHS LATER

"By Hades's bouncing balls is it cold!" I shivered between clattering teeth. I swear I could see my breath freeze and fall to the ground.

"Yeah, well, you were the one who wanted to come out and do the hot cocoa and cookie thing, so you have no one to blame but your stomach." Damen pulled me in tighter to him.

"Hey, at least now when I wear gloves everywhere, no one thinks I'm batshit."

"I wouldn't go that far, oracle." He laughed at his own joke.

"Ha. Ha. So very funny. No, really, you should be a comedian, guardian. I could be your manager," I joked in a robotic tone.

"Cute," he whispered as he slid a finger under my chin. Pinching me lightly, he dipped his lips to mine. Heat started from my mouth and spread like a wildfire to the rest of my body. What started as a chaste expression grew to something more serious.

Before things got too out of hand, I broke away from his teasing tongue.

Out of breath, he flirted, "I know how to warm you up."

"That you do, but this is a family event, and well, cookies," I chattered in a dreamy tone.

"Oh, I see where I stand," he grumbled, though I knew his heart wasn't in it.

"Yup, it goes Hades, cookies, then you," I explained, unable to hide my smile.

We spent the next hour wandering around town, sipping hot chocolate and nibbling on cookies. If I thought the town was magical in August, nothing could compare to December. I'd never really lived somewhere with so much snow. So I thought when it got cold, people hid inside by the fire. I couldn't have been more wrong. The whole town seemed to come alive, as though they were hibernating in the summer, waiting for the first snowfall to wake.

I didn't know it was possible to fall in love with a place, but that's just what happened. I was totally in love with Havenwood Falls.

"My superhero!" a little boy screeched in a pitch I honestly didn't know was possible. I turned to see a bright red streak dart right at Damen. And just like I knew he would, he scooped Jacob up into his arms.

"Hey, little man!" Damen cooed as he held the boy.

"Hey, honey! Where's your aunt? I don't want her to worry." I looked around.

"Over there." He pointed over Damen's shoulder.

I looked over, and Aster waved and mouthed, "Sorry!"

"We're good!" I grinned and waved reassuringly.

"You're Lana?" He giggled, looking at me. I couldn't actually recall if he'd ever known my name.

"Yup!" I affirmed with a smile.

"Thank you."

I frowned at his words, not understanding what he was thanking me for.

"For what, honey?"

He wiggled and moved in Damen's arms, causing him to put the boy down.

He stepped over to me and grabbed my hands. He pulled down slightly, so I knelt down until we were on more of the same level.

His little cheeks were tinged red from the cold, making his dark freckles stand out even more. While his face was framed with his green hood, his wild red hair stuck out every which way. He really was a cute thing.

"For your daddy. He's a nice man." He then giggled and ran back to his aunt, waving back all the way.

I couldn't seem to make my legs work. I just stayed there like a statue, frozen on my knees.

"Lana?" Damen asked, helping me to my feet.

He searched my eyes. Clearly, he hadn't heard what Jacob said. I just stared after the little boy as he grabbed a cookie and did a little spin on the sidewalk.

Blinking tears away, I smiled up at my guardian.

"He was a good man," I choked, trying to keep my emotions at bay.

"Who was?" he questioned in a confused tone.

"My dad. In the end, anyway." For the first time in four months it felt easier to breathe. And like I had a hundred times before, I let out a breath, but this time I let everything go. All of the blame, the guilt, all of it.

"There you are." Damen breathed his own sigh of relief.

"What?" I asked, blinking away the snowflakes that had fallen on my eyelashes.

"The real you," he whispered before kissing me.

Breaking the kiss, I smiled warmly at him.

"But there's more cookies." I giggled.

Holding me tighter, he slid a hand to the back of my head, tanking his fingers in my dark hair.

"Come on, oracle, let's go get cookies."

Ah, the way to my heart: cookies. He knew just the right things to say.

"Oh, and cocoa, too," he added with a wink. All I could do was laugh.

~

ABOUT THE AUTHOR

Emily Cyr is a stay-at-home mom turned writer. She holds a degree in middle grades education with certification in English and social science. She has always had a love of all things paranormal and fantasy, but it wasn't until Emily's husband said the words, "Why not?" that she considered putting her thoughts and ideas into the book, *The Lightning Prophecy*. This trilogy was just the start for Emily. It seemed to open a creative door that had been locked.

Emily has always been an avid reader. Through reading came her love of writing. The more she read, the more she knew she wanted to create her own world. Many of her first works were fan fiction.

Emily and her family currently reside in San Antonio, Texas. She has an incredibly supportive husband, who is also an officer in the United States Air Force. They have three sons, ages 8, 7, and 3. Somehow, even with the demands of being a parent to three little boys, she finds time to escape to her fantasies and write them down.

Currently, Emily has two urban fantasy series out, but stay tuned via her website, www.EmilyCyr.com, for more!

Play list for *Fate's Demand*:
    Juice - Lizzo
    Like a Girl - Lizzo
    Beauty Marks - Ciara
    Almost - Hozier

Movement - Hozier
No Plan - Hozier
Cool Blue Reason - Cake
My Boy - Billie Eilish
Ocean Eyes - Billie Eilish
You Are the Reason - Calum Scott

THE WU & THE WAND

T.V. HAHN

~ A Havenwood Falls New Adult Novella ~
HAVENWOOD FALLS
THE WU AND THE WAND
T.V. HAHN

BOOKS BY T.V. HAHN

The Winged & the Wicked
The Ward & the Wanderers
The Wu & the Wand
Havenwood Falls Short Story Anthology 2018

*To my friend Angela, whose enthusiasm for the story kept me writing,
to my niece Kristie, whose belief in my storytelling encouraged me, and
to my husband Paul, who Wu's me with his own kind of magic.*

PROLOGUE

he bedroom chamber was still as night, though it was only slightly darkened by the oncoming twilight. Four people were in the chamber: the young boy (the poor soul who brought us all here in the first place, or so we thought), his mother, his father, and myself.

A straw of hay rustled across the rice paper floor. That was the only sound that could be heard for what seemed an eternity, until the stillness was interrupted with the eerie raspy rattle of death emitting from the frail body, of whom we stood by the bedside. His skin was waxen and yellow, and so chilled to touch that it numbed one's fingers.

The child had not moved for what felt like a century, but was most likely two or three days. Not a single movement could be detected underneath his sleeping eyelids. That at least might have given us an indication that he was still aware . . . maybe still with us.

Suddenly, the booming command came: "YOU MUST CURE HIM!"

Regardless of the strength of the command, it was easy to discern that it contained worry and grief, and even more—concern for the future of our world.

"Your Highness," I spoke slowly, trying very carefully to phrase the rest of my response so as not to anger but to do my job, "this is no illness I am familiar with." I paused.

"WHY ARE YOU HERE, THEN, IF YOU CANNOT CURE HIM? YOU SHALL BE EXECUTED AT SUNRISE FOR YOUR INSOLENCE AND DECEIT!"

"Your Highness, I am not speaking from either insolence or deceit. There is another force that is upon us. I don't believe this is an illness, but a curse. Someone or something does not want the young prince to survive." And then I bowed my entire body as low to the floor as I could possibly flatten myself.

It must have worked, because fortunately the ruler wavered. It was evident that the poor child had become afflicted too quickly and with no rhyme or reason for its onset. A curse may very well have been the cause.

"WHAT DO YOU NEED?"

"Your Highness, I need time"—the ruler lifted his staff, indicating he had heard enough, but I continued as quickly as I could—"which, of course, I am keenly aware that we do not have. But I have a method of overcoming that." I prayed under my breath. "My devotion and divination with Spirit Crane has put me in good standing with the spirit, and I believe She will assist me in finding out who placed the curse, and, to that end, how to break it!"

The rulers, having reigned so long and becoming so arrogant as such royalty tended to do, had lost their touch with the people. The child prince, however, was blessed with the knowledge and the gifts of his ancestors, and the people loved him. I loved him.

If he died, the people would revolt against not only the rulers, but the mysteries of mankind, and this realm would dissolve into shreds of nothingness.

But that was not my only challenge. I loved him, and I loved my people, but I loved this world too. I wanted—I *needed*—it to survive. There was something very dark, dangerous, and deadly out there, and I needed to use everything in my powers to find it and eradicate it.

CHAPTER 1

TEENY WEENY

*I*t was another perfectly crisp October morning. I absolutely loved this time of year. It was invigorating. The harvest of all the delicious squashes—pumpkins, crooknecks, hubbards, and the like—had come in. There was such an array of colors upon us—the orange maples, the golden-leafed aspens, and of course all of the luxurious evergreens, from the bristlecone pines to the elegant spruces—all of them emitting a fragrance that I could feel.

Havenwood Falls, this small frontier-like town nestled in the cradle of a canyon and cloaked with the mystery of supernaturals and humans cautiously, carefully coexisting, was at its autumn peak, ready to burst with harvest and a few chills and thrills for the Halloweeners.

I grabbed my wool scarf, the latest one given to me by my nephew Mat and his girlfriend Nina, and headed out for my regular rendezvous with my best friend, Barbie a.k.a. Mayor Stuart.

Ah, Mat was not really my nephew, but a cousin. However, with hundreds of years between us, he had always known me as Aunt Siobhan.

My townhome, which housed my palm-reading salon, opened

up to the south entrance of the square. I crossed over Main Street, and since we started our rendezvous fairly early in the morning, it was an easy crossing with no traffic. Town Square Park was accentuated with a fountain in its center. Some modern-day folks didn't believe the story that it was rimmed with real gold flakes that spilled from the floors of the gold-traders, some of whom founded this Havenwood Falls in the first place long ago during the gold rush. I was there, so I knew it was true.

As I approached the Broastful Brew, I could already see the mayor sitting at our familiar table.

The Broastful Brew was more of an artifact, kind of like me, than the best coffee shop in Havenwood Falls. Mabel, the owner and operator, landed in Havenwood Falls maybe twenty or thirty years ago. She was perfectly human, if there was such a thing, but that was what she was. I didn't know if she was one of those souls that were actually summoned to come, or if she just came here by happenstance. I suspected the latter. But you never knew.

The tinkle of the shopkeeper's bell rang a simple chime as I opened the door to the Brew. The flowery scent of Dragon Well green tea smacked me so hard in the face that my fingertips started to tingle, as did the tips of my toes. A distinguished Asian fellow lifted his head from the steaming cup of green tea, noting my entrance. He was very handsome with a neatly trimmed Fu Manchu and dark eyes that seemed nearly black. He appeared to be around my age, my glamour age anyway, but it was hard to tell, especially since I sensed in his eyes something much older, ancient even. I felt he may have been an old soul, reincarnated many times.

I nodded at him, hoping he would accept the greeting, and not think of me as too rude for my intense observance of him, then hurried to the back of the Broastful Brew to join the mayor.

"Good morning, Barbie! Boy, that Manchurian tea still has my fingers and toes tingling!"

"Good morning yourself! Are you sure it's that tea making you tingle?" Barbie winked at me and continued, "You were certainly examining that man up and down. He's really quite handsome, don't you think?"

I sat down, then leaned over the table as far as my four-foot-five frame would allow. Barbie obliged and leaned over her side of the table, meeting me more than halfway, her lemon chiffon bouffant bouncing on the top of my head.

"Who is that chap? Looks can be deceiving, you know, especially in Havenwood Falls," I said in a whisper.

"Don't I know it! Look at us! You have more power in your right pinky fingernail than I do from my heel to the top of my beehive. But anyway, that's Tim Wu, Dr. Wu. The Court invited him all the way from China. Don't you remember the discussion?"

"Well, sort of . . . He's some kind of a professional gamer, right? Well, that sounds pretty much like a professional gambler who already lost a couple of letters. I kind of tuned the whole thing out."

"He's more than just a professional gamer, though all the kids in town are excited about the Grand Master being here because of that. He's also a game developer, and his newest game *Rage of Realms* has an interesting premise—dark forces trying to destroy all magic. The Court felt we may be able to glean something from him."

Then the mayor abruptly straightened up in her chair and said, "That reminds me! Siobhan, you really have to consider being on the faculty of the Academy's College of Guardians. Adelaide is teaching one of the potions classes right now, and you know she's probably not the best choice for that subject. Not compared to you. We need you desperately!"

"I really don't think so, Barbie. I'm no teacher. Even after hundreds of years, I feel I am still a student myself, bumbling around this mysterious world."

My nephew Mat came to the table, carrying my usual chamomile tea. He'd been working morning shifts at the Broastful Brew pretty much since he arrived here two years ago.

"Good morning Mayor, Madame Tahini." He winked at me. *What's with all this winking this morning?*

Mat set down the teapot, steeper, and cup, and no sooner did he leave than the Asian gentleman approached the table.

"Good morning, ladies. I hope I'm not interrupting." He spoke in a smooth voice, but his accent seemed out of place, more British. Maybe he grew up in Hong Kong?

"Dr. Wu! A pleasure to see you this morning. Are your quarters comfortable?" the mayor greeted him, then turned to me. "Our guest is staying in one of the cabins at Whisper Falls Inn."

"And who is this charming little woman with you, Mayor?" Dr. Wu asked.

"I'm sorry. I've forgotten my manners! Dr. Timothy Wu, this is Teeny Weeny Tahini, I mean Madame Tahini, our resident palm reader and healer."

"Enchanted to meet you, Madame Tahini. I've dabbled a bit in healing divination myself. It would be a pleasure to share a spot of tea with you sometime, if you would care to join me."

Oh, dear. The tingling sensation started again, and this time it wasn't the tea, and wasn't just my fingers and toes—it extended to my earlobes, the back of my neck, even my nose!

"I would be delighted," I responded, not having any idea where that came from.

"How about four o'clock tomorrow afternoon? I'll meet you at the inn?"

"Oh, uh, four o'clock . . . tomorrow?" I stammered, trying to backtrack now and regain my composure.

"She'll be there!" the mayor piped in, giving me no room to renege.

"Brilliant! I will see you then." Dr. Wu nodded a goodbye and left.

The bell dangling from the front door tinkled again as the esteemed *doctor* left the shop.

Mat returned to the table and asked if we needed anything else. The mayor requested another cup of coffee, but I was still bouncing my tea steeper in my pot, trying to make heads or tails of what had just occurred.

"By the way, Aunt Siobhan, I'd like to show you the gift I got Nina for our second anniversary. I'll come by after my shift is over?"

Mat meant the second anniversary of their meeting and dating. It was a very slow romance in the making. Mostly because Nina, a very talented Italian tailor, was still quite gun shy because of the death of her lover many years ago.

"That'll be fine, Mat. I'll be home."

The mayor got up from the table and bade me farewell, again asking me to consider the Sun and Moon Academy's new College of Supernatural Guardians. I just shook my head. She was persistent, part of the great politician in her.

I finished my tea in solitude, swirling the brew in my cup and wondering what the tea leaves would be telling me about the town's new guest.

CHAPTER 2

TEENY WEENY

*A*fter my morning stroll through town, I returned home. I decided I'd better do a little homework regarding Dr. Timothy Wu, so I didn't sound like a complete dunderhead at tea tomorrow. Professional gamer? What was that?

I was intrigued about his healing divination comment, though I wasn't exactly sure how one "dabbled" in it. I decided I would start there in my research, since it sounded like something we may have had in common.

I went into the salon and perused my bookshelves. Wonderful leather-bound books filled every slot available, some with colorful ribbons marking important pages of note. Ribbons that the pixie sisters gifted to me regularly as a sign of their devotion.

I fetched the librarian's ladder stationed at the far end of the bookcases and glided it over toward the center. I was grateful for the ladder, as at least three of the shelves would be otherwise unattainable to me, though of course my friend Barbie could reach up and pull anything off even the tops of the cases.

On the second shelf from the top was a leather-and-silk-covered book with calligraphy along the spine reading, *Ancient Arts and Mystics*. A good place to start when delving into the arts of the Orient. I took the book and stepped down off the ladder, placing it on my salon table. The embroidered silk inlaid in the leather depicted a scene with cranes, bamboo, and a tiled-roof temple nestled in a thick forest.

I slid my finger down the table of contents and found the location for "Wizards of the Orient." My fingertip began to tingle once again. *A sign? Of what, I wonder?*

Opening up to the first page of the chapter, I began reading:

"The Wizards of the Orient date back well into the twelfth century BC. The earliest reports treated them as shamans, but as their skills in alchemy, herbal toxicology, and even martial arts developed, they became much more respected, and the royal houses often regarded the wizards, known as the Wu, as high officials, relying on their advice as well as their ability to divine spirits and heal the sick."

Wu. That's interesting, actually even kind of funny . . . Dr. Wu? Wu Who? Dr. Who? Wu.

Right when I was getting hold of my silly sidetrack and going back to my reading, the large metal knocker on my door alerted me to a visitor. Before I could even get to the foyer, Mat was coming through the entryway, bent nearly in half, since he was about six four. Upon each shoulder were two pixies, swinging their feet and taking turns hollering, "Giddy-up."

Once clear of the threshold, he straightened up and brushed the little imps off his shoulders. The pixie sisters simply rolled off him like lint balls, then abruptly began wrestling one another once they hit the floor.

Mat just shook his head and laughed. "Seems I attracted a few hitchhikers."

He bent over once again to give me a kiss on the cheek as I waved him into the living area at the end of the foyer.

We sat down before the fireplace, dormant now, as the weather had not become so chilled that it required a blazing hearth.

"Well, let me see it. Stop keeping your aunt in suspense!" I begged him to reveal the gift he had for Nina, hoping, just hoping, this was it.

He reached into his pocket, pulled out a small box, and handed it to me.

"I got it at Callie's Consignments. Nikita, Callie's cousin, is manning the store, and she just received a new shipment of artifacts from Callie herself. I couldn't resist this one."

I opened it slowly, because really I do like a *little* suspense. The tiny box revealed a golden pendant, the center of which displayed the yin-and-yang motif. Around the edge of the pendant was an array of Chinese characters, most likely an ancient wish or blessing. I turned the pendant over, and the back seemed similar to the front side, but the yin and yang had melded into a solid dark gray color. It too had script around the edge, but even though I didn't read Chinese—Mandarin, Cantonese, or otherwise—I could tell they were not the same characters as on its opposite side. As I touched it, my fingertips, rather than tingling, received tiny shocks, a little like pin pricks, but something more that I couldn't really distinguish. I wasn't really comfortable with this gift he had for Nina, but I didn't want to break his heart.

"Mat, it's really quite beautiful, and maybe something more . . . but don't you think it's time to give her a ring? You know, the type that goes on a certain finger, like a diamond ring?"

"I would love to, Aunt Siobhan, but I don't want to spook her. After that Valentine's Day debacle, I want to take it as slowly as she needs. I love her madly, but I want her to love me madly back."

"That sounds like yin and yang to me, then. In the meantime, let me give it a little blessing to protect it, her, and your love. I'll be right back."

I headed upstairs to get my father's wand—I mean, my wand. I didn't know what it was, but there was something about this amulet that made me uneasy. Maybe, if I got the chance, our illustrious guest, Dr. Wu, would be able to tell me what the script read.

I'd been keeping my special box in my bedroom ever since I discovered that it was originally made to hold the wand. I discovered so many things on that trip to the Isle of Gwynf'l and back last spring, but the box and the wand seemed to have opened up a whole new understanding of my life, my family, and maybe even my destiny.

I passed my hand over the box, tripping the keyless mother-of-pearl latch, and opened the box. My fingers still prickling, I fumbled a little with the wand, but as soon as I held it tightly in my hand, the tip began to glow and the prickly feeling disappeared.

I returned to the parlor only to find that the pixie sisters had moved their wrestling match to the rug in front of the fireplace. *Don't they ever get tired of this? Really, this has been going on for centuries now.*

I picked up the amulet once again, waved the glowing wand over it and under it, and chanted these words:

"Gods, goddesses, and spirits above
Grant this amulet with purest love
For whom its mystery is to be worn
Protect the soul that it adorns
Should anyone dare to steal its grace
This amulet shall remain in place
For all the fae that know—time will tell
Only one's true love can break this spell."

The tip of the wand grew brighter and brighter, and suddenly a flash came from it, enveloping the amulet, and then it extinguished as quickly.

Well, I hope that works.

"Thank you, Aunt Siobhan. I know that makes this gift especially worthy."

"Mat, may I take a picture of it with my phone? Maybe Dr. Wu can decipher some of this writing. I'd like to show it to him."

"Oh, of course. I forgot you are having tea with him tomorrow."

"Does everyone know my business here?"

"No, no. I just couldn't help overhearing the conversation.

Broastful Brew is a small shop and isn't exactly bustling, if you know what I mean. By all means, take a picture."

I grabbed my cell phone from my skirt pocket. Of course, all my skirts have pockets for that very reason. I fumbled with the phone, since I particularly use it to call Barbie, and nothing else, but Mat gently took the phone from me, touched the camera icon, and snapped a photo of the pendant.

"Well, dear nephew, thank you!"

He also showed me where to find the photo he just snapped on my phone. That was smart thinking, because I wouldn't have had a clue.

The pendant placed back in the box, Mat popped the box back into his pocket, then asked, "Well, what about that position teaching at the College of Supernatural Guardians? Are you going to take it?"

Suddenly, the pixies stopped their wrestling and began their yammering.

"You have to be a teacher, Siobhan!" shouted Enya.

"Look at how much you've taught us," added Aeri.

"I want to be your pupil!" emphasized Tierri.

"Haha! I already have two pupils. That makes me a teacher, right? Get it?" Ushka broke out in a huge kind of gurgling laughing fit over her own joke. Needless to say, the remaining pixies joined in the laughter, rolling on the floor, only to be followed by, well, you know.

CHAPTER 3

WU

I knew the amulet was here. I could feel it all the way down to the marrow of these bones. But there was so much interference in this town. There was a lot of magic here, much of which I could not even identify.

Ah, these bones. Such a handsome young man, this Timothy Wu. I hoped he didn't mind that I was borrowing his body for a few weeks. If he was as great and as busy as these people said he was, then he probably needed the sabbatical I was giving him.

The mayor was quite a woman of stature, but it was the tiny woman, Madame Tahini, who concerned me some. She was an ancient. That I was sure of, yet she seemed to be an ingénue at the same time. She was definitely not from any area that I was familiar with, which was why I was pretty sure Tahini was not her true surname. I could not really pinpoint her talents, her knowledge, or whether she could be trouble. Nevertheless, I would stay on my guard, and try to get to know more about her.

I was to meet the little lady in just about an hour. I noticed she was extremely sensitive to smells. Her reaction to the green tea was more than noticeable. I suspected she had synesthesia, as did I. So I wanted her to relax and feel that she could trust me. Chamomile and lavender, I believed, would do the trick. I formulated a cologne of those fragrances.

~

As I headed over to the main building of Whisper Falls Inn from my cabin, I passed what Miss Petran called the conservatory. It looked inviting. Entering into the inn, I headed toward the front parlor, and there she was, such a demure little being. I should not have felt so threatened by her, yet I did. Perhaps, if it were not for this mission, I would have been sensing something else instead, or maybe that in itself was the threat.

"Madame Tahini! Such a pleasure once again."

She did not rise from her seat, but she lifted her hand. *Should I shake it or kiss it?* I took the lithe appendage into my own hand, covering it with my other and letting her feel that I was genuine with my words. *And really, I think I am.*

"As you, Dr. Wu. Tea?" she asked as she slowly withdrew her hand from my embrace.

I took a seat in the overstuffed chair across the coffee table centered in the parlor. "I suspect that you enjoy the Dragon Well green tea, so I took the liberty of having that prepared for us this afternoon. Is that satisfactory to you?" I said.

"It will be a treat, thank you. Maybe I will even get a chance to read your tea leaves before twilight."

"That would be a treat, I am sure." *Actually, it would not, especially if she does have prophetic abilities. I'd better make sure the leaves leave no clue.* "I also managed to smuggle in a flask of Tiger Pond water, so I've requested Michaela to steam the tea with it."

The lovely little lady bowed her head in appreciation. "I am honored to be treated like such royalty. Thank you, Dr. Wu." Her voice was like the song of a nightingale—pure and sweet. It suited her perfectly.

The owner of the inn, Michaela Petran, entered into the parlor at that very moment, with small cups of the steaming brew. There was a scent about the young woman that I couldn't exactly place. It was almost sanguine, but there were undertones of something else. It was possible she was among the creatures in this town that were interfering with my trying to position the exact whereabouts of that elusive amulet.

Michaela—or Kales, as I heard her friends refer to her—shakily placed the tray of tiny tea cups on the table in front of us. She seemed nervous or excited, but I guessed it was this Tim Wu personage I had taken on that had her and so many of the younger folk in town aflutter. Apparently he was a high-tech genius of some sort, and quite the rave around the world. Lucky for me, he came from the Wu clan, making it possible to climb into his skin.

"Miss Petran, by the heady bouquet, I can tell you have brewed the tea to perfection. Thank you for your kind attention."

The young woman was undoubtedly grateful for the compliment, explaining she was nervous about steaming the exotic tea, but after some research, a.k.a. googling, she felt more comfortable.

We engaged in the customary chitchat over tea. Madame Tahini told me a bit about the history of the town, but nothing too enlightening. I told her my family was from Hangzhou, which was actually true, though not in a contemporary sense.

Once we had finished imbibing in the luxuriousness of the tea, she reminded me that she wanted to read the leaves in my cup. I reached for the small vessel to hand to her, and pretended to accidentally knock it over, jostling the leaves around, altering their original arrangement at the bottom of the cup.

"Madame, I'm so sorry. I'm afraid that I've destroyed my own fortune, or at least the telling of it."

"No worries, Dr. Wu. Sometimes the happenstance is supposed to occur. Let me look." She picked up the porcelain demitasse and looked inside. "Hmm . . ." She paused. "And sometimes not. Oh, well, perhaps another time."

"Would you like to take an amble through the conservatory? It appears that there are some interesting plants there." Although our tea had concluded, I felt a tug to spend more time with her. I'm not sure if it was because I sensed she may know something about the amulet, or just because I was enjoying her company.

"Sounds wonderful. It's been a long time since I've stepped foot in it."

The two of us departed the parlor and walked through the dining room and the French doors that opened onto the conservatory. As we entered the sun-warmed glass building, there was an intense contrast to the cold, crisp mountain air. I found this exhilarating.

We walked around admiring the plant life that grew profusely in the domed structure, and I prodded Madame Tahini to tell me about her family. She told me she had a nephew who was really a cousin, who came to live with her a couple of years ago. In fact, he was the server at the Broastful Brew, and he had met a young woman here in Havenwood Falls who had captured his heart. In fact, she went on to tell me, he recently found an oriental pendant that he intended to give her in a day or two for their "sort of" anniversary.

"Oh! I almost forgot!" she said, and started hopping from one foot to the other excitedly while pulling a cell phone out of her skirt pocket. *How cute.* "I have a picture of it I wanted to show you. There are characters around the rim of it. I think they are Chinese, and I thought maybe you would be able to translate it."

Aha! I was right. That tug was telling me she knew something, but this was even better. *As long as I can see the etchings, I may not require the amulet itself.*

She pulled up the picture on her phone, fumbling a bit, as if she were new at this. I was about to assist her, but she managed it herself and held the phone up in front of me.

"Interesting . . ." I said as I pinched my thumb and index finger on the phone, then spread them to make the image larger. This knowledge I seemed to have gained from taking over Timothy Wu's body. His technological savvy had apparently melded into my mind. The photo on the screen showed the dark side of the amulet, the side of which I was already too keenly aware. "Is there an opposite side to the pendant, Madame Tahini?"

"Well, yes, there is, but I only took a shot of this side. Can you tell me what it says?"

Ugh, this is not good. I had to see the other side. I pretended to examine the photo in detail, turning the phone and enlarging each quarter of the circular pendant. "Madame, it is indeed Chinese, but it is a very ancient script. One I am not too familiar with. It seems to be about mythological creatures and spirits. Utter nonsense, of course, but I imagine so many eons ago, they seemed real enough."

I guess this meant I would be having my morning tea at the Broastful Brew tomorrow to have a chat with this nephew of hers.

"Dr. Wu, thank you so much for the tea and the stroll, but it's getting late. If you'll forgive me."

"Allow me to walk you home, Madame." *Maybe that Mat is at her place right now, and I won't have to wait until the morning.*

"Thank you very much, but it's only a half a block from here, and of course Havenwood Falls is quite safe." Then she hurried out of the conservatory, quickly taking a shortcut from the entry to the dining room heading directly to the corner of Beaumont and Eleventh.

CHAPTER 4

TEENY WEENY

*I*t was kind of Dr. Wu to offer to walk me home, but after a couple of hours in his presence, all of my senses, including my sixth sense, were charged up. Walking the half a block from Whisper Falls Inn down Beaumont gave me a chance to let the frosty evening air clear up some of the sensory overload.

As I opened the wooden gate leading into my backyard, I saw Cyllene waiting for me on the windowsill. Her iridescent green wings, so much like a lunar moth's, glistened even in the fading light. I was glad that the little dryad was here, as I wasn't sure all the feelings I was having were going to wait until my morning brew with Barbie.

"Good evening, Silly Annie! So good to see you. Come in." I invited my dear old (like really old) friend into the house as I opened the back door to my kitchen. She, of course, began buzzing about, furious with me for calling her Silly Annie, but as usual, I ignored her complaints.

Once inside, I began to set up the clamp and funnel contraption that acted like a megaphone, so that her tiny voice was audible rather than the hissing and buzzing it amounted to without the device.

"Cyllene! See-lee-nee! Really, Siobhan, I think you

136

mispronounce it just to annoy me," were the first words I could understand now that she had placed herself behind the pipe end of the funnel. *Well, of course I do it to annoy her.*

I opened the icebox and took out some vegetables to make a grab-it—a sandwich, in other words. You slapped your fillings between a couple of slices of bread and grabbed it with one hand. With all this sensory activity going on, I'd worked up quite an appetite! While fixing my grab-it, I began to tell Cyllene about my experience with the mysterious Dr. Wu.

"Everything about him is so vibrant. My fingers and toes never stopped tingling the whole time I was with him. His voice tastes like creamy butter on my lips and tongue. Although I could tell he had some cologne made up of chamomile and lavender, when he touched my hand, all I could smell was an exotic mixture of persimmon, plum, and pomegranate. He looks forty-something, but his eyes are much older than that, older than me or even you, I think."

Cyllene harrumphed at my reference to her being older than me, but she was, by a couple hundred years or so.

"Anyway, I was going to read his tea leaves, but he knocked the cup over, jostling the leaves. Though he apologized as if it were a mishap, I felt in my core that it was intentional. I pretended that the leaves were unable to reveal anything since they had been rearranged, but that wasn't true."

I hesitated, then shook off the shiver that ran down my spine as I remembered the image of the tea leaves.

"So? What did you see in the teacup?" Cyllene prodded me to continue.

"I saw an ancient temple or palace, kind of pagoda style. There was a boy. He was sick. I think he was dying. I am not sure how this connects to the young doctor, but I sense that it does. There was also something very dark and dangerous, but I couldn't make out exactly who or where it was coming from. All I know is that it feels so familiar to me! As if this is something I have been through before."

"Dark and dangerous!" Cyllene repeated, much more emphatically than I. "Oh, Siobhan, you must be careful around this man. Maybe he made the boy sick. One thing I'm sure about, your Dr. Wu is not who he seems to be."

"You might be right. I showed him the picture I had taken of the pendant that Mat is going to give Nina as a present. It is oriental in nature, and has Chinese-like characters inscribed around the rim of it. I thought maybe he could interpret it for me. He said it was an ancient script, and he wasn't too familiar with it, but again, I had my doubts about his veracity."

I bit into my grab-it, savoring the crunch of shredded carrots, sliced turnips, and arugula, and the tang of the vinegar and oil I sprinkled on it. My stomach rumbled back in appreciation. I gobbled up the rest of it quite quickly.

My hunger now sated and my story out of my head and off my lips, I felt much calmer. My sharpened senses had ratcheted down to a more normal level as the comfort of my own home sunk in, my closest confidante Cyllene by my side.

The thought of the *Wizards of the Orient* book popped into my head, and I was wondering just what kind of wizard this Timothy Wu might be. Maybe not the healing type, but maybe something more sinister. In my heart, for whatever reason, I hoped—prayed—not. Regardless, for the sake of Havenwood Falls and the universe itself, I needed to stay on my tippy toes, especially with everything going on. Maybe I'd better rethink that position with the school.

I finished my sandwich and offered Cyllene some peach nectar, which she declined. *Not a good sign. She's fading too fast.* I was getting ready to clean up the crumbs when Cyllene announced through her funnel-trumpet, "Don't bother, Siobhan. You have company!"

And sure enough, through the delivery slot in the back door hopped not one, not two, but all four pixie sisters. They tumbled to the floor through the slot, which only invited a pixie riot, also known as a wrestling match.

"Stop!" I hollered at them. *Just when I was getting my calm, cool, collected Celtic self back.*

Cyllene took charge at this moment. "Girls, there are some wonderful grab-it crumbs available on the table and counter. Help yourself! I know all of you will clean up for Siobhan when you're done."

I let the pixie sisters know that there were also faerie cakes in the fridge if they were still hungry.

"I want one!" exclaimed Tierri, which was expected because she was always famished.

"Me too!" continued Enya, hopping on top of Tierri's shoulders, who was standing next to the fridge, and reached for the door handle.

"Me three!" shouted Ushka, followed of course by Aeiri with "Me four!"

Sometimes I wondered if these little sprites could count past four.

"I'm going to bed. It has been a very long day for me," I announced to my fae and forest friends, as I stretched out an overly pronounced yawn, hoping they got the hint to keep any racket down.

"Oooh, Siobhan, I almost forgot! I have something for you," Enya said, after she and her cohort in crime finished raiding the refrigerator. The little pixie reached into her nest of fiery red hair and pulled out a bit of lacy black ribbon.

"This is for you!"

"Well, thank you, Enya! It's lovely. And . . . black?"

"Yeah, isn't it cool? Nina gave it to me."

"Nina *gave* it to you?"

"No, really. She said I could have it. I didn't take it, really! She made this super cool wedding dress for Jetta Mills, with black lace and skulls, and it was a scrap she had left over."

"I remember seeing that wedding dress for Jetta. Even though it was black, she worked her magical tailoring talents for Jetta's happily ever after. Thank you for giving this to me, Enya."

Now I started yawning for real and couldn't stop. The pixie sisters were merrily nibbling away at the faerie cakes and grab-it crumbs, with Cyllene standing charge. She really made a great nanny for this brood.

I went up to my bedroom and opened the bureau drawer, pulling out my favorite flannel nightgown. Well, actually, all my flannel nightgowns were my favorite, but tonight I chose the dusty-blue one, because the color made me feel relaxed.

I crawled under my feather comforter and did my best to turn off the memories of my tea with the illustrious doctor, and wondering if the black ribbon may be some kind of omen.

CHAPTER 5

WU

I thought I was in luck last night with that tiny woman showing me the photo of the amulet, the very one I was looking for. The good news was that I had been right; the bad news was that it still eluded me.

So here I was, sitting at the Broastful Brew once again. However, I was astounded that this small establishment, in this far-fetched part of the world, whose purveyor was even more far-fetched, actually had Longjing tea. Unusual and . . . interesting.

The young bloke Madame Tahini had called her nephew Mat came to the table and asked me if I preferred my usual. I nodded politely at the boy and thanked him effusively for remembering. After all, I needed to engage him to get him to divulge the whereabouts of the amulet.

Mat brought me a very well prepared cup of Dragon's Well green tea, not quite as good as the last evening's, but after all, I brought my own Tiger Pond water to the mix yesterday.

"Mr. Mat," I started out. "That is your name, correct?"

"Yes, sir!"

"Please, call me Tim."

"Yes, sir . . . I mean, Tim."

"Your aunt, Madame Tahini . . ."

"Oh, you mean Siobhan. By the way, you have a markedly English accent for, well, someone from China. Well, at least, I'm told that's where you are from. Anyway, okay, a lot of folks around town call her Teeny Weeny Tahini, or Madame Tahini, but to me she's Aunt Siobhan. She may be tiny, but she's my superhero!"

He was young, but I was not too happy he caught on with the accent. On the flight over from China, once I took over this Tim Wu's body, I had the blessing to be placed between two very loquacious British gentlewomen, who not only chatted over me amongst themselves, but engaged me in conversation during the laborious twenty-plus hour flight. Apparently, I picked up their accent, but so far it seemed to be working well.

Siobhan . . . Well, that helps me in placing where she's from. I knew she wasn't from any area I was familiar with, but now it starts fitting together. Sounds Celtic or Gaelic.

"Your lovely aunt told me you had a lovely lady of your own," I said.

"Ah, yes, at least I hope so. Her name is Nina, and she is the best seamstress-slash-tailor in town. She just manages to work magic with cloth and textiles like you wouldn't believe! She's a superhero, too, in her own right!" The young man bragged on his woman.

"It sounds like you love and admire the woman. Have you asked her to marry you?"

"I want to in the worst way. But she's a bit skittish on the subject, and I definitely don't want to push her. The good news is I gave her a necklace last night. I was trying to hold out for a few more days, but I was too excited. She loved it! She said it gave her an unusual inspiration, especially for her next project."

Blimey. This poor young man was apparently greener than the tea I was drinking, telling me things I really had no right to know. However, it appeared I was once again thwarted in my quest to retrieve the amulet.

"So you say she is the best seamstress in town. I have a silk jacket that needs a bit of repair. Do you think I could take it to her?" I implored the fit young man.

"Absolutely! She's the only one you would ever want to take it to. Her shop is just around the corner, halfway down Eighth. There's a little alleyway, then her shop is on the second floor."

"Wonderful! I will take my jacket over there this morning."

"Well, that's probably not a good plan. Nina is a bit of a night owl, and unless she has a fitting appointment or something, she is not likely to open the shop before noon or even one o'clock. I can give you her card, and maybe you can set an appointment?"

This young Mat seemed very excited to garner some business for his beautiful talented tailor. Before I could even ask, he pulled a little card out of his pocket and placed it delicately by my teaspoon. He may have been green, but he had class, I must say.

I was not too happy that I had to wait a few more hours in the October chill that reminded me so much of the Wudang Mountains. I guessed I had no choice but to wander around the village for a while. I finished my tea, paid my bill, and as I exited out of the Broastful Brew, I pulled my afghan scarf closer around my neck to fend off the frosty breezes that seemed to come out of nowhere.

Knowing that the amulet was within my reach helped to inspire me and warmed me against some of the more ghastly, chilling elements here.

It was way too early to go to the lovely Nina's shop. I looked at the card the young man had given me. *Dress Perfect.* Since apparently I had a few hours to kill, I checked out the town square and familiarized myself with the territory.

I got to the center of town square, and there was a wonderful fountain flecked throughout with gold chips and flakes. There was a tourist couple also pondering the fountain. The wife was reading aloud from a "Welcome to Havenwood Falls" brochure.

"Henry, it says here that the gold traders donated to the town all the gold dust, flakes, and nuggets swept from their floors to make this fountain!"

The husband was not so gullible and told her he thought it sounded like some made-up story to impress the tourists.

But I sensed immediately that the fountain was indeed speckled with pure gold. One does not become an alchemist without feeling, smelling, and knowing gold. This was the real thing.

The couple moved on, brochure in hand, heading to the next point of interest. Apparently, it was the gazebo at the southeast corner of the park.

I stayed, staring into the glittering fountain, letting the energy of the gold fill me up. I'm not sure how long I stood there, entranced by its power, but when I came out of it, feeling fully recharged, the sun was much higher in the sky.

I scanned Main Street directly south of the fountain and saw a line of shops. Except the north end, where City Hall sat, all the streets around the square were lined with one- and two-story shops, it appeared. The one I noted, however, had a storefront window with mock Arabic lettering that read, *Madame Tahini's Potions, Lotions, Palm Readings, and Other Extra-Sensory Services.*

Well, there's a mouthful. So this is where the little fae works and lives. Yes, I was sure she was fae, not because of her small stature, but because she smelled fae. It almost oozed from her smooth, shiny skin and glowed from her flowing brown hair.

It was odd that her nephew had a slight scent of fae, but that was not his dominant nature. His smell was different, something of a mixture of forest and avian, but I just really couldn't fathom it. It seemed most everyone here smelled like something quite different than how they looked. Well, except for the mayor, other than being unusually tall and well-built, and that quirky little owner of the Broastful Brew. I was not sure what to expect from this Nina person, if indeed she was a human.

It finally began to warm up, and the rustling golden aspens quieted, indicating the breezes whipping through earlier had died down. I loosened my scarf and headed back to Whisper Falls Inn.

My little cottage was quite comfortable. I got the silk jacket out of the wardrobe and took a look at it. It was, of course, perfectly intact, but that wouldn't do at all. I got my straight razor from the bathroom and cut a few threads from the side seam of the jacket, then pulled the pieces of fabric apart to form a gaping hole. There was not too much damage, but certainly enough for the seamstress to repair.

Jacket in hand, I headed back to the center of town. I spotted a tavern on the corner of Eighth and Main and decided to get a refreshment before checking on the tailoring shop. What was it? Oh yes, Dress Perfect.

On my way to the tavern, I passed another coffee shop. This small town must love its coffee. I noted that, unlike the Broastful Brew, this coffee shop, Coffee Haven, appeared to be patronized by the younger generations of the town. A few teenagers in a booth by the front window pointed at me excitedly. I nodded and smiled and continued walking. *The kids these days are so uncouth.*

There it was, the Haven Saloon. Well, that name seemed appropriate. It even had frontier-like batwing doors to enter through. The place was dim, with bare wood rafters, and smelled of beer and what I would have normally said was wine, but there was a tinge of that sanguine scent, like what I sensed from that Michaela Petran.

There was a scruffy, rather scrawny middle-aged man, with a bandanna wrapped around his head, standing behind the bar. He greeted me as I entered, "Howdy, stranger!"

How quaint, how corny.

He took a toke from a fat joint, set it down in the ashtray, then waved his hand, welcoming me to take a seat at the bar. There were rows of wine bottles behind him, all with Stone Falls Winery labels and unusual names. For example: Wolf Pack Pinot Noir.

The glassy-eyed barkeep stuck his hand out to shake mine. "Name's Brent. The locals call me Bent Brent. What's your flavor, my man?"

"Well, by any chance might you have something in the way of plum wine?"

"Sure do! Make it myself every year. Teeny Weeny has a green thumb you've never seen the likes of, and gives me most of the damson plums from the tree in her backyard. You just stuff a big-ass glass jar full of those little beauties, add a bunch of sugar, fill it to the top with water, and of course some grain alcohol, then rotate it every day for a few months. Voila! Best plum wine ever!" And sure enough, he pulled a two-gallon glass jug from underneath the counter filled to the brim with a rich purple liquid. For a scrawny doped-up dude, his strength was impressive.

"Teeny Weeny?" I acted ignorant. *Teeny Weeny, now that really IS appropriate.*

"Oh, yeah, Madame Tahini, the itsy bitsy palm-reader down the street. She doesn't really drink, other than some whacked-up version of a virgin mojito, but we've been friends for a long time."

The wine was indeed good, just the right amount of acidic and sweet. Not a far cry from meijiu back home. I sipped it slowly, enjoying the astringent flavor of the wine.

"Well, my man, your plum wine is heavenly. You crushed it!" I tried using some of the words that kept popping in my head from the brain of the real Timothy Wu.

My new friend, Bent Brent, thanked me for the compliment and went back to his stogie. Hence the "Bent" part of his nickname, I supposed.

Savoring my last sip of this extraordinary plum wine, I glanced at the large clock made of a wagon wheel hanging on the back wall. At least ol' Bent Brent knew how to maintain a motif. It was nearly one o'clock, so I paid my bill, thanked Brent for the libation, placed my silk jacket over my arm, and headed out.

I crossed to the sidewalk at the south end of Eighth, and as I approached a small alley midway in the block, I saw a sign on the wall that read *Dress Perfect* with an arrow pointing upward, indicating the passage up the stairway in the alley toward the second floor flat. At the top of the stairs was a slender woman just entering into the shop. She had jet black hair, cropped short, revealing a long slender neck, and from my angle, I could see there was a gold chain hanging around it. I waited a few minutes before ascending the staircase, to give the seamstress a little time to situate herself.

As I entered the shop, the smell of rich espresso was prevalent. The young woman turned toward me, I believed a bit startled, but she recovered quickly. She was quite beautiful, with olive-toned skin and large dark almond-shaped eyes. And yes, she was wearing the amulet, but unfortunately, it was dangling from the dark side, once again.

"Are you Miss Nina?" I asked.

"Nina Messina, si. Buongiorno!" she replied.

I told her about the young chap from the coffee shop this morning who suggested I bring my jacket to her for repair and showed her the damaged article.

"I'm concerned because it is silk, but this young Mat insisted you were the best and could handle it."

"Si, I can do this, Mr. . . . ?" the young woman prodded.

"Dr. Wu, but please call me Tim."

"Ah, so you are the famous Dr. Wu everyone is talking about." She deftly took my jacket from my hands and placed it on a standing dress form.

"I should have this ready for you later this afternoon, about five?"

"That would be fantastic. I am much obliged. By the way, that's a stunning necklace you're wearing."

"Well, that young chap Mat you mentioned gave it to me, for a bit of an early anniversary gift."

"May I?" I said, at the same moment reaching for the amulet to turn it over. As I placed my hands on its rim, I heard a sudden searing sound, followed by the smell of burning flesh.

The young woman screamed out in pain, and I realized the amulet had melded into her skin. *What kind of curse is this? What's happening?*

She started backing away from me, clutching her chest,

covering the pendant, or perhaps just in pain. I was not sure which, but I had to act fast. *I need that amulet!*

I grabbed the young woman by the nape of her neck, pulling out my vial of *dan*, and forcing her head backward, I poured the poisoning elixir down her throat. Immediately, she crumpled to the ground like a piece of one of her fabrics.

The mixture of cinnabar and mercury should have only caused a state like a temporary death, I hoped, but I needed time to figure out how to remove the amulet.

CHAPTER 6

TEENY WEENY

*T*he morning light streamed brightly through my bedroom window. It woke me up in a near panic. I never slept past the break of dawn. I looked at my cell phone, and it was nearly eight o'clock. I texted Barbie immediately to let her know I would be running late.

BS: No prob. Got paperwork. 9:30 ok?
TW: C U then
Hehe, I'm getting the hang of this.

I had so much to tell Barbie this morning, not only about my tea for two with Dr. Wu, but about the weird dream I had last night. Barbie, my go-to oneiromancer, would likely be able to interpret its meaning.

I was moving rather slowly, kind of all achy, but I guessed that was from a sensory overload from last evening's tea. It seemed to take me forever to just brush my teeth and wash my face. At the rate I was going, I felt I might actually need a cup of coffee this morning, just to get jump-started.

I did make it to the Broastful Brew by nine thirty, and of course I spotted Barbie at our usual table as I walked into the shop. The first thing I smelled was not coffee. It was that lavender and chamomile fragrance. I whipped my head around to see if Dr.

Wu was in the Brew, but alas, all the tables except Barbie's were empty.

I didn't order coffee, of course. It's not my cup of tea. Mat was already coming over with the teapot, cup, and steeper before I could even sit down with Barbie. I was grateful the shop was otherwise empty.

"Mat, was Dr. Wu here this morning?" I asked my nephew, still bothered by the flowery aroma.

"Why, yes! He really likes that green tea that Mabel brews up for him. In fact, he was looking for a seamstress. Apparently, he has a silk jacket that needs mending, so I gave him Nina's card." He answered my question and then some. Poor boy, he just spilled his heart out.

Barbie grabbed my hand. "So . . . are you going to fill me in on your tea with Timothy?"

I basically reiterated what I told Cyllene the night before, though not quite in such detail, since I had already gotten the raw feelings off my chest by talking to the dryad. Then I told her I had a dream that maybe she could make sense of.

"Okay, hurry up. Let me hear about it." She eagerly invited me to share.

"I'm in some place very far away, in place and maybe even in time. There is a young boy lying on a large throne-like bed, dying. His parents are beside him, worried sick. The mother is doing everything in her power to keep from crying. The child is barely breathing, and it does not look like he has very much time left.

"The father came over to me and grabbed me by my shoulders, shaking me and hollering 'YOU MUST CURE HIM!'

"There is something about the color of the child's skin. He's not dying from an illness. I can see his veins through his nearly paper-thin waxy skin, and the veins are green. There is a smell about him too, something like five spice, but I'm not sure. One thing I am sure about—this child has been cursed.

"I sensed there is something special about this child. It seems that his parents are worried about something else too. Not just this child's fate, but something larger. The child has or had special powers. I could feel them surrounding me like a swirling light, but dimming fast and slowing down. My heartbeat almost came to a standstill when I touched him. Is he fae?

"I tell his parents that I believe there is a dark force responsible for his illness. I tell his parents that I need time . . . but really, I think I need my wand.

"Then I woke up."

Barbie took a long slow sip of coffee, uncharacteristically making a slurping sound in the process. "Hmm . . . Is this like your dream with your brother? Maybe it is a remembrance of something you've done before?"

"I wish. Then it would make some sense to me. I know it's been eons, but I don't have any recollection of anything like this. Does it have some alternate meaning? Or do you think the goddesses are trying to tell me something?"

"Ah, that could be it! Maybe they are trying to tell you to be a professor of Healing Arts at the college! Classes have already started, but you could come in for the spring semester." Barbie, bless her heart, was trying to use my dream to get her wish. Then again, maybe she had something there. "Don't worry, Siobhan. I'll think more on it and see if I can divine some inspiration for you." She patted my hand, finished her coffee, and bid me farewell.

Well, the day had gotten off to a late start, and I had plenty to do back home. I had a palm-reading appointment in the afternoon, and the had pixies devoured my stash of faerie cakes, so I needed to replenish my stock, and then of course Halloween was just around the corner. Hopefully, Mat and Nina would help again this year.

I waved goodbye to Mat and thanked Mabel for the tea as I headed back home to finish my chores and get ready for the couple coming in for their fortune-telling session, Henry and Grace.

Cyllene, of course, was waiting for me and floated in behind me as I entered the townhome and headed for the kitchen. I set up my beakers and flasks, pulled out a bowl and whisk, and searched the cupboard for the daisy flower flour.

While I was baking the third batch of faerie cakes and wondering if I should start on some pumpkin spice cookies, Nina dropped in for a brief moment on her way to work to show off the anniversary gift that Mat had given her last night.

Once Nina left, I realized there was a slight chill in the house, so I stoked a small fire in the fireplace to begin warming the place before my clients arrived.

Henry and Grace showed up at four o'clock sharp for their palm-reading, just as I finished placing the last of the faerie cakes on the cooling rack. I welcomed them in and led them to the salon. I noted the *Ancient Arts and Mystics* book was still on the table, and I grabbed it quickly and placed it on my chair.

An hour later, Grace was satisfied with her reading, and Henry the Unconvinced reluctantly pulled a few bills from his wallet. I left them with a blessing and hoped they enjoyed the rest of their visit in our lovely town. As I opened the door for them to exit, I saw the pixie sisters running down the block. I diverted Henry and Grace's attention to the clock on City Hall, and gave them some ridiculous story of how on Halloween the clock only ran backward, all of its own accord. While the couple was staring up at the clock, the imps ran underneath my legs and rolled into the foyer. Henry gave a harrumph at my outlandish tale, as I shrugged my shoulders and closed the door quickly behind them.

"Well, that was close! You gals need to be more careful. What's all the excitement about?" I asked the pixies, who were dusting off their knees and rabbit punching one another.

"We're going to apply to the College of Supernatural Guardians!" spouted Ushka.

"Are you now? And what makes you think you are qualified to go to college?" I asked.

"Well, we're supernatural!" Tierri stated matter-of-factly.

"Yeah, and we were your guardians in Gwynf'l, sort of, maybe, kinda, I think," Aeri said a bit skeptically while shaking her cloud-like white-and-pink locks about her head.

Hands on her hips, Enya insisted that they were smart, and they were going to write a story that would get them into the college.

"Really? Well, you are at least imaginative, I can admit that. Can you count to ten?"

"One!" cried Enya.

"Two," said Tierri.

"Three," added Ushka.

"Four," huffed Aeri.

Well, they got that far.

"Two!"

"Four!"

"Three!"

"One!" and back and forth between the four pixies, all the numbers out of order, continuing on for nearly ten rounds. *The closest they can get to the idea of ten, I guess.*

"See! We can count," Tierri exclaimed with a big grin on her face. "But we may need your help with the story, Siobhan."

"I can't help you write a story. You have to write your own story."

"We know, but we only know how to write in runes. We will need your help to translate it," Enya explained.

I grabbed some paper and pencils for the sprites and set them down in the living room, now pleasantly warm from the fire I started earlier. I left the sisters alone, saying a little prayer under my breath that this would keep them busy enough for me to clean up the kitchen and maybe have a nice quiet cup of chamomile tea. *Hmm . . . Maybe not chamomile tonight. That might be more stirring than calming.*

My tea brewed, I sat down at the small kitchen table, still clamped with Cyllene's megaphone, to take a sip when all four of the pixie sisters proudly strutted in, each with a sheet of paper in their hands, all waving them at me to look and read.

153

Enya and Tierri always seemed to take charge, so I took one of the sheets from Aeri, who was a bit shy to have hers read first, but handed it to me delicately.

The paper was full of rune-like figures—geometric shapes, wavy lines, a circle, a cross. These were indeed our ancestral runes. Aeri's read in English: *Fire 1 Earth 2 Air 4 Water 3*, and continued repeatedly throughout the page. I did not dare take her second sheet.

"Very nice, Aeri! Enya, let me see one of your pages." That of course did not take any cajoling whatsoever, as the imp slammed her paper down on the table proudly, triumphantly, and almost with an attitude that said, how dare I not choose hers first anyway.

Well, because in English it read like this: *Fire 1, Fire Fire 2, Fire Fire Fire 3, Fire Fire Fire Fire 4*

Not wanting to bore myself to death with reading all their pages, but trying to be supportive, I sent them back to the living room to compile their "story."

"You gals put your pages together, figure out what page is first, second, third, fourth, first . . ." *Jiminy criminy, I'm starting to sound like them.*

Fortunately for me, that's all it took. They delightedly threw all the pages into the air, each one grabbing another's, and off they rolled into the hearth room.

Ahh! I can finish my tea, maybe with a little peace and quiet.

BANG . . . BANG . . . BANG . . .

Holy junipers, WHAT THE HECK?

It was my door knocker, but never ever in my century and a half years here did it ever bang so loudly. Worse yet, I heard the etched oak door bang against the wall, and I knew intuitively that there would only be one person that would enter my home so boldly, and yet so humbly.

My poor dear nephew Mat charged into the foyer, nearly taking out the door frame with him. He was obviously distraught, to say the least.

"What's the matter, Mat?"

"Oh, Aunt Siobhan, I think Nina has stood me up. Maybe she's breaking up with me?" he responded in near tears.

"I highly doubt that, dear. What would make you think so?"

"She was supposed to meet me for dinner over an hour ago. I sat at the restaurant all that time waiting for her, but she never showed up, and she's not answering my calls or texts. Maybe the pendant I gave her wigged her out. If so, I'm glad it wasn't a ring."

"Mat, honey, Nina did not get 'wigged out' over your gift. In fact, she came by to show it off on her way to the dress shop this morning—well, actually, early afternoon. She loved it and told me how she was as happy the past two years as you. She's quite attached to the pendant."

"Oh. OH! Then she might be in trouble!"

I tried to calm this strong young man, now falling apart before my very eyes, and assured him we could find her. I sent him back to the restaurant, just in case she had the time wrong. Meanwhile, since I had a key to her shop, I told him I would go there to check it out.

"Maybe she fell asleep. I've caught her snoozing behind her bolts of fabric before," I informed Mat as we both headed out to search for Nina.

I checked in on the pixies before grabbing my wool coat and noted that they were now wrestling one another over whose pages went where. I called Cyllene into the living room to keep an eye on them, then rushed out the door. Something in the pit of my stomach told me Nina did not fall asleep.

I started to grapple for the key to the shop in my skirt pocket once I got to the top of the stairs at the end of the alley, but I saw the door was ajar.

"Nina? Yoohoo! Nina?" I called out, but no reply.

Nothing really seemed out of order, but there was a scent all mixed in with the usual espresso aroma that permeated Nina's shop. It was lavender and chamomile. *Again? Oh yes, Dr. Wu was supposed to see her.*

I noted the silk jacket Mat mentioned was still hanging on the dress form mannequin, and as I touched the jacket, an entirely different smell seeped into my nostrils. It was a metallic smell, part mercurial and what was that other thing . . . sulfur? The hairs raised up on my arms, telling me it was poisonous. This was a bad sign, I feared.

I texted Mat to meet me back at the salon, locked the door to the dress shop, and headed back home. Mat was already at the door waiting for me, and I suspected he had shifted into his owl self and flew back here to have arrived so quickly.

I raised my hand to place it gently on his shoulder—well, right below his shoulder, because I couldn't reach quite that high.

"I think Nina is with Dr. Wu," I tried to tell him calmly, especially since I didn't really have a lot to go on. *Dabbled in healing divination, my eye!*

Mat nodded. "She told me she heard about the town guest from the kids at Coffee Haven, where she gets her espresso. They were all excited about him being here, and she seemed just as excited, but then, that could have been the espresso talking."

"I think maybe it's not a good thing if she's with him. Now we need to find Dr. Wu, too. But at least I think I know where to find him. We need to go to Whisper Falls Inn. Stay here; I will be right back!"

I dashed into the townhome and scurried up to my bedroom. Grabbing the wooden box with the mysterious mother of pearl latch, I passed my hand over it, and the latch popped open. The wand nestled inside the case glowed dimly. *Just in case.* I wrapped my fingers around its shaft, lifting it out of its bedding carefully, then hurried back down the stairs to join Mat.

CHAPTER 7

WU

I waited until night had fallen to move the girl. My studies in the mystic arts had allowed me to master gravity and, in doing so, overcome it. It was a blessing for me this night.

As I exited the second-story flat, I scanned the surroundings and planned my escape route. I saw a snowy owl flying northeast, away from me. I didn't want anyone to see me, and though it was only a bird, I could not be sure in this town if it was indeed just a bird or something else—a familiar who may reveal my destination? A fae in disguise? I could take no chances.

Determining the coast was clear, the unconscious seamstress underneath my arm, so light and limp it was as if she were nothing more than a pillow, I leapt from the top landing of the staircase, across the alley to the top of the roof on the opposite side, and moved swiftly to the end of the row of shops. With the momentum of my run, I was able to jump catty-corner across the intersection. I continued swiftly across the roof of the Haven Saloon and westward toward Whisper Falls Inn, making a second leap across another alley, then once I was at the pawn shop, I took a deep breath, closed my eyes, and let my mind's eye soar me across Beaumont and Eleventh, where I moved stealthily, quietly to my cabin at the backside of the inn.

I gently placed the slumbering beauty on the bed in the back of the cabin and fetched my straight razor from the front room where I had left it after ripping my jacket open. I would use my surgical skills to remove the amulet that was now seared to her breast.

As I was about to make the first delicate slice between the amulet and the woman's skin, a piercing bolt of lightning flashed into my head, blinding me with pain. I heard the razor clatter to the floor as I regained my vision. *I have not had that happen since . . .*

Oh, divine spirit, thank you for your blessing and your protection! I had nearly forgotten in my haste that when one is under the influence of the Elixir of Immortality, a single drop of blood would destroy the spell and the soul would die. I could not have another death on my hands. I needed to come up with a different method to remove the amulet.

In the wardrobe was my black alchemist bag, and I fumbled through it to see if there was something among my mixtures, tinctures, and powders that would accomplish the task. Just as I was about to give up on this idea, my hand touched a small bottle. I could feel the tiny mosaic pieces that adorned it. It was my vial of Royal Water, what the Romans called *Aqua Regia*.

I pulled it out from the bag and held the bottle in front of me. The mix of acids that had been placed in this little glass jar, carefully lined in wax, held a precise three-to-one solution that would allow me to melt the gold from Miss Nina's chest without spilling a single drop of blood. It might burn her a little bit, but it appeared that had already happened to the unfortunate woman anyway.

I had to be careful with its application, though, as I could not take the risk that the script etched on the unrevealed side of the amulet melted in the process. I fumbled in the bag some more, as I was quite sure my glass straw was in there, and it would allow me to draw out the smallest amount of Royal Water from its special flask. My fingers identified the slender glass tube with its one end pinched so that only a tiny pinhole was present.

My index finger covering the wide end of the straw, I dipped the needle nose end into the vial of the caustic solution, then slowly I lifted my index finger to siphon up a small amount of the fluid. It was vital that I applied this sparingly around the rim of the amulet, so as not to destroy any of the engraving, but just to soften the metal enough to lift it from the lovely lady's chest.

I leaned over the sleeping beauty and cautiously, slowly allowed just the smallest amount of the liquid to drip upon the edge of the prized pendant, and continued to do so around its perimeter.

WHOOSH! WHOOSH! THUMP, THUMP, THUMP!

"Augh! It's too much! What was that?" The sudden noise coming from the living area startled me so that I lost my touch on the straw, and far too much of the liquid leaked on to the golden disk.

I quickly released the remainder of the fluid back into the vial and went to see what was the cause of all the commotion. But before I could even turn around, a sooty owl flew into the bedroom, swooping over my shoulder heading for the bedpost. My quick reflexes allowed me to grasp the creature's leg, and I swung it back through the door into the front room.

I heard the front door open, and realized Madame Tahini had just intruded.

CHAPTER 8

TEENY WEENY

*M*at shifted into his owl self and led the way to Dr. Wu's cottage, then disappeared momentarily before I saw him dive into the chimney of the cabin.

I ran as fast as my tiny feet could take me and attempted to charge into the cabin, but the door was locked. I could hear shuffling inside, a few squawks from Mat, then a loud thump and silence. I pointed my wand toward the door knob, letting its power overwhelm the lock, and the door flew open.

Mat was now a sooty grayish owl lying unconscious on the floor. Ash, soot, and feathers were drifting around the living area of the small cabin. But I saw no sign of the Wu. The door to the bedroom in the back of the cabin was open, and I could see Nina, but she was perfectly still, eyes closed and barely breathing.

I heard the front door slam shut as I rushed into the room, taking me by surprise, but I did not hesitate. As I entered the bedroom, I was struck from behind. I turned to see where the blow had come from but saw nothing. I scanned the room, and it was not until I looked up that I saw Dr. Wu crawling across the ceiling. I smelled melting flesh, and in a flash, I realized that the not-so-good doctor had been up to something very vile.

I pointed my wand at the man, and as I did so, the tip glowed brightly and a flash of electricity bolted from it. But the Wu was quicker and moved stealthily out of its way. He leapt from the ceiling in a midair somersault, landing directly in front of me. No sooner had he touched ground than his right foot took flight from the floor, connecting with my head in a painful blow.

I fell to the ground, but I kept a tight grip on my wand, which was a good thing, since I thought it protected me from any real injury the hit may have caused. I saw him once again running up the wall and across the ceiling, upside down. Again I pointed my wand in his direction, and again I missed the mark, as he did a double flip to the other wall. *Dang! I can't even do that!*

"You, little lady, are no match for me! Game on, sister!" He snickered as he said this.

"And you, Dr. Wu, are nothing more than a glorified alchemist, more of a sham than a shaman!" I shouted as I aimed my wand, this time with both hands on the shaft, and shouted as loud as I could, "*Wu Begone!*"

Several bolts of lightning flashed brilliantly from the wand's end, making the globe tip appear like one of those plasma balls the science nerds were so fascinated with. The strands of electricity surrounded the Asian man, trapping him like a giant claw and then knocking him to the ground.

He slowly got to his knees, and before I could take aim again, he pulled a small vial out of his pocket and threw it to the ground. The vial smashed into hundreds of tiny shards as a dense red smoke filled the entire room. I could barely see a dim glow from my wand right in front of me. My heart was pounding, but I could not give him a chance to hit me again, or worse, get a hold of the wand.

Tiny bubbles began to emerge from my skin, my fear and anxiety spinning them into motion far faster than usual, and I shrunk into my faerie form, looking much like a wispy fairy moth. My skin, hair, all of me, including my feathery wings and my wand, had gone completely white. This time it was I who flew up to the ceiling.

The smoke began to thin out, and I realized Mat had awoken from his stunned state, transformed into his human body, and opened the front door of the cabin, letting the red fog dissipate into the great outdoors.

I spied the shaman in the southeast corner of the room, moving nearer the napping Nina (at least I hoped she was just napping). He was searching the room, looking for me, unaware of my transformation.

"You cannot escape, Miss Teeny Weeny! This is *not* a game," he uttered, but this time without all the snickers. *Good, I think he's nervous.*

I was unsure of the energy of my wand in my faerie state. It was so small, and I was so new to its powers. I didn't want to give away my position, so I remained totally still, trying to think of a strategy.

The crimson fog was now only a thin veil, and I saw Mat grab the wizard by the nape of his neck, catching him totally off guard. Mat lifted him off the ground, but the Wu was swift, and with a chop of his hand to Mat's wrist, the grip was lost. The Wu spun out of his way and onto the northwest wall, swiftly climbing to the top. It was from that vantage point that he spied me directly diagonal from him.

I could see for a moment he was not sure if I was just an unsuspecting insect that had accidentally flown into the situation or something else. But that moment vanished in an instant as he realized that it was me in the opposite corner.

He reached into his pocket again, pulling out yet another vial. So much for strategy. I didn't have time to come up with something fearsome or clever, not with both Mat and Nina at risk too. Clinging to the ceiling with my wings pressed to the rafter, I aimed my now tiny wand at the Wu and whispered softly, "*Wu Begone.*"

The sensational streaks of electricity that occurred previously did not appear this time. Instead, a stream of silky threads spewed from the glowing orb at the top end of the shaft, and within seconds, the wonderful wizard of Wu was trapped in a spider web in the far corner of the room, along with his vile vial.

I took another shot at the shaman, adding a second layer of the webbing. *Just in case!*

Mat was standing over Nina, wringing his hands, deep crevices of concern appearing on his brow. There was dripping gold and flesh on Nina's chest, although most of the pendant had retained its shape. He reminded me of the worried people in that dream with the dying young boy.

I effervesced back into my human glamour, the bubbles now becoming rainbow colors rising from my form as the paleness of my fae faded away and the colors of this world returned to my skin and hair.

"What have you done, Wu? Why are trying to kill Nina?" I interrogated the imprisoned imposter.

The webbing was now so thick that Tim Wu could only mumble as the threads of the web tightened their hold upon the struggling sorcerer.

At that moment my cell phone vibrated, and I pulled it from my pocket to see a text from Barbie.

BS: Not U! It's Wu!

What the heck does that mean? I punched her little avatar above the message and let the phone dial her directly.

"Barbie, what does this message mean? I have Wu trapped here in his cabin. He kidnapped Nina, and I don't know what he's done to her. Maybe you need to bring Sheriff Kasun here."

"Siobhan, your dream! That's not you in the dream. That's Dr. Wu who was ordered to cure. It was in the tea leaves you told me about. I'll be there in just a few minutes. If we need to, we'll call the sheriff later. Just keep Dr. Wu busy for now."

No worries! I plan to keep Dr. Wu tied up for some time.

I joined Mat by the bedside to evaluate Nina's condition. Like the boy in the dream, her skin was becoming waxen and pale as she drew weak breaths erratically and too far apart for comfort.

I returned to the Wu and cautiously pointed my wand at the

area in the web where the mumbles seemed to be coming from. A delicate glow emitted, and a small circle burned through the webbing where the doctor's mouth would be.

"Again! Why are you trying to kill Nina?" I pressed him.

Barbie entered the cabin just in time to hear this villain's lame excuse.

"Madame Tahini, I am *not* trying to kill Nina! I am a healer, not a killer! But we must act fast, or else the *dan* may take over, and she may not be able return to our world. You must set me free now!"

"How can I trust you?" I screamed at him. This took me by surprise, and I jumped at the sound of my own voice. "You are a deceitful devil, a shamming shaman, a wicked wizard, a mean magus, a pathetic parasite . . ." I ran out of awful things I could throw at this atrocious alchemist . . . "Oh yeah, and an atrocious alchemist!" I added.

Barbie cut in, and in her officious demeanor, questioned him. "Dr. Wu? Who are you? Really?"

She asked this with such fierceness of authority that even I felt like there was something I had to confess.

"Madame Mayor, I am Tang Wu from the Zhou Dynasty. I am the Master Wu for the royal family. Their son, a young boy, has been gifted by the spirits with special powers that will heal and protect the people of the kingdom, and in fact, the world. But he is dying. A significant evil, determined to destroy the mysteries, mystics, and spirits, has placed a curse on him. I was ordered to cure him, but the only antidote, the spell that will break the curse, is on the other side of *that* amulet. I have failed, and to that end, I know not what will happen to your world, if mine becomes extinct."

I could feel the anguish and heartache in his voice, and it cut me to the core. That tingling sensation in my fingertips and toes began again. I didn't know what to make of it. The truth of his words spun twinkling stars in my head.

"If we can get you the amulet, will Nina be okay?" I beseeched him.

"I can only hope I have not ruined the amulet when I used a Royal Water solution to solve the problem of removing it. But, yes, your Nina should be revivable," he replied woefully.

"Should be? I'm afraid, Dr. Wu, that is not good enough!" Mayor Barbie stated matter-of-factly. "If she does not revive, you have a very serious charge against you and you will face the Court! You will be facing the Court nevertheless, since you failed to inform us of your powers for the Registry."

"The pendant has a protective spell on it. Only Nina's true love can remove it," I began to explain, and looked at Mat still standing beside Nina's prone body with a questioning look.

"I don't know, Aunt Siobhan. She is my true love, but I cannot say that I am hers. What if I make it worse and embed the pendant even deeper into her?" he responded.

"You have been with Nina for two years. As the blessing says, time will tell. Remove the amulet, Mat," I gently commanded my dear lovesick nephew.

His large hands shaking, he stretched his fingers around the circle of the amulet. Nervously, he touched its rim.

CHAPTER 9

TEENY WEENY

*W*e all kept perfectly still as Mat gently attempted to lift the pendant from Nina's chest. It began to glow with a golden light around its entire circumference. With his eyes squeezed shut, too fearful to see if he might be causing his love any injury, he lifted the coveted charm from her chest with ease.

I took the amulet from his hand as he gave a heavy sigh of relief and sat down on the bed beside Nina, who was still in a deep state of slumber, or whatever it was the Wu had placed her in. The amulet was now safe, albeit not sure how sound it was, as it appeared to have suffered some damage from Wu's so-called solution.

Nina, however, had not come to. She was still in her restful repose, and it was clear that it was Wu's elixir that kept her in this state, and not the necklace that had adorned her. I was relieved that it was not something I'd done with the protective spell I'd placed on the piece of jewelry. Then again, since Mat was able to remove it from her neck, if it had been part of the spell, Nina would be back with the living.

"Well, Mr. Tang Wu, what do you propose to do to revive her?" I implored him.

"I can do nothing if you don't release me from this web!" he replied.

I was just about to unravel the silky cocoon still containing the mysterious Wu when Barbie stopped me.

"Siobhan, let me call Sheriff Kasun over now. We don't want any surprises without him standing by." She took her cell phone out of her purse and punched in a direct code for the sheriff. Explaining the situation briefly, she asked him to get to the cottage as soon as possible.

Aside from the fact that the town was relatively small, it was still a wonderment that the supernaturals could move so quickly, and the sheriff's "as soon as possible" was almost instantaneous, utilizing his wolf's swiftness.

I gave the sheriff a quick rundown of the battle that had ensued between the Wu and me, which led him to his current imprisoned position. The sheriff nodded, understanding the danger, and placed his hand on his holster, not inconspicuously, even though I doubted the wizard was able to see his movement through the thick gauze that enshrouded him.

I twirled my wand around the exterior of the wrapped Wu, allowing the silken threads to disintegrate, freeing the master.

Tang Wu began to move toward the closet, but the sheriff grabbed him by the shoulder, stopping him in his tracks.

"I need my bag in order to prepare the Elixir of Life. That is the only thing that will revive the young woman. Hopefully, it is not too late, as it is nearly midnight and the stars will align themselves in a way that may make it impossible for her to come back," he explained.

"Come back? Come back from where?" I asked, my voice now edged with heightened anxiety.

"She is entranced with the Elixir of Immortality. It allows the subject to enter a higher plane, a plane of enlightenment. It causes a temporary death, so to speak, as her soul enters this elevated level. The timing is essential to administer the Elixir of Life, which will return her soul back to this plane. If she is too long in the temporary death and the stars realign, the cord between the two planes will be broken."

Mat held up a black medicine bag that he had garnered from the closet while Mr. Wu gave his dissertation.

"Is this it?" he asked.

"Yes, quickly, bring it here."

The sheriff maintained his grip on the shaman's shoulder as Mat placed the bag at his feet. Wu rustled around in his bag and took out a copper vial and a blue silk bag embroidered with a white crane and multi-color starbursts, then cinched closed with a red braided string. He also removed a small wok-shaped bowl and placed it on the floor. The master wizard opened the bag and poured a pinch or so of purplish flakes into the bowl, then with an eyedropper, he withdrew a brownish liquid from the copper container and added it to the mixture. It began to bubble immediately as the chemicals interacted with one another, the flake mixture dissolving, and a violet plume arose from the simmering stew. Within a few moments, the bubbling had ceased, and the Wu once again used the eyedropper to withdraw a portion of the mixture from the bowl.

The sheriff did not trust the Asian stranger, especially now, knowing that there was an attack on one of Havenwood Falls' oldest citizens, and refused to let the man budge. I took the eyedropper from his hand and went to Nina's bedside. I gently placed the open end of the dropper on her lips, letting the small tube part them somewhat. As the City Hall clock tower began to strike its midnight toll, I released the liquid into her mouth and held my breath, just as it seemed Nina had been holding hers for the past few hours. I could sense that everyone in the room had ceased to breathe for the entire tolling of the twelve chimes.

On the last ring of the clock tower, a cumulative exhale came from all except Nina. It appeared that Tang Wu's potion either did not do the trick or we were indeed too late administering the antidote.

Mat began to cry.

"Nina, Nina, Nina. Please come back! I am your true love, and you are mine. You must be in this world!" Then he pressed his lips to Nina's just as the echo of the twelfth bell dwindled into infinity.

Sheriff Kasun was unfastening his cuffs from his belt when a loud gasp shattered Mat's cries, and Nina's eyelids fluttered, then opened slowly, her eyes drowsily taking in the wet-cheeked Mathieu. She lifted a weak hand to his cheek and uttered, "Ciao, mi amor. What are you doing here?"

Clearly, Nina had not yet realized that she was back in our world, but that mattered not to Mat, who wrapped his large arms around the lithe frame of the Italian seamstress, seeming like he might knock the wind right out of her again. But like his love for her, the hug was gentle and kind.

Interrupting the lovers' display of affection, Barbie requested the sheriff put Dr. Timothy Wu or Master Tang Wu, or whatever his name was, into the lockup.

Tang begged me to hand over the amulet, but I refused. It would remain in my safekeeping for now, and we would discuss it tomorrow in front of the Court of the Sun and the Moon. Tang Wu looked miserable, and that made me happy, but not really. I suspected we would all be more enlightened come tomorrow.

CHAPTER 10

WU

The bars on the cell they placed me in were obviously more than just a physical barrier. There seemed to be some spell placed on them, since I couldn't even use my mind-bending to budge them. Or perhaps it was just me. After all, it had been a long night, I was still no closer to accomplishing my task, and I was so weary.

Hmm, that little fae had some big power. I had underestimated her. In fact, I thought, I had underestimated her in more ways than one. She seemed to affect me in a way that I could not really fathom. There was something about her that made me feel I needed to have her close by. I certainly hoped she would forgive me for the wallop I gave her, but I had a duty to perform. Even though I was a total failure.

The overhead lights in the jail cell kept the area brightly lit, but I was the only prisoner this evening, which was just as well. It would give me some solitude to call on my spirit.

I knelt in a corner of the cell facing the wall opposite the bars, imagining there was a window near the ceiling. Closing my eyes, I envisioned the moon shining brightly amongst a sea of glittering stars, then cleared my mind and began my divination chant.

"Qǐzhòngjī, mighty spirit. Wings of Wisdom, Feathers of Faith."

I repeated this chant over and over again until my head began to swirl and my body was lifted from the ground. I floated in midair in the center of the cell, enveloped by the velvety darkness of the night and surrounded by the twinkling stars—at least in my mind. My glorious Spirit Crane flew in and made a circular flight around my body before landing. As she did so, the crane's body transformed, melding into the shape of a tall, lean woman whose skin and robe were completely white. My floating body declined back to the floor, and I arose. She stood before me, her right leg bent with her right foot propped on the other leg, in a crane's stance.

This is my divining spirit the great Qǐzhòngjī, the great white Crane. She is my protector and my healer, my spirit teacher and my guide.

As I looked at her now, in her non-celestial form, I noted she looked remarkably like Madame Tahini in her fae form, the one I spotted right before she pointed her tiny wand my way and wrapped me in a web. Perhaps this might have something to do with why the little woman affected me so much.

"Tang Wu, loyal servant, how may I assist you?" the crane-woman prodded me gently.

"I have been set with the task of curing the young prince, but rather it is more un-cursing than curing that is needed, Mighty One. There is an amulet that holds the spell to break the curse, and I have tracked it to this place. In fact, I nearly had it in my hands, but I am thwarted at every turn. There is magic and mystery abounding here, but it is beyond me, Great Spirit."

"Ah, Tang Wu, you are here because it is part of your journey. You will need to draw from the strengths you learn here to help the Zhou prince of your past."

"Great Crane, I thank you for your wisdom." I bowed my head in a grateful gesture and continued, "I am also confused about a woman who has been involved with the amulet, a spell that protected it, and a wand that has more power than I have ever seen."

"Tang Wu, I sense in your voice that your confusion is more than just her spells and wand. I sense she has a power over you. I will grant her blessings this night, and in the daylight, perhaps both of you will see clearer."

"Again, I thank you for your wisdom and the blessings you bestow." I bowed again before the Great Spirit, this time all the way to the floor in total servitude. She placed her soft hand upon my forehead, and I could feel that she was gleaning my thoughts and memories. As she did this, she transformed once again into the mighty white crane, and her hand became her wing. She took flight, circling above me and out of the channel, taking the stars and the velveteen night sky with her. I was left once again in the glaring light of the jail.

I wondered what blessing the Great Spirit Crane would bestow upon Teeny Weeny. I prayed that it would be forgiveness.

CHAPTER 11

TEENY WEENY

I had a fitful night's sleep with so many things dancing in and out of my head all night long. I must've awoken at least twelve times during the night. It was almost like my brain was tolling the stroke of midnight, but every half hour.

Cranes invaded my dreams constantly, and that was bewildering. Great white flying birds, with brilliant moon beams spraying off their downy wings. Cranes watering at a shining aquamarine pond, not so dissimilar to our own Peacock Lake at Smalls Falls. The pond lay in front of a pagoda-type building. It seemed Master Tang Wu and his little bag of tricks left an indelible impression.

His face kept swimming in and out of my dreamy head during the sleepy/sleepless night, but it wasn't always the face we had seen this past week. At times it was an older face, with gentle lines creasing his forehead, a long flowing white Fu Manchu mustache melding into a goatee made up of silken threads like those I had entrapped him in, and soft dark almond-shaped eyes that seemed to glimmer with love and hope.

I found these two contrasting visions of Wu very disturbing. Then there was the vision of him running up walls and across ceilings, doing somersaults in midair, with colorful smoke fading in and out of the picture.

Every time the vision of the older Wu came waffling into my head, my fingers and toes wriggled with that funky tingling sensation I had experienced so many times in the doctor's presence.

I supposed doctor was appropriate. Although he was a wizard in its most explicit terms, he did far more than just dabble in divination and play with potions. He obviously knew not only his alchemy but herbs, elements, spirits, spells, and healing ointments.

And speaking of elements, there was something elementary about the effect he seemed to have on me, regardless of our differences, battling or otherwise.

After about six hours of non-sleep, I gave up and got out of bed. I was exhausted, apprehensive, excited and concerned, mostly about the assembly at the Court, but also about seeing Timothy/Tang Wu. I was looking forward to seeing the Master Wu and didn't really know why. I was definitely in need of a strong cup of chamomile tea this morning to calm my nerves. *I'm almost thinking that a touch of lavender might not be a bad idea either. Then again, maybe NOT.*

I padded my way down the stairs and into the kitchen that doubled as a laboratory at the back of my townhome. Cyllene was already by the windowsill. I set the kettle on the stove, opened the window just a smidge to allow my dear friend to waft in, and closed it quickly behind her, as the late October chill was still present this early.

Like an automaton, I instinctually set up her funnel and clamp contraption so that we could converse.

"Siobhan! Where have you been? Why do you look so, well, so tired?"

"Ah, Silly Annie, it was a long night, and I did not get to bed until after midnight."

"Midnight! You can't stay up later than eight o'clock, or sundown even, depending which comes first!"

Well, actually she was right. She'd known me for over a hundred years, and that had not changed, other than of course, the changes that seemed to keep occurring since Mat arrived more than two years ago. *Or maybe it IS something else?*

Cyllene deserved an explanation, and I proceeded to tell her about the adventures of yesterday—the disappearance of Nina (she gasped), Mat's flight down the chimney (she gasped), Nina's coma (she gasped), and my battle with Dr. Wu (she double gasped). At this point, I had to slow down, as I was not really sure how much gasping a poor little dryad could take.

I finished brewing my tea and went over to the small kitchen table where Cyllene and her "microphone" were set up. But when I looked at her, she was not the same sunset moth-styled dryad with whom I was familiar. She looked almost like a white crane, and I was so taken aback, I spilled my tea and knocked over my chair.

I righted the chair and cleaned up the spilt mess from the floor. *Maybe I should pay attention to my own tea leaves.* I sat down, trying not to stare at this miniature white crane. But the tiny white bird wasn't there. Cyllene was exactly that—Cyllene.

"Siobhan! Are you okay?" came her lilting voice from the wide end of the funnel.

"For just a second, you looked like something else, like a bird —a crane to be exact. I guess my mind is playing tricks on me. Probably due to the restless night's sleep I had."

"Restless night?"

I continued with my story while brewing another cup of tea, since my last cup wound up on the floor. I told her about wrapping up Dr. Wu in a cocoon, the sheriff's arrival, Wu mixing the Elixir of Life from the flakes he shook out from the mysterious little crane-embroidered bag, Mat kissing Nina, and the sheriff taking the wizard off to jail. I took a deep breath and sat down with a fresh cup of steaming chamomile tea while Cyllene was absorbing my words.

"After I got home and went to bed, I kept having visions of Wu, cranes, and all sorts of strange places. I'd fall asleep briefly, and then another apparition would wander into my head. It appears I will need to do a little research before we assemble at the Court. I've got the amulet now, but I don't know how damaged it is, or how exactly it plays into this scenario. I also need to see if I can find some information about what the crane symbolizes. I know it's linked to Wu somehow."

I got up from the table and was headed toward the salon when my cell phone vibrated in my pocket. I took a look, and it was a message from Mat.

MM: Nina has this scar now. Is there something you can do for it?

A picture of Nina's emblazoned chest followed the text. The pendant that had seared itself to her chest when Wu tried to take it had left an imprint of the design on her skin. The photo showed her skin a bit reddened, but it did not seem too serious.

TW: will chk HOHUM & get back 2 u. Any pain?

Yeah, I got this.

MM: She said no.

I knew my *Handbook of Healing Unctions and Mixtures* (HOHUM) should have just the right recipe to heal Nina's scar. So I added this to my research list and continued into the salon and my extensive library of spellbound books. Of course, they were not really spellbound, but they were bound, and most contained spells, so there you had it.

I kept HOHUM fairly handy, as healing was my nature and the reason why my backyard garden was so thick with herbs, plants, and fruit trees. I placed the manual on the round table that sat in the center of the salon, next to *Ancient Arts and Mystics*, which I had left out earlier in the week.

I thumbed to the index to search for *crane*, and no surprise, it led me back to the chapter on "Wizards of the Orient." I continued where I left off the last time, and it read:

"The Wizards of the Orient typically use spirit divination in their arts and practices. They align themselves with one of the spirits, such as the Spirit Turtle, Spirit Dragon, and Spirit Crane. *See additional reference material: Spirits & Totems.*"

Ah, it just so happened I had that book! It was on a lower shelf of my wall of books, so I did not need the ladder. I pulled it out and again placed it on the table and searched through the index for *crane.*

I found the page on Spirit Crane and read:

"The Spirit Crane totem represents longevity and the creative connection with the eternal and divine. When a crane totem appears, it means that you need to use the power and strength from the past to deal with the present. The specific crane denotes specific attributes.

"The white crane symbolizes faithfulness and wisdom. It is one of the most powerful healing spirits in the oriental arts."

Well, that certainly explained a lot. This Spirit Crane was obviously connected to Wu. He must use its divination to achieve his goals. Since cranes appeared to me last night, I needed to keep in mind that I would have to use my past strengths—*my wand?*— to deal with him now.

Next I looked to see what HOHUM had for Nina's wound.

It didn't take very long to find the right recipe for the salve that would heal her scar and rejuvenate her skin to its original silky smoothness. But of course the recipe called for chamomile and lavender, however, this time mixed with the milk from dandelion stems, all of which I had in abundance in my garden. *Darned dandelions. Well, in this case, darling dandelions.*

I took a look at the amulet now. I had been apprehensive to look at it since last night's episode. The side with the colorful yin yang was indeed damaged. There were parts around the rim where the Chinese characters were blurred and one or two were totally obliterated. If the Wu did indeed need the spell on this charm, I was afraid it wouldn't be of much help now. Nevertheless, I planned on taking it to the Court, and maybe he could make something out of it.

CHAPTER 12

TEENY WEENY

I dressed as quickly as I could; time was running short before I had to be at the Court. I was so nervous that I had trouble just pulling a skirt on. I took a linen handkerchief from the bureau drawer and placed the pendant in the middle of it, then wrapped it carefully before placing it in the pocket of the skirt I finally managed get on. I grabbed a thick pullover sweater, since buttons were out of the question this morning, and a thick wool scarf, as the weather was getting colder day by day.

Once downstairs, I pulled on a pair of fleece-lined Sherpa boots and a down sleeveless vest. I remembered Cyllene was still hanging out in the kitchen, so I ran in to open the window so she could flit out and join her beloved tree Maximus. Thankfully, no pixies visited this morning.

I hurried out the front door, locking it behind me, then crossed Main Street and the square to get to City Hall. I of course did not go through the front door. I headed around to the back of City Hall, double checking to make sure no one noticed me, to a most unobtrusive looking entrance to the Court—a large metal door that looked like a maintenance door, except there was a relief of a moon and a mountain hammered into it.

I pulled the heavy door open, went down a flight of stairs,

then through the long hallway before entering into the large courtroom. A few small rows of seats made up the gallery that faced a large wood-paneled dais. In front of the gallery was a table and a single chair—that would be the "hot seat."

I noted that all the chairs behind the table on the dais were occupied, except of course mine. I bade good morning to each of the Court members assembled for the emergency meeting—Michaela Petran, Saundra Beaumont, Roman Bishop, Barbie Stuart, and the rest of the cast—as I scampered past them toward the last chair on the panel and took my place.

Sheriff Ric Kasun was standing in the back of the room, waiting for the signal. Roman banged a gavel, alerting the Court members that the session had now begun. Mayor Barbie nodded at the sheriff, who opened a door in the back of the courtroom, and Ric's deputy escorted Dr. Timothy Wu—now known to most of us as Tang Wu—hands cuffed behind his back, to the hot seat.

The sheriff recited from his notebook the events of yesterevening that led to the wizard's arrest. The Court members were intrigued, and a few of them even looked over at me, nodding their condolences or giving me an admiring smile. They certainly were not used to me defending myself, but then I'd rarely been in a position to do so, other than the episodes with the she-cat Shayin Pisik.

After the sheriff finished reading his notes, Roman Bishop nodded at Barbie. She cleared her throat and began to speak.

"Sir, you are before this Court not only on the charges that the sheriff has just described, which include but are not limited to putting one of our citizens in an induced coma that practically killed her and attacking one of our oldest and dearest Court members, Teeny Weeny Tahini. But you, sir, deceived the Court by pretending that you were the famed Dr. Timothy Wu, when in fact you are a wizard, an alchemist to boot. That is something you failed to inform the Court, let alone register with us. What do you have to say in your defense?"

"Madame Mayor, let me first start off by apologizing to the

entire Court. When you offered the invitation to the prominent Dr. Wu, it was the opportunity I needed to find the amulet that will save my kingdom and the world as you know it. Timothy Wu is a descendant of mine. That is why I am able to inhabit his body. I had already tracked the amulet down to this place, Havenwood Falls, and this time. It was just a matter of getting here.

"I am on a mission. My emperor's son is dying. As I told you before, I am from the Zhou Dynasty. The young prince was blessed by all the spirits with a special gift, one of love and compassion that transcends our normal understanding of such things. He was destined to rule the dynasty and keep intact the teachings and healings of the spirits so that the mysteries and magic of the universe would not be destroyed. But there is something viciously evil in my time, and perhaps even yours, that placed a curse on the young boy. This curse is inscribed on an amulet, as the spell that can break the curse is inscribed on its opposite side.

"The amulet is the very reason I am here, because it is. The young woman Nina, who was simply the unfortunate recipient of a gift, was wearing it, and as I went to examine it, the amulet became nearly surgically attached to the poor girl. I believe a protective spell must have been placed upon it for something like that to happen. Unfortunately, the exposed side of the amulet is the curse, which I already know too well.

"If my young prince dies, there is a chance that the evil that is trying to destroy the mystery and magic of the world will succeed, and then even Havenwood Falls may not exist as you know it. All of you, in fact, may cease to exist. It is a paramount mission, and I appear to be failing at it miserably.

"Truly, I intended no harm, but I was at a desperate point and was at odds on how to solve it."

Mr. Wu bowed his head and added, "Madame Tahini, I hope you can forgive me, most of all."

He could not even look me in the eye when he said this, but I was glad he didn't, because I might have fallen apart right on the spot. First, because it was I who placed the protection on the pendant in the first place, and second, because I was afraid I would have seen the truth, despair, and caring in Wu's eyes as I heard it in his voice.

Barbie asked me if there was anything I wished to contribute to this tribunal. I stood and reached into my pocket, pulling out the kerchief-wrapped charm. I motioned to the sheriff to take it and show it to our defendant.

"Mr. Wu," I started, "is this the amulet?"

"Yes, the very one. It is thousands of years old."

"And the inscription you are seeking? Is it of any help?"

I was hoping for his sake that it was not too damaged to decipher, but as he turned it over, his face was crestfallen, and I knew that it did not reveal all that he needed to break the damned curse.

"I'm afraid, Madame, that I continue to fail, as I am the one who caused this damage. The essential elements of the spell are too obscured to make out." His disappointment and pain were loud and clear. I remembered feeling that kind of pain when my father had cursed my brother Grenfold, and I felt I could do nothing to stop it.

"Your Honors," he addressed the entire court, "do with me what you will, as I am no good to my people. My emperor has already warned me that if I cannot cure the prince, I will be executed. And I am surely no good to your people, as I have already hurt some of them."

I heard Barbie and Roman whispering, then the others chattering back and forth. I wondered if they would send him back to his own time to be beheaded or whatever they did there. His infractions here were not so serious as to warrant execution.

Roman once again banged the gavel. The Court members shushed each other, and the room fell silent.

Barbie ordered the Wu to stand while she laid down the law and pronounced his sentence.

"Mr. Wu," she began again, "though we sympathize with your

predicament, the Court feels it is best that you be returned to your original home in your original time. We anticipate that you will cooperate with the Court so that they can make the appropriate preparations to send you back."

The agonizing doctor simply nodded his acquiescence. My stomach became a leaping frog, bouncing up into my throat and back down. The tingling in my fingers and toes became a violent burning. My head was pounding so furiously with the sound of rushing blood, as if every vein in my brain had become a rogue wave. I felt I was about to vomit, but then my cell phone vibrated. *Oh my gods and goddesses! The phone, the photo, the pendant, it's all here, all clear.*

"WAIT!" I shouted out so uncharacteristically that Lilith Blackstone and Mathilde Augustine were startled out of their seats.

"Siobhan?" the mayor addressed me. "You have something to say?"

"I have a picture of the amulet. It's on my phone! I mean the right side of it, truly the *right* side. The one with the spell that could break the curse." I pulled out my phone and opened the photo that Mat had sent me this morning. I got up from the dais and walked the phone over to Tang Wu. This was probably dangerously close, considering how he made me feel, but I felt I must try to save him.

For a brief moment, a flash of hope fleeted across his features, but then he looked at the picture on my phone, the one of the imprint in Nina's skin, with all of its intricacies and delicacies. Alas, he shook his head once again in dismay and what I sensed was frustration.

"What? What is it? What's wrong?" I begged him.

"It doesn't make any sense. The characters are all wrong. It's unintelligible. Even the yin yang is backwards!"

"It is? The yin yang is backwards? Is that even possible? Wait! This is a picture of the amulet emblazoned on Nina, of course it's backwards! Really we should say reversed."

Ric Kasun came to my rescue, taking the phone from my

trembling hand. He downloaded the picture into my photo album, then played around with some of the tools in the app and managed to flip the photo. He posed the phone in front of the master, and joy lit up his face. For a moment, I saw the true face of Tang Wu—his white hair, his wizened skin, his beautifully compassionate eyes—the face that appeared in and out last night.

"That's it! That is the cure, the spell! I must study this and be sure that I have it right before I return. Your Honors, please give me a little more time here before returning me to the Zhou Dynasty. I'll register. Whatever it takes!"

Roman looked at me and at Barbie, then at the other members of the Court. They all seemed to be in congruence for a change, except maybe Lawrence Mills, who could often be a bit of a curmudgeon, but even his nod came.

"Mr. Wu," Barbie once again laid down the law, "we will give you four days. You will register immediately after this meeting with Adelaide Beaumont, and you will be under house arrest until the end of your four days. You will work with Siobhan, that is Madame Tahini, to discern this spell, and anyone else she feels may be necessary to assist. And you will cooperate fully!"

Roman Bishop banged his gavel once more, and spoke for the first time, which was unusual to say the least. "Dismissed."

CHAPTER 13

TEENY WEENY

I was so excited that Tang would not be executed. I mean relieved, of course. I was happy that he would be here for at least a few more days. I was terrified that he would be here for at least a few more days. *Sheesh, I'm so conflicted!*

The Court disassembled, and as I headed back to my townhome, I remembered the cell phone had vibrated while we were in session. I checked my messages again, and of course it was from Mat. He was only asking again about Nina's scar. I had completely forgotten to let him know that I found the right recipe for an ointment that would not only help the scar, but that she might want to use religiously, all over her body, and he may want her to too, since it was like an anti-aging cream.

TW: Yes got it! B ready by 4

As soon as I got home, I headed to the back of my house and out the back door from the kitchen that led into my garden, grabbing my snippers from the counter on my way out. I had to push back a few blackberry brambles, as they had taken over most of the walkway all on their own. We had already experienced a bit of snow, but a little fae magic and a touch of Addie's helping witchcraft went a long way. The garden was still bright and green, and yes, overflowing with dandelion weeds.

This day, I was grateful. The fronds of lavender protruded every which way they chose, but there were plenty. The backyard was so overgrown, I had to rack my brain to remember where the chamomile was planted, or had chosen to plant themselves was more likely. *Oh! There they are, right next to a great patch of brilliant yellow dandelions.* The small flowers of the chamomile, like tiny daisies, were so easily disguised amidst the brilliant yellow of the dandelions that they could be easily confused to an unaware eye as just another weed. But both plants were essential, and they needed to be protected and properly utilized, rather than dismissed as weeds and discarded.

I kept a gathering basket handy by the water pump and used it to collect my clippings. Poor Nina, so human. I would have known this salve like the back of my hand if I needed it, but being fae and glamoured, the aging process was, well, weird. Thankfully, I had my "cook" books for the likes of our darling girl.

I followed the distinct instructions in the HOHUM, which really weren't so distinct, a pinch of this here and shred of that there, a squirt of the dandelion milk, simmer for however long, and voila! A salve. This was one cookbook that relied on the cook to know what to do.

At four o'clock sharp, there was a knock at the front door. My skin salve for the seamstress had just finished curing.

"Come in! It's open!" I hollered at the foyer, assuming they could hear my teeny weeny voice. But of course, it was Mat, and he had the keen hearing of an owl, so the door creaked on its hinges as he opened it and led his beloved Nina in before him, ducking his head very low to maneuver the threshold.

What wasn't included in the recipe for the ointment was faerie dust, but I added a pinch of it to speed up its progress.

Nina was in a black cashmere sweater with pearl buttons up to the neck. She daintily unfastened the exquisite buttons to reveal the imprint imbedded on her sternum directly above her breast.

"Are you sure you want this to disappear, Nina? This mixture will do that. No matter what happens to the necklace, you can always have this," I warned her in advance of applying the aid.

She and Mat glanced at one another, with that special knowing look between true loves.

Mat responded on her nod, "You are probably right, Aunt Siobhan."

"No worries, this keeps for a long time. If you change your mind, let me know. If you don't, someone else will probably desire it! It may even contain a little something special for your later years." I winked at Mat.

We enjoyed a bit of tea together. Well, Nina was having espresso, but no matter. After a while, I had to rush them on their way. I knew they thought they were accommodating "the old lady," but really, I had things to do!

Wu only had four days. I assumed the first day started tomorrow, but I should double check with Barbie. Nevertheless, that didn't give anyone much time. It was now close to dusk, and Wu must already be registered with the Court and returned to his quarters at the inn.

I had no way of getting in touch with him, and even though I didn't want him to get the impression that I was anxious to see him, I didn't want to waste a spare second figuring out what needed to be done so that he could accomplish his mission.

Wait! I do have a way! I'll call Michaela at the inn. He either has a house phone or she can relay a message to him.

"Michaela? This is Teeny Weeny," I responded to the answer on the other end of the phone, pronouncing her name "Mi-hae-la" like her aunt Luisa, her "mammie" did.

She confirmed that there indeed was a house phone in Wu's cabin, and that she would connect me.

I took a big gulp, not really knowing what I was going to say, but hoping it would come to me when I heard his voice.

"Hello?" And there it was, that tingly feeling in my fingertips, toes, earlobes, and nose.

"Dr. Wu, it's Madame Tahini. I was thinking, well, uh . . . maybe we should get started examining the amulet right away. I mean so we don't waste any time, since the Court limited you to four days. Oh, and by the way, how did the tattoo go?" I added the last bit so he didn't think that I was so anxious to see him or anything.

"I agree with you completely. I'm obviously not going anywhere, since I am under house arrest, so you can come by whenever you would like. The tattooing went well. Miss Adelaide Beaumont is quite the talent. I now have a tattoo of a crane. It is beyond me how she knew that is my spirit guide."

"Yes, Addie has a special gift for that sort of thing. I can be there in about an hour. Goodbye." I clicked off and went about preparing for my meeting with Tang Wu.

CHAPTER 14

TEENY WEENY

When I arrived, there was a nice little fire blazing in the small hearth in the living area of his cottage. He took my coat and offered me some tea. Naturally, I accepted. The green tea was really quite good.

I had the amulet with me, but as it was damaged, it really was not going to be of much use to us, so we were stuck with trying to manipulate the small picture on my phone.

"Maybe I should ask Michaela if she could print this out?" I suggested.

We were sitting side by side on the settee in front of the fireplace, and it was nearly unnerving the vibrations I felt and that creamy buttery taste on my lips when his hand met mine holding the cell phone.

"We may need to do that, but for now, let me get a notepad and jot down what we can see in this photo."

He got up and left for a brief moment, returning with a hotel-style pad and a pen both inscribed with the words "Whisper Falls Inn" with a simple but stunning logo. He sat right back down next to me and began to write the characters that appeared in the flipped photo version of Nina's embedded scar.

"Siobhan . . . oh, I'm sorry, may I call you Siobhan?" he began, and then stopped himself.

He says my name so delicately, pronouncing it more like chiffon, that I can almost taste a creamy chiffon pie with extra whipped cream on top. It makes me downright woozy when he says my name that way.

"Oh yes, please do! I'm not sure how I should address you, though, given you have more than one name?" *Look who's talking.*

"My given name is Qiángdà. It means powerful. The dialect is a bit difficult to maneuver, so Tang Da or Tang for short is fine. As to the amulet, typically these spells begin at the north edge of the amulet. The yin-yang is the guide for the north and south. Yin is north and yang is south."

He was actually writing down the ideograms as they appeared in the photo, keeping them in their circular motif. I watched, mesmerized and silent, as he made quarter turns with the photo using his fingers and then manually turned the Whisper Falls Inn notepad in the same quarterly fashion. He made a rough sketch of the yin-yang in the center of this circle of figures.

When he completed the entire circular chart of characters, an almost blank stare overcame his demeanor. I could practically see a giant question mark above his head as he quizzically pondered the symbols he had scripted.

"What is it?" I finally broke the silence, and the trance to which he had succumbed.

"It appears this is not so much a spell to break a curse as it is a recipe."

I'm good with that! I can do recipes, even when my cookbook doesn't really give great direction.

"What does that mean?" I was trying to be patient, but between tingling and creamery butter, I wasn't sure if I could hold out much longer. I needed a rest!

"It is talking about the *Dan* of *Běnzhí*. It is the Elixir of Essence. I have heard about it, but as far as I know, no one actually knows how to make it. This apparently is the recipe."

"What does that mean?" I was starting to sound like a broken record.

"Essence is everything about a person, more than just their soul. It is their life, blood, innate characteristics, their spirit, their beliefs, and even their destiny. The Elixir of Essence can only be used when one's essence is taken from them unnaturally. Some of this makes sense, but some I am not sure what it means. Like here." He pointed to a grouping of swashes and slashes. "Translated it says Hair of Crane. But cranes do not have hair. If it meant feather or down, it would have said that, but this is specific as to hair. It bewilders me. Then there is this . . ." He pointed at another set of hieroglyphs that made no sense to me, so I was just intrigued that he even knew what it represented. "This says the light of *Xiānnǚ*. I really don't know what that means at all. I mean, I know *Xiānnǚ*, but I am not sure what the 'light of' is really referring to."

He said this word *Xiānnǚ* something like tschen gnu (like the wildebeest) but it was so foreign to me, I had no idea.

"What does that mean? That word, tschen gnu?" Okay, I kicked it up a notch so as not to sound like a total broken record.

"Ahh, well, interestingly enough, it means fairy or sprite. Like you, I'm guessing." And he said this with a jesting spirit and a twinkle in his eye that sent me reeling.

That was my opportunity to bid him goodnight before I did something really dangerous, like kiss him. "Then I think we should both sleep on those words tonight. Maybe the Spirit Crane will enlighten you, or my fae spirits will send me a message."

He stood up and offered me his helping hand in a gentlemanly gesture. I did take it, cringing inside all the time, knowing what his touch did to me, and now not only creamy butter but sweet honey was piercing my tongue. *What a mess I am!*

Now that he had his little map of the pendant, I took my phone and placed it in my skirt pocket, as he got my coat and assisted me in donning it. We both agreed that I would contact him in the morning, after breakfast, and I exited as quickly as possible.

CHAPTER 15

WU

I hoped I had not offended her. She left in such a hurry that I feared she did not wish to be near me. She always seemed to have the strangest reaction when I so much as touched her hand. But her hand was so soft, so small, so wonderful, I couldn't help myself.

She was small, but she was so powerful. She was *Qiángdà Xiānnǚ*, a powerful fae! But she had a power over me that again I could not explain. I'd never felt this way with anyone, let alone a teeny weeny woman.

I needed to concentrate on this Elixir of Essence. I would only have one chance to get it right. Like this evening might have been my chance to get it right with Siobhan, but I was sure I botched that one.

Really, you HAVE to concentrate!

I looked at my drawing of the amulet on the pad I had jotted on. It began from the north of the ornament, "The *Dan* of *Běnzhí* only when *Běnzhí* is stolen. Dram of Dragon's Water, one Hair of Crane, light of *Xiānnǚ*."

Really the only thing I understood was the Dram of Dragon's Water. That was the water from Tiger Pond. It was believed that the Dragon drank from the pond; that was why it was used when making Dragon's Well tea. It was the same pond that the great Spirit Crane drank from, but I could guarantee she had never left a hair behind, even as an apparition. So even if it was speaking of her appearance in human form, how could I have obtained a hair from an apparition anyway? And then . . . there was the light of fae.

Ah, Siobhan, you are my light, but I am not sure how that is going to translate into an elixir.

Stop it, man! Concentrate!

Really, it was no use. I could only think of her this evening. Her big eyes, far too large for her face, with those long dark lashes. Her little pursed lips, always puckered like she was tasting something she was unfamiliar with. The way she constantly wiggled her fingers and her toes. Oh my, it might just have driven me to insanity, but if nothing else, it had all worked up an appetite.

I guessed I was stuck with ordering room service or delivery. I heard the teens in town talking about the taco truck. It sounded interesting enough, maybe not so different from a good mu shu pork. They kind of acted like it was a new invention, this food truck thing. Centuries ago, we always had at least one or two carts in the town square. How else was a young man to survive if there were not purveyors of pot stickers and pork buns?

I picked up the house phone and dialed the front desk. The lovely voice of Miss Michaela came from the other end of the wire.

I asked her about the food truck, and she informed me that Tacos for Daze was run by Sky Spill Water. *Sounds like a combination of Hollywood and Navajo . . . I like his name.* I could hear her rustling through papers, then she started reeling off the short menu. I picked out a pulled pork something or other, then thanked the young woman for her assistance and hung up.

A little food, a little sleep, then maybe I would be able to concentrate on the Elixir of Essence and my mission.

~

TEENY WEENY

Why was it I always seemed to be running away from Tim Wu, or Tang Da, or well, *him*? I really only wanted to stay, but it felt, sounded, tasted, and smelled so awkward to me. He was even upsetting my already screwed-up sensory system. I just never seemed to be able to think clearly when I was near him.

Well, I was home and safe in my little place. I grabbed my fleece nightgown, wrapped myself in my robe, curled up with a good book (*Ancient Arts and Mystics*, naturally), and settled my body into my comfy down mattress to rest this weary head of mine.

I fell asleep somewhere on page 322 or thereabouts (the number may or may not be of importance, one never really knew for sure) of my encyclopedia. I was reading about the *Xiānnǚ*, the fairies of the Orient, when I nodded off.

The crane in my dream from the other night returned again, but this time as a woman. She stood next to Wu, in his natural state, with his white hair and long beard. Actually it wasn't so much that she was standing beside him. It was more like she was in him, around him, and through him.

The next vision of the night was of my own Goddess Brid. My guide, she was the fire of hearth, forge, and inspiration. It was through her and her fellow gods and goddesses that I existed still today. She appeared in her ethereal form, carrying a flame upon her open hand and an olive branch in the other. She was adorned in a tapestry that depicted the essence of spring.

Light of *Xiānnǚ*—was this it? The flame that Brid held in her palm? She and her flame were my guide, but I did not believe that was something that could be captured and used. Certainly not in a country thousands of miles from here and certainly not in a time hundreds and hundreds of years ago.

That was the last vision of the night. After that, I slept as if I hadn't slept for a week, which certainly felt like it was the case. I awoke well after the dawn's light broke through my curtains. I felt like the sunlight pouring into the bedroom was all the enlightening I need. I found myself heaving a calm sigh, as if a heavy weight had just been lifted from my chest. That was, until I heard the clamoring of four pixies in my kitchen. Did I leave the door unlocked? They were pixies, so they certainly could manage the little crack under the door that never quite was flush with the doorstep. They had never done that before, so I was guessing it was due to my own absentmindedness from this entire calamity.

I hurried downstairs and found Tierri and Aeiri over the sink, trying to work the latch on the window above it to allow Cyllene in, who was not so patiently waiting to enter. This was well past my normal wake-up time; in fact it was eight o'clock. *Eight o'clock? Oh geez, what the heck happened?*

Enya and Ushka were trying to figure out how to brew my morning tea, and it even looked like they had it covered. *There is hope!* The good news, I guess, was that I had been so busy between Wu, the Court, Nina and Mat, and of course, the amulet, that Cyllene's megaphone was still in the exact place we left it yesterday morning. So really, all I needed to do was sit down at the table and let everyone take their places. That equated to the pixies going into the parlor to presumably wrestle one another, and Cyllene alighting by the funnel.

"Well? What's going on? You are out late! You slept in late! You have a funny look on your face!" Cyllene's admonishments and questions came barreling through the funnel.

"Silly Annie, everything is fine!" I said to her, but I didn't completely believe it myself, especially the "funny look" comment.

"Cyllene! See-lee-nee! And it's clear everything is not 'fine.' What happened at Court? Where were you last night? Why aren't you up at dawn like normal?"

Sheesh, she is now sounding like she's my nanny and not the pixies'. Wait . . . What? Weren't the pixies letting Cyllene in and making my tea too? Maybe I am the one who needs a nanny.

I apologized for my behavior and continued to tell her about the whole proceeding in Court, the ruling they made on Wu's term here in Havenwood Falls, the salve for Nina, the meeting with Tang Da . . .

"Tang what?" Cyllene stopped me at that point. So now I had to fill her in about how Tang Da Wu was posing as Dr. Timothy Wu and why.

I would tell you she lifted one of her eyebrows suspiciously, if she had eyebrows, but her complexion was so multicolored she looked like an illustrated lady. There was a colorful menagerie of hues above her vibrant eyes that gave the same impression as raising an eyebrow.

After explaining the task that Wu and I had been assigned by the Court, I told her about the visions I had last night.

"So you said Addie gave him a tattoo of a crane? And he said that's his spirit guide?"

I nodded in response while sipping a pretty well-brewed cup of tea.

"Then I think that part of the visions I understand. The crane actually represents your Dr. Wu, or I guess the real Wu. He and his spirit guide are meshed. His hair is the Hair of the Crane," Cyllene stated rather matter-of-factly.

"Silly Annie! I mean, Cyllene, you are brilliant!"

"One doesn't live some eight hundred-odd years being a soul of a tree without learning a thing or two along the way," she said proudly, and for a moment, her mosaic skin took on all its former radiancy.

"Well, this I have to share with Tang! Hopefully, he has determined the other piece of the puzzle."

"On a first name basis, I see." She harrumphed. "Explains your funny look."

I guess she was right about learning a thing or two over the course of a few centuries, because she might have nailed this one too.

I ran upstairs to change clothes and just as I reached the top landing, I heard my cell phone buzzing on the end table. I ran to the phone expecting to see Barbie's name, or even Mat's, but the caller ID revealed "Whisper Falls Inn."

"Hello?" I answered the call.

Michaela was on the other end, and she said that Dr. Wu was calling, and wanted to know if she should transfer his call. I of course said yes, and she connected us, or whatever it was—merged the call, swapped the call—it was all new to me.

"Siobhan?" the inquiring voice came through after a clicking sound.

"Tang, good morning! Sorry, I'm running a bit late."

"I took the liberty of having some blueberry scones delivered from Coffee Haven. I hope that's okay."

"Perfect, they are the best! I should be there in about fifteen minutes." Then I added, "I received a little inspiration this morning that might help us move this mysterious mixture along. See you soon!" I hung up quickly, since I was practically drooling with a taste of the butter and honey on my lips just from hearing his voice, let alone the thought of Coffee Haven scones for breakfast.

As I entered the cottage, the smell of freshly baked blueberry scones was wafting in the air, and Tang was busily nibbling away at one of them.

"These are incredible! I've never tasted anything so divine!" he said waving a half-eaten scone in the air while motioning me in.

"Of course they are. They have a touch of magic." I smiled, knowing these were far better than my faerie cakes.

"Speaking of which . . ." He paused, finishing the biscuit in his hand. "I believe I have determined the part of the spell regarding the Light of *Xiānnǚ*. This morning I remembered our little fight—again I humbly apologize for that . . ."

I waved my hand as if it were nothing. "Forgiven, forgotten . . . forge on!"

"The wand that you wield, it has a tip that glows like a nebula. I think that is it—the light of the fae, a fairy's wand. There's only one problem . . ." He hesitated.

197

"Yes?"

"You are the only fae I know. Back home, in my time, it is not a realm I associate with. When I return, there will not be enough time for me to find a *Xiānnǚ* to help, assuming one would be willing. I think I am going to need you to come with me. That is, if we can figure out the other meaning of the amulet's message."

I was taken aback by his suggestion that I go to China with him, and not only China, but a China way before I was even born. I would deal with that idea later, if it were something that could even be accomplished. First I wanted to share with him what Cyllene had discerned.

"Ah, the Hair of the Crane! I think you are correct. It is not a feather, but neither is it a crane. You are the crane!" I told him excitedly.

"Me? Why me?" he bewildered.

"You live in the divination of the Spirit Crane. She is your guide, as Brid, the goddess of spring, is mine. She is a part of you. In you and around you always. You are her manifestation in this earthly realm. It is *your* hair that is required."

Then the light dawned in his eyes. He stood up quickly, spreading scone crumbs all over the floor. *The pixies would have a feast with those.* He hurried over to the table where he had left the notepad with his rudimentary drawings, and re-read the scripture.

"I see it now! It is more detailed than just hair of crane. It says specifically 'the white hair of a crane's neck.' I was focusing on the wrong thing. That would be a hair from my beard. Well, the beard I will have when I return home," he said as he stroked the finely trimmed dark goatee of Timothy Wu. "The other part makes more sense about it being your wand, now that I am reading the details. It says a 'touch of the Light of *Xiānnǚ*.' Spirit Crane told me that I will need what I learn here to accomplish my journey in the past. You, dear Siobhan, you are my teacher! I definitely need you!"

"Say I would go with you, how do you propose that be accomplished? You told the Court you were able to enter this time because Dr. Wu was your descendant. I am quite sure I have no

Chinese ancestry in my blood." He raised an eyebrow, and I stopped him before he could even say another word. "No! I'm not taking a DNA test!"

"Then I fear I am right back where I started, failing." He turned away, but not without me seeing the forlorn look on his face. He uttered as he returned the notepad to the table, "If only you had some fae magic that could move you to another place."

"Well, I can ripple," I responded, "but I don't know about in time. I've only rippled in space."

He turned about again to face me, his eyes bright once more. "Time and space—they are relative. One cannot be without the other. Tell me about it."

So I explained to him about the ripple. How I could go from one place to another in a matter of minutes, or less, sometimes more. I got into the stipple in the ripple, that little wrinkle that does not guarantee that I will arrive in the new space without losing or gaining time, sometimes minutes, days, even weeks. If I could use the ripple to move in time, it may have a similar (or opposite, depending on how you looked at it) effect on the space. Maybe I could get to the right time, but perhaps I'd be in Timbuktu instead of Tiger Pond, or whatever the place was he said he was from.

He massaged his chin again, then said, "I know the exact time I will return. It will be nine p.m., 13th of October 3519."

"3519? It's only 2019 now. I thought you were going back in time!" I heard myself screeching this.

"So sorry, that is the Chinese calendar year. For Westerners, it would be 800 CE. You will be able to find Tiger Pond by letting the crane constellation guide you, as it will point you directly to its location."

"I don't know that I have ever heard of the crane constellation. I will have to review my charts."

"I believe you may find it by the name Grus. In fact, the only star that will be visible then will be the Alpha Grus, or Alnair."

"I see, so you want me to go back more than one thousand

years, then find you by a constellation that I may only be able to identify by a single star. That's what you're saying, right?"

"Uh, correct," was all he could say.

"Well, that's a lot to take in, and a good deal more to think about. We still have a few days, and if I do agree to go, and I'm not saying I do, I have plenty of studying to do first." With that, I grabbed a scone and left.

CHAPTER 16

TEENY WEENY

I spent the rest of the day and night reading everything I could find about time travel and reviewing my own sky charts. I did find the crane constellation he spoke of, but even if I did go, I had to familiarize myself not only with it but also its location on that day and time.

I had arranged with Barbie to meet her at the Broastful Brew the next morning, and this time I was more than prompt. I sat at the table waiting for her for a change.

I wasted no time. As soon as she sat down, I filled her in on the amulet, the spell—rather the recipe—and what Wu and I had come up with. Naturally, that included his grandiose scheme of my traveling in time to meet up with him in some land far far away, like a faerie tale that even I had a hard time swallowing.

She took a sip of coffee, then leaned back in her chair. After a minute or so of contemplating my words, she said, "Seems like the two of you are moving right along. What do you think about this time travel thing? Is that something you can do? Is it something you want to do?"

"Well, if saving the poor child is truly essential to our very existence, then yes, it is something I want to do. Is it something I can do? I'm not really sure. It's a little frightening." *Actually, it's a lot frightening.* "I'm assuming I can get there and back again. I've been thinking about whether the ripple would work with time, but I've never done that, so I just don't know."

"You do have a couple of days left. You might want to start practicing. Meanwhile, I'll talk with some of the Court members, maybe even Dr. Sam Fraser, the new professor at Halvard Campus —he teaches interdimensional exploration and time travel and has some experience himself. He might be able to provide a portal, or something of the sort, just in case." I wasn't sure if she was mimicking my *just in case* to tease me, or if she really meant a portal just in case.

The Luna Coven did a time travel spell for Joe Greg, a young wolf shifter, over the summer, but that was only a few years backward and nowhere near the distance. They only sent him to Houston for the year 2012. Even that was a big risk for the Luna Coven.

After our meeting, I just kept repeating on my way home, "Practice, portal, portal, practice." The portal idea was intriguing, and for some reason I felt it was safer, mainly because it would be here in Havenwood Falls, where I belonged, when I belonged! But that was a "just in case," like Barbie said, so the practice part had to come first, and I had to get started right away.

I decided to try it out with just a few months ago, when I broke the curse on my brother Grenfold and reunited him with the mermaid Coralie at Peacock Lake. When I got home, I went straight into the salon, wasting no time. I closed my eyes and concentrated on the image of that moment with Gruff by my side, ready to break the curse. The ripple began, the atmosphere around me started to waver, and as it did, so did I, melting into that wave. In an instant I was at the edge of the lake, looking at Gruff's forlorn face and the red-haired beauty poking her head out from the turquoise and teal waters.

It worked! I can do it!

I was about to say the words that broke the curse when I realized I did not have my wand with me. *Oh dear goddesses, what have I done? Did I mess this whole moment up by rippling without being prepared?* I panicked and immediately reversed my concentration back to the salon and the moment I got home from the Brew.

The ripple returned me to my home once again. Without wasting a second, I ran to my bedroom and the bedside table where my wand was stored in the keyless safe. After passing my hand over the pearlescent latch to pop it open, I grabbed my wand from its velvet bed. I closed my eyes once again and placed the scene at Peacock Lake from last May into my mind's eye, praying that it was still there.

The air around me vacillated as I slipped into the ripple and appeared at the precipice of Peacock Lake, with everyone in place as before. *Whew! That was close!*

I touched the glowing tip of my wand to Gruff's head and said the magic words that broke the curse. I witnessed once again the serene transformation of Gruff into my beautiful brother Grenfold, who then kissed me on the forehead and said, "Thank you! Make amends with Father! I'll love you always, sister!" With that, he joined the lovely sea maiden in Peacock Lake and swam away.

I was so relieved that I had done no damage to their destiny. This time-space continuum was going to be tricky. I also realized that I'd better take my wand with me when I tried this again, just in case.

Home again in the right time, well, the present time anyway, I decided to relax and have some tea. I also found myself starving, so a snack or a grab-it was in order. But with such little time left before Wu must depart, I would have to practice the time ripple again, but farther away and further back in time. A few months and nearby did not seem to be a real challenge. Hopefully, it would be the same with a more difficult journey.

∿

Later in the evening, I reminisced about Grenfold and Coralie, and how in love they were and how patient that love was to remain so strong after hundreds of years apart from one another. I decided to try to return to the moment when Father, the great King Ian of the spring fae, was about to curse my brother. This time I would stand up to him and stop him. I realized that now! Maybe I could save the two lovers eons of heartache, and maybe my mother, Queen Rose, in the process.

I stood by the wardrobe in my bedroom, holding my wand in both hands, not about to take the chance of losing it in some tidal wave of time and space, and focused on the Isle of Gwynf'l and the emerald fields of shamrocks that flocked the hillside. I imagined the moment my father began his chant more than 550 years ago, the one I dreamed about every year on the spring equinox. The space around me undulated, and I was gently pulled into it.

This time, however, when I appeared on the other side of the ripple, I was not on the hillside with my father, mother, and Grenfold. Instead, I found myself in our home, a quaint thatched hut, which was quite a distance from that field. The surroundings were familiar—a kettle of soup simmered in the hearth and my mother's strings of flowers she made each morning for our necklaces and bracelets were aligned on the table. At least this told me that the time was somewhat close, and I was on the right island, if not the exact place I had intended to be.

So there was a stipple in a time ripple too. I figured I'd better explore the area and determine how far off in time I might truly be. Last time I traveled from here in a ripple, I had lost weeks! As I exited the cabin, I grabbed one of the daisy chains and placed it around my neck. I couldn't help myself. I had forgotten all about them.

I headed toward the hill where the incident occurred, and right before I got out of the wooded section where our home was lodged, I heard my father already halfway through his curse. I ran as fast as I could, but I could not reach them in time to stop him. I came to an abrupt halt as I saw and heard my poor brother Grenfold turn into a misshapen soul and scamper away as my father ordered him to crawl under a rock.

The agony and grief I felt that day came back to me, as it did every time the dream recurred. Unlike the first time, when I turned away from my father and went after Grenfold, now poor Gruff, I was watching my father from this distance. Father had fallen to his knees and began to weep.

"What have I done? Oh dear lords, what have I done? This power is not for me!" I heard him crying into his hands. Then I saw him thrashing at the dirt, digging up the soil with his bare hands. He placed his wand in the hole he had created, stood up, and kicked the dirt back onto it, then rolled a large rock over the top.

I guess it was not meant to be for me to save Grenfold and Coralie from their estrangement. Perhaps this was necessary for them to be together in Havenwood Falls. I ran to my father and hugged him, telling him it would be okay, and Grenfold and I would always love him. My mother was grabbing her stomach in pain, and tears flowed from her beautiful azure eyes. I heard my father telling her if the pain was still that bad, they should go see the witch for another dose of brew. I had no idea my mother was ill. I thought she died from the heartache of her only son being cursed to live as a troll.

My father wrapped his arm around my mother and gently led her back home. After they abandoned this fae-forsaken site, I sat on the rock and cried an eternity of tears for all I had misunderstood. As I lifted my hand to wipe my tears, wishing I were in my own room with a good down pillow to soak up this mess, I accidentally touched my wand to my the tip of my nose.

There came an enormous boom, like the sound of a volcanic eruption. The air puckered and ruffled, but not anything like a ripple. A bolt of bright purple lightning flashed down from the clear blue sky and hit the ground next to the spot that Father had buried his wand.

There was now a large glowing amaranthine colored hole, but not in the ground. It was standing right before me, in midair, like a doorway to a deep dark tunnel. *Is this a portal?*

I took a chance and walked through the threshold. I felt my body swirl through an amethyst sea of time and space, all glowing with sparks of yellow, blue, and green. Bolts of white lightning flashed before me and beside me.

I heard a tremendous rumble and another explosion, then suddenly I was blasted through another hole, and found myself standing beside the wardrobe in my very own bedroom in Havenwood Falls. *It was a portal!*

CHAPTER 17

WU

*A*s uncomfortable as it was to be under house arrest, I was delighted that Siobhan was working with me on this project. When she was in my company, nothing else seemed to matter. I had full confidence that she was a strong fae. How else could she have such power over me and my affections? She called early this morning to let me know that she could indeed ripple in time and space simultaneously. I had no doubt, but the diminutive dear did not have enough faith in herself.

She said she had a few questions for me, so that she could prepare for the journey, though she hadn't quite yet decided if she was going. I guessed that wasn't true. Otherwise why would she be experimenting with her ripple?

I heard a tiny rap on the door, and I knew it was her sweet little hand knocking upon the wood.

"Come in; it's open!" I responded to the sound.

There she was, all four foot five of her. I noticed her hair looked different. It seemed like there was glitter in it or something. I asked her about it.

She stroked her hair, and I watched as it seemed to glow with a glistening white undertone, the colorful sparkles moving about.

"Oh, this? Well, apparently the time-space travel has some

unusual effects. I doubt there is a hairdresser who could quite accomplish this technique."

I found it enchanting, as I did her.

"On to business," she interrupted my musings. "So, first, I'd like to know what happens to Dr. Timothy Wu when you return?"

"Currently, Dr. Wu is in a fugue state, in his own home. When I return, he will awake from that state, without any memory of the last week or so. No harm will have come to him other than the loss of a few days. He will feel extremely rested and recharged, as if he had been on the best vacation ever."

"Well, I'm happy to hear that, and I suspect the teenagers in town, who are all infatuated with him, will be too. Next, I'm going to need an image of the place that I'll be able to fix in my mind's eye. I don't even think a photograph will work. So I'm not sure how we will overcome that obstacle."

"Let me get my compass. That might do the trick," I replied as I headed to the closet for my black bag.

"Uh, Tang, if a photograph won't do it, I doubt a compass will."

"I said *my* compass." I returned to my favorite fae. Now I was glad that I never had any dealings with a *Xiānnǚ* before, as I doubted I would ever have been able to concentrate on my profession.

I held the round gold box before her, which looked everything like a pocket watch or navigator's compass, until I pushed the little button that popped open the lid. Instead of finding a minute and second hand, or the twelve points of the compass and a magnetic needle to gauge the direction, the inside revealed something similar to a mirror, but not exactly. The image of Tiger Pond, the temple, the plum and cherry blossom trees, and a myriad of birds including cranes came into view. But this was a living image, the water shimmering, hummingbirds twittering around the cherry blossoms as their petals flowed to and fro in the wind, and bright gold-and-white koi jumping in and out of the water.

"This is how I will find my way home." I placed my finger on the glass, and the image changed to the Wudang Mountains, lush with greenery, the mists from the multitude of secluded waterfalls rising and working their way like a fog throughout the upper edges of the dense forest. A falcon was flying high above the treetops. Again with my finger I traced the cover, and the image turned into one of my small village, with children playing near the community well, and carts of fruits and vegetables lining the dirt paths.

"This is amazing! I think I can work with these moving pictures. It feels like I am really there," she responded, while doing that little jig of hers I found so charming. I guessed this meant she was really going.

"You can take this for tonight to familiarize yourself with the area and get a fix in your mind of where you are going." I handed her the imaging contraption.

"Yes, thank you! I will study it the rest of the day and evening, then we should be able to report to the Court that we have figured out how to accomplish our mission. I mean, your mission."

She's going! Thank you, Great Spirit Crane, for your blessings!

CHAPTER 18

TEENY WEENY

I spent the entire rest of the day mesmerized with the impressions that wafted in and out of the circular frame of the compass. *I think I'm going to call this the Come Home Compass.*

It was a truly amazing little gadget. I even saw the poor young boy on his luxurious throne-style bed, on the brink of death. A lot of good all that luxury did for him now. It looked like a white-haired shaman and a teeny weeny woman were what he was going to need most. I saw the emperor and empress fretting over the sickly child, and another woman—at least, I thought it was a woman—in a simple flat black jacket, with a long braid trailing down to her waist from the nape of her neck. She was not much taller than I, maybe an inch or two.

I texted Barbie right before I went to bed to let her know that we were ready to report to the court.

BS: Great! And you?
TW: Yes, I'm going w/
BS: Woohoo! LOL WuHoo!

Sheesh! I'm not sure this texting is a good thing. WuHoo? From Barbie?

I met up with Tang Da Wu at his cottage the next morning.

Sheriff Kasun was already on the porch, waiting for my arrival. He would escort us to the Court. After all, Wu was technically still under arrest.

We kept it pretty short and simple, explaining how we were able to use the reversed photo, and how between the two of us, we figured out the elements for Dr. Wu to return to his appointed time and place and perform the cure. I acknowledged to the Court that I was aware my part of this journey had a few wrinkles, a.k.a. stipples, but regardless, I should be able to return in a day or two —well, a week tops. *I hope!* So I should be safe within the memory ward boundaries.

We also recited how the real Dr. Wu would reawaken once Tang had returned. Maybe the Court would still want to offer him the invite, as he sounded like a good fit with Sun & Moon Academy and its students.

We received the blessing from the Court to proceed. Barbie and Ric were to oversee Wu's departure (to ensure he actually did depart). I was to take care of my individual "travel" plans, as I saw fit.

As we exited the Court, I returned Tang's compass to him and asked him about the other woman in moving picture.

"Oh, that is Mai Li. She is my Mickey Mouse."

Ah, I was right. It is a woman! "Your Mickey Mouse?"

"When the two English marms weren't chattering away, I had the privilege of watching Walt Disney's *Fantasia* on the airplane. Mai Li is my sorcerer's apprentice. She has been assisting me and learning the arts of the Wu for many years. She is almost ready for her mastery."

We agreed that I was to meet him in the prince's chambers, as close as possible to nine o'clock in the evening. He showed me on the sky chart where that one stupid star was supposed to be in the sky at that time. *Yikes!*

I prepared myself as best as I was able. Cyllene was literally hovering over me as I skittered around, trying to decide what I needed. She buzzed incessantly above my head, trying to tell me something.

We went into the kitchen, where the funnel ensemble was still in place. *Dang, this has been a busy week!*

She set herself up to her megaphonic instrument. "Siobhan, you are going to a place and time you have never been. You are not taking a trip on a bus! Trust me on this—you need yourself and your wand. That's it! The rest is up to you and your magic. By the way, I like your hair."

She's right, of course. Gotta hand it to a dryad of eight hundred years, give or take a score or two.

I left Cyllene in charge of the pixies, which she was extremely delighted about. Why did it take me so long to figure that one out?

My cell phone vibrated, and there was another text from Barbie.

BS: Done! WuBeGone!

Okay, that's really weird, because she wasn't there, and I was pretty sure I didn't tell her that part. I will have to think about that later. This meant it was my turn.

TW: K! C ya! Sooner/Later/Whatever

It really was my turn.

I went to my bedroom and looked at the new radiating portal next to the wardrobe—well, almost embedded in it. *Can I use this to get back from China's Zhou Dynasty?* I took a chance again and entered the portal.

I found myself swirling through the complexity of purplish-red gases and prismatic sparks and bolts, only to find myself back on the hillside of the Isle of Gwynf'l. *Well, that won't work.* Apparently this was a doorway between then and now, and here and there.

So much for my entryway to above and beyond. Seemed I was stuck with the ripple and my wand.

I made sure I had my wand held tightly in both hands. I focused on the living image of the young boy on his death bed in a land far away, in a time far behind, as it appeared in Wu's Come Home Compass. I also concentrated on the sky chart path with that crazy Alnair that was supposed to be my guiding star.

Oh my gosh! I'm here! At least, I think I'm here. Well, I wasn't exactly in the emperor's mansion, nor at Tiger Pond or the temple. I found myself standing under a waterfall, getting drenched. But it was definitely not the Great Havenwood Falls, and it was not the three sister falls at Peacock Lake. I looked around, and the area was thick with tall, fibrous bamboo, and I even saw a panda bear munching on a stem! Heavy dark green vines looped from each and every tree in this lush forestry.

I made it to China! Not where I was supposed to be—there was a stipple. *That's one!* I hoped the timing was at least close. Now I had to see if I could even find the bright crane star Wu told me to follow. If it wasn't even visible, I definitely had the wrong time. Really? What was I thinking?

WU

I am home again! Thanks again to you, Great Spirit Crane.

There was a peace and serenity in that knowledge. So why was I feeling nervous and apprehensive? I had no idea when Siobhan, my teeny weeny fae, my *Xiānnǚ*, was going to show up. Or where she would show up, even if she did. Without her, I could not cure the boy. However, I had no choice but to leave; the Court made sure of that.

Without her, I felt lost! This emotion was on a completely different plane than I had ever experienced. If she arrived, we could cure the prince, we could save the dynasty, and as long as my people were diligent, we could save the faith.

I wanted to be with her always. This would be the end for me as a shaman. I had served my rulers well.

"Master Wu!" my apprentice, Mai Li addressed me. "Where have you been?"

"On my mission, Mai Li! I have found the cure, and we must get everything ready. The boy has not a minute to lose. I need you to fill this beaker with water from Tiger Pond, then meet me in the child's chambers forthwith. There is a *Xiānnü* that is required. I am waiting for her arrival."

"*Her?* A *Xiānnü?* What is this? You have nothing to do with *Xiānnü*."

"It is not your concern, Mai Li! She is necessary to heal the prince and let him have his destiny!"

"Very well, Master Wu. I will get the water and bring it to the palace." She bowed to me in acquiescence, or so I thought.

Sometimes that woman could be so difficult! No wonder I never married!

~

TEENY WEENY

I had no idea when I was. I definitely knew I was in the right place, well, country at least. I didn't have a clue if I was anywhere near the right century, let alone the right day and time.

Everything I read told me that this crane star, the Alnair in the Grus constellation, was rarely visible in China. *Yet Tang Wu insisted it could guide me? I am crazy!*

Perhaps he was right. The day and time I was supposed to be here was the day and time you could actually see that star. I started thinking about Mat, my nephew, and his joyous compilation of fae and owl. How he could see and hear things, even in the dark, that no other could see or hear. How he could soar through the Havenwood Falls night skies without fear or worry, the moon reflecting on his perfectly white wings, able to navigate all of it by the stars and his pure love.

With all of those thoughts in my mind, and not even realizing it, I stepped into the ripple.

I found myself no longer in the waterfalls somewhere in the Wudang Mountains—*I guess that's where I was*—but actually on the edge of Tiger Pond. Better yet! That crane star thing was not only reflecting off the pond, it was magnified! It was magnificent!

WU

I arranged all of the necessary items to cure the boy in accordance with the spell divulged on the amulet. The temple held not only my equipment, but my secrets as well.

I sent Mai Li to retrieve the Dragon Water from Tiger Pond. I looked up at the sky and saw the Great Crane's beak shining brightly through the misty night sky. It was time. I was here when I was supposed to be here. I hoped my love—I mean, my little fae —would also arrive on time.

This had always been a little iffy.

There was a strange waver in the air, and Tiger Pond emitted an ambiance that was almost like a mirage effect. There she was! She had just rippled to the edge of the lake! The cranes drinking from the water took flight upon her arrival in this unusual appearance.

The next thing I saw was Mai Li running toward her. I assumed that she was greeting her, as Mai Li knew we needed her to ensure our destiny.

Oh, Great Crane! Mai Li just pushed Siobhan, my love, into Tiger Pond! Blasphemy!

TEENY WEENY

This pond was astounding! It almost seemed like diamonds were floating and glistening in the lake. I thought I could love this place. In so many ways, it reminded me of the Isle of the Gwynf'l, but far more lush and brilliant. I saw my own reflection in this sylvan pond. It revealed that I was now cloaked in a white robe, my hair totally white, except there was a rainbow effect, and it undulated of its own volition. I looked into the water and admired the most beautiful koi I had ever see—

Ack! I can't breathe! Oh my Goddess Brid, I'm drowning! I am not supposed to be in a lake. Nor in any water. A little waterfall is one thing, but I am not Coralie! I'm a spring fae. I am the queen of the spring fae of Gwynf'l! Ack! I can't breathe!

I gulped for air but all that I ingested was water.

Goddess Brid, I'm drowning! Help!

My vision went black, and my whole body was becoming numb. Then I felt myself being pulled by the collar of the white robe, trying to gasp for air on the side of a foreign lake. I heard yelling in some language I didn't understand. It sounded choppy yet sing-songy.

While I was doing my best to spit water out of my lungs and pull air back into them, I heard Tang yelling at someone in that foreign dialect. He grabbed the woman in the flat black jacket and long braid with one hand by the shoulders and was shaking her and wagging a finger in front of her face.

WU

"Mai Li! Are you crazy! What do you think you were doing?"

My apprentice just pushed Teeny Weeny into Tiger Pond! If Tiger Pond were just any normal pond, and Siobhan—Teeny Weeny—were just any normal person, it would not have been a catastrophe. But this was not the case! Tiger Pond was sacred! Xiānnǚ were sacred! Had I not taught Mai Li anything?

"Mai Li! Do you realize that if she died, the ruler would execute you for killing her? Not to mention execute me, as she is necessary to cure their son? I fear you have lost your mind!"

"I'm sorry, Master Wu!" she kowtowed to me. "She is trying to steal you from me!"

"I am not yours to be stolen, Mai Li. You are my apprentice, and you have been a fine one thus far. You should be proud of what you have learned and how you can help our people. But this is unforgivable!"

TEENY WEENY

The woman in black crumpled to the ground, crying and pulling at the hem of Tang's robe. It looked as if she was begging for forgiveness, and even though I could not speak their language, I was positive that was the crux of the confrontation.

"Stop, Tang!" I hollered at the top of my water-soaked lungs. *Father, Gruff-Grenfold, Mother Rose, Coralie—everything! Amends, forgiveness. That is what the centuries need to survive. I see it now!* "We have a mission! We need to do it now!"

WU

I grabbed Mai Li by the arm and led her to the palace. Siobhan, bless the little fae, seemed to have recovered from the Mai Li incident and was right behind us. Even more astounding, she was still holding her perfectly wonderful wand, clutched in both hands. *That's a woman who knows how to focus on a mission.*

~

TEENY WEENY

I was standing in the massive bedroom, the one that was described as the prince's chambers. There was a reflecting shield, not exactly a mirror, more a finely polished sheet of silver, and I saw myself now as the others saw me. The white robe I found myself cloaked in was embellished with multicolored starbursts, just like the ones that seemed to flow in and out of every strand of my now totally white hair.

Tang appeared exactly as I saw him in my visions. He was wearing his crane robe, a small cap upon his head of pure white locks. The more recent closely cropped fu manchu of Dr. Timothy Wu was now a long mustache that melded into an even longer snowy goatee.

Mai Li was holding a flask of teal-colored water, and Tang plucked a hair from his own goatee, placing it in the flask. He nodded at me.

It's my turn, again.

I took out my wand, which also seemed to have undergone its own transformation. It fit into my hands perfectly, but the shaft felt like it was made of alabaster, rather than the wood I was used to handling. *I have to let go. If I overthink this, I will get it wrong, that I am sure of.*

I murmured a prayer under my breath:
Please, Goddess Brid, be my hand and sight
And touch this task with your guiding light

The small orb at the tip of my wand began to glow brilliantly. Suddenly, the entire room was filled with a blinding white light. Not even the smallest corner of the room was spared a shadow.

The mixture in the flask became effervescent, popping with tiny champagne-like bubbles. Tang took the flask from Mai Li and gently pressed it to the lips of the pale prince. The liquid trickled into his mouth as we all held our breath, hoping and waiting.

Color slowly began to flow back into the child's skin, a pink blush appearing on his cheeks. His long black eyelashes fluttered, then his eyes opened wide. He took in the sight of his mother and father, peered at Tang and Mai Li, then looked at me. He smiled gently and said something in Chinese.

Tang laughed and turned to me and translated. "He said 'Xiānnǚ? What are you doing here?' I told you he was gifted."

~

WU

We left the prince and his parents to celebrate his regained health. Both Siobhan and I were exhausted. Especially my precious fae, for not only did she come from far away into a land completely unknown to her, but she nearly drowned in the process.

I escorted her to the guest quarters of the palace after the emperor gave us leave and commanded we meet him and the empress in the throne room in the morning.

I could not help myself. I opened the door to the guest chamber for her, and I was not sure what came over me, but as I looked into those deep hazel eyes, gold flecks flashing about, I could not help but place my hand under her chin and lift her face up to mine. I gently kissed her soft lips.

She was obviously taken aback, and I was afraid that I had overstepped my bounds. She had taken a small jump backwards. I could not tell if she was astonished, insulted, or what. Then she gave me a quick peck on the cheek and said goodnight, hurriedly shutting the door behind her.

I supposed that was a good sign.

I had been the rulers' shaman for some thirty years now. Never had I cared for anything but my profession and my people, but now it was different. I thought I would like nothing better but to spend as much time with this tiny lady as she would possibly

219

allow. I doubted I could convince her to stay here, so I was at a loss.

❧

TEENY WEENY

Oh my goddesses, he kissed me! It was frightening and wonderful all at the same time. What was I to do now? He lived in a time and place that was so foreign to me. If only there were some way he could come back to Havenwood Falls. Of course, he might not want to come back. After all, this was his life here, and Havenwood Falls must have been so foreign to him. Although, he did fit in pretty well as Dr. Timothy Wu.

Well, I was just dreaming. We each had our own place and time to be, and they were not together, at least not anymore.

❧

WU

We were all gathered in the throne room. Even the young prince sat beside his father on a smaller throne.

My teeny weeny fae looked as if she had had little sleep last night. I myself did not sleep well. I tossed and turned, dismayed that today would be our last day together.

The emperor raised his hand. Everyone became still and silent before he spoke.

"Tang Da Wu, you have served the kingdom well as our Royal Wu. You have not only saved our child, but the future of the dynasty. For this you deserve a reward. What is your wish?"

Well, I certainly wasn't expecting that. I had done many things for the rulers and for the people over the decades, but never had I been rewarded. It was my job; the satisfaction in that was reward enough.

If only the emperor could wave his staff or his mighty sword and make it so Siobhan and I could be together.

"Your highnesses! I thank you for your generosity. It has been many years that I have been nothing other than your wizard. That has been all I had ever wanted, and it has been my pleasure always to serve you and the kingdom. However, if I were to wish for anything, I wish that I could spend all the rest of my days with this little *Xiānnǚ*, if she would allow me."

The young prince smiled and nodded his agreement. The empress stood behind him, patting him on the shoulders in affirmation.

"Who would take your place?" the emperor asked, contemplating the request, but I felt unsure that he was liable to grant it.

"Mai Li can take my place as the Royal Wu, your excellency. She has been under my tutelage for well over fifteen years, and is ready to become a Master Wu."

The empress was delighted with this suggestion. I believe she was keen on the idea of the palace wizard being a woman for a change.

"Father," the young prince spoke up, "Tang Da Wu is the best Wu ever, but I think he will be an unhappy Wu if he is not with the one he loves. Mai Li is fair and kind to me, and I've seen her in practice. She can do this. Please, Father!"

The love and compassion that was bestowed upon the boy by the great spirits shone even more brightly at that moment. He said "the one he loves," and I knew he was completely right. *I do love Siobhan.*

"Very well. Make your preparations. Your wish is granted if the *Xiānnǚ* will have you."

We bowed to the rulers, all three of them, and were dismissed with a wave of the emperor's hand.

~

TEENY WEENY

"What was all that about? I heard you say *Xiānnǚ* several times. You were talking about me?"

"The emperor asked me what I wish as a reward for curing his son. I told them I wished for nothing more than to spend the rest of my days with you, if you would have me."

"Well, I don't know if I would have you or not. But I do know I have to go back to Havenwood Falls. That is my home, my family, and I must go back soon."

He looked at me in such a heartbroken manner, I was choking up, but I blurted out anyway, "Would you come to Havenwood Falls with me?"

"Why yes, of course! But I would not know how. It is one thing to occupy another person's body for a short period of time, but I certainly could not do it for the rest of my life. That would be unconscionable."

I looked down at the ground and made little circles in the dirt path with my foot as we stood outside the palace. I did not want Tang to see the tears welling up in my eyes.

"Let us go sit by Tiger Pond. There is great power that emits from the temple, and the Great Spirit Crane may descend upon us to give us some guidance. At the very least, we will have these moments together."

His words were soft and gentle, but I could hear and feel the pain, so much like mine. He took my hand in his and led me to the temple in the forest. We sat at the edge of the pond on a finely hewn stone bench. I stared into the dark blue-violet waters of the pond, watching the koi swim lazily around on a course only they understood.

I closed my eyes, trying to hold back the tears, so much like the ache I felt when I rippled to Gwynf'l only to find that I could not change that history and learning there was more to my mother's death and my father's pain.

When I opened my eyes, the tears that had welled up blurred the purplish pool before me, and I saw it! The answer!

"Tang, I think I can take you back with me!"

"In your ripple?"

"No, in a portal! My portal! It might work! I hope it will work!"

"Great Spirit Crane has blessed you with inspiration! Thank you, Great Spirit!"

"And thank my Goddess Brid!"

I told him about the wand and how I accidentally formed a portal that led me from Gwynf'l back to my own bedroom, and how it seemed to have an effect on my hair, I guess to warn him. Then I just burst out laughing at myself for even mentioning it. This was not the Timothy Wu who appeared in Havenwood Falls. I was looking at Tang, my Tang, whose hair was already totally white.

I touched my wand to my nose, concentrating on the memory of my bedroom with the purple portal next to the wardrobe. The blast resounded throughout the forest, and the bolts appeared as if a giant amethyst had just exploded. An undulating circular opening appeared before us, the same dark violet that I knew waited on the other side.

"Take my hand!" I said to him, and without hesitation, he did.

We walked into the portal together, Tang gripping my left hand tightly as I hung on to my wand with my right. We entered the swirling mist of colorful sparks that wound us through the dark purple vortex, whooshing us to our destination.

EPILOGUE

TEENY WEENY

*E*veryone was gathered in the parlor, while Cyllene and I were in the kitchen. I was preparing some teacakes and little sandwiches for everyone to snack on. I could hear the pixie sisters yammering to Mat and Nina about how Wu and I were both going to teach at the "Sun & Moon Academy of Guardian something or other," as Aeiri was calling it.

Cyllene was staring at the rainbow that was weaving in and out of my snow-white head of hair.

"I know, Silly Annie, I'm going to have to glamour it back to my normal brown. I can't very well go around town with all this racket going on in my hair. Funny how Tang's hair came out a purplish black color. He almost looks like when he arrived as Timothy Wu, save for needing a bit of trim on that beard and mustache."

Cyllene nodded in agreement, flying behind me as I carried the tray of treats into the parlor. Wu was on the settee before the hearth, and Mat stood behind Nina, who had her legs curled up in the overstuffed chair.

"I'm sorry about you girls not getting admitted to the Academy," I said, not really sorry at all. "I'm sure there is something we can find for you to help out with, though."

"It's okay," replied Enya.

"Yeah, we decided to start our own Pixie University," stated Tierri.

"We're going to call it P.U. for short," spoke up Ushka.

Then Aeiri began to giggle and blurted out, "Yeah, like P.U., you stink!"

That started the ruckus, the pixies all saying "you stink" to one another, a rabbit punch here and there, and the next moment they were rolling all over the floor wrestling one another.

Mat cautiously stepped over a couple of wrestling pixies and knelt on one knee before Nina. He took her hand in his, looked into those big black eyes of hers, and said, "Nina, would you please be my wife, and share this humble owl's life?"

My breath caught. Cyllene stopped in midair and nearly fell to the ground, and even the pixie sisters came to an abrupt halt. All of us waited anxiously for Nina to answer.

"Si! Si! Mio bel gufo! My handsome owl! I thought you would never ask!"

The pixies became a band of cheerleaders, whooping and hollering, doing somersaults and all kinds of acrobatics, making up songs about weddings and flowers and bells and bows.

Mat beamed with joy, and I looked at Tang, who had a big smile on his face.

Did I just see a twinkle in Tang's eyes? Uh oh, there goes that tingling feeling in my fingers, lobes, nose, and toes again!

❀

We hope you enjoyed this story in the Havenwood Falls series featuring a variety of supernatural creatures. You might also enjoy T.V. Hahn's other stories in the Havenwood Falls universe:

The Winged & the Wicked

The Ward & the Wanderers

ABOUT THE AUTHOR

T.V. Hahn has loved the fantastical and whimsical since she was a child, which may or may not have been that long ago. A creative soul, she enjoys making art with her hands, her voice, and her words. She finds humor in everything and is the first to laugh at her own jokes. During her downtime, you may find her tending her floral beauties, writing poetry, working on her faerie gardens, or watching *The Dark Crystal* or *The Princess Bride*. All of this, combined with her petite stature, has made more than one person wonder if she is, indeed, a faerie. It may be no accident that her first published book is about Teeny Weeny Tahini, a spring fae living in Havenwood Falls. Hahn is self-employed and lives in Florida with her husband and pup. She can be reached through her publisher, Ang'dora Productions.

ACKNOWLEDGMENTS

My readers, who I know are loyal and put up with me being "invisible," thank you for your reviews and your enthusiasm, and I hope I can cast some faerie dust your way.

Regina, for getting Dr. Timothy Wu spot on for the cover!

All the great writers in Havenwood Falls who share so much, and the SUPER characters that make it so exciting and fun.

Our publisher who works tirelessly to make Havenwood Falls the place all of us want to be!

To Paul, who supports me, gives me the time off needed (and some I don't really need but want), and helps me put it all together (even reading about faeries).

A DEMON'S REDEMPTION

JD NELSON

A Havenwood Falls New Adult Novella

Havenwood Falls

A Demon's Redemption

JD Nelson

BOOKS BY JD NELSON

Wicked Ways Series

A Night of Wickedness

All I Want For Christmas Are My Two Front Fangs: A Wicked Ways Companion Novel

Wolves Will Be Wolves

Too Cute To Spook: A Wicked Ways Companion Novel

Night Aberrations Series

Night Aberrations

The Fire within the Night

Stand Alone Novels

Control: A Tale of Desire

Havenwood Falls

Plans Laid Bare

Soul Laid Bare

A Demon's Redemption

To Nels, always Nels.

CHAPTER 1

*E*very demon has a breaking point, and as it turns out, my breaking point was the sixty-seventh time Penelope Osbourne told me to go fuck myself.

She didn't even ease me into it. She verbally pounced on me while I was waiting to cross the street at Main and Eighth, chewed me up, and spit me out as if I wasn't worth the effort it took to swallow. All I could do was stare as she stormed away, the fury and heat of a thousand suns in her usually cheerful brown eyes.

And, to think, before I came along, she used to be such a nice woman.

"How does one go about redeeming oneself?" I asked aloud, throwing myself onto the nearest bench and burying my head in my hands. I was tired, so tired, of trying and failing. My confidence was shaken to my core. And for me—hell, for any demon—that was really saying something.

To my surprise, someone answered my exhausted query. "In my experience, you start with flowers and work your way up to the hard stuff."

Mouth quirked into a suppressed grin, I looked up to find a violet-eyed woman with a sleek silver-blond bob smiling down at me. I hadn't realized anyone had been close enough to overhear me, but I guess I should've. This was Havenwood Falls, after all. I knew to expect the unexpected when dealing with its citizens.

Sliding over, I offered the lady a seat next to me on the park bench and asked, "Do you have much experience in redeeming yourself?"

She grinned as she sat. "No, but I do have experience with flowers. My sister, Reagan, and I own Fairy Tale Florists over on Fifth Street."

"Well, if you're willing to help me out of a hopeless, no chance of succeeding, ridiculously horrible situation, I'm willing to try anything." I stuck out my hand. "I'm Rayonus Rixa."

"Rhiannon Underwood. Nice to meet you, Rayonus."

"Likewise," I told her, genuinely meaning it. "So, tell me a little more about how this flowers-to-redemption thing works. Because for the life of me, I cannot get the hostile woman I love to see me as more than someone who has betrayed her trust."

"I saw that, and I have to ask—do you deserve to be seen as anything more than that?"

I sighed, staring down at my black leather boots, embarrassed, not for the first time, that I had been such a schmuck. "Truthfully, Rhiannon, in the beginning, I didn't."

She nodded in understanding. "But you're different now?"

"Decidedly so." I met her kind eyes. She was so easy to talk to; I felt compelled to tell her the truth. "I feel absolutely nothing but remorse for what I've done. I love her. I'll never do anything to hurt Penelope again."

And it was true. Every single word of it.

Seemingly satisfied with the honesty in my answer, Rhiannon said, "Well, Rayonus, I think I can help you. Or, at least, I can try."

Sighing in relief, I gave her a grateful smile. "You're too kind."

"Nonsense," she said, waving away my gratitude. "You can thank me when *and if* you get back into your Penelope's good graces."

"I will do that," I told her, suppressing another grin. I was going to like Rhiannon Underwood.

After a few more minutes of chatting, Rhiannon invited me to walk with her from the town square to her flower shop, a dark gray three-story Victorian with whimsical eggplant purple trim, complete with turrets and an odd, beguiling charm that made me feel instantly at home. The interior was just as delightful, with colorful butterflies and small chirping birds flying about the lush greenery and flowers in perfect harmony.

I stood still, nearly gaping at the enchanting sight. "This is lovely."

"Thank you," she said, gesturing to a petite brunette with striking blue-green eyes behind the counter. "Allow me to introduce my sister, Reagan Fairchild. Reagan, this is Rayonus Rixa."

"How do you do, Mr. Rixa?" Reagan asked.

"I am very well, now that your kind sister has agreed to help me in my quest to win back the heart of my beloved."

Brows raised, Reagan gave her sister a quizzical look and stuck a pencil behind her ear. "Has she? Then I wish you luck."

"I need all the luck I can get," I told her, noticing the *Help Wanted* sign displayed next to her. "And speaking of that, are you, by chance, still hiring?"

"Yes, we are. Are you in search of a job?"

I nodded. "Sadly, my job giving the occasional ghost tour doesn't quite allow me to pay my way. I've been living off my savings and staying with friends until something steadier comes along."

"Well, if you can be reliable and show up on time, I think Reagan and I can give you a shot," Rhiannon said. "On a trial basis, of course."

"Of course. Thank you. You don't know how much I appreciate everything you're doing for me."

She winked. "You should. This will give you the perfect opportunity to see your Penelope."

Grinning conspiratorially, I said, "I see you and I are of the same mind."

Interest piqued, Reagan fingered the fine pearls around her neck and asked, "Is Penelope your beloved?"

"Yes. It may be an impossible task, but I'm trying to earn back her trust, and hopefully, her regard."

Reagan nodded sagely. "Then you're going to need roses. Rhiannon's arrangements have a way of changing even the hardest of hearts."

I retrieved my wallet from my back pocket and pulled out my debit card. "You'd better ring me up for a few dozen, because, after what I've done, this particular heart may be a little harder than most."

I left Fairy Tale Florists and headed home feeling both lighter and conflicted. While delivering flowers for the ladies would give me a much-needed chance to see Penelope outside of her job at the Chinese buffet, it was also just a front—one that made me feel like a great big douche for lying about my circumstances to the ladies to get the job. It was true I did need steady employment, but it was only for appearance's sake. I didn't need money. After six hundred years of devious deals and double-crossing demon activity, I'd amassed quite a bit of wealth and wouldn't be strapped for cash for the next millennium or so. What I was strapped for was a reason to stay in town. The more Penelope saw me around, making an effort to call Havenwood Falls my home and not just my occasional crash pad, the better.

I shook my head as I internally berated myself. It seemed funny to me now—the way I used to be. I had been the most cunning and deceptive demon I knew, save for a few megalomaniacal examples. There hadn't been a creature—demon, human, or otherwise—that I cared one fig about. Then I met Penelope, and everything started to change. I started to change.

My priorities, once selfish and self-centered, were becoming focused on the one thing that really mattered—the sweet and funny half-demon woman that had no inkling she wasn't one hundred percent human.

Sadly, as much as I had wanted to do the right thing by her, my careless, reckless demon nature made a wreck of everything. Once I had gained everything I wanted in Penelope—her reluctant admiration, her trust—I traded it all away on a crazy roundabout plan that nearly got her killed because I was prone to go into every situation with guns blazing instead of thinking about what the outcome could end up being.

Kidnapping her? Taking her to be imprisoned (however temporarily) by a demon I knew wouldn't care if she ended up a casualty? I honestly didn't know what I had been thinking, and if she never forgave me, I wouldn't blame her.

CHAPTER 2

"Hey, Mrs. Claus! I'm home!" I yelled, opening the holiday-bedecked door of a house that had been painstakingly decorated more than a full month early.

The Homes for the Holidays tour was a big deal in Havenwood Falls. At least, that was what I was always told and retold by my benevolent benefactress when she deigned to speak to me.

My best incubus friend, Cameron DeSalle, and his Christmas-obsessed wife, Mavis, had been gracious enough to allow me to stay with them for almost a year, both here and at their apartment in Havenwood Village. As grateful as I was for the hospitality, the absolute best part about the arrangement was that I got to annoy Mavis pretty much all day, every day. Getting her riled up to the point she was angry enough to use her rarely seen ice demon abilities was one of my favorite pastimes. Though I have to say, those ice balls she'd learned to create hurt like a bitch when she aimed for my head.

"Oh, super," Mavis grouched, coming into the living room with a pink apron tied around her waist and a smudge of flour on her cheek. "It's you."

I grinned at the tiny blond beauty and used my thumb to wipe away the flour. "The one and only. Did you miss me, or did you and the elves keep yourselves occupied this morning?"

I grinned at her feisty little expression of indignation as she swatted my hand away. As much as I gave her shit for it and as bizarre as it was to see a demon so domestic, I really did love coming home to the extravagant Christmas display she'd created. I planned on helping to make it an even bolder one by hanging about a million and a half strands of sparkly lights outside after Halloween. She tolerated the very sight of me every day, so I figured, at the least, she deserved pretty lights to make up for it.

"Me? Miss you?" She harrumphed and headed back to the kitchen. "Yeah, I missed you—like a human misses the flu. What are you even doing here, Ray? I thought you were out for a walk."

"It's Rayonus," I corrected, teasing her with our usual argument over the use of my nickname. It was more fun with Penelope, but Mavis always did well in a pinch.

She rolled her eyes. "Fine. Rayonus."

"Thank you," I said, preening at my little battle won. "And I was out for a walk. But something quite unexpected happened while I was out."

"Penelope told you to go fuck yourself again?" she guessed. "She said she saw you this morning."

I took a freshly baked sugar cookie off a cooling sheet pan and popped a piece of it in my mouth. "No. Well, yes, but that's not that unexpected, is it?"

She pressed her lips together and let out a long-suffering sigh through her nose. "Not lately."

"So, what happened?" Cameron asked, walking into the kitchen to join us. He kissed his wife on the cheek and stole a cookie before lifting himself onto the opposite counter to watch her work.

Making myself comfortable on a barstool, I smiled at the pair. "I got a job today."

"Don't you already have a job?" Cam asked, dark brows furrowed over his amber-colored eyes.

"I do, but twice-a-week ghost tours aren't exactly keeping me in the lavish lifestyle I deserve."

"Lavish lifestyle?" Mavis asked. "How're you going to manage that? Are you planning on picking up Cameron's old line of work?"

Cam burst out laughing. "I don't think Rayonus would make a good escort. He lacks a certain . . . um, let's call it 'finesse.'"

She shrugged and cocked her head to the side as she examined me. "I don't know. Look at him, babe. The lean, muscled physique, the tight ass-hugging jeans, that one blue eye and one black demon eye—as much as I hate to say it, he's got that tall, dark, and intriguing thing going on. Who wouldn't jump at the chance to get him into bed?"

"Penelope, for one," Cam answered, jumping off the counter to pull her away from me. "And you, for a second. Have you forgotten what an asshole he is? You have to be nice to people to make the kind of money I made."

"You know, I am standing right here," I griped, though I was incredibly bemused at Mavis's surprisingly positive assessment of my appearance. "You'd think you guys would be more excited about the prospect of me moving out."

Mavis perked up. "Move out? You didn't mention moving out. Where are you working? When can you leave?"

I rolled my eyes. "Your caring and compassion for my feelings really know no bounds."

"Hey, I didn't kill my evil fake grandfather and buy this gigantic house with the money I inherited for no reason," she said. "I want to spend some uninterrupted time with my husband that you can't hear . . . or ridicule."

"Or critique," Cam added.

"So you can christen every piece of furniture in the house?" I asked. "You know, you could say I've been doing your future guests a great service by staying here."

"How do you know we haven't christened the furniture even

with you living here?" Cam asked, wrapping his arms around his wife and planting more than a friendly kiss on her neck.

I shivered at the thought of the two naked demons on the settee where I read my copy of *Sun & Moon Tribune* every Sunday. "Can we get back to my job at Fairy Tale Florists?"

Cam's mouth dropped open. "You're working for Reagan and Rhiannon?"

I nodded. "I'll be delivering flowers on a trial basis, but regardless of whether it works out or not, I'm moving back into your old apartment in Havenwood Village. I should have done it already. I signed the lease right after you bought the house."

Mavis gaped at me, her blue-gray eyes wide with shock. "You cannot be serious. Tell me you're not serious." She groaned. "Penny is going to flip her shit when she sees you've moved in next door to her."

"She can flip whatever she likes. I liked that apartment. It was home. I should've just stayed in it when you guys moved here."

"She will not thank you for this," Cam warned.

"Tell me something I don't know."

"I'll tell you something you don't know," Mavis hissed. "If you steal another cookie off this sheet to eat your feelings, I'm going to stab you with an icicle."

I looked down at the two small Christmas-tree-shaped cookies in my hands and smiled winsomely before shoving them in my mouth.

"Get out of my kitchen!" she yelled. "Both of you!"

"Yes, ma'am," I said around my ill-gotten sweets. "Love you, Mom."

She threw an oven mitt at my head as Cam started to bodily drag me to the living room. "Fucking annoying but lovable demons."

Once we were out of throwing range, Cam said, "Speaking of parents. Have you thought any more about the Penelope situation?"

"Can you be more specific?" I asked, hedging a bit. "I have many Penelope situations at the moment."

"Her parentage," he clarified.

I winced. I had been hoping they would give up on their mission to be the saintliest demons in Colorado until I had a chance to make Penelope love me again. Or, at the least, until she liked me again. I needed more time to make sure she would be safe if she ran off all half-cocked to find her asshole of a father. The demon's intricate world of brokering souls and bullying each other into whatever was the scheme du jour wasn't a place I wanted Penelope in. She was an innocent. She didn't realize her best friends, Cam and Mavis, were an exception to most demons. As demonic as they thought they were, they were different. They had consciences. They were raised to value life and be kind, just like Penny was. The majority of demons didn't value anything but themselves.

"Well?" he pressed.

"I have thought about it, Cam. You know I have. I just don't think right now is the time to spring that kind of news on her. She's already pissed at me. I don't want her pissed at you guys, too."

"I feel like a schmuck for keeping this from her for so long. She's not a kid anymore. We have to tell her soon."

"I don't want to lose her, Cam. Just give me a little more time."

Cam threw up his hands. "It's been more than seven months since she's spoken anything other than insults to you!" he hissed, glancing furtively in Mavis's direction. "Has it occurred to you that you may have already lost her?"

"Only every fucking day," I told him, my voice flat.

His face grew sympathetic as he calmed. "We have to do it soon, Rayonus. It's killing Mavis."

I sighed, hating that I had to keep secrets from my friends. I wanted so much to be able to tell him and Mavis the truth about my procrastination, to explain the reasons why telling Penelope would be a monumentally bad idea. But I just wasn't ready to expose myself because, as always in the case of demons, ignorance was definitely bliss.

Instead of doing the right thing and telling him all that, I said, "You know, Cameron, life was a lot easier when I had no morals. I was happy. I was carefree. I got laid. Wait. Why am I doing this again?"

"Because you love our fair Penelope," he said, clapping me on the back. "And you're not the half the jerk you used to be."

"Yeah, well, I wish I believed that."

Leaving Cam to his thoughts, I grabbed my jacket and stepped out into the cold October air, angry and desperate. The rage that had been building inside of me for the past year was a nearly tangible thing. I wanted out of this. I wanted a life—one without lies and deception.

But that was impossible and always would be. Because, though I might be walking around a free demon, in reality, I was caged— not by my secret assignment here in Havenwood Falls or the hierarchy of demons—by my fear, the fear that I would lose them all from my life if I told them the truth. They'd forgiven me after my first significant betrayal without any explanation. Another revelation could sever their faith in me forever. That was something I wasn't willing to risk.

CHAPTER 3

*T*he next day, I arrived at Fairy Tale Florists early, hoping to learn as much as I could about the process before my first actual delivery. Finding the first floor empty, I climbed the stairs to find the second-floor offices much the same.

"Hello?" I called, listening for any noise.

"Rayonus? Is that you?" Rhiannon answered, climbing down from what must have been the turret. "I was just doing a little meditating. Are you ready to get started?"

I gave her an eager smile. "I am. What do we do first?"

"Follow me," she said, returning the smile.

It turned out there wasn't much to my job as a delivery driver. The names and addresses were checked and double-checked by a meticulous Reagan. The flowers were artfully arranged by the skillful hands of Rhiannon. It seemed my only tasks were loading the flowers into a specially designed van bearing the Fairy Tale Florists logo and driving them to various businesses and residences in the town tout de suite. I could do that. For Penelope, I could do any number of things.

The paperwork Reagan gave me a few short minutes of instruction later showed that my first delivery would take me straight to the source of all my stress. It was a hell of a way for the ladies to start me out, but one thing was for sure—every delivery after Penelope's would be a piece of cake. If I survived the interaction with all my appendages intact, that was.

After I loaded the massive arrangement into the van, I took a deep, steadying breath and drove straight to Havenwood Village. I knew Penelope would be home right now. She never went in to her job at Sakura Buffet before eleven. If my calculations were correct, she'd be smack in the middle of applying her makeup and trying to do something with her mass of beautiful long brunette curls right now.

I pulled into the parking lot a scant two minutes later and took another deep breath. And when I struggled to remove the vase from the contraption that kept it upright, I took another. Turning away from the flowers, I stared at her door. I had walked in and out of that door a hundred times, and during every one of those times, I had been the happiest I'd been in more than six centuries. Penelope was the most important thing in my life, and I would earn back her trust. Maybe it wouldn't be today or tomorrow, but it would come eventually. The weird relationship we'd fostered together was too important to both of us to stay like this forever.

In a better headspace, I turned my attention back to the task at hand and had to admit, while insanely huge and hard to manage, the roses and soft white flowers Rhiannon wove together with just the perfect amount of greenery were a thing of beauty. As soon as she told me orange roses indicated enthusiasm and passion, I knew there would be no other choice. I passionately and enthusiastically wanted Penelope back in my life. She had taken that sentiment to heart, creating an arrangement nothing short of a masterpiece.

Smiling wanly, I finally popped the vase loose and hefted the flowers onto one hip to knock on Penelope's door, waiting as patiently as one could for what was sure to be a disaster of epic proportions.

The door swung open almost immediately. "Hi! Oh, my gosh! They're stunning! Come in!"

I knew she would most likely react badly when she realized the identity of her delivery person, but I stepped in and took the chance, praying that this wouldn't be the last time she invited me into her apartment with that level of happiness.

"Just set them on the coffee table," she instructed, pure sunshine in her voice.

Fuck me; I didn't want to take that away from her. The absolute joy was like a balm to my aching soul.

Setting the flowers on the table, I had a mad urge to snatch the card from the holder before she saw it. This was too much. It was too soon. She wasn't ready to forgive me. What had I been thinking?

But it was too late. She'd plucked the card out of the middle before I had a chance to make my move.

"Thanks," she said, her eyes going from the tiny envelope to mine. "Ray."

I stiffened at the coldness in her voice but wanted to bask in her radiance like a housecat in the sun. Her hair was in a messy bun, and she had only lined one eye, but she was more beautiful than anything I'd ever seen. "Hello, Penelope."

Her gaze moved from my eyes to the logo on my chest. "You work for the florist now?"

I nodded. "I just started this morning. This is actually my very first delivery."

Her expression unreadable, she opened the envelope and pulled out the card.

"A secret admirer?" she asked, holding it out to show it to me.

"That is what it seems to say," I agreed, breathing an inward sigh of relief and thanking my lucky stars Rhiannon had the foresight to leave my name off the card.

She frowned. "Really, Ray. Are these from you?"

I shrugged and shook my head, hoping like hell that I looked innocent for once in my long life. "I'm afraid not."

Penelope knew me better than anyone else and probably didn't believe a word I was saying, but instead of fighting me on it as she was wont to do, she turned her attention to the flowers, stroking her index finger lightly over the delicate petals of a rose. "Thanks, Ray."

"It's my pleasure."

She didn't look up. "You need to go now."

"Of course," I said, giving her a ridiculous little bow that I would berate myself for later. "Have a good day at work."

Finally drawing her eyes away from the roses, she said, "You, too, Rayonus."

My name. She had used my name.

I beamed as I turned to leave. This felt like a win, and after the incident that had ruined things between us, I would take any progress I could get.

The incident . . .

What a colossal cock-up that had been.

Every time I thought about how close I'd come to losing everyone that meant anything to me, I wanted to sink into a deep, dark hole and wallow in my stupidity. But, at this point, so many months after, there was nothing I could do that hadn't already been done, no apology that hadn't been made. I'd made my bed with my choices, and it was time to stop hoping for Penny's forgiveness and start putting an actual plan into motion to gain that forgiveness. Nothing less would work with her, and I felt like an idiot for not realizing that from the start.

Moving back into the apartment I'd shared with Cameron and Mavis turned out to be much easier than I expected it to be. Partly because I chose a time in the early morning when I knew Penny would still be asleep, and partly because I was ecstatic to be so close to her, especially after what I was choosing to assume was an overture of civility the day before. I had practically hurtled everything I had to my name the short way to Havenwood Village with a genuine smile on my face.

Once I was done and sitting on the floor with my pitifully few belongings, though, I did feel a keen sense of loneliness, it wasn't something I was unused to; I'd always been alone before I came to stay in Havenwood Falls, but over the last year, I'd become so accustomed to Mavis's sarcastic and sometimes hurtful and painfully accurate quips and Cam's brotherly honesty and reprimands, I knew living on my own again would be an adjustment. They were, unequivocally, my family. Of course, family could be a giant pain in the ass, and I did have the comforting assurance that I could always visit Mavis for my daily abuse, so there was that.

Sighing, I picked myself up and shook off the feelings of dread and worry. I needed furniture and a lot of other little things that I should have taken care of a long time before I moved in. As much as I wanted it to, that kind of thing wasn't going to happen by itself.

Setting out on foot, I walked the short way to Room and dropped in on Melissa Lewis, where she helped me spend an exorbitant amount of money on things to make my living space homey. She assured me that was important, and I wasn't about to argue. After living with Mavis for so long, I knew better than to second-guess a woman who knew her stuff about decorating. After that, I made my way over to Callie's Consignments, where I spent an hour or so picking out furniture with Nikita, an unfamiliar death spirit. I arranged all of my purchases to be shipped to my apartment by CDI in a couple of days, though after I made the spur-of-the-moment decision to visit the human, Joshua, at Havenwood Falls Garage & Tow Service to buy the shiny silver pickup truck he had for sale, I had the means to move them myself. I figured the less time I spent traipsing in and out, the less chance of Penny imploding when she found out.

In the driver's seat of my new-to-me truck, I felt better, almost stronger. *I can do this,* I thought. I could live here full time in Havenwood Falls. It would be easy to become one of the fold. It would always be a little tainted by my secrets, but I could do this.

For the chance to spend my life with Penny, I could do just about anything.

I showered and set up the TV on the bedroom floor after I returned to the apartment. Turning on a mindless sitcom, I rolled my puffy blue sleeping bag out on the carpet in front, stopping still, then landing heavily on my ass when the memory of the last time I'd used it—or hadn't used it—came barreling back.

It had been in the igloo, Mavis's wild idea of roughing it on the mountain in late March. Penelope and I had gotten drunk on Fireball and each other, both of us falling into her two-person sleeping bag to snuggle after Cam and Mavis went to "sleep." That had been the first time she'd kissed me, and it had met every expectation and desire I'd dreamed up inside my head. Her lips had been warm and soft, despite the cold. The taste of her? Cinnamon, whiskey, and Penelope. She had been a goddess that night, unabashedly telling me her secret fantasies and whispering things so dirty, I thought my brain would overheat from my desire for her.

I shook my head, ridding myself of the image of her flushed cheeks as she let go of her inhibitions that night. I couldn't dwell on what had been between us. Starting tomorrow, I was saying fuck it. Screw any fear I felt. I was starting fresh. Anything my friends asked, I would tell them. Anything they needed from me to prove myself trustworthy, I would give it to them. My decision had been made. After hundreds of years of lies, fake identities, and coercion, I wanted something real. The demon hierarchy be damned. They could find someone else to do my job.

CHAPTER 4

$\mathcal{O}$n my way out to work the next morning, the first obstacle in my grand plan hit me. Or rather, a hurricane of déjà vu hit me as I walked out my door to see the same cross look on Penelope's face that she wore the entirety of Mavis and Cam's beautiful gazebo wedding in the square this summer. She had looked stunning in her pale blue maid of honor dress, but it was that look that had nearly stopped my heart. That look had haunted me and had distracted me so thoroughly, I almost missed it when an amused-looking Addie Beaumont dropped the f-bomb as she pronounced my favorite demon couple husband and wife.

Arms crossed, which only served to compound that angry look, Penelope asked, "Seriously?" bringing me out of my reverie.

Like a dumbass who had learned nothing from his past mistakes, my first instinct was to feign ignorance. "Pardon?"

"Forget it," she said, angrily stomping back toward her door.

Lurching forward, I put a light hand on her shoulder to halt her escape. "Wait a minute, Penelope."

She stopped but didn't face me. "What?"

The need to be honest with this young woman was a brute force inside me, a constant banging in my head and heart telling me to do the decent thing. It screamed at me to not be stupid this time, to tell the truth for once in my miserable life.

"I'm done lying to you," I said, finally finding my voice. "I want to earn your trust."

Turning suddenly, she poked my chest, her eyes ablaze with rage. "Bullshit."

"I'll tell you anything you want to know," I swore. "Anything."

Penelope stared at me. Then she hastily grabbed my hand to drag me into her apartment. "Come on."

Once the door was closed behind us and we were away from prying ears, she dropped my hand and whirled on me. "Why did you do it? Why did you kidnap me and set up Cam and Mavis to get captured last March? Just tell me the truth, Rayonus. I have to know."

I took a deep breath and began, more than ready to get this off my chest. "Ever since the day Severin brought Cameron to Havenwood Falls as a child, I've been tasked with keeping an eye on the activities of the cambions and other half-demons here. I am what the demons call a watcher."

A furrow creased her forehead. She had not been expecting that. "What?"

"There is a hierarchy within the demon ranks," I explained. "Those above me asked me to befriend demons who have children in Havenwood Falls to make sure they toe the line, and in return, they would forgive certain indiscretions of mine."

"So, you're like a spy?"

"A mole would be more accurate. I blend in, see what they're up to, then try to covertly stop them if they're using their younglings as weapons of mass destruction."

"That makes no sense," Penny said. "Weren't you Severin's evil henchman for like a hundred years?"

"Yes, and I'm not going to say aligning myself with Cameron's father didn't serve me well. Not all of what Severin got up to was world domination. We had our hands in a lot of pies and made a lot of money."

"So, what does that have to do with Severin's master plan to own Mavis and you kidnapping me to get her in his grasp?"

"Everything, really," I told her, taking a seat on her couch. "What I did was a means to an end. And as stupid, illogical, and hurtful as my plan was, it worked. Severin is dead, and you all are safe. I did what my assignment dictated me to do."

She sat next to me. "Do Cameron and Mavis know about this? About you?"

I shook my head. "I'm not supposed to tell the younglings or the parent, though sometimes it's unavoidable."

She pursed her lips. "So, you're telling me because it's unavoidable?"

"No, I'm telling you because I don't want to keep secrets from you anymore," I told her, risking rejection and a missing limb to cup her face in my hand. "I can't bear to hurt you more than I already have, and honestly, that angry, disappointed face you wear when you see me is making me feel . . . well, things—things I don't want to ever feel again."

Penelope stared at me, her face softening. "I want to trust you, Ray."

"Then trust me," I implored.

Shaking her head, she pulled away and stood. "How can I? You're basically telling me you're a glorified demon babysitter, which, by the way, makes you the absolute worst babysitter in the world. You almost got Cam and Mavis killed."

"Technically, Mavis was never in any danger. Severin would have roughed her up, but he wouldn't have done any permanent damage."

"Severin shot Cameron!" she exclaimed. "He could have died if he wasn't half-demon. And then you disappeared for two weeks after you brought me back to town. Where did you go? Didn't you care what happened to Cam and Mavis after we left them there with Cam's crazy-ass dad?"

I stood up and took her hand in mine. "Of course I cared, Penny. Who do you think cleaned that whole mess up? Do you think all of Severin's foot soldiers just disappeared after Mavis disintegrated him with her demon-killing power? Do you think they forgot she was the fabled Exitium Daemonium? Severin told everyone in his circle about her and his plan. I had to make sure they didn't come to Havenwood Falls for her themselves. Her safety—the safety of all of you—depended on them being taken out of the equation."

"I didn't think of that," she admitted.

"I didn't want you to think of it. And it would have been easier to tell you, but I wanted you guys to feel safe in your homes. I had already put you through enough to end that asshole's reign of terror."

She sighed. "If you just would've told us all this from the start, we could've stopped him some other way. We could have saved so much heartache."

"I couldn't tell you, Penny. Severin had a clairvoyant working for him." I pulled the ability-curbing amulet out of my shirt. "I was protected, but your minds would have been wide open to her."

"It's been seven months since all that. Why are you telling me now?"

I brushed a wild curl back from her face with my free hand. "I want you."

"Me?" she asked.

Lost in the beautiful brown of her solemn eyes, I said, "It can't be a secret, how much I care about you, how much I care about all of you."

"Then you need to tell Cam and Mavis. They deserve the truth."

"I'm pretty much an imposter, Penny. Do you really think Cam is going to be okay with me lying to him for a hundred years?"

Penelope threaded her fingers with mine. "You're not an imposter, Rayonus. You're his best guy friend. Friends forgive each other."

"Do you forgive me, Penelope? Are you my friend? I'm a demon. I do thoughtless, dangerous demon shit. Look how easy it was for me to lose you. Do you think he's going to overlook this right after I almost got him killed?"

She hesitated, biting her lip in thought before answering my questions. "Yes, I forgive you. And of course you're my friend. But it's going to take some time to trust you again fully. It will be the same for Cam. Trust me; I know him much better than you do. He'll sulk and be pissed for a day, but then he'll come around."

Unable to stop myself, I pulled her into my arms and hugged her to my chest, reveling in her scent and the warmth of her body against mine. "I have an eternity. I can wait as long as it takes."

She grinned up at me. "Well, I don't have an eternity, so I don't think it will take quite that long."

"About that . . . ," I replied, only to be cut off by the ringing doorbell.

With an apologetic little smile, she pulled away and opened the door. Standing there were a grinning Cam and Mavis, both carrying takeout bags.

"We have breakfast burritos!" Mavis chirped, before her eyes fell on the unexpected demon in the room. "Ray? What are you doing here?"

While every part of me wanted to barrel through the couple and run far, far away, I knew that wasn't what was needed right now. It was time to come clean to the people I cared about. "Guys, we need to talk."

Wary, they both stepped into the apartment.

"What's going on?" Mavis asked, her eyes darting from me to Penelope.

I froze. How was I going to do this? I didn't even know where to start.

"Oh, for fuck's sake!" Penelope cried, throwing her hands up. "Ray is secretly some kind of super demon babysitter, and he's been assigned to Havenwood Falls by his demon bosses or whatever."

Cameron barked out a laugh. "Demon babysitter, huh? I don't recall you telling me any bedtime stories when I was a boy."

"It's true," I told him. "The hierarchy assigned Havenwood Falls to me when you were a toddler. There was an inordinate number of children that belonged to demons here at the time."

Stunned, Cameron sobered. "You're not kidding, are you?"

I blew out a heavy sigh. "No. I'm sorry I didn't tell you sooner. I should have, but it just got harder and harder as the years went on."

His voice ice-cold, he asked, "Because you were working with my father?"

"No!" I exclaimed. "I only worked with Severin because it was my job to know what your parents are up to."

"Our parents?" Mavis asked. "Ray, tell me you didn't know my grandfather was fake the whole time."

"I didn't," I swore. "I didn't know anything about you. I only found out you existed when Leon LeGrand came to Severin the day you ran away from him to ask him to use his clairvoyant to locate you. Utah wasn't in my jurisdiction."

"But you knew after?" Cam asked.

"Yes. And I did try to do what I could to help keep you both safe. Severin was so secretive about the whole Exitium Daemonium deal at the beginning. It was all I could do to keep one step ahead of them."

"One step ahead?" Cam growled. "My wife had to kill a pervert demon that broke into our apartment."

"Franco Ross was that demon," I supplied. "And the jerk was only there because I convinced Severin to send him in his stead to see what Mavis was capable of. She would have been taken if Severin came himself. He'd already had the Alchemist make an amulet to repel her magic. I made the only choice I had available to me." Turning my attention to Mavis, I said, "I'm really sorry you had to kill someone. That is not what I had hoped would happen."

"Apology accepted," Mavis replied, shrugging as she stood to start pacing the living room. "But I don't get it. Why didn't you tell us about this?"

Then she stopped, her mouth dropping open as the pieces clicked into place. "That was the woman who got in my head right before I killed Severin that day. That was his clairvoyant."

I nodded, relieved at the noticeable lack of anger in her voice, and pulled out the amulet around my neck again. "This is the only thing that saved my ass while I was there. It blocked her mindreading ability."

"I didn't know she could read my mind," Cam said, clearly thinking back to how much he'd unknowingly given away without even realizing it. "I just knew she was dangerous. How could I have been so careless?"

"Who would've guessed psychic?" I asked. "I was just lucky I had the amulet. Don't beat yourself up about it now that all that's behind us."

"Is it behind us, though?" Mavis asked.

"If you're asking if she's dead, then yes, I killed her. I killed them all. And I have no regrets for doing it. You guys' safety was and is my only concern."

Penelope sat on the couch and fished a breakfast burrito out of one of the bags, looking nonplussed. "Yeah, great. Everyone is dead. But let's back this thing up here." Taking a bite, she chewed for a moment, then asked, "If you didn't know about Mavis's parent, who are the other demon kids you referred to? You said, 'your parents' in the plural earlier."

Cameron and Mavis both gave me significant looks when I didn't answer Penelope's question right away. I returned it with a meaningful look of my own.

Alarmed, Penelope watched our game of facial charades for a moment, then her face crumpled. "Oh, fuck. It's me, isn't it?"

"Yes," we all answered in unison.

I added, "Only on your father's side. Your mother was human."

She rose, throwing the burrito on top of the paper bag. "Get out," she said, shooing us none too gently toward the door. "Now!"

Mavis sniffled. "We wanted to tell you, Penny. Please don't be mad."

Turning away from us once we reached the door, Penelope whispered, "Just go, Mavis. Just leave me alone."

Without another word, we did as she asked, though leaving her and hearing all the pain in her voice nearly broke me.

Outside, Cam stared at her closed door and asked, "What just happened?"

I checked my watch and sighed. "I happened, Cameron. I asked you not to tell her. If it's not perfectly clear, that's my demon gift. I fuck shit up. I destroy everything I fucking touch, and fuck me, it's fucked up timing, but duty is calling me in the form of a tasteful arrangement of posies due to be delivered to a human woman from a lovestruck werewolf. Apparently, time is of the fucking essence with these wolfy courtships."

Despite the shitty situation, the corners of Mavis's mouth quirked up. "That was an admirable number of fucks, Ray."

I smiled down at the petite little ice demon, surprised by her composure with the whole situation. "I can assure you. I meant every single one of them."

She returned my smile for only a moment, thinking better of it. "Dinner. Tonight at seven. Okay? Come prepared to talk. You've been excessively sneaky, and that ends tonight, or I'm putting you in timeout. Capisce?"

Hugging her to my side, I kissed the top of her head. "I'll be there, Mom." I held my hand out to Cameron. "Are we okay, Dad?"

After a second's hesitation, he shook it. "See you tonight, asshole."

Mavis rolled her eyes and looped her arm with her husband's. "Fucking annoying but lovable demons."

With one last look at Penelope's closed door, I saluted the two and ran for my truck, yelling, "Thanks, guys!"

CHAPTER 5

*a*fter my deliveries for the day were made, I didn't go home right away. Penelope was hurt, and if my history with her had taught me anything, it was that hurt eventually turned into seething hot anger. I would need to give her a wide berth for as long as I could. At the very least, until she stopped shooting the invisible laser beams of death out of her eyes.

Ducking into Howe's Herbal Shoppe, I took my time hand-picking bath bombs to be put in a fancily wrapped sage green gift box. Then I ran over to Sanguine Elixirs to get a bottle of the French champagne she liked. My plan was to get Penelope something I knew she'd love; something so lovely, it wouldn't end up in some weird science project on my doorstep the next day. Baths and booze were her two favorite things after the TV series *Supernatural* and pretty much every character from *Supernatural*. Except for Dick Roman, of course. Because, well, he was a dick, and she had season seven issues.

After splurging on the champagne and a couple of nice bottles of red wine for dinner, I took the things I'd bought for Penelope over to the OutPost Pack & Ship and had them carefully boxed together with a handwritten card I signed *from your secret admirer* in a moment of pure, unadulterated cowardice. I was not the proud, sardonic demon I usually was on this day. No. This was a new day, and on this day, I felt just as insecure as anyone else whose future relationships hung in the balance.

By the time I was done with my errands and back in my truck, I had just enough time to get to Cam and Mavis's house for dinner. With only a few moments to spare, I pulled into their driveway to find a frustrated Cam trying to unravel the various twinkle lights he was pulling out of a giant box. He looked absolutely miserable.

"Hey," I called, sliding out of the truck with the bottles of wine. "Need some help?"

"Yeah, go get two glasses and a corkscrew. No, fuck it. Just bring the corkscrew. We can drink out of the bottles."

"Things going that well out here, huh?"

He growled in frustration as he threw the twisted and tangled mess back into the box. "Why does she insist on reusing everything she found in the attic? These lights look like they saw their heyday in the eighties."

"Then this would be an excellent time to tell you about the multitude of brand new LEDs hidden in the garage?"

"Don't toy with me, Rayonus. I'm a man on the edge."

I laughed. "It's true. I had Blaekthorn Lumber and Supply call me as soon as they put them out on the shelf. I thought they might appease Buddy the Elf in there until we could get the actual trees."

Cam rolled his eyes in exasperation. "I ask you. Who decorates fake Christmas trees, then takes them all down to put up real ones? A year ago, she didn't even decorate. I don't know what's happened to her."

I shrugged. "We had a nice family moment, picking out that tree last year and decorating it."

"Hmph," he muttered. "Don't think I've forgotten that you also perpetuated Penelope's obsession with *Supernatural* with that nice family moment. Didn't we have enough of Castiel in our lives without looking at him on the top of the tree every day?"

"No," I retorted. "Because, unlike you, I'm not jealous of some fictional character. You know, just because Mavis had super-secret fantasies about doing it with Misha Collins, and you were too much of a horndog incubus to tell her no, doesn't mean you have to hate on Penelope's favorite character."

Disgusted, he said, "Ugh. You sound just like her."

I inclined my head. "I will take that as a compliment and hang on to it like a lifeline, thank you."

"You haven't heard from her, then?" he asked.

"Not at all, but I didn't really expect to. You?"

"Yeah, she called a couple of hours after we left and asked for more burritos to be left at her door."

I smirked. "Weren't there three burritos in each of those bags you left behind?"

Cam nodded. "Yes. Which is why she called an hour after the original burrito delivery with a request for ginger ale and Pepto Bismol."

"She's taking this to the extreme a bit, isn't she?"

"This *is* Penelope we're talking about," he reminded me. "It's your classic high drama, then sad, then angry, then over it scenario."

Grinning at the highly accurate description of my lady love's emotional process, I clapped him on the back. "Come on. We'll put this mess away after dinner and a few drinks."

He looked at the jumble of different styles of string lights and kicked the side of the box. "We're going to have to bury this thing like a body."

"Drinks first," I called from the porch. "Disposal of the Ghost of Christmas Past later."

Mavis had set a lovely tablescape for dinner—white candles, a pine cone and holly centerpiece, and actual crystal wine glasses to go with the delicate white gold detail of her wedding china. She was even using the gravy boat I bought to match—which, for her, was a bit disturbing.

"This is stunning, Mavis," I said, kissing her on her cheek and simultaneously taking the basket of what smelled like butter rolls covered in a white cloth napkin from her hands. "I would have changed out of my work clothes if I'd known we were having a fancy dinner."

"This isn't a fancy dinner," she corrected, pointing to where she wanted the bread placed. "It's a celebration. And I like seeing you in your work shirt. You don't look as shifty and useless as you usually do."

"Uh, thanks?"

"Don't mention it. Now give me that wine and go wash up for dinner. Our guest of honor will be here in a minute."

I groaned. "Please don't tell me it's Penny. You know she isn't past the initial shock. It will end badly."

"No, it won't," she insisted. "Because we're going to go out of our way to tell her all the good things about being a demon, and I'm going to get really, really drunk."

"There are good things about being a demon?" I asked, scrunching up my face. "Can you fill me in on some of the finer points before she gets here?"

She gave a martyred sigh. "Just go wash your hands before I put this meat fork to good use."

Grinning, I stepped out of her reach and blew her a kiss. "Am I going to have to call child protective services on you, Mom?"

"Either that or I'm going to end up smothering you with a pillow by the end of the night."

"Hey, that hits too close to home, Mavis. My mother did try to smother me with a pillow."

She gasped, horrified at her choice of words. "Oh, my gosh! I'm so sorry! I didn't mean anything by that!"

"I'm just kidding," I said, laughing as I walked to the sink. "She tried to drown me."

Narrowing her eyes, she shook her head. "I can't imagine why."

Penelope showed up only a few minutes after we popped the cork on the first wine bottle. Avoiding eye contact with me, she slid into her usual spot at the table and held out her glass.

"Are you sure drinking is a good idea, Penny?" Mavis asked, hesitantly picking up the bottle. Clearly, she was having visions of a drunk demon crying on her shoulder all night.

"Yes, it's a good idea," Penelope snapped. "As a matter of fact, you drink your shit wine over there on the counter. I'll drink the two bottles Ray brought."

Puzzled, Cam asked, "How did you know Rayonus brought wine?"

"As I said, you buy shit wine. Ray is the only one with an eye for the good stuff."

"It's not so much the eye as it is the price. If it's over thirty-five bucks and foreign, it's a safe bet that it's a good bottle of wine."

She stared at me, her face shocked. "You are much less suave and debonair than I thought you were. Why am I not surprised?"

"Because I'm a demon?"

Penelope scoffed. "I'm a demon, too, and I'm refined as fuck."

"Without a doubt," I said, not about to engage with her while she was hovering between the angry and over-it stages of her demonic revelation.

"You may not be as urbane as I thought, but you can't deny that you're smart," she said, tipping her glass to me.

Smiling, I held her gaze. "I will take that as a compliment."

"And hang on to it like a lifeline?" Cam muttered under his breath.

I shot a glare at him as a too-bright Mavis jumped out of her seat and asked, "Who wants rolls?"

After a surprisingly explanation-free dinner and too many glasses of wine, Cam and I went in search of the LED lights to hang while Mavis and a pensive Penelope continued their boozefest in the living room. Because booze, plus demons, plus ladders were always a fine combination.

"Are you sure they're here?" Cam asked, looking in his fourth box to no avail.

Moving another box out of the way, I cursed. "They were here! They were in a brown box with green and red print on the outside. I don't get it!"

"Wait," Cam said, spying the box on the opposite side of the room. "There they are." Wading through the piles of boxes we'd moved, he picked it up and shook it. "I know LEDs are lightweight, but this seems a little too light."

I sighed upon noticing that the box had been tampered with. "I don't think you want to open that box."

He furrowed his face. "Why?"

"Oh, just a hunch."

Setting the box down, Cam nudged it like there was a live snake hidden under the lid. "Hold me, Ray. I'm scared."

I snickered as I knelt to rip off the loose tape. Peering inside, I fell back on my ass, cackling with laughter. Inside was a note written in black Sharpie that read, *I TOLD YOU TO USE THE LIGHTS FROM THE ATTIC.*

"Mavis!" Cam yelled. "You suck!"

Immediately following this proclamation, we heard intoxicated giggles from the living room.

"Never get married," Cam warned. "It's all downhill after the wedding."

I shrugged. "If anything, that makes me want to get married more."

CHAPTER 6

*H*ours later, with the ancient lights detangled, hung, and lit, I went inside to say my goodbyes to the ladies. Both were sprawled out on the couch watching *Aquaman* for the hundredth time this year.

"I'm leaving. Penny, can I give you a ride home?"

Mavis sighed, staring at Jason Momoa's bare chest. "I know who I want to give me a ride."

"Then you should've thought of that while I still had my full incubus abilities," Cam said, scooping her off the couch. "You'll have to settle for riding me tonight."

She made a show of pouting, but mouthed, "Yay!" to Penelope and me.

We both shuddered.

"You know," Penelope slurred. "I think I will take that ride, Ray."

"I thought you might," I said, getting her coat from the rack in the foyer. "Night, guys."

There was no answer.

"Hurry," Penelope urged, nearly stumbling into me. "Before we hear something."

Laughing, I helped her over the threshold as she wobbled and steadied herself.

She broke away and skipped to the passenger side of my truck, all smiles and excitement.

"I like your truck," she said as I opened her door.

"Thank you," I told her, making sure her long flowy skirt was tucked into the truck.

When I rounded the hood and got in the driver's seat, she added, "I think this suits you."

"How is that?"

"It's big and manly like you. And it's shiny and pretty, but you know, not too pretty. It's basically you in truck form."

My smile was tight as I backed out of the driveway. "I'm not a man, Penelope. I'm a demon—a dumb-ass demon that makes huge mistakes and hurts the ones he loves."

"Nooooo," she whined, holding her hands out in the stop position. "I don't want to talk about that. Talk to me about something else. Like literally anything else."

I pursed my lips, trying to think of a safe topic, but all I could think about was how much I loved this woman and how fucking amazing she was. I finally settled on, "Well, I can talk about how downright delectable you look in that red top."

She traced a finger down the V-neck of her sweater to her cleavage and asked, "This red top?"

My cock punched up painfully in my jeans, reminding me just how long it had been since I had been able to touch her. I cleared my throat. "Yes, ma'am."

"Do you want to see what's underneath it?" she asked, toying with the bottom hem.

I didn't take the bait. Eyes straight ahead, I ignored the temptation and drove us as fast as I could down Eighth Street, swinging into my parking place less than a minute later. Without a word, I turned the engine off, jumped out of the truck, and ran around to open her door.

Penelope laughed at my theatrics. "Is that a yes?"

"That's a 'hell yes,' you beautiful, sexy woman. But it's also a little bit, 'I think you're too drunk to make good decisions, so I'm getting you out of the public eye before you get yourself arrested for public indecency.'"

"I like handcuffs," she mused, pressing her breasts against my chest as she slid her arms around my neck.

"So I've heard," I said, trying to coax her out of her seat.

She wrapped her long legs around my waist and nipped at my neck, biting hard enough I knew it would leave a mark. "I want you to handcuff me, Rayonus."

I gripped her ass and blew out a shaky breath as pure lust pulsed through my body. "I want to bend you over this seat, rip your skirt apart, and fuck you until you scream out my name."

When I pulled away to look at her face, I had to fight the need to do everything I'd just said. Her eyes were fiery, hungry, and all-consuming. She wanted that. She wanted me. But this was Havenwood Falls, not a porn set. Irene Beckett would be sure to walk by and have the whole town buzzing before church tomorrow if we so much as removed one shoe. It was risky enough just doing what we were doing.

"We'll talk about all the sexual fantasies you like once you're in your apartment," I bribed, lifting her up to carry her to her door.

"That's going to be hard, since I seem to have left my purse and keys on the coffee table," she purred, smiling like the cat that ate the canary. "Wherever will I sleep?"

I shut the truck door with a foot and laughed at the absurdity of the situation as I carried her koala-style to my apartment door. I had my hands on Penelope's perfect ass. Her legs were around my waist, putting her in a very favorable position against me. And if the nuzzles and nips to my jawline were any indication, she wanted to do a good portion of the filthy things she'd mentioned that night in the igloo.

The only problem was I was a fucking gentleman—gentledemon—whatever.

I groaned and leaned back away from her roaming lips,

tongue, and teeth. "Penelope, as much as I'd like to give you that ride you asked for earlier, it can't happen tonight. When and if we ever fuck, I want you to be sober. I want to know you won't regret it, that you won't regret me."

Rolling her hips, she closed her eyes and breathed out a little contented sigh. "Trust me, Rayonus, regret is nowhere on my mind right now."

Hating what I was about to do, I eased her down to her feet and steadied her as she swayed slightly. "Penelope, I lied to you, put you in danger, and kept the biggest secret of your life from you. Tomorrow, when you're sober, you're going to remember that. You're going to remember all the pain and anger I've caused you."

I unlocked the door to reveal the empty apartment as she absorbed my words, all the while mentally bracing myself for her to revisit that anger, to strike out to hurt me as much as I hurt her, to give me the ass-kicking of an immortal lifetime, even. But she only cocked her head to the side and leered at the not-so-little problem in my work pants.

"I don't care," she said. "I want that."

I raised my brows and quickly shut the door behind us. "Say again?"

She bit her lip before speaking, but her eyes never strayed from the erection now throbbing in time to the beat of my heart. "I know I should care about all that. And I do. I'm drunk, not stupid. And I am mad. So, so fucking mad. And hurt. It took me so long to be able to trust you, and you fucked that sideways. But I realized something tonight at dinner."

"What's that?"

"I always held back when I thought I was human. I was scared of you—whether you'd be too much for me sexually or if you'd walk away once your overtly disturbing innuendos got you what you'd been after since we met."

I tensed as she spoke, my body taut with the need to show her who I truly was.

"What's changed?" I asked, closing my eyes and letting the façade I held onto for so long dissipate into nothing.

Penelope took an involuntary step back. "Rayonus, is this you? The real you?"

This was the real me, all right. I was showing her the form I hadn't seen for myself in decades. And I knew it might frighten her to see me as the black-eyed, seven-foot-tall, red-skinned demon I was born as. To human eyes, I looked like a thing of nightmares. But I needed her to see me as me, to see what was inside of me.

Reaching out, she touched the exposed skin at my collarbone, and I looked down, suddenly realizing that I'd ripped my shirt at the collar when I transformed.

"I'm sorry," I said, pulling off the shirt, then realizing I'd popped the button off my jeans. I held the shirt remnants low, covering myself.

She stared at me for a second, then did something wholly unexpected. She pounced on me, holding nothing back, knocking me to the floor and straddling me with her skirt bunched around her waist.

"What did you tell me you wanted to do earlier?" she asked, undulating her hips.

I spoke through clenched teeth as she brought all of my focus and resolve to a screeching halt.

"I want to bend you over," I said in a rough voice, fisting my clawed hand in her hair. "I want to rip your skirt apart," I continued, tearing open her red sweater to reveal a black lace bra.

She gasped as she moved against me. "And then what?"

Flipping her to her back, I growled, showing her my fangs as the heavy weight of my erection found her center. "I want to fuck you until you scream out my name."

Breathing heavily, we lunged for each other, both of us fighting for control in a clash of tongues, teeth, and fangs. Breaking away, I got to my knees and ripped my frayed pants open at the fly. A moment later, I was sheathed and ready for her. "Tell me to stop, Penelope."

She shook her head, slipping off her skirt and panties. Nearly naked, she rose to her knees in front of me, defiant as she met my tortured gaze. Her eyes were dark, fathomless, but her voice was as steady as stone as she smoothed her hand down the latex-covered length of me and said, "Never."

Every bit of restraint and self-control I had in me disappeared when I heard that word. In the fantasy I'd dreamed up over the past seven months, I'd pictured this moment to be a tender thing between us. I'd thought it would be slow, shy touches and languid kisses leading up to us making love.

Oh, how wrong I was.

This was rough. This was Penelope crashing her body into mine. It was me jerking her up to let her wrap her legs around my waist. It was her sex feeling like a blistering hot vise as she sank onto my cock. It was a year of wanting and need brought to an end.

"Fuck," she whispered, rolling her hips to grind against me. "Oh, fuck."

I stopped thinking. Hell, I stopped breathing. She was so impossibly beautiful with her lips parted, eyes closed in pleasure, and hair falling wildly around her. I wanted to own this demon woman. I wanted her to own me. I wanted us to be in each other's skin, for what we had together to be bone-deep within us, to be untouchable.

Grabbing her hips, I held her against me as I lay back on the carpet. She yelped in surprise at the sudden movement and opened her eyes to reveal the most predatory glare I'd ever seen on a lover. It was as if her hunger was consuming her from the inside out.

And that's when I noticed she had my amulet—the only thing that kept me together—wrapped around her hand.

CHAPTER 7

I woke to the unrelenting brightness of the sun in my face and a ringing in my head. Groaning, I rolled away from the window and opened my eyes, realizing the ringing was coming from the cell phone lying on the carpet next to me.

I picked it up and mumbled, "Hello?"

"What did you do?" a sly voice asked.

"We could be here all day with a vague question like that," I answered. "Want to narrow it down some?"

Mavis chuckled. "Oh, no. You know exactly what I'm talking about."

"No, I really don't. And honestly, I feel like I've been hit by a truck, so can we postpone this Q and A until later?"

"Rayonus, are you seriously not going to tell me how you managed to get Penny into your bed last night? Wait. Do you even have a bed yet?"

I sat up and dropped the phone, my hand going to the amulet that was, thankfully, back on my neck. Then my eyes widened in horror.

Penelope. Penelope had been here with me the night before. Frantic, I searched for the dropped phone and jammed it back to my ear. "What did she say? Is she okay?"

"Okay? Hmmm. Is she okay? Well, she moseyed all the way over here John Wayne style this morning because she couldn't walk right. I guess you could call that okay. And she's done nothing but sing the praises of your otherworldly demon dick every five seconds, so I'd say it's a pretty safe bet that you'll be getting a ten out of ten for your performance last night."

"I am relieved to hear it," I said truthfully.

"Then why do you sound like you've done something wrong?"

"That's the thing. She ripped off my amulet. I have no idea what I did."

She paused, and I could tell she was trying to decide whether or not she wanted to get involved. Finally, she said, "Explain, please."

"There's really not much to it. I'm chaotic without the amulet. I can go into a kind of frenzied state where I black out and, uh . . . do things."

"You lived with me a year, and you're just now deciding to tell me that's something that could happen?"

"You already knew that could happen, Mavis. Remember the igloo I took care of for you in March? No amulet, things get destroyed—that's the way it works."

"Well, I've seen what you 'destroyed' last night," she said, laughing at her joke. "And she's currently over here carb-loading French toast so she can make it through her work shift today. If you want to see her before she realizes what a terrible mistake she's made, now is the time."

"I can't this morning. I have furniture coming, but I'll stop by Sakura for lunch or dinner later to see her. Don't tell her I'm coming, okay?"

"Why?"

"Just don't. I want to see her reaction. She was buzzed last night."

"And you think that's why you got lucky? Oh, please. Penelope doesn't do anything she doesn't want to do. And I'm sure that includes you."

"I'm saying goodbye now, Mom."

She gave me a world-weary sigh. "Don't fuck this up, Ray.

I hung up the phone, looked down at what I'd just realized was my naked demon form, and prayed that I hadn't already fucked this up.

~

My new furniture started to arrive only moments after I'd showered and dressed for the day. As I assembled what little needed to be constructed, I tried to talk myself into going to Sakura Buffet for lunch. When I couldn't summon the courage for that, I moved the furniture around into different configurations and tried to talk myself into going there for dinner.

It was no use.

For the first time in my life, I was petrified. I didn't know what Penelope and I had done or even what we'd said to each other. There was no way I could possibly play this whole thing off. I was going to have to tell her the truth. But for someone like me, that wouldn't come easily. The truth bared a side of me that I'd kept hidden for excellent reasons.

But by four thirty, I realized I had moved the couch eight times and had to slap myself mentally. I couldn't fight the urge to see her anymore. I was driving myself crazy.

Jumping into my truck, I drove to Miller's Plaza as fast as the law allowed, hopping out as soon as I shifted it into park. Since it was relatively early for dinner, there were only four people inside the restaurant—Penelope, looking like a fucking goddess in her uniform; Dao Pham, the darkly seductive and well-dressed female owner that I hoped I never had the misfortune of running afoul of; Mavis, who was smirking at me like it was her job; and Dade, the guy from Hey, Nice Glass! who shone like a beacon to the soul-sucking demons in town, but didn't really seem to stand out to the humans in his almost constant attire of novelty T-shirts and jeans.

Every one of them looked up from what they were doing when I walked in.

Silently cursing the fear I felt as I approached the counter, I smiled sweetly at Penelope. "Can I get a to-go plate and the license plate number of the truck that ran over me last night?"

The corner of her mouth quirked up as she punched the order into the register and took my money. "Hey, you aren't the one whose sore thighs were making her waddle around like a duck this morning."

"No." I reached up to stroke the tiny white flowers she'd woven in her braid. They were from the arrangement I'd given her. "But I was the one who was left to wake up alone, wondering where you'd gone off to."

"Well, you won't have to wonder where I'm at tonight. I'm coming to your place when I get off."

I lifted a brow at her choice of words and leaned in close, unable to let an opportunity for sexual innuendo pass by me unchecked. "Penelope, I cannot wait for you to get off."

Pink-cheeked and smiling, she handed me a container for my food. "See you shortly after ten."

"Yes, you will."

Mavis and Dade were both smirking at me when I turned around. I narrowed my eyes at Dade, expecting him to look away, but he merely grinned, speared a piece of sweet and sour chicken, and popped it in his mouth with a sarcastic little fork salute.

"Dude, do you know how long I've been waiting?" Mavis asked, drawing my attention away from the odd young man.

I gave her a perplexed look and filled my plate before I sat down across from her. "Want to fill me in on why you're waiting for me, weirdo stalker?"

She pursed her lips like she had been sucking on something sour. "I didn't think you'd show up is all. I might have made a wager on whether or not you'd show."

It was my turn to smirk. "I told you I would be here. Why would I not show up?"

She gave me a droll look. "You know exactly why, Ray."

I shook my head and stood. "You need a hobby, Mavis."

"Your guys' relationship drama over the past seven months has been my hobby," she hissed. "I'm invested now. It's like witnessing a real-life soap opera. You can't take that away from me."

"I'm telling Cameron," I told her, picking up my plate to leave. "You need an intervention."

"I can quit anytime I want!" she yelled at my back.

Dao looked up from where she was counting the till and cut her eyes at me. I shrugged apologetically at the distinctly nonhuman woman and picked up the pace. Even to a demon, Dao Pham was more than a little scary.

CHAPTER 8

*P*enelope didn't show up as promised after she got off from work. Instead, she texted.

COME OVER AS SOON AS YOU GET THIS!!!

I frowned as I read the text. I didn't know why, but those words were screaming, "There's something terribly wrong that's going to disrupt our already precariously balanced lives" to me.

"This is going to be bad," I groaned, grabbing my coat.

There was no answer at her door when I knocked. No sounds or noises either.

I sighed, not knowing what to expect as I fished out the key she'd given me many months before and stuck it in the lock. Stepping in, I shed my coat and closed the door behind me. "Penny?"

"Ray?"

I held a hand to my chest when my initial panic eased a bit. She was coherent. That was always good.

"Where are you?" I called.

"The bathroom. Can you come here, please?"

In the back of my mind, I knew that what I was about to see wasn't going to be one of those "Dear Penthouse" scenarios, but I certainly didn't expect to see what I saw.

"Holy shit," I said, taking in everything.

"That's all you have to say?" she asked, throwing her loofah at me.

I stared down at the naked demon sitting in the bath. "I'm trying to decide what I'd like to talk about first."

"Oh, I don't know. How about the fact that I'm a demon?"

I sat down on the edge of the tub. "Yeah, but you were already a demon. I think you naked in this bathtub might be the bigger story here."

She slapped the bathwater to get my attention. "You know what I mean!"

I did know what she meant. But fuck me, she was so stunningly beautiful right now; I couldn't stop gawking at her. I shook my head as I reverently looked over the amazing transformation of her body. Her body was always long and lean, but now her skin was bronzed, her frame more muscled, and there were new angles on her face, each as sharp and defined as the fangs in her mouth and the claws on her fingertips. "Penelope, you have no idea how beautiful you are to me right now."

Her breath quivered. "And you have no idea how much I am freaking the fuck out."

I cupped her cheek. "Tell me how I can help, demon lady."

She glared at me, but said, "I need three things from you."

"Please tell me one of them is my seed," I pleaded. "Because damn." I frowned, suddenly remembering who I was talking to. "Oh, wait. This isn't going to be some kind of riddle, is it? Or a quest?"

"Stop trying to make me laugh," she said, poking out her bottom lip, which was a little harder with her shiny new fangs.

"What will you have me do, milady?" I asked, grinning as I leaned in to kiss her pouty lips.

"First, you're going to tell me whether or not you're my secret admirer," she said, giving me a hard stare. "The next two things will depend on that answer."

"Yes, I am your secret admirer," I admitted. "Are you surprised? You didn't think it was Dade, did you?"

"What?" she asked. "Who?"

I waved the thought away. "Never mind. What are the other two things?"

"Can you get me the champagne and bath bombs you sent from the table?" she asked meekly, batting her eyes.

I sighed and jumped up to do her bidding. "Do you need a glass or are you going to just drink out of the bottle like you normally do?"

She groaned in annoyance. "Shut up and go get it."

Closing the door behind me, I leaned my forehead against the wall and sighed in relief. Since we'd apparently had more sex than the Kama Sutra had positions, I shouldn't have been so shocked by her complete nudity, but I was. I was a six-hundred-year-old demon who was acting like I'd just seen my first naked lady.

"Get yourself together," I whispered, pushing away from the wall and running to grab what she'd requested. She needed more from me than my dick right now.

When I came back in, she was rewarming the water and looking a little more chipper. Handing her the box of bath bombs, I set her glass on the edge of the tub and popped the cork out of the bottle.

"Are we going for taste or speed of drunkenness?" I asked, pouring a bit into the glass.

"Speed," she said. "And I'm kind of sad that you had to ask me that."

"Not at all." I filled the glass up to the top and handed it to her. "Here you go, lushie."

Still a little shaky looking, she hugged her knees with one arm and took a sip out of the glass with the other. "Thanks."

I took a swig of the warm champagne and gagged. "I know it's been a hard night for you, but how the hell are you drinking this warm?"

"Trust me. After what I've seen today, it's easy," she said, dropping a fizzing orb into the water then downing the contents of her glass. "Really, really easy."

I gave her a refill and gestured to her naked body. "Are we talking about seeing more than the extreme sexiness you've got going on right here?"

She nodded. "I'm talking about my boss having six tails. I'm talking about the werewolf that came in for a late dinner just before closing. I'm talking about the red-skinned demon I'm looking at right now."

I stared at her for a second, then jumped up to look at myself in the foggy mirror. Nope, no red-skinned demon, just the façade I wore while I was around others. "Penny, how do you see my form while I'm not wearing it?" I held out a hand. "No, wait. Dao has six tails?"

She choked back a laughing sob. "I don't know how I see it. I've always been able to tell when people weren't quite human. It was a gift I didn't want but couldn't get rid of. But this—this is the gift on steroids. I can see everyone's forms flickering around them as if they're almost but not quite tuned in. And to top all that off, I can't figure out how to make my human form come back out."

"Man, Cameron is going to be pissed when he sees you're able to shift forms. Most half-demons can't."

"Not really my concern right now," she deadpanned.

I laughed. "I know, but there's not much you can do about it that you haven't already done. You've already gotten the tattoo from the court, so there's no worry about the humans."

Her mouth dropped open. "I have a tattoo?"

"Yes." I pointed to the invisible ink on her shoulder. "It was done when you were first placed here in the Falls. Otherwise, this may have happened while you were in school or somewhere else in public. Can't have you demoning out at recess."

"Not that I'm complaining or anything, but we really should have talked more last night. There's still so much I don't know."

"About that," I began.

She held her hands up in the stop position. "Nope. I don't want to know."

I gave her a sheepish look. "But you need to know."

"Damn it!" she growled. "Isn't my day going bad enough?"

"Yes? No? I honestly don't know how to answer that, Penelope."

She glared at me, held up a finger, then downed her glass. When I refilled it with the rest of the bottle, she said, "Get naked. There's enough room for both of us in this tub."

"Do you really think us both being naked will improve the situation?"

"Get. Naked," she reiterated.

"Okay, but once I'm naked, I get to come clean about everything. No pun intended."

She grinned excitedly and bounced up and down, which didn't do anything to help me in the staring department. "Deal."

With a reluctant groan, I kicked off my boots and socks and stood to take off my shirt, jeans, and underwear. Getting certain sensitive body parts close to her when I was about to tell her things she didn't want to know was probably the worst plan ever. But it was apparent Penelope thought the opposite. She never stopped watching me as I undressed. Her face never lost that stunned, amazed expression, as if she couldn't believe what she was seeing.

That expression did not suck for my ego.

I kicked my clothes into a little pile and stood up straight in front of her. "Do you like what you see?"

She leveled a stare at me. "Do I like what I see? Are you kidding? Fuck, yes, I like what I see. If I weren't so sore from last night, I would climb you like a fucking tree."

"Good to know," I said, easing into the hot water behind her.

Settling in between my legs, she laid her back against my chest and sighed as I cupped her breasts.

"That didn't take long," she said, laughing.

"Sorry, it's instinctual to me, like breathing."

"And the erection against my back?"

I kissed her temple. "Same goes."

She closed her eyes, relaxing against me. "I'm glad you're here right now. You're a nice distraction."

"I've been called worse."

"I'll bet you have. What do you think I'll call you when you 'come clean'?"

"Hmmm . . . honest? One would hope, anyway."

"Not something I would normally expect out of you," she said. "But you do seem to be trying it out lately. Okay. Shoot. Be honest with me."

"Okay." I blew a long slow breath out of my nose. "When I woke up this morning, I couldn't remember most of last night."

She turned in my arms to look up at me. "What parts of last night?"

"Every part after you took off my amulet."

Her forehead wrinkled in confusion. "What do you mean?"

I sighed and lifted the amulet to look at it before dropping it back down against my chest. "Having this thing is a double-edged sword. It protects me and diminishes my abilities to keep me from making catastrophic mistakes, which is great, but because I've become so used to having my power dampened, it's really easy for me to slip into a kind of frenzied state when it's off. During those times, I can't remember much of what I do."

"What do you remember from last night?"

"You looking like you were about to fuck my brains out with my amulet wrapped around your wrist."

She looked horrified. "I'm sorry, Rayonus. I guess I just ripped it off in the heat of the moment. I don't even remember doing that."

"No, I'm sorry. If I was honest with you like I should have been, you would've known that was a possibility."

"So, we can just agree we're both sorry and leave it at that?" she asked hopefully.

I laughed. "No freakin' way. I want to know what you did to me while I was out of it. Anything kinky?"

"You mean, what you did to me," she retorted. "I didn't get a chance to do anything."

I cringed. "That does not sound good."

"Good doesn't even come close to it, Ray. You were an animal for three straight hours. And I don't speak Renaissance-era Latin, but you do, and I was pretty into whatever you were saying. It all sounded like an orgasm for the ears, and by the end of the night, an orgasm for every other part of me."

Trying hard to tamp down the smug smile spreading across my face, I asked, "Do you remember anything I said?"

"Yes. You kept whispering *te amo* into my neck and something that sounds like *uxor mea*."

"I love you, my wife."

She smiled. "That's what you were saying?"

"*Omnia mihi es,*" I told her. "You are my everything."

"I'm not going to lie. You were pretty focused last night. I felt like I was your everything. I just wish you could remember it."

I wrapped my arms around her stomach. "Honestly, I'm just thankful I didn't bring the building down on top of us. Usually, when the necklace comes off, bad things happen—bad things like property damage and demon murder."

She laughed. "You did shake the room for a brief second, but it wasn't bad enough to do damage. You tried to be as gentle as you could through it all."

"So, I didn't hurt you?"

"Only in very good ways—a light bite on my neck, the tips of your claws digging into my ass—the only thing that's still sore is my well-used . . ."

"Okay," I said, interrupting her. "That's enough of that talk."

She laughed. "I'm just saying, A plus for effort. And also for skill. You pretty much ruined me for all other demons."

I lifted the heavy weight of her hair away from her neck and scraped my fangs across the delicate wet skin. "Good, because I don't plan on letting any other demons have you—ever. I want you as my mate."

CHAPTER 9

With a much calmer and drier Penny fast asleep in her bed, I made a phone call I hoped I would never have to make.

The Alchemist answered after only one ring. "Rayonus Rixa. I haven't heard from you in almost a year."

"Yeah, well, I've been busy," I told him.

"With my little girl?"

"She not a child anymore, Draz, as you well know," I said. "She's almost twenty-four."

"Even so, you know it's frowned upon for someone in your capacity to fraternize with our younglings."

"I do. Just like I know it's frowned upon to fraternize with their parents. But I'm calling you for a reason."

"And that is?"

"I need an amulet made."

He sighed. "Not for you, I hope? Your amulet wiped my magic out for a week after I made it."

"No, not for me. Do you really think I'd be coherent enough to make a phone call without my protection?"

"No, I suppose not. But you do know I don't make these things for just anyone. I would need to deem them worthy, and

286

they must align themselves with me in the event I should ever need their power."

"No."

Draz chuckled. "Those are and have always been my terms."

"Not with me and not with the owner of this amulet. She needs it, and you will give it without expectation, just as you did for me."

"It's for Penelope, isn't it? She has my power."

The way he said "my power" made my skin crawl. "It's nothing that could help you," I told him. "She only sees the creature underneath. She can't seal their powers away like you can."

"Not yet, she can't. But it will only take a few lessons."

My voice unwavering, I said, "We're not doing that again. You tried that, remember? With your son. The one that had to be killed when you pushed him to the brink of insanity."

"Think of it as trial and error," he said, dismissing my reminder of his all-too-recent failure.

"I'll think of them as your younglings, Draz. You only have one left. Do not attempt to sway her to do your dirty deeds. If you hurt her—if you so much as lay a finger on her—I will be the end of you. Testor ego eam."

After a long pause, he finally said, "Bring her to my shop in Patriam tomorrow evening. I will make the stone, and I will not mention our relation. But after this, I will ask that you will cease to watch over my child."

"Do as you must," I said, not giving a tin shit what he wanted. Penelope was mine to protect whether it was my assignment or not. She was going to be my mate. The demon in me—in both of us—had chosen.

I hung up with Draz and peeked in the bedroom door at Penelope. Back in her human form, she looked peaceful and content as she slept—all the worry and fear she'd felt just a few minutes earlier absent from her mind.

Frowning, I silently stepped into the room and sat on the foot of the bed. I wanted to just live in that quiet moment and keep her away from all of the demon bullshit she was about to be immersed in. It was for the best that she knew what her father was capable of, I knew, but that didn't mean I had to like it.

Shifting slightly, she opened her eyes and smiled at me. "You look worried. That's becoming a thing with you."

"I'm not worried at all," I lied, stretching out beside her and pulling her into my arms. "But I am thinking about taking you someplace tonight. Can you get off from work?"

She nodded against my bare chest. "I'm already off tonight. Where are we going?"

I sighed. "To what we demons call Patriam."

She propped herself up on an elbow. "Patriam? Like, in the demon underground? But didn't Cameron say that place was dangerous?"

"For him, yes. It's quite dangerous. He's half-human."

"I'm half-human," she reminded me.

I tucked her hair behind her ear and pulled her back into my embrace. "You'll be with me, love. And we aren't going to hang around long enough for anything to get dangerous. We're going to see the demon we call the Alchemist and then we're going home. He's willing to make you an amulet to seal your power away."

"Oh, thank God," she said, relief coloring her voice.

"But, before we go to all the trouble of going there and having to deal with some inevitable demon-related shit, I will say that I think you could perform that magic yourself without exposing yourself to the others, especially one as dangerous to you as the Alchemist."

"How do you know?"

I pressed my lips together. "Because you undoubtedly have similar powers to your father. That's the way it always is."

"Still, shouldn't we err on the side of caution and get the amulet anyway, just in case things take an unexpected turn?"

"I'm not sure seeing the Alchemist would be considered erring on the side of caution. Seeing him puts you in much more danger."

"Why?"

I rolled onto my back, taking her with me. "Because he wants to own you, just like he's wanted to own all of his children."

Her brows furrowed as she looked up at me. "Are you trying to tell me my father is the Alchemist?"

I closed my eyes and nodded. "That is what I'm saying."

"And you've known this for how long?"

Sensing the storm of her anger rumbling in the distance, I cracked an eye open. "Around a quarter of a century."

"So, my entire life, basically."

"Basically."

She groaned and flopped her head onto my chest. "Why do you tell me things I don't want to know, Ray?"

"Because you get violent when I don't tell you and your fists of fury hurt . . . a lot."

"Stop bringing logic into this conversation. You know that's not the way you do things."

I laughed. "Have you ever thought that maybe that's why I always get the demons I love into bad situations? I think logic *should* be brought into our conversations."

"Pssshh . . . where's your sense of adventure?"

CHAPTER 10

The trip we took to Patriam was the work of a moment. One second we were standing in my living room, dressed and ready to leave, and the next, an amazed Penelope and I were standing in the weakening evening sun on a nearly empty street, just outside the entrance of the demon settlement.

She narrowed her eyes at me. "Next time, warn a girl! I didn't even know you could do that!"

I shrugged, checking around us to make sure no one had overheard her human decree. "There's a lot about me you don't know," I said, wrapping an arm around her shoulders. "I plan on giving you little tidbits of information over the next two hundred years or so to keep you guessing."

She stared at me. "You are so fucking weird at the oddest of times, Rayonus."

I kissed her forehead. "You using my real name negates the insult. Just so you know."

"I think you're immune to my insults anyhow," she said, turning toward what appeared to be a group of black-shawled demons heading our way. "Friends of yours?"

"Scavengers," I told her, leading her down a path in the direction of the town. "Best to avoid them."

"Noted." She glanced behind us. "Anything else I need to worry about?"

I grinned, enjoying myself a little more than I probably should have. "Do you want me to put it into some pop culture references you might understand?

"Do you really have to ask?" she retorted.

"Okay. Where we're going is like Diagon Alley. It's full of interesting demons and magic. Where we are now is like Knockturn Alley. Here, you don't want to stray from the path. If you do, don't let anyone try to show you the way back. And whatever you do, don't make eye contact. Just stay near me and try not to get separated or buy any owls . . . or magic wands . . . or books that try to eat you."

She smirked. "So, keep my half-blood ass in line and let you eat me?"

I pressed a kiss to her hand and led her into the dozens of demons milling about the stands and stores on the street. "You do have a way with words, my love."

"I can't believe you said that instead of coming up with some kind of sexual innuendo about oral sex," she said, looking up to me as I led her through the crowd of increasingly inquisitive demons. Either she was so cool that she hadn't noticed their stares and whispers, or she was willfully ignoring them to show no fear. Either way, she was killing it. Nothing was more respected in this town than a demon who had balls, so to speak.

Meeting her halfway, I kissed her lightly, then captured her bottom lip between my teeth and bit down ever so slightly, just hard enough to make her gasp and pull me closer. "I will talk to you about oral sex as much as you want, once we've completed our business here," I whispered against her mouth. "Count on it."

Her lips quirked up into a smile. "Trust me, Rayonus. I will."

I met several greedy eyes when Penny and I separated and continued walking. I gave every last one of them a look that said in no uncertain terms that the demon in my arms was my mate, that I had claimed her, and that she wasn't up for grabs. One by one, they turned away, showing defeat. No one wanted to fuck with the watcher. Stories of the demon before the Alchemist helped me restrain my power still circulated around the fires. I was too wild, my magic unpredictable. I was to be feared.

And I was . . . for the most part.

There would always be someone out there who wanted the recognition, the glory, of defeating the undefeatable. Those demons, I let be. But that's not to say I didn't keep an eye on them.

"Where is this place?" Penelope asked. "None of the stores have signs."

"That's because these stores cater to people who live here. Outsiders aren't usually welcome."

"Sounds quaint. When can I expect to be murdered by a local?"

I shook my head. "As long as you're with me, never."

She threaded her fingers with mine. "Then consider us joined at the hip."

"You just can't stop yourself from giving my dirty mind openings like that, can you?"

She shrugged. "It's more like I don't want to."

Laughing, I wove us around the crowd and down to the narrow alleyway that led to the Alchemist's home. "Here we are."

Penelope eyed the worn door and the surrounding dirty walls. "This is where I could have grown up?"

"Not what you were expecting?" I asked.

She shook her head. "Not even close."

"Oh, it wasn't too bad, growing up in Patriam. There are much, much worse places to live in our little demon underworld. Ones I hope to never have to show you."

"I will do everything I told you I wanted to do in the igloo if you never show them to me," she said, fighting a shiver.

"Deal," I told her, reaching to knock on the door. "Ready?"

"As I'll ever be."

I'd warned Penelope earlier that Draz said he would keep their relation a secret and that she was under no obligation to mention she knew the truth, but somehow, even before the door swung open, I knew she'd blow that whole thing wide open. That was Penelope's style—shock and awe.

"'Sup, Dad," she said, stepping in the doorway before he could invite us in.

I bit my lip to keep from laughing at Draz's stunned face. I was guessing he was in his demon form to try to intimidate her, but his wasn't much different than her own, and compared to mine, it wasn't even remotely terrifying. If anything, it probably pissed her off more.

"Hello, daughter," he said in return. "How do you fare this evening?"

Rolling her eyes, she said, "Cut the shit, Draz. I need the amulet. Give it to me, or I'll make one for myself."

Looking to me for an explanation, Draz held up his clawed hands in a *what gives* position.

I shrugged. "Draz, meet your daughter, Penelope, and her wildly inappropriate temper."

Not sure whether I was joking, he smiled at her, fangs on full display. "It's nice to meet you, Penelope.

"Is it?" she asked, staring him down.

He shot another dumbfounded look my way.

I stepped between them, hoping to defuse the situation. "Okay, I can see this is going nowhere fast. Draz, we've come for an amulet for your daughter. Will you make it for her, or is she going to have to shove her size nines up your ass?"

He turned an overexaggerated bright smile on his offspring. "Of course! I'd be happy to help her! Just leave it to us, and I'll have her ready and back on the road to Havenwood Falls in a jiffy."

Did he just say *a jiffy*? I narrowed my eyes at him. "I'm not leaving her alone with you."

Clenching his jaw for a moment to get his temper under control, he spat, "I told you, Rayonus, you aren't to watch her anymore. She's my daughter. I will request another watcher, one who hasn't become enmeshed in the lives of his wards. You have no rights to her."

Alarm bells went off in my head. Draz was usually civil with me, though it was more likely that he was afraid of me than because of a mutual respect. After all, he alone knew how powerful I was. If he was choosing to stand up to me like this now after centuries of near-cowering, something important was in the works. Something he didn't want me to impede.

"Rights or not, Rayonus does whatever he wishes to me," Penelope purred, tangling her hand in mine and throwing gasoline on an already out-of-control flame. Clearly, she wasn't used to dealing with demon politics.

"You dare to defile my daughter without my permission?" Draz shouted.

Penelope smiled frostily at the angry demon. "Like you even care. Make the amulet, Draz. Or don't make the amulet. I don't give a shit. But I'm tired of you wasting our time."

Draz's shrewd, calculating eyes roamed from me to his daughter. "I have no problem making it for you, daughter, but I will not give our secrets to him. You may have them, but he will not. He will use what little power we've gained against weaker demons. Surely, you can sense how powerful and dangerous he is."

"He stays," she said plainly, her voice almost bored.

"Then, I'm sorry, Penelope. I cannot make the amulet."

Penelope turned on her heel and walked to the open door. "See ya, pops."

"It appears we will not be needing your services," I said, following her to the door. "Until next time."

"Don't either of you dare darken my doorstep again!" he screamed after us.

I turned and raised an eyebrow at this unusual display of anger, but Penelope just continued walking, her middle finger held up high as she went.

When the noise of Draz's roars were shut off by the closing

door, Penelope hurried back to me and looped her arm in mine. "I might have gotten a little carried away there. I almost forgot where I was."

"I'd say you got just enough carried away."

"How so?"

"Well, any less and Draz might have noticed that we took his book with the instructions for your amulet." I patted my pocket. "Did I mention that I have excellent sleight-of-hand abilities?"

She grinned up at me as we quickly made our way down the street. "You did not. Am I to assume that's one of the tidbits you mentioned that you'd be sharing over the next two hundred years?"

"You are. Impressed?"

"Very. But how do you intend to play it off once he realizes it's gone?"

I stopped at a secluded ivy-covered staircase and led her down. Unlocking the hidden door, I pulled the chain of an old lamp to illuminate the small but clean parlor and locked the door behind us.

"He won't realize it's gone," I told her, taking out my camera to snap pictures of the pertinent information. "We're going to take these pictures, and then I'm going to return it using teleportation. Even if he already knows it's gone, he'll just think he overlooked it when he finds it. But chances are, he's so mad, he won't even think to look for it."

Her eyes were wide as she stared at me. "You're some kind of evil genius, aren't you?"

I chuckled. "Not what you expected in a mate?"

Her brows furrowed. "Yeah, about that. What is all this mate stuff?"

"It just means I've chosen to mate with you. If you're willing to accept me," I added lamely.

"Mate? As in a sexual partner?"

I nodded. "Sort of, yes. Demons aren't really into the whole monogamous thing; they usually just fuck anyone—human, demon, or other—no strings attached. Mates stay together.

Sometimes not forever, but generally, for a few decades or centuries."

"So you were serious about that Latin wife stuff the other night?"

"I can't be anything else without my amulet. When it's off, you get the real me."

"I like the real you," she said, putting her arms around my waist. "He's hot."

"Hold that thought," I told her, disappearing for a split second to slip the book back into Draz's home.

When I returned, she smacked my shoulder. "Stop doing that!" she exclaimed. "I don't know where I am!"

"You're in my home," I told her, rubbing my shoulder. "Did you really think I'd leave you somewhere where you could have been in danger?"

Her interest piqued, she glanced around the parlor. "This is really your home?"

I watched her as she took in the paintings in gilded frames on the wall and the vintage furniture from decades past. "My home when I'm in Patriam, yes."

"What's back here?" she asked, pointing at the closed door that led to the rest of the house. "Dungeon? Demon torture chamber?"

"I hate to disappoint, but that's the hallway leading to the kitchen, bathroom, and my bedroom."

Brows raised, she walked to the door. "May I?"

"Feel free to roam wherever you'd like. We have time. According to Draz's book, we have to gather a few materials before you can make the amulet anyway."

She nodded and stepped to the door, hesitating for a second before she reached for the knob. "Is there anything dangerous back here?"

"There might be some twenty-year-old Pop Tarts in the kitchen. I'd stay away from those."

She shook her head with an expression of exasperated humor on her face. "There's something really wrong with you."

Laughing, I swung the door open to the darkened hallway and flipped on the lights. "You're not the first to say it."

"That does not surprise me," she said, stopping in front of the door at the end of the hall. "Bedroom?"

I nodded, wondering what she'd think about the ridiculously ornate demon-sized bed within.

"Wow," she said, marveling at the room when I turned on the lights. "This is your bedroom? It looks like a gigantic king lives here."

"Not a king, just a giant demon."

"Is this where you lived before you moved in with Mavis and Cameron?"

"Yes. I still live here off and on, though I haven't been here for a month or so. I just come back every so often to dust and change the sheets. I like to keep it ready and maintained in case my situation ever changes, and I have to return."

To my surprise, she kicked off her sneakers and ran to the bed to dive on top of the duvet. "I love it," she said, stretching out her arms. "We could sleep together and never see each other in this thing."

I unlaced my boots and climbed onto the bed after her. "I don't care what bed we're in. We will be seeing each other in it. And hopefully, you'll be naked."

She laughed sultrily as I grabbed her leg and yanked her under me. "Naked in human form or demon?"

I feigned thought. "You know, when it comes to us having sex, I don't think I have a preferred form. I'd be delighted to take you any way I can."

"I've never had sex as a demon," she reminded me, unbuttoning her shirt and unclasping the front clip of her bra to expose her breasts. "Is it any different?"

"I'm not sure," I said, getting to my knees to pull my shirt over my head. "Think we should give it a try?"

"For research purposes?" she asked, reaching down to unbutton my jeans.

I closed my hands over hers to stall the hurried movements she was making and stood to shed my clothes. If she continued like this, I would burst out of them Hulk-style and have to dig through my closet in hopes of finding some from this decade.

A pounding on the door rang out into the silence, startling us both.

"Who's that?" Penelope asked, her fingers flying to clasp her bra as she sat up.

"I don't know, but I'll get rid of them," I told her, pulling my shirt over my head and shoving my feet into my boots.

"Should I stay here?"

"Yeah. It's safer out of sight until we know what we're dealing with."

She slipped on her sneakers and grabbed the fireplace poker. "Okay. I'm ready."

Amused, I eyed her fighting stance. "Ready for what? Who do you think is going to be out there?"

Penelope glared at me. "Just go answer the door, jerk. I want to know what a centuries-old demon does in a centuries-old bed."

I bowed, leering at her. "I am your servant to command, milady."

She smirked. "I want you to remember that you said that."

"I will," I promised, pressing my lips to hers before appearing before the door.

"I hate it when you do that!" she muttered from the bedroom.

Grinning, I unlocked the door and only had a split second of recognition before a blur of motion tackled me, pushing me a couple of steps back into the parlor.

"Rayonus!" the beautiful young demon cried. "You've come back!"

Of all the demons I thought might knock on my door, this female was one I hoped would have forgotten I existed. She had an uncanny way of showing up at my door when I came into town, and an even more mysterious way of getting me into her bed each time she did.

I cast a furtive look over my shoulder toward the bedroom. "Helisa, what are you doing here?"

The demon sighed and flicked long locks of white hair over her bare red-skinned shoulder. "My mother had a vision that you'd be in need of some of the spring water salt she brought back from her travels in Austria last year. I thought I'd make a house call and give it to you myself." She bared her fangs in a seductive smile and trailed a clawed finger down my abdomen to my waistband. "Along with anything else you want, of course."

Grabbing her wrist, I stopped her downward motion. "Helisa, I'm mated now."

She pouted prettily. "So am I, but that doesn't mean we can't have a little fun. Not that you've ever really been *little*."

"As much as that bolsters my ego, you know what you and Toraris have isn't a true mating. It's a convenient financial arrangement at best. My mate is for life."

She stepped back as if I'd slapped her. "You can't mean that, Rayonus. No demon mates for an immortal lifetime."

"I did, and so did my mate," Penelope said, coming out of the hallway in her demon form. With her long brown hair tousled and wild around her shoulders, her shirt still unbuttoned to show the sheer black bra she wore, and nothing but black lace panties covering her bottom half, she looked satisfied and well-laid.

Incredulous, Helisa asked, "Her, Rayonus? You're giving up our dalliances for a half-human?"

"Don't worry," a black-eyed, pissed off Penelope simpered. "I just *dallianced* his fucking brains out. He's all set."

Howling with rage, Helisa threw the burlap bag of salt at my chest and stormed out, yelling, "Find another salt supplier, Rayonus Rixa!"

In shock and in complete and total lust with Penelope, I closed and locked the door before turning on her. Her face was the picture of innocence.

"Dallianced my fucking brains out?" I asked, ripping my shirt off and stalking toward her.

Penelope shrugged as she quickly backed down the hallway. "You're my mate or whatever. The days of her enjoying your . . . uh, attributes are over. You're mine now."

"You want these attributes, little demon?" I growled, kicking off my jeans mere moments before I let my body change into its natural form.

"Why?" she sassed, slinging her bra and shirt to the floor and climbing onto the bed. "Are you going to give them to me?"

She let out a little yelp as I flipped her onto her back, then her lips parted in a very feminine gasp as I pressed myself between her legs. I shook my head and chuckled. "Oh, Penny, you have no idea how bad I'm going to give it to you."

CHAPTER 11

or two demons with jobs, responsibilities, and a task to do, Penelope and I were shameless in the way we whiled away the hours, learning each other's bodies as we frolicked in my oversized bed. It was somewhat of a novelty for her. For me, as well, but not in the same sense. The novelty for me was feeling that the woman in this ridiculously massive bed was made for me and me alone. No female I had ever known in the biblical sense had ever made me feel—had ever made me want—more from them. Penelope did. She was it for me. Woe be the idiot that ever tried to take her.

I let Penelope sleep for a few hours before I roused her into the shower and made us breakfast with items I popped out to get from my apartment. It wasn't out of the norm for me to be domestic at times, but waking up here at my home—my real home—with her in my arms had done something to me. It felt so surreal. After more than six hundred long years, I woke up with an overwhelming need to nourish my lover's body, to please her, to protect her in any way I could, even if that meant with my own life. These feelings scared me, and yet, they felt right.

"Morning," Penelope said, yawning as she toweled her hair dry.

Struck by how beautiful she was, I rounded the counter and fell to my knees. "Marry me, Penelope," I begged. "Be my wife and my mate."

"What, no ring?" she asked with amusement in her eyes.

Without a second thought, I took her hand and transported us to the master bedroom in my apartment in Havenwood Falls. Standing, I opened the top dresser drawer and grabbed the red velvet box containing my great-grandmother's ring.

When I faced Penelope, her eyes were wide with shock. She hadn't realized how serious I was about this, about us.

I opened the box and stared at the blood-red cinnabar crystal. "This ring has been passed down through my family for thousands of years. It hasn't always been a ring. It began as a pretty bauble in the hilt of a sword. It has been an amulet, talisman, a brooch, and even bargaining chip for someone's life in the years since. My grandmother passed it down to me. She didn't trust my mother not to sell or pawn it. Now I want you to have it. I want you to pass it down to our son or daughter when it is time and for them to pass it down to their sons and daughters." Meeting her eyes, I knelt again. "Be my wife. Dalliance my brains out on a regular basis."

She laughed and nodded with tears gathering in her eyes as she held out her hand. The metal sizzled as I settled it onto her finger, the magic protection spell conforming to her particular essence before glowing bright red and then dulling to its normal shade.

"Is that a yes?"

"Yes," she said, bending to give me a smacking kiss. "I will dalliance your brains out on a regular basis."

Standing, I gathered her into my arms and kissed her properly, our breath mingling, our tongues sweeping against each other's until she melted against me and I was panting with the effort to control the raging need to take her right here on the bedroom floor—again. "I love you, Penny."

"I love you, Rayonus," she replied, giving me another sweet kiss. "But didn't I smell pancakes at your other place?"

I laughed at the sudden change of topic. "My plans to ravish you are foiled by the siren call of pancakes. I should probably get used to this sort of thing, shouldn't I?"

She shrugged. "That probably wouldn't be such a bad idea."

~

Thirty minutes and four pancakes later, I coaxed Penelope away from the platter of bacon and into the street. With the sun shining and the merchants' wares laid out for everyone to see, it wasn't nearly as ominous as it looked when we arrived the night before. During the day, I didn't mind letting Penelope explore the stands and stores, oohing and aahing over every little thing she found interesting. She was adorable, really, my little demon mate.

Letting her visit every store she fancied, I kept a watch out for the items we needed and demons I knew that sold them. We had wound our way down to the river when I found just the demon I'd hoped we'd find easily. She had moved her shop from where it was the last time I'd stopped in, which was a very regular occurrence, but she couldn't hide the flashing green of her eyes under the red wool hood she wore. Even in her demon form, those eyes were unmistakable.

"Fyrira," I called, greeting her with a small bow. "It has been too long."

Her voice was hoarse and low when she answered but just as friendly and warm as it had been since I was a youngling. "That it has, Rayonus. That it has." She eyed Penelope, then gave me what I could only describe as a *you sly dog* look. "Who might this lovely half-demon accompanying you be?"

"This is my mate, Penelope. Penelope, this is Fyrira. She has sold Sicilian brimstone at the markets for as long as anyone can remember."

Penelope curtsied, making Fyrira and me chuckle with delight.

"Sorry," she said, laughing at herself. "I'm not sure what the procedure is when meeting new demons yet. Rayonus, as you can imagine, isn't the most thorough of teachers when it comes to manners."

"Truer words were never spoken about our little trickster, Rayonus," Fyrira croaked. "He does have quite the bad reputation."

I shook my head. "Hey. That hurts my feelings. I've always been good to both of you."

They both stared at me, stunned at what I'd just said.

"Okay, maybe not, but my heart's always in the right place."

They continued to stare.

Laughing, I held my hands up in defense. "Okay. Okay. I'm a recovering terrible demon."

"That's more like it," Penelope said, grinning at me like I was her whole world.

I liked that look. No. I loved it. I wanted her to never stop looking at me like that.

Fyrira watched us stare at each other for a long moment, then shook her head. "You two are more smitten than any demons I've ever seen."

"You haven't met Cameron and Mavis DeSalle," Penelope told her. "Those two are so sickeningly sweet, they'll give you a toothache."

"I find that hard to believe about the Exitium Daemonium and the son of Severin DeSalle," Fyrira replied sagely.

"Oh, no. It's true," I concurred. "They are disgustingly affectionate."

She barked out a rusty laugh and motioned us into her tent. "Come, younglings. If it's brimstone you need, it is brimstone you shall have."

After only a few minutes inside the tent, Penelope and I left to find the next piece to our puzzle, but not before Fyrira warned us that we had better watch ourselves while we were in the marketplace. "There are eyes and ears everywhere," she said. "Say anything interesting, do anything interesting, and they will hear and see you. Do not forget, younglings."

We agreed to stay on course after her dire warning, only visiting the tent Fyrira had directed us to for the African gum arabic made from an acacia tree. The salesman, Arlennear, a demon I'd known for decades, sold us the item without any conversation at all, handing it over immediately after accepting my offer of four gold coins with a nod.

The only thing left was for us to choose an amulet to hold the magic.

After looking in a few more stalls, Penelope pulled me to the side to whisper into my ear. "Do you think it's possible for me to use my ring as the amulet? It doesn't have to strictly be a necklace, does it?"

I grinned. "Of course it is. The cinnabar the ring is made from is a perfect conductor for demon magic."

With our last step decided, we hurried back to my home and collapsed on the stiff settee with our purchases laid out on the table before us.

"That was a bizarre day of shopping," Penelope said, rubbing her socked feet. "Demon shopping is not like human shopping."

"I agree wholeheartedly. There is a distinct lack of food courts in Patriam."

"Food sounds so good," she moaned, then she sat up suddenly. "Oh, my God! I forgot to tell Dao that I needed the night off!"

"What time is your shift?"

"Four to ten."

I checked my phone. "We can make it in time. But what about the seeing everyone in their true form thing?"

"Shit. I forgot about that. Nearly everyone here is already in their true form."

I nodded, agreeing with that assessment. Here they had nothing to hide, so most of the population didn't bother.

"So, what're you going to do?"

"What choice do I have?"

"This may be the terrible demon with the bad reputation in me, but you could call in sick and spend the night eating exotic demon delicacies with your fiancé. Technically, you are having a problem that keeps you from completing your work as usual. It's not that much of a stretch."

Penelope chewed her lip. "Can our phones work from here?"

"No, but the trip back to Havenwood Falls will only take a second," I said, standing up. "Ready?" I asked, pulling her to her feet.

She grabbed her shoes in one hand and threaded the fingers of her free hand with mine. "Ready."

We arrived in Penelope's apartment to a severely pissed off ice demon.

"Where the fuck have you been?" Mavis cried as soon as we popped into existence. "I've been worried out of my mind. Dao said you had to leave early the other night and asked me to check up on you yesterday. Yesterday! Where have you been?"

I rolled my eyes. "Calm down, Mom. I've been with her the whole time. She's perfectly fine."

"Funny, but that doesn't really do anything to calm me," she spat, yanking Penelope away from me.

"Are you okay?" she asked my mate. "He didn't put you in any danger, did he?"

"No. Actually, he's been helping me track down the items to help me make an amulet. The Alchemist refused to help and was all sketchy, so I'm just going to try to do it myself."

"You took her to Patriam to see her father?" Mavis asked me, her face incredulous. "Wait." She turned back to Penelope. "Why do you need an amulet, Penny?"

"Because I can see you. Like, the real demon you right now. Horns and all."

Mavis patted the top of her head and frowned. "How?"

Penelope shrugged and shook her head. "Apparently, it's my talent. That's why I had to leave work so abruptly. Dao's six tails were freaking me out. Not to mention, did you know there are werewolves in this town?"

"Just the sheriff and a shit ton of others," Mavis answered. "Can you see Ray's demon form right now?"

"Yeah, but I'm pretty used to that by now. It doesn't really freak me out. And that's a pretty good thing, since he's asked me to marry him."

Mavis's mouth dropped open with a squeak.

"Uh oh. I think we might have broken her," I said, waving a hand in front of her shocked face. "Quick, show her your demon form to snap her out of it."

If possible, Mavis's eyes widened even farther.

"You're scaring me," Penelope said, taking her arm to lead her to the couch. "Say something."

"Go get Cam," Mavis demanded of me. "Right now. I'm calling a family meeting."

CHAPTER 12

*O*nce we explained the situation and the shock of the engagement and seeing Penelope as a bronze-colored, fanged demon wore off, Mavis and Cam finally gathered enough sense between them to congratulate me and ask if Penny was out of her ever-loving mind.

"The ring is beautiful," Mavis whispered to Penelope. "And it's powerful to be sure; I can feel the magic pulsing in it. But are you sure Rayonus is the demon you want to spend an eternity with? We're talking about someone who has sold us out, betrayed us, and left us in the dark."

"Yes," she agreed. "But we're also talking about someone who risked his own life to end Severin's madness, worked hard to get back into our good graces, and loves me beyond reason."

"I just want to remind everyone that I'm sitting right here," I said sourly. "I also have feelings."

"Since when?" Cam asked.

I held up a middle finger to my best friend. "Right here, Cameron."

"Okay, that's enough of that," Penelope said, moving from the couch to the loveseat to sit with me. "Rayonus is a douchebag."

"Was a douchebag," I interrupted.

Mavis harrumphed. "Debatable."

Penelope rolled her eyes. "You guys know what I mean. He's changed, and not in the *I want to get in your pants* way. He's really an entirely different demon than we used to know."

"Regardless, he's not good enough for you," Cam said. "No offense, Rayonus."

I glared at him. "I'm taking full offense. You guys are supposed to be my friends."

"To be fair, it is Penny we're talking about," Cam said. "I'm not sure there's a creature, demon or human, that's good enough for her."

Penelope grinned at him. "Awww . . . I didn't know you cared."

"Yes, you did," Mavis countered. "He says it repeatedly."

"Okay, maybe I did, but it still makes me all squishy inside when he says it."

I sighed heavily, looking over my friends. I knew they meant well, and I knew they would come around, but it hurt me to know, when it came down to it, they didn't trust me. It was deserved—I knew that—but it still pained me in a way I never expected to feel.

"Getting back to the task at hand," I said. "Penny, unless you're okay with seeing a hell of a lot more creatures on your work shift, I suggest you go ahead and call in sick. Mom and Dad, are you coming to Patriam with us to see if we can make the amulet, or are you going to worry yourselves into an early grave?"

Cam shot a glowering look my way. "We're immortal, dickhead."

"I put nothing past you guys," I retorted.

"I've never been to Patriam," Mavis said, looking at her husband with excitement. "Can we go?"

"Is there a reason we have to do this in Patriam?" Cam asked.

"Well, not technically, but the ingredients are there, and the spell will most assuredly attract attention."

He sighed. "It's against all of my better judgment, but yes. We can go." When Mavis jumped up and down with excitement, he added, "As long as you don't wander off and get yourself in trouble.

Mavis scoffed. "I'm the Exitium Daemonium. Who's going to bother me?"

"Do you need a list?" I asked, thinking of the many, many demons who had protection amulets just like Severin DeSalle did before I took it.

"Exactly," Cameron said, pointing at me. "Let's not get too big for our britches."

Penelope laughed. "Cam, you're so old! Who says that anymore?"

"I'm old? Have you stopped to think about how old your fiancé is?" he retorted.

"I prefer experienced when it comes to Ray. Because wow, his—"

Cam held up his hands to stop her from speaking while Mavis plugged her ears with her fingers and started singing "Jingle Bells" as loud as she could.

I might have preened a bit.

Kissing my love's temple, I stood and pulled her to her feet. "If you guys are coming, let's do this. I have work tomorrow myself."

"Please?" Mavis pleaded. "You never take me anywhere."

"That's because we were kidnapped the last time I took you out of town. And you want to go to the demon underworld with the very guy who set that up?"

"I'm out of the kidnapping game," I told Cam. "You don't have to worry about that from me anymore."

He narrowed his eyes. "What do I have to worry about, then?"

"Premature balding? Impotence? How am I supposed to know?"

Penelope blanched. "And on that note, I say it's time to go." She held a hand out to Mavis. "Coming with us?"

Mavis batted her eyes. "Please, honey?"

"Fine," Cam growled. "But if we have to kill any demons, you're never going anywhere with Rayonus again."

She clapped her hands together and jumped up and down. "Yay! Underground trip!"

After Penelope made her phone call to Dao, I transported her to our home in Patriam, followed by Cam, and finally a giddy Mavis, all in the span of less than a minute. We weren't in a huge hurry, but the less time we all spent in the underground, the safer we would all be. Cam was right to be leery. Mavis was a weapon that any demon would love to possess.

Once everyone was there, the tour of the home was complete, and the laughter died down about the massive bed in the bedroom, we got down to brass tacks.

"Do I need to take the ring off for this to work or do we do it while it's on?" Penelope wondered aloud, nervously twisting my grandmother's ring around her finger.

I checked the pictures on the phone, translating the Latin as fast as I could. "I think we need to put it on a natural, non-synthetic surface."

"What about the slate fireplace?" Cam suggested.

I nodded, reading a bit more. "That should work."

"What's next?" Mavis asked, her eyes alight with excitement. "Sacrifice a goat? Dance around naked under the stars?"

We all stared at her.

"What? Isn't that what demons do?"

"In the movies, maybe," I said, laughing at her crestfallen expression. "This is a little more straightforward. We're not depending on anything else to give us the power. It's all inside Penelope."

Mavis looked expectantly at me.

I frowned. "What?"

"No sexual innuendo? You literally just said, 'It's all inside Penelope.' I'm finding it a little hard to believe that you were able to control yourself with that kind of opening."

"You said opening," Penelope told her, giggling so hard she fell into me.

Mavis slapped a hand across her eyes. "Never mind. I see Penny has picked up the passed torch with the innuendos."

"Hey! Someone has to do it!" she exclaimed. "We cannot live in an innuendo-less world. Right, babe?"

Cam gave me a look of disgust. "You did this."

I kissed Penelope's smiling mouth and shook my head. "No, Cam. Some things are just meant to be."

He rolled his eyes. "Can we move this along before Mavis decides to venture outside of your, frankly, quaint home? The giant-sized bed will only keep her entertained for a few minutes."

Mavis rolled her eyes, then shrugged. "He's probably right. So, we've got the ring in a pure, non-synthetic place. What's the next step?"

I handed the bag of salt to Penelope. "Sprinkle the salt over the cinnabar and the silver ring. When it's completely covered, say *purgo* to purify it."

She nodded and started pouring the salt. "Mavis, remind me to tell you about Ray's demon ex-girlfriend that literally threw this salt at him. That exchange was one for the books."

I laughed. "That it was. Helisa is probably still fuming over it."

"A good demon dick is hard to find," she said in a commiserating voice. "I almost feel sorry for taking hers."

"Second that," Mavis piped up. "But, you know, not the taking your dick part, Ray."

Cameron groaned. "This will never get done with the two of them together."

"It's a distinct possibility," I agreed, handing Penelope the gum arabic once she had spoken the first word of magic. "Make a well in the middle of the salt and add this. Once you're done, say *sorbere*. That will make the spell stick."

Her eyes widened as she spoke the second word. "I can feel it, Ray. It's pulling the magic from me."

"That means you have the same abilities as your father. Let us thank the stars he didn't raise you here himself. If he had, you would be enslaved. I have no doubt about that."

"What's the next word?" Mavis asked, leaning away from the red-glowing salt pile.

"*Simil.* It means to combine. You should be able to really feel the magic pull when you say this part, so immediately after, I want you to say *duco.* That will draw the extra power needed from the brimstone. Otherwise, there's a strong possibility that it could drain you for an extended amount of time."

Penelope spoke the words fast and deliberate, one of her hands holding tightly to me. As soon as she was done, a whoosh of heated air swept across the room, covering us with fine particles of the salt.

"What now, Ray?" Penelope asked, the light of the magic making her eyes glow in the semi-darkness of the parlor.

"*Minuas,*" I told her. "That will diminish the magic that allows you to see a creature's true form. *Protego* will add protection."

"*Minuas!*" she exclaimed, her voice reverberating inside my head. "*Protego!*"

An explosion of light blinded us as the magic coursed from Penelope to the ring, and I felt her tighten her grasp against my forearm.

"Ray! I can't see!" she screamed.

I felt for her face and rained kisses over her tear-stained cheeks. "This will pass, my love. The same thing happened when Draz made my amulet."

She tucked her face into the crook of my neck. "I'm scared."

"I'm right here," I said, feeling around for Mavis and Cam without being able to see them. "Is that you, Mavis?"

"Why did I think this was a good idea?" Mavis groaned, wrapping her arms around us to join our person pretzel.

Cam sighed and threw his arms around the lot of us. "No one ever listens to me."

Penelope started to laugh. Then continued to laugh until our eyes adjusted and the tears on her cheeks were no longer tears of fear but mirth. She lifted her head and looked at us before picking up the ring. "Here goes nothing, I guess."

We collectively held our breath as the ring sizzled and popped down the length of her long finger.

"Well?" I asked expectantly.

She squinted at each of us, then grinned and threw her arms around me. "It worked!"

We all breathed a sigh of relief.

"Awesome," Cam said. "Not that this hasn't been fun and your house isn't lovely, Rayonus, but can we get the fuck out of here? Having Mavis in the underground is making me nervous."

I smiled at my old friend and clapped him on the back. "Sure, but I might remind you that you married this firecracker. You'll be dealing with her wants and wishes for the next few millennia, no matter how crazy they are."

Mavis slid her arms around her husband. "I knew I should've added that to my vows."

He cupped her face. "You missed your chance, you little hellion."

She smiled and stood on her tiptoes to give him a peck on the lips. "Drat."

"I can take you back when you're ready, Mavis."

"Wait a minute," she said, running toward the bedroom. We all heard the telltale click of her phone's camera before she ran back into the room, grinning from ear to ear. "Okay. I'm good."

"Don't get any ideas," Cam told her. "Neither one of us is a seven-foot-tall demon."

She shrugged and winked at him. "Not since you got your soul back, no, but I can think of a few ways to use that giant bed to our advantage . . . a few dirty, sexy ways."

I shivered. "Let's take that grossness back to your apartment, you two."

"Bye, guys!" Penelope called. "See you tonight for Napoli's and *Supernatural*?"

"Sounds good," Mavis said. "If you can tear yourself away from Mr. Wonderful for two seconds."

I beamed at Penelope. I'd never seen such a beautiful face on anyone before. "I have an eternity to spend with Penny watching *Supernatural* reruns," I told Mavis. "She can do whatever she likes as long as she comes home to me."

Cam held up a finger. "Speaking of that. You two have an extra apartment now. What are you going to do?"

Everything had happened in such a blur, I hadn't even considered the implications of our engagement, much less what our life would be like after the wedding. My place was nice here and I would never give it up, but Penny belonged in Havenwood Falls. She grew up there. It was home for both of us now.

"Penelope is the boss," I told him. "All decisions filter through my bride-to-be."

"Wow," Mavis marveled. "You have it really bad, Ray."

I smiled at Penny. "It doesn't look so bad from where I'm standing."

"Me either," she said, pulling me down to whisper in my ear. "I'll meet you in the bedroom when you get back."

Pulling her to me, I kissed her hard. "Give me thirty seconds and be naked."

"Ewwwww," Cam and Mavis chorused.

CHAPTER 13

I transported Mavis back to her house in Havenwood Heights, followed by Cam. They surprised me by giving me a hug before I could go back to Penelope.

"I'm really happy for both of you," Cameron said. "I know we've had our differences over the last year, but deep, deep, DEEP down, you've always been a stand-up guy."

"Don't lie to the demon," Mavis said, rolling her eyes. She put her hands on her hips and stared me down. "If you hurt her, I will make sure you suffer before I murder you right where you stand. Got it?"

I smirked. "Yes, Mother."

She smacked my chest. "Don't sass your mother."

I laughed. "Yes, ma'am."

"Now go back to Patriam before she thinks you've forgotten she's naked and waiting on you."

"Ugh," Cam groaned. "I wish *I* could forget about that."

With a wave, I stepped back from the pair and traveled back to my house in the underground.

"Penny? I'm back," I called, knowing before I even got the words out that something was wrong.

"Penelope?"

When there was no answer, I appeared in the bedroom. She wasn't there. Popping into the bathroom to find it empty broke something inside of me. Where was she? Had she left of her own volition, or had she been taken?

"Penelope!" I screamed, hearing my voice crack. I'd never been so scared, so panicked. I had to find her.

Racing to the front door, I found something I hoped I wouldn't find. Antimony, also known as kohl to humans, was semi-poisonous to demons of every kind. Most were wary of even touching it, for fear they would succumb to its sedative properties accidentally. But there was one demon that used common poisons all the time. I would delight in watching the light leave his eyes if he was behind this.

The Alchemist.

"Fuck!" I yelled, punching the wall as I shifted into my true form. If he hurt her—if he did anything to her—I would make what Sam and Dean did to demons on *Supernatural* look tame.

Snatching the door open, I slammed it behind me and stormed down the packed street. No one tried to stop me. Some even pointed me in the direction of Draz's home to stay on my good side, assuming I had one. The demons who had witnessed my raw power centuries ago knew better than to hide her from me. Demons were devious and selfish, not stupid. They knew that immortality could be snuffed out in less than a second.

A block away from the alleyway, I bellowed, "Draz! Show yourself to me or suffer my fucking wrath! I will only ask once!"

The demons interested enough to have followed my path at a distance scurried away from me when they caught sight of the raging lunatic I was rapidly becoming. Even with the amulet on, my magic surged, twisting and turning, coiling like a snake within me. It stole my reason, my sanity. All my magic knew was that he had kidnapped its mate. The mate we'd fought for. The mate we'd killed for. The mate that completed us unlike any other female ever had. Our vengeance would be an ugly, horrible thing to behold, and it would hurt.

"DRAZ!" I screamed outside his door, pounding on it so hard the hinges were buckling under my fists.

When he didn't answer, I snapped. Ripping the dampening amulet off my neck, I threw it to the ground and crushed it beneath my heel. The time for asking was over. I would destroy everything he held dear, everything he'd worked for. He would know destruction, and its name would be Rayonus.

For the first time in centuries, the real power that resided in me flared to life and vibrated wild and untamed. The hunger of the destructive beast released. It wanted to taste the blood of my enemies, rip their bodies to shreds, and bring the world to collapse around their broken and battered corpses.

Focused like I'd never been before, I roared as I shot my magic into the door. It disintegrated.

Smiling with malevolence, I ducked to step into the space where the door had been and caught Draz's arm as he came at me with a blade. His bloodcurdling scream was the thing of nightmares as I crushed his arm into fragments with nothing more than a thought. Shoving him to the ground, I kicked the blade aside and loomed over him, fangs bared.

"Where is she?" I demanded, grabbing his hair to keep him from scrambling away from me. "WHERE?"

"I'm here, baby," Penelope's tired voice answered. "But I'm not sure where here is and why this black powdery stuff on my face is making me so sleepy."

"Penelope," I breathed out, taking in every single, minute thing about her. My eyes couldn't get enough of her.

She frowned. "Where's your amulet?"

"I destroyed it, just like I will destroy all the demons that try to keep you from me." I turned to look at a cowering Draz on the floor before bringing my attention back to her. "Starting with him."

Her brows shot up. "Is there any way we can *not* do that?"

My growl shook the bricks around us. "He drugged you with antimony! He took you away from our home! On my honor, I will crush his bones to dust!"

Penelope held her hands in the universal position for a time out. "Rayounus, you don't need to do that. There are worse ways to hurt him," she said, glaring at him with fury as hot as lava in her eyes. "Much more long-lasting and permanent ways."

Draz whimpered as he clutched his shattered arm to his chest. "Please, child. I'm sorry for what I've done. Believe me, daughter."

"He lies!" I thundered, lifting him up by his throat and slamming him against the wall. He collapsed bonelessly in a heap at my feet. I reached for him again.

"Rayonus! No!" Penelope shrieked, throwing inky powder in my face.

I only had time to realize that she'd used the antimony on me before my legs crumpled and I crashed to the floor.

I woke to the sound of angels. Well, if angels sang like a cross between a rabid cat and Alanis Morissette on her worst day.

"Oh, good," Penelope said, turning down her iPod. "You're finally awake."

Groggy and disoriented, I sat up and looked around. We were in Penelope's bedroom. "What happened?"

She climbed onto the bed, kissing me on the cheek before she settled cross-legged at the end of her bed. "What do you remember?"

I furrowed my brow, thinking back to what I'd done—everything that had happened once I found out she was missing. "I remember . . . everything. How is that possible?"

"I'd tell you if I knew," she said, shrugging. "Your amulet is right there."

I followed her line of sight to the crushed amulet laying on the bedside table. "But . . . I'm lucid. I'm focused."

She held her hands up. "I don't know how. I don't know why. But I'm not about to look a gift horse in the mouth."

"What about Draz? I didn't . . ."

"No. He's currently super pissed and wondering how his little girl knew how to bind his power without him sharing any family secrets."

My mouth dropped open. "You sly thing. You didn't."

Penelope scoffed. "The fuck I didn't. I ran and got Fyrira from the river, and she found a suitable crystal while I gathered the ingredients that we left at your house. It was said and done in less than five minutes."

Suitably impressed, I grinned at her, though my head felt like someone had screwed it on wrong. "Is he still bound?"

Shaking her head, she leaned onto her knees to reach a rolled up parchment next to the broken amulet. "I traded it back for this."

Unrolling the document, I squinted my blurry eyes and tried to make out the calligraphy.

"I can't see it quite yet," I told her, handing it over.

"It basically says that Draz is selling me to one Rayonus Rixa in exchange for his magic to be unbound—in blood, which is fucking gross."

I shook my head, not understanding. "What do you mean, he sold you to me?"

"He was powerless. I made him an offer he couldn't refuse. My freedom for his. All he had to do was sever the ties to my blood with his blood on the contract, and it was a done deal. I was pretty offended by the whole selling part at first, but Fyrira assured me it's a pretty common practice between parents and younglings within the demon community. She's a smart lady."

"Smarter than I realized," I said absently.

"She also advised me to keep our little arrangement just between us and not tell Mavis and Cam. Well, she called him the incubus. At first, I thought maybe it was because Mavis might be pissed enough to go to Patriam and strike down demons like it was some biblical reckoning, but I think she just knew they'd be over here telling us 'I told you so' until we both went into convulsions. Either way, the demon is a literal lifesaver."

I chuckled, sitting up straighter as I started to regain my strength. "It seems we owe Fyrira a debt of gratitude."

Penelope curled into my side, wrapping my arm around her like a security blanket. "Definitely. And she also kind of insisted we name our first daughter after her, but honestly, I can't think of a better name than that of the demon who saved us from certain doom and had a hand in me gaining my freedom from a real douchebag." She leaned away from me to look me in the eyes. "If you know any other jackass demons like him, I don't care what we think we might need. I don't want to meet them—ever."

Pulling her close, I brushed back the mane of tangled hair in her face and kissed her as tenderly as I could manage with the emotions growing inside of me. "That is a promise I would love to keep. As is naming our child after Fyrira. But I hope you know that I never want you indebted to me. If we didn't need this paper, I would burn it to ash right now."

Penelope shrugged and nipped at my lips before straddling me and laying a kiss on me so hot it sent shockwaves through my body. "That's too bad, you know, because as my mate, you're always going to own a piece of my heart."

Sliding my hands down to cup her ass, I said, "If that's the case, we're indebted to each other."

"Good," she purred. "Because I want to dalliance your brains out for the rest of my life."

I grinned, flipping her onto her back. "Not if I dalliance your brains out first."

We hope you enjoyed this story in the Havenwood Falls series featuring a variety of supernatural creatures. The series is a collaborative effort by multiple authors. Have you read them all?

Also try the YA line, Havenwood Falls High; the historical paranormal line, Legends of Havenwood Falls; and the darker, sexier side of town, Havenwood Falls Sin & Silk.

Find the full list and sign up for our reader group at www. HavenwoodFalls.com

ABOUT THE AUTHOR

JD Nelson is a Bestselling Author of Fantasy Romance and Adult Paranormal Romance. An avid time-waster, JD enjoys watching TV and listening to audiobooks when she really should be writing.

JD loves to hear from her readers. You can contact her through her website, AuthorJDNelson.com, or on Facebook, where she spends an alarming amount of time chatting with her many author and reader friends, much to the dismay of her continually neglected manuscripts.

ACKNOWLEDGMENTS

To the readers, thank you for asking for more of Ray and Penelope's story! I couldn't have written this without your support and feedback!

www.ingramcontent.com/pod-product-compliance
Lightning Source LLC
Chambersburg PA
CBHW020934260626
47169CB00006B/1723